DARKEST BEFORE DAWN

GEORGE WALLACE

DON KEITH

Severn River Publishing
www.SevernRiverBooks.com

ISBN: 978-1-64875-712-9 (Paperback)

ALSO BY THE AUTHORS

The Hunter Killer Series

Final Bearing

Dangerous Grounds

Cuban Deep

Fast Attack

Arabian Storm

Warshot

Silent Running

Snapshot

Southern Cross

The Gibraltar Affair

The Tides of War Series

Argentia Station

Darkest Before Dawn

Also by George Wallace

Operation Golden Dawn

The Cold Sea Series

Also by Don Keith

A Call to War Series

PROLOGUE

Lieutenant (Junior Grade) Alistair MacLean III hopped off the motor launch onto the stone quay just as the little vessel pulled away, and promptly headed off toward the Fleet Landing to disgorge the remainder of its passengers. MacLean—"Trip" to his friends—strolled casually through the familiar parklike maze of lush palms, flame trees, and rambling bougainvillea. His destination, a couple of hundred yards ahead, was the white, three-story Manila Army and Navy Club, which now peeked out at him through the teeming foliage with the promise of a pleasant evening for the young US Navy officer.

An ice-cold gin and tonic would be only the first pleasure that beckoned, but the submariner was in no hurry. A tropical breeze blew in from the Sierra Madres to the east, enveloping him in a cloud of vibrant jungle scents. It was the late fall of 1941 and Trip MacLean was living his dream. The Army and Navy Club, as the nexus of all social life for the US Navy's Asiatic Fleet, provided a perfect backdrop for all the Philippines offered a handsome, unmarried young officer with limited duties in peacetime and the willingness to explore his options. Lazy days when he had no responsibilities at the submarine base were filled with tennis or golf or just lying around the pool. That often proceeded to evenings at the well-stocked—but male-only—Officer's Bar at the club. Or dancing to the music of a live band in the pavilion, which was decidedly *not* male only. Even early on, back at his previous billet at the submarine base at New London, Connecticut, MacLean had discovered that his dress white uniform, sporting his gold dolphins—signifying he was a qualified submarine officer—was irresistible to unattached female customers. That was true not only at the ritzy spots along the Connecticut coast but also for those who frequented the Manila Army and Navy Club. And for many of the attached ones as well. The fact that he was the only son of Alistair MacLean Jr., a wealthy businessman and New York's junior Senator in the US Congress, only added to the appeal. Which was the reason he made certain to casually work that fact into the conversation with the ladies he met along the way.

As the Torpedo Officer on the old *S-55* submarine, MacLean happily found himself in a position that allowed him to enjoy life in the tropics to the fullest, even if this particular duty assignment had been dealt to him as punishment. That came not only for being far too cavalier about his sub school classes but because his father had attempted to exert his considerable influence to get his boy the choice assignment that he lusted after. Significantly annoyed by the impertinent attempt to go over their heads, his Commanding Officer and Squadron Commodore arranged to have MacLean assigned to a rusty, beat-up submarine at the absolute far end of the world. He soon realized he could not have picked any more pleasant "punishment" had he chosen it from a catalog.

The submarine to which he had been assigned was the long-in-the-tooth *S-55*. That boat and her sisters were the products of a submarine building boom that came in the early 1920s, just at the end of the Great War. Six of these boats, along with seven newer *Porpoise*-class subs, made up the entire Asiatic Fleet submarine force at the time. The *S*-boats—commonly referred to as *Sugar*-boats, "sugar" being the phonetic in radio transmissions for the letter "S"—were the first submarines to be built for blue-water operations instead of just for harbor and coastal duty. But they had not been designed for operations in a hot, humid tropical climate. Nor were they equipped for the very long distances required for any vessel involved in Far East operations. The *Sugar*-boats quickly developed a reputation for being unreliable. That especially applied to the *S-55*. She was jokingly known as "Building *S-55*" since she spent more time in Cavite Navy

Yard undergoing repairs than she did at sea. The ancient submarine's recalcitrant MAN diesel engines were only one reason. There were many other issues. The engineers, wrenches in hand, expended untold hours trying to nursemaid the reluctant boat back to sea, only to have her limp back in for more shop time. MacLean, who was responsible for the torpedoes lying quietly in the torpedo room, quickly realized that he had plenty of time to explore the ancient Spanish city of Manila and its manifold delights. The Army and Navy Club was just one of those. And a gateway to so many more.

MacLean walked up the steps to the club's main entrance. Sammy Wong, the establishment's long-serving and venerable "Number One Boy," greeted MacLean as he walked through the huge mahogany double doors into the relative coolness of the interior. Built in 1908, the building was not air-conditioned. It depended on shade and catching the breezes off the bay to cool the old pile.

"I have your table ready in the Officer's Dining Room," Sammy told him as he held the door open and bowed, ushering MacLean inside. "The chef has a fresh-caught lapu-lapu done up in a sweet and sour sauce tonight. Pure heaven. And we just received a shipment of mangosteens from Pitogo. Best in the Philippines."

"Thanks, Sammy, sounds delicious," the young officer said with a smile. "But I think I'll eat out on the pavilion this evening."

MacLean strolled out onto the broad, open-air, covered structure. The sun was just setting over Manila Bay out to the west, bathing the scene in shades of orange and yellow. The club's staff was busy, lighting *tanglaws*, Filipino torches, adding a flickering, almost romantic illumination to the scene.

Much better than walking through a sleet storm to Solomon's Tavern back in New London, he thought.

"Hey, sailor! Buy a lady a drink?"

MacLean turned. The invitation came from a table back in the shadows of a rather large and luxuriant flame tree. The voice was familiar.

Madeleine Forester, the XO's wife. The Executive Officer, second in command on *S-55*. Madeleine seemed to always be on the prowl. She was trouble.

But, as it happened, that was precisely the kind of trouble LTjg Alistair MacLean was looking for this most pleasant evening.

∞

Lieutenant Geoffrey Chandler, Royal Navy, stood on the signal bridge and gazed out to the east. That was where a tropical sun was just starting to peek over the low green line on the horizon that formed the coastline of the British Crown Colony of Ceylon. The spicy scent of the tropical isle tickled the senses even this far from land. Positioned almost fifty feet above the main deck, the signal bridge of his ship was Chandler's favorite spot to enjoy a cup of coffee while watching the sunrise.

Like Trip MacLean, Chandler, too, was much more pleased with this new duty station where he proudly served King and country. Sailing on the battleship *Prince of Wales* in the warm, peaceful waters of the Indian Ocean was quite different from battling German U-boats and destroyers from the deck of a tiny ASW trawler in the cold, storm-tossed North Atlantic.

He was aware, however, that the peacefulness of the scene could be deceptive. The *Prince of Wales* was Admiral Sir Tom Phillips's flagship. Together with the battlecruiser *Repulse* and a half dozen destroyers, they made up Force Z. Their mission was to reinforce Great Britain's far-flung Eastern Fleet while doing what they could to intimidate the so far peaceful but certainly threatening Imperial Japanese Navy.

Being the Assistant Communicator on the battleship while it functioned as the Force Z flagship kept Chandler hopping. With the constant stream of messages to and from the Admiralty in Whitehall, back in London, combined with all the orders flowing back and forth from the various Eastern Fleet commands and the myriad administrative postings, Chandler and his team had precious little downtime. That made him appreciate the coffee and the sunrise even more this morning.

"Lieutenant!" Chief Telegraphist Ian Murphy's thick Irish brogue disturbed Chandler's revery. "Sir, message just in from HMS Trincomalee. We've been cleared to enter Trincomalee Bay and to anchor abreast the Navy Dockyard. Time at anchor is 0330 GMT, 0900 local time. That damnable half-hour time thing's just to confuse us, I say. Anyway, I've already routed the message to the Captain and the Admiral."

Chandler nodded as he watched the Aldis lanterns flashing the orders for entering port to the other ships in company. The destroyers raced to their assigned stations while HMS *Repulse* slid over astern of the *Prince of Wales* to follow the flagship into the Royal Navy's largest and oldest naval base east of Suez, His Majesty's Station Trincomalee.

"Murphy, you ever have the feeling you are being watched?" Chandler blurted out.

"Not since me girl's daft old man back in Limerick used to trail me home," the radioman replied. He was accustomed to the Lieutenant's off-the-wall queries and comments. "Old bastid had eyes in the back of his head, he did. Why ye be askin', sir? You got that feelin' about now?"

Chandler took a sip of his coffee. "I do. But we got nobody shooting at us in this part of the world that I know of, so I suppose it don't matter. Let 'em look." He drained the last of the coffee and tossed the remaining grounds that came with it over the side of the signal bridge. "Now back to your key and radio set in case the boss has got something urgent to relay as we make port."

"Aye, sir." And Murphy was gone.

The rising sun had fully broken free from the surface of the Bay of Bengal aft of the *Prince of Wales*. The warm, fragrant breeze, the placid sea state, and the color-laden early-morning sky were all peaceful, calming.

Even so, Lieutenant Geoffrey Chandler could not suppress the sudden chill that climbed up his backbone.

∞

Kaigu Shosa (Lieutenant Commander) Riku Ito kept his eye to the periscope. His vessel, the *Kaidai*-class Imperial Japanese Navy submarine *I-53*, had spent the last two weeks patrolling the waters off Trincomalee, Ceylon, just for a chance to find what was now parading across the sea directly in front of them. He allowed himself the barest smile. But then he frowned. Frowned because he could take no action against this assemblage of prime targets sitting in the crosshairs of his periscope.

No, Japan was still ostensibly at peace with Great Britain. The Type 95 torpedoes, in his torpedo tubes ready and waiting to be used, would have to wait for another day. Then they could strike a blow against the so-called British Empire on behalf of the Imperial Japanese Navy, the Emperor, and the Empire of Japan.

Kaigu Shosa Ito carefully watched as the unsuspecting British warships steamed by, then he lowered the periscope and ordered the *I-53* to turn and head due east. He wanted to be well over the horizon and away from any potential aircraft before he surfaced and reported sighting the British fleet entering Trincomalee. It would not do for an Imperial Japanese Navy submarine to be detected lurking off a British naval base six thousand kilometers from Formosa, the nearest IJN base.

Ito leaned against a chart table and watched his crew efficiently carry out his orders. He had no way of knowing if or when he might be called upon to attack a British or US or Australian or some other potential enemy ship.

But he was ready. So was his crew.

∞

Lieutenant (Junior Grade) Fred Wurster stepped carefully over the tangle of cables, lines, and pipes that littered the wing wall and draped over it. Somewhere down there in Drydock Four, hidden under the maze of scaffolding, lay the USS *Wolffish*. The *Gato*-class submarine was slated to be Fred Wurster's new home, just as soon as the shipbuilders at Mare Island Naval Shipyard on San Francisco Bay finished putting her together and zipping her up. But first Wurster had to find the gangway and report aboard. And in the maze of pipes, air lines, scaffolding, and tarpaulins, that looked impossible.

"Freddy! Freddy Wurster!"

The voice sounded familiar. And friendly. Wurster looked around. "Jim Shelton, you old sea dog!" Wurster answered as he spotted a former shipmate from the old *S-52* emerging from the scaffolding and charging across the gangway. Wurster and Shelton had served together on the *S-52* in the Atlantic, based in New London, then Argentia, Newfoundland, Canada. It had been out of the latter port where the two men shared a harrowing experience. Their boat was badly damaged when it deliberately rammed a U-boat in a highly classified fight off Placentia Bay. The Navy had told everyone involved that, due to the nature of the operation and the fact that the US was not at war with Germany, the incident would likely be classified well into the next century. And maybe never declassified. With the *S-52* facing a long shipyard repair period, President Roosevelt himself had promised to reassign her crew to active, war-fighting boats, just in case there might be a war.

Wurster was thrilled he had drawn duty aboard "new construction," one of the Navy's most technologically advanced warships, the *Gato*-class *Wolffish*. But his first look at the submarine left him unconvinced such a mess would ever be ready for sea duty. And certainly not for a shooting war.

Wurster enveloped Shelton in a bear hug and clapped him on the back. "Great to see you, shipmate. But what are you doing in the far reaches of Northern California?"

"It's Lieutenant Shelton now, thank you. But you can call me 'XO,'" the young officer shot back, pointing to the "racetracks" adorning his collar and with a stern look on his face. "And I expect the proper respect and courtesy demanded by my rank and position." He kept a straight face for about one second before they both burst out laughing.

"Come aboard," Shelton said as he guided Wurster on board the boat. "You arrived just in time. Despite the confusion you see here, the good ship *Wolffish* is scheduled to join the fleet and become a war-fighting denizen of the deep by the end of the year." He waved at all the shipyard clutter that surrounded them and effectively hid the submarine somewhere underneath it all.

"You are talking about this year, 1941, right?"

"Damn well better be. The way Japan's huffin' and puffin' all over the Pacific. Skipper's not aboard right now. He's over at Twelfth Naval District Headquarters. He and the Shipyard Commander are meeting with the Admiral, going toe-to-toe, discussing why the *Wolffish* is behind schedule and what needs to be done to catch up."

The pair of naval officers dodged shipyard workers, found their way around piles of gear, and stepped over hoses before dropping through a hatch and climbing down into an equally cluttered and confusing space belowdecks. Wurster could vaguely identify a submarine control room, but it was filled with a couple of dozen workers running wire, connecting hydraulic piping, or painting anything that did not move. Between cigarette smoke, the paint fumes, and the sparking and spitting of the welders' torches, Wurster could hardly breathe. The cacophony of banging, shouting, and grinding was to the point of being painful. How could anyone build a submarine in this den of confusion?

Shelton pulled Wurster through a hatchway into the boat's wardroom. At least in there they could hear each other if they shouted loud enough.

"Jim, this thing's never gonna float!" Wurster yelled.

"To the contrary, it will. It'll also sink when we tell it to and come back to the surface on command as well. And you'll have a big part in seeing that it does." There was a pause while some worker noisily seated a rivet nearby. "Freddy, I'm making you the Engineer," Shelton told him, still at the top of his voice. "We need the engineering plant ready to light off as soon as we get out of the drydock. Diesels, main motors, freshwater still, the whole shebang. That's scheduled for next Friday, so you got your hands full, buddy."

"Damn, XO! This is a whole different boat from the *S*-class. I don't know a thing about these babies."

"That's one reason I managed to shanghai Chief Wankel as your engineering chief. The Navy had him down at Electric Boat there in Groton observing early development of the *Gato*, so he knows more about them than any of us. Besides, he didn't want to spend a couple of years rebuilding the old *S-52*. He'd rather be going to sea on a brand-new *Gato*-class."

"Thank you for that!"

A horn blasted from somewhere topside. Shelton glanced down at his wristwatch. "1700. Shift change," he yelled. "Let's get you settled in at the BOQ and then grab a beer at the O'Club. Skipper'll join us there."

As they started for the hatch, Wurster tapped Shelton on the shoulder.

"Jim, I just want to tell you how glad I am to be sailing with you again." They shook hands. "And, if there's going to be a war, I can't imagine anybody I'd rather go to war with."

Shelton nodded, then said, "Freddy, remember, we went to war together already. Up there in Newfoundland. And we lived through it, too, even if we can't brag to anybody about it. Hell, we can't even tell Skipper that you and I..."

Somebody started up a loud grinding tool of some kind then. That brought their conversation to an abrupt conclusion.

1

LT(jg) Brad Johnson stood on the platform, waiting impatiently. His train would depart from New London's Union Station in five minutes.

Where the hell was she?

Johnson checked his watch yet again. Here he was, heading off in five minutes to somewhere in the far reaches of the western Pacific Ocean. It would almost certainly be a long time before he came back Stateside. Before he once again saw the girl with whom he had fallen in love.

He frantically looked up and down the long platform. Dozens of other sailors were saying goodbye to their girls. But his lady, Debbie Schultz, was nowhere to be seen. He had already considered the worst of the possibilities, then tried, with no success, to dismiss such depressing thoughts from his mind.

The conductor, holding up the inevitable railroad pocket watch, walked impatiently up and down the platform, hollering, "All aboard! Pennsylvania 177 for New York's Penn Station leaves in two minutes. All aboard!"

The big K4 4-6-2 locomotive belched a massive cloud of steam, like an impatient sigh, then sounded its whistle, alerting all the world that it was ready and raring to go. Johnson shouldered his seabag and was just turning to board his train car when he spied a flash of pink racing out a platform-side door of the station.

Debbie! And she was coming his way across the platform at full tilt. She almost knocked him over as she leapt into his arms.

"Damn Ford wouldn't start," she explained between kisses. "Dad had to push me down Cottage Street Hill to get it started!" She kissed him again, deeply. "Oh, God, I almost missed you."

Johnson returned her kisses and stroked her hair. "Shush," he whispered. "You're here now. You made it."

The conductor walked past them, heading down the platform toward the last car. He slowed just long enough to turn to the couple and say, "Finish your goodbyes. You really must get aboard. The train is leaving. Now."

As if to confirm the conductor's words, the big PRR locomotive blasted its whistle once more. Johnson reluctantly let Debbie go, hoisted his seabag up onto his shoulder, and grabbed the stanchion on the railcar's loading steps. He leaned down and kissed her one more time as the train lurched ahead, pulling them away from each other. Both of them knew that kiss would have to last them a long, long time.

"I'll write to you every day," he promised.

"I love you!" she shouted as the train headed on down the tracks. And she continued to wave as long as she thought he had any chance of seeing her. The train picked up speed, skirted the waterfront, and crossed the Coits Cove Bridge. Then it was out of sight. And Brad was gone.

Wiping tears from her eyes, Debbie Schultz slowly made her way back to the parking lot and her beat-up Ford coupe, which she had left running rather than risk having to get a push to get it going again. She was half hoping somebody would steal the damn thing. She was not looking forward to her shift as bartender at Solomon's Tavern in Groton tonight. It just would not be the same without her favorite sailor there. Or Brad's best buddies, either. They had all gone to their own new—and very secret—assignments. No matter how busy the bar would be this night, she knew Brad was getting farther and farther away from her all the time. He had not even been able to share with her exactly where his new port of call would be, other than a cryptic "pretty much on the other side of Planet Earth."

The tears and the pain of separation kept Debbie from noticing two men watching her with great interest from separate points deep in the shadows of the big train station building. Each had also made a great effort to prevent her from seeing them.

George Klemp was the Naval Intelligence agent who had been assigned to watch over her. He stood just past the taxi stand, making a pretense of reading the morning *Herald Tribune*. When he saw she was safely in her car and pulling out onto Water Street, he folded the paper and headed off toward his own car to follow her, to make sure she got to Solomon's safely. Klemp's superiors had not told him the full story of Miss Schultz and her father. Just what he needed to know to do his job. He knew she was a barmaid and that her daddy worked at Groton's sprawling Electric Boat facility where a number of new submarines were under construction beneath an almost impenetrable veil of secrecy. And that the father and daughter had been contacted by what appeared to be members of a German spy ring to attempt to cut through that veil, to get the elder Schultz, an immigrant from Germany, to supply them with details about those subs. But the Schultzes had—out of patriotism and the desire to do the right thing—voluntarily become double agents, working for Naval Intelligence. And Klemp's job was to see that no one—no one from either side—tried to hurt Debbie or her dad.

At the far end of the parking lot, a workman emerged from behind a delivery van. He also kept an eye on Debbie Schultz's car as it merged into traffic and disappeared down the street. Then the workman, maybe taking a break for lunch, kept walking on up State Street. He spent almost an hour weaving a convoluted route through the streets of downtown New London, all to make certain that he was not being followed. Then he doubled back to the Greyhound bus terminal. Ducking inside, he seated himself in the phone booth most distant from the terminal entrance, dropped some coins into the slot on the phone, and dialed a number. The call was answered on the second ring. The "workman" briefly told the answerer what he had seen.

In a guttural voice and with a pronounced Bavarian accent, the man on the other end of the phone line replied, "You vill make contact with the *junge frau* tonight. We must have them assist us in obtaining those documents and drawings. You vill convince them of the urgency on behalf of the cause of the Fatherland, *ja*?"

∞

The *Broadway Limited* departed Penn Station in New York City at precisely six p.m. Chicago was sixteen hours away. From there, Brad Johnson faced another forty hours on the *City of San Francisco* before he finally arrived on the West Coast. He thanked his lucky stars that he—or at least his father, Admiral Devin Johnson, who was so proud of his boy graduating Annapolis and choosing submarine service—could afford for his son to travel while enjoying a little comfort. Most US Navy sailors, as well as officers, typically traveled third class, sitting on bench seats and packing their own food. Brad was in first class.

The porter settled Johnson in his roomette as the train passed through the tunnel under the Hudson River. He had a late reservation for dinner in the dining car, so he walked back to the club car for a drink. As the train raced across New Jersey and approached Pennsylvania, he sat and sipped a Scotch as he reread his orders one more time.

Report to Transportation Officer, Naval Operating Base Terminal Island, San Francisco, California, on or before 1 November 1941, for forwarding transportation to the port where USS Tigerfish might be located. Upon arrival, report to Commanding Officer, USS Tigerfish for duty.

Even if the orders were vague on the matter, Brad Johnson had been able to learn that the *Tigerfish* was currently homeported in Pearl Harbor, Hawaii, but she was scheduled to head west, eventually making it to Cavite Naval Base in the Philippines. There was no doubt about it now. His assignment confirmed it. War with the Empire of Japan was coming and he was headed right into what would likely be the heart of it. He was not at all sure how he felt about it. After his recent harrowing submarine experiences off Greenland and in Placentia Bay, Newfoundland, against German U-boats, surviving vicious battles in a non-war, fighting had lost most of its glamour. However, it was something that needed to be done, considering what he was hearing that the Japanese were doing around the Pacific Rim. Brad was more convinced than ever that he had the training and the experience for doing this job. Not to mention having grown up in a Navy household with a father who was an Admiral, who now worked at the highest level of the military and alongside the nation's leaders, and who had instilled "the Navy way" in his son.

"Mind if I join you?"

Johnson had been lost in his thoughts. The voice startled him out of his revery. He looked up and saw a young Navy officer wearing Lieutenant bars and gold dolphins. Brad jumped to his feet and said, "By all means, glad to have company. I'm Brad Johnson." He offered his hand.

"Hi, I'm Isaac Sternman. I see you're wearing dolphins. I just got orders to the *Tigerfish*. Where you headed?"

Johnson grinned. What were the odds? "Same vessel, as it happens. Looks like we're going to be traveling companions for a bit. Care to join me for dinner?"

Without waiting for an answer, Johnson signaled the porter. No doubt the two officers had much to discuss.

2

The honky-tonk piano blasted into the warm night air where it battled with the jazz horn that blared away from next door. The flashing neon lights strewn across the façade of the tacky little structure spelled out “Felipe’s Chicago Bar.” It was only one of a dozen or more establishments that lined Del Pilar Kayle, strategically located right outside the main gate of the Cavite Naval Yard, Philippines. The ideal location to efficiently separate a military man from his money. Army Sergeants Gus Arnett and Stan Lamoille had secured themselves a table in the far recesses of the crowded dive, effectively shrouded by cigarette smoke. The rows of empty squatty green Balintawak bottles gave testimony to the fact that the two had been at it for a while now.

“Damn, I’m glad to be out of that cave for a few hours,” Arnett said, his words slurred by the Philippine pilsner. “The Lieutenant won’t even allow me to open a window to let a damn breeze through. The place’s a steam box.” He took a long draft from a full bottle even as he used his free hand to wave to the barkeep to send over more.

“It wouldn’t be so bad if we just had a clue of what we was doin’.” Stan Lamoille’s Cajun drawl had not diminished one iota in the twenty years since he left Theriot, Louisiana, to join the US Army. “They be given us them papers full o’ gibberish to log in and pass on to dem egghead occifers.

Ain't got no idy what dey do wit it." He shook his head and took another swig. "But dem occifers be speakin some kinda furren talk all da time. Shore ain't Tagalog. We been here long enough, I picked up 'nuff of dat lingo I knows it when I hears it. I'm bettin' they be speakin' Japanese 'mongst theyselves."

Gus Arnett nodded in agreement. "Stan, you may be right for once. Bill Schott, over in Admin, tells me he overheard a couple of them officers talking about what a hard time they're having, trying to figger out what them Japs is up to. I reckon we must be breaking their radio code and listening in on 'em."

Manny, the barkeep, was taking his time clearing the table next to theirs. Grabbing an armload of empties, he sauntered around behind the bar and then disappeared into the stockroom. Once out of sight, he pulled a slip of paper from his pocket and carefully dialed a number from it on the wall phone. What he had just heard from the two half-lit American soldiers would surely be worth a few pesos.

The phone rang once and then was answered. The voice was gruff, guttural.

"*Hai!* Japanese Consulate."

∞

Major Frank Tanaka sat and stared at the mound of paperwork covering his desk, then overflowing into piles on the floor. From his tiny, windowless office, Tanaka supervised a small group with a very large task. His Station CAST team, made up of a dozen cryptologists, about the same number of radio operators, a half dozen Japanese language experts, and a rotating assortment of clerks, messengers, and typists, were tasked with intercepting, decrypting, and deciphering Japanese radio messages. OP-02-G, back in Washington, had tasked Tanaka with two specific ciphers, the Japanese diplomatic code, called PURPLE, and the Japanese Navy code JN-25.

The PURPLE code was pretty basic. Station CAST had one of the Signal Intelligence Service's PURPLE machines, built specifically to decipher that brand of messages. Tanaka kept his junior, less experienced people busy with the PURPLE message traffic. The problem was that most of what they gathered turned out to be drivel: diplomatic postings, updates on traffic congestion in New Delhi, the poor quality of the sake in Batavia. That stuff was all easily available from various sources. It rarely revealed information on Japanese plans or intentions. Analysts could only try to detect tendencies or get hints of more crucial operations from the vanilla transmissions. War clouds were hanging heavy, so any data was better than no data. But strategic insights were vital. It had become clear of late that the Japanese diplomats and military leaders were no longer relying on PURPLE to communicate about the more crucial matters.

OP-02-G and Tanaka were certain that the JN-25 code contained the more critical military intel. The big problem was that JN-25 was infinitely more complex than the PURPLE code. They had just begun to make headway in the spring when the Imperial Japanese Navy suddenly changed from JN-25 to JN-25A. It was possible the IJN became aware of the Americans' progress and made the switch. Or it may have been yet another pivot, like moving away from PURPLE, to avoid eavesdropping. Regardless, Tanaka and his team had to start all over again.

It was exasperating, mind-numbing work. Many, many hours spent trying to sort the signals into anything decipherable, and then to try to decode the gleaned bits into Japanese. Inevitably, something failed along the way, and Frank Tanaka was left with pages full of gibberish, all neatly written in *Kanji*. He needed help. A lot more help, and soon.

As the Major sat and drafted the message to his boss, General Olmstead, back in Washington, he thanked his lucky stars that he did not need to worry too much about security. There appeared to be no indication that the Japanese had any clue that his team was working in the Philippines, let alone that they were busy trying to read Japan's mail from there.

He could only hope it would stay that way.

∞

The *S-55*'s twin MAN diesels hammered away, obliterating the morning calm and wreathing the gray submarine in a cloud of thick black diesel smoke. The harbor water was dead calm. No breeze disturbed the placid surface. Trip MacLean stood on the bridge, his headache hammering in time with the throbbing of the engines. The previous night's party at the Army and Navy Club had been legendary, and Madeleine Forester had kept him awake most of the rest of the night. Now he was paying for it dearly in the dawn's early light.

MacLean looked up and down the pier. Underway was scheduled for 0630. If there was one thing that he had learned about LCDR Tony DiCarlo, the *S-55*'s Skipper, it was that he was a stickler for absolute promptness. An 0630 underway meant exactly that. Not 0629. And most assuredly not 0631. Line handlers were standing by the lines, the shore power cables were neatly coiled on the pier, and the brow was already rolled back well clear of the boat. Motor Machinist Chief Anthony Watson, the *S-55*'s gruff, burly Chief of the Boat, had personally made sure that everything topside was, as he termed it, "Ship-shape and Bristol fashion."

MacLean checked his Rolex. 0627. All was ready for underway.

All except the Skipper was not yet on the bridge.

MacLean reached down and keyed the 7MC microphone. "Control, Bridge. To the Captain. The ship is ready to get underway."

Sam Forester, the XO, answered, "Bridge, Control. Captain has the word."

MacLean checked his watch. 0628. Okay, where was he? A ship's whistle added to the cacophony. He stole a look over at Alpha Pier. The *Porpoise* was noisily backing away from its berth. The two boats were scheduled to operate together, making a sweep of the Luzon Strait and attempting to see if the Imperial Japanese Navy was up to anything. The *Porpoise* was soon pulling out into Manila Bay, and he was still sitting there, tied to the pier.

0630. Still no Skipper.

MacLean leaned over the side of the bridge and yelled down to the COB at his place on the deck. "Chief, cast off all lines." Then he grabbed the 7MC. "Control, Bridge, to the Captain, the ship is underway."

Tony DiCarlo exploded through the bridge hatch three seconds later, his face a livid red and his arms swinging wildly. "Mr. MacLean, just what the hell do you think you're doing! The very idea of getting underway without my permission! I should have you up on charges!"

"But, Skipper," MacLean sputtered, "underway was scheduled for 0630. I know how you hate to be late for underway." He pointed down toward the pier. "We haven't moved an inch yet. I can have the COB drop lines back over the cleats and we'll be right where we started from. Or I can answer bells and get us out of here and we'll be precisely on time."

It took a few seconds, but DiCarlo visibly calmed down. "Mr. MacLean, twist us away from the pier and make a course for the harbor entrance." Under his breath, so only he and MacLean could hear, he added, "You think you're pretty slick, don't you? You try another trick like that and I'll have your balls in a little glass bottle. We understand each other?"

Somehow Alistair MacLean understood that DiCarlo was not this pissed off over his getting the *S-55* underway without permission. He just had no idea what the actual reason could be.

The Skipper stood over on the starboard side of the tiny bridge and silently watched as the *S-55* headed out. He folded his arms and stolidly stared toward the western horizon. The submarine pulled away from Bravo Pier, out into Bacoor Bay. The piers around Cavite Navy Yard were crowded with the ships of the Asiatic Fleet. The waters around the yard were busy with ships, boats, captains' gigs, and lighters of all descriptions servicing the various ships. The *S-55* steamed around Sangley Point and out into the broad and almost-as-busy Manila Bay.

MacLean had to weave the surfaced submarine through hundreds of banca boats, the tiny outrigger canoes that the Filipinos used for fishing or just general transportation. They darted every which way and seemed to take particular delight in seeing how close they could get to the American submarine without getting rammed. A tramp steamer, laden with produce and heading inbound, sounded one short blast on his whistle and dipped his Philippine ensign, signaling that he intended to pass the *S-55* on the port side, and, at the same time, rendering honors to the warship.

MacLean shook his head in wonder that the Skipper of the tiny, rust-streaked scow could be that squared away. He reached down and gave one short acknowledging blast on the whistle, telling the steamer that he agreed to a port-to-port passing. Then he yelled back at the lookout to dip the *S-55*'s ensign and fully raise it again.

The Skipper of the *Mindoro Belle*, dressed in the traditional *baro* shirt and *tapis* wraparound skirt, stood on the steamer's bridge and waved as the two ships passed. MacLean smiled and returned the greeting.

He glanced over at Tony DiCarlo. The Skipper had not moved a muscle.

Caballo Island was abeam to starboard when DiCarlo finally turned and said, "Come to course two-seven-zero. When you are well clear of Bataan Peninsula, come to course three-two-zero." He stepped over to the bridge hatch and the ladder down into the conning tower. "If you think you can carry out those simple orders without screwing things up, I'm going below for some breakfast."

"Yes, sir, two-seven-zero, then three-two-zero," MacLean answered, but DiCarlo had already dropped below. MacLean shook his head. He still had no idea what he had done to mess up, but he was very clearly on DiCarlo's shit list. All he knew to do until he figured that out was to drive the boat as ordered and not cut a banca boat in half in the process.

∞

US Navy Lieutenant (junior grade) Stan Ward grabbed the clipboard and riffled through the day's stack of intercepts. He was sitting at his desk in the Operations and Intelligence Center for the Commander, Submarine Patrol Force. The Ops Center was hidden behind double locked and guarded steel doors deep in the basement of COMSUBPATFOR's brick-and-cement headquarters building on the New London, Connecticut, Submarine Base. The Ops Center was responsible for correlating and analyzing all of the German Naval messages that various American Navy radio stations intercepted around the Atlantic.

Ward shook his head. German *Kriegsmarine* Admiral Karl Dönitz and his flock of U-boats were certainly being talkative of late. Ward thumbed through the messages, counting them, and then studied the big map of the North Atlantic that covered most of one wall of the room. It looked like there were at least four wolf packs out hunting convoys right now. Hunting, shooting, killing. With the various individual scout submarines steaming around, there could be as many as forty of the deadly undersea killers hungrily prowling the shipping lanes between North America and Europe.

The frustrating thing—and one that was regularly costing lives of Americans, even if the US was not at war with anybody—was that intelligence operators were no closer to decrypting and reading the German messages than they had been when they first started trying almost two years ago. The information they did have on not only Hitler's submarines but other German warships as well was almost entirely based on the HF/DF intercepts of those messages and the reports of a very few well-placed spies. And what little had proved useful to this point depended on young Lieutenant Ward's rapidly developing techniques for radio traffic analysis. Through radio direction-finding and observing the unique quirks of the various radiomen when sending Morse code, US Navy intelligence could tell where the messages were coming from. And then they could track individual boats and their movements in response to that traffic as they plied along the shipping lanes. With that, the Navy could deduce at least a small part of what was being transmitted back and forth. Even so, it was not reliable enough to allow for much strategic action. It was guesswork for the most part.

The German Naval ENIGMA code continued to be a tough nut to crack. The Brits had some of the best minds working on it. The US did, too. But it was slow, demanding, and brain-numbing work. For every brief moment of brilliant, actionable insight, untold hours and immeasurable effort were wasted poring over meaningless gibberish. And to top it off, cooperation was not exactly the order of the day. The Brits did not entirely trust the Americans and were unwilling to share any headway that they were making. And the Americans were not sharing with the Brits, either.

Ward walked over to the office's stainless steel coffeepot and poured himself a cup of whatever the sludge was that came out of the carafe. Coal tar? Asphalt? The foul brew must have been stewing for a while. The thick, dark stuff was no longer liquid. Oh well. It didn't matter. It contained caffeine and that was exactly what Ward needed at the moment. Between the long, tedious hours there at the COMSUPPATFOR Intel Center and his new baby boy, Jonathan, just starting to teethe at home, the Lieutenant was dragging tail.

Even so, Ward smiled at the thought of his son. And of his wife, Karen. Things could be worse. He could be stationed a long way from his family like some other naval officers he knew. One benefit of his job and its high security clearance was that he could take a peek and keep up with three of his buddies, close friends since their days together at the US Naval Academy. They were living their dreams of being submarine officers, maybe someday commanding their own boats, but they were doing so while far, far away from home.

All four young officers had chosen submarine duty upon graduation from Annapolis. Trip MacLean, son of a US Senator, had gotten into trouble one too many times and was promptly exiled to the wardroom of an old *S*-boat way out in the Philippines, half a world away. Brad Johnson, son of an Admiral, was heading to Pearl Harbor, about to take the USS *Tigerfish* thousands more miles, all the way to Cavite, the same navy base as MacLean. Fred Wurster, a star athlete at the Academy but much less skilled in academics and thus supposedly the least likely of the four to find success in submarines, had already served heroically in a dicey, highly classified operation in Newfoundland. Now, he was about to help with final prep and take a new *Gato*-class boat from San Francisco Bay, beneath the still-new Golden Gate Bridge, and out to Pearl Harbor, Hawaii.

But Stan Ward's submarine service aspirations had been rudely redirected.

At least Ward, the son of a Colorado farmer, could go home most nights to wife and son. But his work at the Intel Center was arduous and required long hours away from his family.

Being a submarine officer had become an impossible dream for Ward when he was badly injured in a bus accident while en route across the country from the Colorado high plains to sub school in Connecticut. But the horrible accident that ended his hopes for submarine duty had also given him some huge positives. He met Karen, a nurse, during his recovery in a hospital in Kansas. And then he—and the right people in the Navy—discovered he had a knack for helping to solve the multi-dimensional puzzles presented by Naval Intelligence. Even if he did have a bum leg that prevented him from going out on normal sea duty, from ever commanding his own submarine, he was enjoying a pretty good life with his wife and boy. He was also contributing as best he could to trying to figure out what Herr Hitler and his Kriegsmarine were doing with their U-boats.

Now, if he could just help break this damn ENIGMA code!

"Hey, Stan, come in here a moment," Ollie Oglethorpe called from his tiny office, interrupting Ward's thoughts. "Need to talk with you."

Commander Ollie Oglethorpe was the Skipper of the Intel Center and Stan's boss. Though he could be a bit of an eccentric and he was stubbornly set in his ways, Oglethorpe was a brilliant and insightful intelligence officer, and one of the first to notice Stan Ward's unique skills. The rumor was that the Commander could figure out what the Germans had planned before they even decided on it themselves.

Ward grabbed his coffee cup and stepped into Ollie's office. He had to beat his way through the thick cloud of pipe smoke to find a place to sit. Oglethorpe had his favorite old briar puffing away like a steam engine.

"What ya need, boss?" Ward asked as he removed a stack of files from a chair, put them amid stacks of other files already on the floor, and plopped down.

Oglethorpe stopped sucking on the pipe long enough to scrape the smoldering tobacco from the bowl, open a new bag, and tamp in a fresh load. When he was satisfied that the tobacco was sufficiently tamped, he took his time lighting it afire, setting off another billow of smoke. Ward sat patiently but wondering why the Commander was stalling.

"How is little Jonathan doing?" Oglethorpe finally asked. Still buying time, delaying whatever it was he actually wanted to discuss. "You look like you ain't gettin' much sleep and I expect it's not just Nazis and ENIGMA."

"That's a bit of an understatement," Ward answered with a chuckle. "The rascal's teething and he ain't real happy about it. I don't think Karen or I have had a solid night's sleep in weeks." Ward studied Oglethorpe carefully. The intel officer's demeanor was an open book. Ollie had something on his mind besides the baby's dental progress and Ward's bleary eyes. And Ward most wanted to get on back to his desk and look for common threads on all those reports on his clipboard. "So, what's up, boss?"

Oglethorpe shoved a folder full of papers across the desk to the Lieutenant.

"What we got here?"

"Your orders," Oglethorpe answered. "Stan, they're shutting us down and moving us all the hell out to the Philippines. Somebody in Washington seems to think we'd be a lot more useful trying to read the Japs' mail since we are clearly stymied by what the Nazis are using. They're going to leave ENIGMA to the Brits. You ever hear of a program called MAGIC?"

Ward thought for a moment and then shook his head. “Nope, can’t say that I have.”

Oglethorpe took another drag on his pipe and blew out a cloud of fragrant smoke. “Well, MAGIC is the name for our project to crack the Jap JN-25 code. I understand that it’s damn near as hard to break as the German ENIGMA. And besides that, here’s a surprise. It’s in Japanese. Somebody with some clout is thinking the Emperor of Japan poses a bigger threat to us at the moment than *Reichskanzler* Hitler does. Anyway, we’re scheduled to fly out there the end of next week, so don’t buy any green bananas. We’re going to flesh out an Army operation called Station CAST in a place called Cavite.”

“How long you think we’ll be there? At...what’d you call it? Cavite?”

“Who knows? I don’t suspect we’ll be back for a bit, though. Look, Stan, you best get home, break the news to Karen, and get the home life set up.”

Ward stood but he was suddenly dizzy, disoriented, as if the ground beneath his feet had become unreliable, the smoky air in the room unbreathable. He had no idea where Cavite was. Or where the words would come from when he told his wife he was about to go there, and she and Jonathan were not.

3

Trip MacLean was thoroughly enjoying the warm tropical breeze that gently wafted out of the east. The black night sea was calm. A full moon blazed a silver trail across the water. He had the bridge of the *S-55* all to himself with only the lookouts up in the periscope shears above him to keep him company. Meanwhile, somewhere twenty miles ahead, the *Porpoise* was steaming to their rendezvous off Caunayan Point, the northernmost extension of the Philippine Island of Luzon.

"Bridge, Control, normal battery charge complete," the 7MC blasted, muddying his revery.

MacLean grabbed the microphone and answered, "Bridge, aye. Inform the Captain that the normal battery charge is complete. Answer bells on both main engines. Answer ahead full."

"Bridge, the Captain is being informed. Answer bells on both main engines, ahead full, aye."

MacLean took a sip from his coffee cup and stared up at the sky. From the Southern Cross, well down on the southern horizon, to the Little Dipper, low in the heavens to the north, millions of stars pricked holes in the nighttime canopy when the moon was occasionally curtained by clouds.

"Mr. MacLean, sir, I have a contact," Seaman First Class Thurgood

Williams called out. He pointed off toward the northwest. "Low down on the horizon, fine on the port bow. I'm not seeing any lights, though."

MacLean grabbed his 7X50 binoculars and scanned the horizon in the direction that Williams pointed. Yes, there was something there. He could just make out what looked like a dark shadow. Glancing down at the compass repeater, he estimated that the smudge was at a bearing of three-five-zero true.

"Control, Bridge, we have a surface contact on bearing three-five-zero. On the horizon. Report contact to the Captain," MacLean reported over the 7MC. "Can you see it through the scope?"

There was a short pause before the XO's voice came back over the 7MC. "Bridge, Control, we see the contact. Unable to classify yet. Too dark right now. Captain has the word. Commenced tracking the surface contact."

MacLean glanced up to where Seaman Williams clung to the periscope shears a good ten feet above where the Lieutenant stood. "Good catch, Williams," he shouted. "Keep an eye on him. Probably some tramp steamer hauling rice down to Baguio."

"Reckon why he's running with no lights, sir?"

"You know these Filipino sailors. Most likely forgot to turn them on."

MacLean had just settled back down, pouring himself a fresh cup of coffee from the Thermos, when the 7MC crackled once again. "Bridge, XO, we're getting a better look at the surface contact. Best guess is a warship and it's closing pretty fast. It now bears three-five-seven true. Best range, six-five hundred yards."

Quickly throwing the coffee over the side, MacLean grabbed the binoculars and took another look. Whatever it was, it could not be more than five thousand yards away from them. Less than three miles, and it was on a course to cut them off. He regretted that he had not paid more attention when they were teaching ship recognition at sub school. He figured he would always have access to recognition posters and manuals. But not in the dark, on the bridge of a submarine, with a mysterious ship barreling down on him.

At least he remembered enough to conclude the vessel that was quickly filling his binoculars was a warship. The clearly visible guns told him that. From somewhere in the recesses of his brain, he decided that he was staring at an Imperial Japanese Navy *Mogami*-class heavy cruiser. And from the bow wave it was kicking up, it had to be making twenty-five knots or more. But what was a Japanese heavy cruiser doing in American waters just off the Philippine coast, and why was it running with a darkened ship straight at *S-55*?

MacLean was pondering those questions when he saw a brilliant flash of light, then a bright streak arrowing up from the warship. *Jesus, was that...?*

Then he heard something that sounded almost like a freight train rushing past them, directly overhead. A huge column of water geysered upward a couple of hundred yards beyond the stern of his submarine.

It took the young submariner only a short second to realize that he was being shot at.

In the meantime, the Japanese warship fired off another round. This one fell short by a mere one hundred yards. Another fact somehow got pulled from the recesses of MacLean's brain. A heavy cruiser like this one packed eight-inch main guns. Just one direct hit would blow the little *S-55*—and the forty-two men aboard her—into tiny bits.

"Mr. Maclean...uh...dive the ship." Tony DiCarlo's quavering, unsure voice came over the 7MC.

MacLean turned his face up toward the lookouts, cupped his hands around his mouth, and yelled, "Clear the bridge!" The three lookouts had heard the Captain and were already diving for the hatch as MacLean grabbed the 1MC microphone and ordered, "Dive! Dive!" He yanked the diving alarm twice for two blasts before he followed the lookouts down the hatch.

He dropped into pandemonium. The submarine was angling down sharply, her bow aimed toward the safety of the deep, trying to get a protective cover of water overhead before a shell found them. Watchstanders were running around aimlessly, seemingly not sure where they were supposed to be or what they should be doing. Sam Forester, the XO, stood by the navigation plot with a blank expression on his face, staring at the depth gauge as if it held the answer to life. Or might suddenly tell him what to do to try to dodge the next incoming round.

Another very close explosion rocked the submarine. MacLean looked around. He saw no apparent damage, but the air in the control room was instantly filled with dust and bits of cork hull insulation.

Skipper Tony DiCarlo, who stood in the shadows behind piping in the corner of the control room, ordered, just loud enough to be heard, "Make your depth two hundred feet. Ahead flank."

They were diving deeper and running as fast as the ship would go. The *S-55* took an even sharper angle downward and simultaneously raced ahead. Crewmembers had to grab hold of something solid to keep from falling as the deck slanted dangerously. What the hell was DiCarlo thinking? Why weren't they even trying to fight back? MacLean stepped over to stand beside the Captain.

"Skipper, recommend going to Battle Stations," the Lieutenant said in a voice that only the two of them could hear. With that simple command, they could clear up some of the chaos and be ready to defend the ship. Crewmen would know where they were to go and what they were to do. DiCarlo stared back blankly. It was as if MacLean was speaking Japanese. "Captain, we need to be ready to defend ourselves."

No response.

MacLean looked carefully at DiCarlo. The man was staring straight ahead. His eyes were fixed on the forward bulkhead. And his hands were shaking uncontrollably. The young officer had a sudden realization. Tony DiCarlo had been a submariner for a dozen years, had traveled in subs for thousands of miles, dived and surfaced hundreds of times.

But he had never been shot at before.

Now, his submarine was running as fast as it could go on battery power, and it was doing it as deep as they could go in the ocean.

"Control, Maneuvering, battery is at maximum discharge rate."

The 7MC reported that they were draining the sub's battery as much as it was possible to do. They needed to slow down. Soon. At a flank bell, their tired, old battery could not last more than fifteen minutes before it was totally depleted. That was only half the issue. Once the battery cell voltages fell too low, the weakest cells would reverse, actually sucking charge from other cells. Then there was a real danger of the battery short-circuiting and catching fire. That would be catastrophic! Explosive!

MacLean looked over at DiCarlo, his face barely visible in the shadows. There was no response from the Skipper.

"Captain, we need to slow down before we drain the battery and reverse cells," MacLean implored, still quietly enough that no one else could hear him explaining things to the CO.

DiCarlo was mumbling something MacLean had to strain to hear: "Gotta get away. Gotta get away."

"Battery at minimum voltage!" the voice on the 7MC called out urgently. "Recommend slowing!"

The electrician back in Maneuvering had also recognized the predicament they were in. But MacLean still saw no response from DiCarlo. They had already run more than three miles from where they first ducked underwater. The Japanese warship was long gone astern, no longer a threat. MacLean came to a conclusion. He had no choice.

"Ahead one-third," he ordered. That would lower the discharge rate a lot and hopefully buy some time.

"Control, Maneuvering, recommend all stop. Individual cell voltages show three cells already reversed."

Explosive situation! At two hundred feet below the surface, every bit as dangerous as the shells of the Japanese warship. Maybe more so.

DiCarlo was shaking his head, but his eyes remained closed tightly, as if he was in denial of their dire situation. MacLean steeled himself for the angry reprimand he knew was coming. He had just directly countermanded the CO's orders. He would pay a heavy price for that. And he was about to do it again. His naval career was likely over.

Then DiCarlo seemed to abruptly wake up. He calmly looked around the control room and ordered, "All stop." Glancing over at the young officer, he said, "Mr. MacLean, we will discuss this in my stateroom later."

Just then, Sam Forester slid down the ladder from the conning tower. DiCarlo told him, "XO, let's stay down deep until daybreak. Then we can go up and report this attack when everything is safe and it has calmed down topside."

MacLean started to protest, to make the case that they needed to report immediately. That murderous Jap might next shoot at the unsuspecting *Porpoise* or some other innocent vessel. And even if that did not happen, the other submarine would certainly report *S-55* overdue for their rendezvous, setting off a serious search operation.

But DiCarlo merely shook his head and said, "Later, Mr. MacLean. We will discuss this later."

∞

Kaigun Chusa (Captain) Akito Saito smiled as he ordered, "Cease fire."

He supported his heavy Nippon Kogaku 10X80 night vision binoculars on the bridge railing and carefully scanned the horizon. Nothing out there but calm, tropical water and a few lights dotting the distant coastline of Luzon. The forward 127mm guns of his *Asashio*-class destroyer *Kasumi* had done their work. The submarine, most assuredly an American one, had been sunk.

"Officer-of-the-Deck, resume course one-zero-zero, ahead full," Saito ordered.

Saito stepped into the enclosed bridge and back to the chart table. Carefully shielding the dim red flashlight so that he did not night-blind anyone else on the bridge, he studied the chart. Only thirty-five kilometers to Bangui Bay. That was less than an hour steaming. Then two hours reconnoitering the shallow bay before racing back out into the South China Sea well before daylight. That should be plenty of time to determine if Bangui Bay could support an amphibious assault landing.

Looking at his watch and doing some quick mental arithmetic, Saito smiled again. By the time the sun was fully above the horizon to the east, the *Kasumi* would be over two hundred kilometers to the north, better than halfway across the Luzon Strait. Then they would be back home in Kaohsiung, Formosa, in time for an afternoon *onsen* in the hot springs above the city. He felt more relaxed simply by thinking about it.

Saito stepped up to the forward bridge window and gazed out at the open sea for a few seconds. Then he said, "*Kaigun Chui* Kato, send a message to the Squadron Commodore. Inform him that we encountered an American submarine that we sank with gunfire before he had a chance to report. The *Kasumi* remains undetected. We are proceeding with the mission."

Sub-Lieutenant Kato snapped to attention and sharply answered, "*Hai!*"

Saito headed toward his little sea cabin. There was just enough time for a celebratory cup of tea before they started their covert and invaluable survey of Bangui Bay.

∞

The roar of four turbo-charged Wright R-1820 Cyclone engines made conversation on the aircraft next to impossible. Most of the US Navy Intel team, passengers on this flight, were curled up on the deck, dozing. Or at least attempting to. The group had luckily managed to hitch a ride with a squadron of B-17 bombers being deployed to Clark Field in the Philippines. Such transportation did not exactly provide first-class accommodations, but a week spent bunny-hopping across the US and then the Pacific Ocean sure beat the month and a half it would have required to make the same journey on a train and then a steamer, plodding along across that same endless expanse.

The team was small. Only a half dozen cryptologists, a couple of signal analysts, along with Ollie Oglethorpe and Stan Ward. They left the linguists and the radio operators back since there would be little need for German language experts in that part of the world. Plus, the Army assured them that they would have plenty of radio operators at Cavite.

The team first met up with the twelve planes of the 30th Bombardment Squadron at the brand-new Windsor Locks Army Air Base in northern Connecticut. They took off from there before dawn and expected to arrive at March Field outside of Riverside, California, just after sunset. The next day, they would make the long hop to Hawaii. Then Midway, Wake Island, Port Moresby, New Guinea, and on from there to Darwin, Australia, before finally arriving in the Philippines.

Stan Ward spent most of his time looking out the oval-shaped side gun window. It would without question be a very long and very boring flight. That was especially the case now as the flight of twelve B-17E Flying Fortresses were winging along ten thousand feet above the flat Kansas plain. Somewhere down there, he knew, a train was making its run across the same flatlands, taking Karen and his son Jonathan to Salina, Kansas, and her family.

Ward experienced a brief moment of sadness and loneliness before feeling relief. His young family would be safe and secure there with the Kamp family. And it was not that far from his own family farm outside Lamar, Colorado, so his parents could have time with their daughter-in-law and first grandson. Karen had already signed on for a job at her former place of employment, the Asbury Hospital, too. With a possible war looming, there was no telling how long they would be separated. Both he and Karen realistically knew it could be a while. And agreed that her childhood home in Kansas was the place for her and young Jonathan.

"Sure is flat," Ollie Oglethorpe yelled as he plopped down beside Ward. He pulled out a Thermos and a couple of mugs. "Coffee?"

"Thanks." Ward happily took a cup. "Yep. Beautiful country, ain't it?"

It really looked more like a dusty brown tabletop with a few sparse patches of green fields. Ward pointed off to the northwest. "I grew up just a little ways north of here. Out here, sometimes it feels like you can see forever." He pointed off to the west to a cloud-covered mountaintop beyond the plains. "That's Pikes Peak. We're over two hundred miles away and that lump of granite still dominates the horizon. I suspect we'll skirt around to the south, down over New Mexico. That way, we don't have to go on oxygen to climb up over the Rockies."

As if on cue, the big bird swung to the southwest.

"I made my departure call on Admiral Edwards yesterday," Oglethorpe said, changing the subject.

"I hope you ditched that cardigan and wore shoes this time," Ward scoffed. Ollie was notorious for his "informal office attire," usually including a ratty old cardigan sweater and bedroom slippers. "Comfort trumps protocol," he maintained. "The Navy wants me to think, and I think much, much better when I'm comfortable." He had been known to absentmindedly rush upstairs to the Admiral's office when summoned, forgetting to change into a uniform in the process. The boss always gave him grief about it, but so far, nothing formal or hurtful. "Double-O," as the Admiral called him, was simply too important to Naval Intelligence to allow fashion or formality to get in the way.

"Yes, you precocious young whippersnapper," Oglethorpe retorted with a chuckle. "What I was trying to say, before I was interrupted by your disrespectful sartorial comment, was that the Admiral related some directions from Main Navy that don't appear in the text of our orders."

His voice had quickly lost its playful tone. Main Navy was the headquarters building for the Department of the Navy in Washington, DC. Directions emanating from there, whether official and on paper or otherwise, were serious stuff. "Evidently, the Navy powers-that-be recognize that we are being lent to the Army on a liaison basis and since, for all practical purposes, we will report to the Army chain of command, we are instructed to not lose sight of the fact that we are a Navy operation. I'm supposed to set up a back-channel communications path back to the Navy command in Pearl Harbor. We're all on the same team, but..."

"Sounds to me like Big Navy doesn't exactly trust General MacArthur," Ward mused. "I understand that MacArthur does have a reputation for kingdom building and for not playing nice with others. My dad is still boiling mad with the way MacArthur handled the Bonus Army thing in '32. You're not allowed to even mention his name in the Ward house."

In 1932, General Douglas MacArthur, then the Army Chief of Staff, had used infantry, cavalry, and tanks to forcefully chase thousands of Great War–veteran demonstrators, upset about how their benefits were being withheld during the Depression, out of Washington. Many of the veterans and their families were injured or killed in the ensuing clash with the Army.

Ward rubbed his chin. "We'd best be real careful. The guy has a reputation for getting more than even with anyone that crosses him. And he's wearing enough stars to make that 'getting even' real painful for us minions."

Oglethorpe nodded. "Point taken. Let's be real careful. You know, get it done, but get it done the Navy way."

"Yeah. The Navy way."

4

Freddy Wurster picked up his pace a bit. A cool, misty morning fog had rolled in off San Pablo Bay overnight, enshrouding everything in a cottony pillow rising up over the Napa River. The fog would quickly burn off in the late-autumn California sunshine, revealing the bustling shipyard down the hill and the gritty industrial town of Vallejo just across the river.

The short walk down from the BOQ to the fitting-out pier gave Wurster a precious few minutes to think. The previous several weeks had flown by, shrouded in a blur of frenetic activity. The Shipyard Commander had abruptly decided that getting the submarine *Wolffish* to sea was a priority. That pronouncement immediately opened the floodgates. It seemed that every shipyard worker that could be mustered spent all his time on or around the boat. There were so many bodies crammed onto the deck and inside the confined submarine that Wurster could not see how anyone could move, let alone get any work done. But before it seemed possible, the *Wolffish* was determined to be complete and ready for sea trials.

Today would be the day for the new vessel's first taste of saltwater.

Wurster strolled down Nereus Street and out to Berth 15 beyond, to where the *Wolffish* was tied up. He had to nimbly step around a shipyard crane that was swinging a pallet load of gear off the submarine's still-cluttered topside. Shipyard workers had formed a human chain on the after brow to pass tools and loose gear off the boat while the crew had formed a similar line on the forward brow to pass groceries on board.

The young submariner shook his head. He could see no way that the *Wolffish* could break free from the shipyard's clutches today. Too much to still accomplish and too little time to get it done. Any underway from the Mare Island Shipyard was a balancing act between the clock and the tides. The Napa River was shallow. To safely navigate the mud flats that formed where the river flowed into the Carquinez Straits, they needed as much water as they could get. The only window that was safe for an underway was about an hour either side of high tide. Even then, the naval engineers' calculations showed that they only had a couple of feet clearance between their keel and the muddy bottom. It would not do for the bright, shiny, new *Wolffish* to find herself ignobly stuck in the silt and sand. Especially on their first underway. But the clock was not going to do them any favors. Maximum high tide at this spot came at 1313. Missing that two-hour window meant waiting until midnight. That would be the next high tide.

Wurster carefully made his way across the forward brow and down the hatch into the forward torpedo room. Sure enough, belowdecks was just as crowded and frenzied as topside. He had to scoot by men passing boxes and cans down the line to their eventual storage locations. "Cookie" Ramirez, the head cook, clutched a metal clipboard and yelled out directions for where each box and can was to be stuffed. There was definitely a method to his madness.

Wurster smiled as he made his way aft. There must be some kind of rule in the submarine service that every cook had to be named "Cookie." Every Corpsman is "Doc." And the Engineering Officer is "Eng."

"Hey, Eng," Jim Shelton, the XO, hollered as Wurster stepped past the wardroom. "You have the engine trials plan all worked out?" Shelton was seated at a table stacked high with paperwork and littered with empty coffee cups and an overflowing ashtray.

Wurster stepped into the tiny space and poured himself a cup of coffee from the shiny stainless steel pot. "Yeah, XO," he offered. "All planned out. We'll do most of the tests on the run down San Pablo Bay past Richmond and out through the Golden Gate. Then we'll do the full-power run once we are in deep water and well clear of land. That's two hours at a flank bell running north past Point Reyes and back. That's a pretty good check, I'd say."

"Okay." Shelton nodded. "Just so we're through the Gate an hour before sundown. I'm not really comfortable running through there at night." He grabbed another file and began scanning it. Then, remembering something, he glanced up and added, "Oh, and Chief Wankel was looking for you a little bit ago. Says he wants to show you something." Then he remembered something else and passed Wurster an envelope. "And this came in the mail for you."

Wurster nodded, stuffed the envelope in a pocket, and turned to head aft. He would read the letter later.

He knew without asking that Chief Wankel, the leading engineman, would be back with his beloved diesels. The man positively breathed Fairbanks-Morse 38D8⅛ diesels. This would be a big day for him, and the Chief would be making sure that his four babies were ready to roar. Literally and figuratively. Sure enough, Wurster found him changing out the oil filters on number two diesel.

"Mornin', sir. I wanna make sure these are all clean and ready to sing," the Chief said as he grabbed a rag to wipe his oily hands. "Wouldn't do to have a clogged strainer on engine trials, now would it, Eng."

"That's for sure, Chief."

Then, with a frown on his face, Wankel reached up to grab a wadded-up cloth that was stuffed in a cranny in the overhead. "Here is what the XO sent you back to take a look at." He unwrapped the cloth, revealing a small pile of shiny metal filings. "I found this in the filters on number three engine. And I just now found the same thing on two. The boys are checking one and four right now."

Wurster rubbed some of the metal between his fingertips. The stuff was hard and sharp. "What is it?" he asked. "Doesn't feel like bearing babbitt."

Bearing babbitt was a soft alloy of tin, lead, and antimony. It was used to provide a low-friction, wear-resistant surface for rotating shafts, like a diesel crankshaft. It was not uncommon to find a little babbitt in the filters while breaking in a new engine.

"It's not," Wankel said, shaking his head. "It's steel grinding filings. Someone had to intentionally dump this in the oil sumps."

"Sabotage?" Wurster asked, dreading the answer.

"My guess," Chief Wankel said with a nod. "We'll have to drain and flush all four engines. That'll take all morning, but me and the boys will get it done. Better break the news to the XO."

Lieutenant Wurster found XO Shelton and Steve Leland, *Wolffish*'s CO, in the control room reviewing the navigation charts. He unwrapped the little pile of metal filings and showed it to them. After explaining what Chief Wankel believed they were and how they got into the oil sumps, Wurster explained that the underway would have to be delayed at least until the next high tide.

Lieutenant Commander Leland, his usual clipped Boston accent even shorter and sharper than usual, said, "XO, move the underway to midnight. Eng, make a thorough inspection of those diesels. We got to make damn sure this was the only sabotage. Right now, I'm going to call the Shipyard Commander and get them investigating. Tell the Chief to keep this quiet. I doubt it's anybody in the crew, but we don't want the sneaky, conniving bastard to know we caught this before it could do any damage. We leave on the midnight tide if I have to carry this boat down the channel on my back!"

His face contorted in anger, the Skipper stomped off to his stateroom to make the call.

It was almost 1700 when Chief Wankel reported that the oil flushes were complete. They had not found any more metal filings or any other signs of sabotage attempts.

Two ONI agents from the shipyard District Intelligence Office came over the *Wolffish*'s brow just as the sun slipped behind the Marin Headlands to the west. They took custody of the metal filings and questioned Chief Wankel and a couple of his machinists for a good hour before getting back in their car and driving away.

The *Wolffish* officially got underway for the first time when all lines were cast off at 2315. The submarine twisted out into the Napa River, made the sharp right turn into the Carquinez Strait, and then eased out into the broad-but-shallow San Pablo Bay. The channel was well marked and lighted so the navigation was easy. Low-power engine trials filled the time it took to transit down to Point San Pablo. Once they rounded the rocky promontory, Chief Wankel was ready to open up the throttles. He carefully watched his four rock-crusher babies as they pushed the *Wolffish* down across San Francisco Bay and then out through the Golden Gate, passing under the orange-painted bridge of the same name.

Fred Wurster felt the first Pacific rollers lift the submarine's bow as they passed Point Bonita to starboard. Looking out over the broad Pacific, all he could see was a dark, black sea and a million stars. San Francisco's bright lights were behind them, hidden by the Presidio. Out ahead was empty ocean. Then, five thousand miles away, the Empire of Japan.

Wurster grabbed the 7MC and reported, "Control, Bridge, to the Captain. Clear of Point Bonita. Request permission to commence full-power run."

The response was immediate. "Bridge, Control. Captain to the bridge."

Steve Leland's head appeared through the hatch as Wurster was putting the mike back in its holder. "Mr. Wurster, commence full-power run."

"Commence full-power run, aye." Wurster grabbed the 7MC again and ordered, "Ahead flank. Commence full-power run."

With a broad grin on his face, Leland lifted himself up so that he could take a seat on top of the fairwater, above the bridge enclosure and just below the periscope shears. The fairwater was the metal enclosure that surrounded the conning tower, all the mast-hoisting mechanisms, and the diesel induction piping. It housed essentially everything above the submarine's main deck. The narrow, rounded top of the fairwater was as high as a person could get without climbing up into the shears.

"I can get a better view up here. One of the advantages of these *Gato* boats. Would you hand me my coffee, Freddy?"

It was the first time in their weeks of working together that Leland had called him by his given name. It was always "Mr. Wurster" or "Eng" or "Lieutenant." Wurster grabbed the Skipper's mug and handed it up to him.

The deep-throated roar of the four diesels took a higher pitch as they shoved the twenty-four-hundred-ton submarine forward. The *Wolffish* leapt ahead, plunging into a wave crest and then rising clear out into the trough. The waves would slam the boat almost to a stop before it punched free and raced on to the next one.

"Bridge, Maneuvering, all engines running normal." Chief Wankel's voice sounded positively happy, almost giddy.

There was a voice on the bridge speaker. "Bridge, XO, recommend we slow until we clear these waves. Should be smoother when we turn north into the Gulf of the Farallones. Ten minutes to turn."

As fun as the ride was up on the bridge, it was probably tossing folks around below. They could not see and brace themselves for the upcoming waves. Wurster glanced back and up at Leland. From his perch above the bridge, the Skipper shook his head and yelled over the rushing wind, "Hell no! Right full rudder. Steer course three-one-zero. Let's see what she'll do!" He laughed as the wind blew his usually carefully combed hair askew. The CO was having himself one hell of a good time showing off his new hotrod.

The submarine's bow swung sharply to the right just as a particularly large wave slammed into it. The combination of the turn and the massive wall of water slammed the submarine sharply over to starboard and drove the bow under. Wurster's previous experiences on an old *S*-boat in the winter North Atlantic paid off. He seized the chance to take a quick gulp of air and wrapped both arms around the bridge railing before the water rolled over him. After what felt like an eternity under the cold, dark deluge, the submarine snapped back up and he found himself once again in the clear night air.

The Navy had promised that the new class of submarines would be much better vessels on the surface than previous boats had been. That certainly appeared to be the case.

"Skipper, you okay?" Wurster called out. No answer. "Skipper?" He looked up to the fairwater, then around the bridge. No sign of Steve Leland. A horrible image flashed through his mind of another cold, dark night, during Wurster's previous duty in the North Atlantic.

Another man overboard.

"Man overboard! All stop!" he yelled into the 1MC. "The Captain's overboard!"

Wurster looked up into the periscope shears. The lookouts dangled crazily from their safety harnesses but were busily scrambling back up to their perches. At least he had not lost them over the side, too.

He grabbed his binoculars and carefully searched the water. No sign of the Skipper. The ocean was empty.

"Control, Bridge, I'm going to do a Williamson turn and head back down our track. You seeing anything through the periscope?"

"Bridge, XO, we were turning when the Skipper went overboard. Recommend an expanding circle search. Contacting Coast Guard now. Launching a red flare from the forward signal ejector."

Wurster thought for just a second. Shelton's recommendation made sense. There was not much "track" to go back down. The circle search had the advantage of the current setting the boat in the same direction as a man in the water would be swept along. "Left full rudder," he ordered. "All ahead one-third."

A red flare illuminated the night sky as it arched up and then slowly parachuted back to earth.

They started a slow, careful search, but nothing was visible in the pitching and heaving seas.

"Bridge, XO, Coast Guard reports that they are scrambling an RD-4 Dolphin seaplane now. They'll have a patrol boat underway in an hour. Seaplane is twenty minutes out. Patrol boat ETA is 0530. Two more planes at dawn and another patrol boat."

Wurster looked at his watch. It would be twenty minutes before they got any help at all and two hours before a boat arrived. Not much hope of an airplane finding a man in the water at night or even a boat doing much better once it got there. Even if he was a good swimmer, the chances of Leland staying alive and afloat in the cold North Pacific waters until dawn were slim at best.

"Bridge, aye," Wurster answered. "XO, can you get some more lookouts up here?"

Even with a dozen sets of eyes scanning the horizon from the navigation deck forward and the cigarette deck aft, the search was futile. The clumsy looking RD-4 twin-engine seaplane soon buzzed overhead and started a slow circular search around the *Wolffish*. A couple of civilian fishing boats, heading out for a day's work on the water, answered the emergency flare and volunteered to join the search. When dawn came, three seaplanes and a dozen watercraft of various kinds were slowly searching and re-searching the seas between the Marin Headlands and the Farallon Islands.

It was noon before anyone was willing to admit defeat. There was nothing else to do. The *Wolffish* made its slow, sad return to Mare Island.

All along the way, Fred Wurster thought to himself what a bad omen this was for the new warship. And wondered if somebody was going to get washed off every submarine he might ever take to sea.

∞

The SS *Lurline*, a great white passenger liner flying the Matson Line flag, eased against the fenders at Pier 9. The ten-story-tall Aloha Tower rose high above the pier, welcoming the ship's passengers to Honolulu, Hawaii. Brad Johnson stood at the ship's rail, watching the leisurely bustle as brows were put in place for the passengers to disembark. Meanwhile, a group of grass-skirted hula dancers lined up to perform at the base of the brow, and several vendors with their carts piled high with flower leis vied for the best locations to set up shop. The warm tropical air brought scents of jasmine and ginger, adding to the laid-back island vibe. He wondered if the Chamber of Commerce might be piping in the signature aromas to make a good impression on the tourist and military passengers. Then he decided he would try to be less cynical and get off on the right foot on this new assignment.

"Ready to head for the boat?" Lieutenant Isaac Sternman asked as he plopped his seabag down next to Johnson and took in a deep breath of the fragrant air. "First time to the Islands? Beautiful, ain't it?" He pointed down at the line of cabs queued up at the end of the pier, all with their trunks agape, passenger doors open, and drivers standing by. "Wanna split a cab? They charge a buck to deliver you to the pier at the subbase."

"A buck! You gotta be kidding!" Johnson was aghast. "That's worse than Times Square."

"Welcome to the Islands," Sternman deadpanned. "Everything costs more here."

The two officers hurried down the gangplank, put their seabags into the open trunk of a bright orange cab with "Charley's Taxi" painted on the side in big black letters, and then climbed into the back seat. They did not even have to tell the cabbie where they were going. He had spotted their dolphin pins. The taxi shot down Kamehameha Highway toward Pearl Harbor but immediately slowed to a crawl. The busy street was clogged with trucks delivering supplies and material to the many construction sites that claimed the land on either side of the busy highway. The move of the Navy's Pacific Fleet headquarters to Pearl Harbor beginning in mid-1940 had certainly caused a construction boom all over Honolulu. The seven-mile journey took almost half an hour, but eventually Sternman and Johnson were dropped off at Pier S-1 on the Submarine Base.

Brad Johnson stared at his new home waiting for them there at the pier. The USS *Tigerfish*, a brand-new *Gato*-class submarine, floated quietly in the aqua-tinted water. Johnson could not help but take note of how very different this boat was from his last one, the old, battered *S-54*. That vessel was now languishing at the Portsmouth Navy Shipyard in freezing cold Kittery, Maine, undergoing repairs after some very tough duty—top secret duty, back in August—in the operation near Argentia, Newfoundland. To Johnson, the *Tigerfish* looked as if she was crouched there at the pier, ready to spring forth, if only someone would slip the lines and allow her to prowl.

Isaac Sternman slapped Johnson on the back and laughed. "Stop drooling, Brad. It's unbecoming an officer in the US Navy, don't you know?" He hoisted his seabag over his shoulder and walked toward the brow. "Let's get aboard and take over this fine yacht."

The two had just dropped down the ladder into the forward torpedo room and were picking up their seabags when they were met by a deep, booming voice. "You boys must be the new XO and the new Nav. Welcome aboard the *Tigerfish*."

Johnson's eyes had adjusted just enough from the bright sun topside to be able to see a short, balding man coming their way. His appearance did not match his voice. But he wore a Lieutenant Commander's gold oak leaves. He shook hands with the two new arrivals and introduced himself. "I'm Wayne Schacter, but you can call me 'Skipper.' Glad you two are aboard. I hope you didn't plan on any island sightseeing or going surfing. You're gonna have to hit the deck running." Schacter brandished a sheaf of papers. "We just got orders to get underway bright and early Monday morning, destination Cavite Navy Yards in the Philippines to arrive on or before 20 December in the year of our Lord 1941. And to make life interesting, COMSUBPAC has ordered us to conduct a simulated war patrol on the way."

Turning to Sternman, he went on, "XO, I need for you and the COB to have the boat ready to go by then. Stores loaded, fully fueled, full weapons load-out, and the crew ready for underway. We still got guys that need to qualify, so we'll be doing that during our little cruise. And you need to put together a training plan to get the crew ready for a war patrol before we put into Midway for our refueling stop."

Sternman was flustered. "Uh...yes, sir," he stammered, "but where's the XO? Don't I need to conduct a relief with the current Exec?"

"Sorry, XO," Schacter replied. "Hate to report that Lt. Wilson is up at Tripler Hospital. He was in a car accident yesterday and he hasn't regained consciousness yet. He's in pretty bad shape. You got this one cold. COB is back in after battery setting up the stores load, so that's a good place to start."

Sternman gulped before he answered. "Yes, sir. I understand. We'll be ready to go. Guess I'd better go meet the COB and get crackin'." With that, he turned and headed aft to find the Chief of the Boat. He forgot to pick up his seabag. Johnson let him know and he trotted back for it, a sheepish look on his face.

The Skipper watched him go, then looked over at Brad Johnson. "You're a little luckier. The Leading Quartermaster is in Control. He'd better be breaking out the charts and beginning voyage planning."

"Skipper?" Johnson had a curious look on his face. "I gotta ask you. Navigator is normally the job of the XO on most boats, right?"

"Yes, it is, Mr. Johnson," Schacter explained, "but the XO is going to have his hands full getting the *Tigerfish* out of here on schedule and getting the crew fit to fight this war everybody but me thinks is coming. I'm thinking that making you the Navigator relieves him of that responsibility and he can concentrate on the details. You're going to find the Navigation department on this boat plenty complicated enough to challenge both your skills in the art of navigation and your leadership abilities. I know you'll do well. For now, though, I suggest that you throw your seabag into your stateroom and then go meet your department."

Brad Johnson, who could normally size up a man quickly and accurately, was not yet sure how to categorize his new Commanding Officer. When it came to submarine Skippers, the only comparison he really had was Stephen Brewster on the *S-54*. Brewster was always direct and no-nonsense. Nobody had to guess what Brewster was really saying. What he said out loud was always precisely what he was thinking. Somehow, Wayne Schacter just did not strike Johnson as being that way. He could not quite put his finger on the doubts he was having about the CO. But he could not for the life of him imagine Schacter ordering the *Tigerfish* to ram a U-boat when all the torpedoes he had just fired at the target had missed. To do whatever it took to sink the other vessel as ordered regardless of the risk to his boat, his crew, or himself.

That was exactly what Johnson had witnessed Stephen Brewster do with the *S-54* only a few months before.

5

The sun was just making its daily debut over the eastern horizon, promising another hot day on lonely, isolated Wake Island. A large colony of red-footed boobies with nests alongside the primitive airfield complained vociferously about the disturbance to the early-morning tropical calm caused by a sizeable formation of big airplanes preparing to take off.

Stan Ward, in the first B-17 in line, sat on the deck and braced himself against one of the plane's ribs for support. If the landing was any indication, takeoff from Wake Island's crushed coral runway would be bumpy as hell. It was hard to believe that he was already five thousand miles away from Karen and little Jonathan back in Kansas. And there was no way to know when he would see them again. Would Jonathan even remember his dad by then?

At least the long journey was nearing its end. They still had twelve hours from Wake Island to Port Moresby, New Guinea. Then a mere six hours to Darwin, Australia, followed by a final ten hours to Manila. With layovers in Port Moresby and Darwin, they should be in Manila on Tuesday, 3 December, on this side of the International Date Line.

Captain Greg Tillson, the pilot, taxied the big B-17E—nicknamed *Little Girl*, though the pinup painted on the plane's nose was hardly little, especially her eyes, her hair, and her other "attributes"—to the end of the runway and spun it around to line up with the long stretch of blinding white coral. The rest of the 30th Bombardment Squadron, all the other eleven planes, lined up on the taxiway behind *Little Girl*.

"Okay, children, hold on. This may be a bit bumpy," Tillson announced over the plane's intercom. As he always did when defying gravity in this aircraft, he patted the top of the instrument panel and muttered, "All right, *Little Girl*, it's time to do your stuff." Only then did he shove the four throttles ahead to full military power.

The quartet of huge Wright R-1820 Cyclone engines bellowed as *Little Girl* raced down the runway until the plane reached rotational speed. As the red-footed boobies fussed at them from their nests, Tillson pulled back on the control yoke and *Little Girl* reluctantly lifted off. Clawing for altitude into the crystalline blue sky, Tillson maintained the runway heading of two-eight-zero until he reached five thousand feet. Easing back on the throttles, he slowed to one hundred and eighty knots to allow the rest of the squadron to catch up and get into formation. At the same time, he swung the bird around to a bearing of two-zero-zero, the heading to Port Moresby, and edged the nose up to climb to ten thousand feet.

LT Sam Beyers looked out the right-hand window as they made the turn, took a quick count, and then reported, "All the birds are airborne."

Tillson keyed the radio microphone and ordered, "*Little Girl* to Flight, form up on me. Cruise speed two hundred, course two-zero-zero, angels ten." Then he eased the throttles forward to bring his own speed up to two hundred knots. Reaching over, he flicked the autopilot to "Engaged" and then sat back in his seat. "Now, for some coffee and a sandwich." He reached behind his seat for his Thermos and a bag of bologna sandwiches.

The flight was smooth until they were almost a thousand miles outbound. That was when the weather started to turn. Giant thunderheads rolled in from the southeast. A massive wall of roiling cumulonimbus clouds that towered to well above forty thousand feet. The dark, gray-black mass lit up with frequent flashes of jagged lightning. And the whole mess was coming toward the flight, threatening to cut them off and force them to fly through the violent winds and dangerous updrafts hidden in the darkening clouds.

"I ain't liking that," Tillson said, looking at the storm. "Let's come around to west and see if we can skirt all that mess." He keyed the radio and ordered, "*Little Girl* to Flight. Let's dodge that weather. Change course to two-seven-zero. Execute now."

He flicked the autopilot off and swung the big plane around to the new heading. At two hundred knots, they should be able to outrun the storm and then resume their southerly course to Port Moresby when they were past it.

Little Girl had just steadied up on the new course when LT Jim Swits, the plane's navigator, stuck his head in the cockpit. "Boss, this ain't a good course," he announced.

"Tell me, Jim. Why not?"

"This heading...well...it has us aimed directly toward Truk. The Japs aren't going to like a flight of US B-17s disturbing their afternoon tea ceremony."

"How far?" Tillson asked.

"Three hundred miles, give or take," Swits answered, rubbing his chin. "I haven't taken a fix since we took off. Winds aloft could have blown us a bit off course, so we could be closer."

"Shouldn't be that much of a problem," Tillson answered. "If we go west for an hour, we ought'a be clear of that storm." He jerked his thumb toward the ominous wall of dark clouds behind them. "And we'll still be a hundred miles from our Nipponese neighbors."

"You reckon they'd actually shoot at us if we got too close to them?"

"Who knows? They can be awful touchy, so let's don't tempt 'em. We'll keep our distance." Tillson chewed on his sandwich for a moment. "God willing," he added.

A few minutes later, Ollie Oglethorpe stuck his head up on the flight deck. "We seem to be jinking all over the sky, Greg. What gives?"

Tillson looked around at the tall, overweight Commander hunched down beside him. "Hey, Ollie, apologize for disturbing your nap time. We're just trying to skirt some heavy weather, but it has us heading right at the Jap base on Truk. I figure Truk is maybe a little over an hour's flying time ahead. We may be forced to come around into the storm to avoid the place."

"Good idea, from what I hear," Oglethorpe said. "They seem to be in a bad mood of late and have even shot at some of our aircraft and ships, declaration of war or not."

Tillson knew Oglethorpe was Naval Intelligence and likely knew what he was talking about. "Well, we won't give them a reason. But if we have to fly through that storm, you best tell your guys to hang on real tight. It'll probably be worse than anything the Japs might decide to throw at us."

He had just finished when something flashed dangerously close to the B-17's windscreen.

"Jap fighter!" Sam Beyers yelled. "Looked like a Zero!"

Sure enough, the dark-green fighter plane roared right down the middle of the bomber formation and then pulled up, climbing high above them. Bright red "meatballs"—the distinguishing rising-sun insignia of the Japanese warplanes—were clearly visible on each wing and on the fuselage. The plane made a large, lazy circle high above the bombers.

"Scout plane," Tillson announced. "He's calling home for orders." He keyed the radio and said, "*Little Girl* to Flight. We got unwelcome company. Be alert. Break out the guns but absolutely no shooting unless they shoot first. Coming left to course south."

"Calling for more of his buddies," Ollie said quietly.

"Naw, he's just messin' with us," the pilot offered. "Some lone wolf having some fun." He watched the Zero, circling around in the sky high above them. Turning to Oglethorpe as he banked *Little Girl* to the new heading, he said, "Ollie, just in case, get your boys strapped down. I got a bad feeling that this could get hairy if he really is calling in the cavalry."

"Here he comes!" Beyers yelled. "God, he's fast!"

The Zero screamed down directly at them. The fighter's two 20mm cannons spat fire as he abruptly opened up on *Sweet Sue*, the second B-17 in the formation, the one just to the right and slightly behind Tillson's plane. Smoke and flames belched from that bomber's number two engine. The plane abruptly veered to the left, then fell out of the formation and slowly spiraled toward the sea, ten thousand feet below.

"They got *Sweet Sue*!" Anson Hopper, the top turret gunner, yelled.

The Zero roared past *Little Girl* again, as if taking a victory lap, and then climbed once more.

"He's got friends!" Beyers yelled. "Half dozen of 'em."

Sure enough, six more Zeros now swooped in at the bombers at blurring speed. The lead plane came in blasting away at *Little Girl.*

Ollie had just stepped back to find Ward and the rest of the team looking out the gun windows, trying to figure out what was going on. Suddenly, a row of bullet holes were stitched across the fuselage. Both gunners, who had just gotten into place and were starting to swing their .50 caliber machine guns into action, were hit.

Stan Ward jumped up, pulled the wounded gunman out of the way, and grabbed the port side gun. He hollered, "Ollie, take the other gun." Ward aimed at the onrushing Zero and opened fire. The Japanese fighter roared by, missing colliding with the bomber by scant feet.

Oglethorpe grabbed the starboard side gun. "Stan, I've never shot anything before. How the hell do I do this?"

"I reckon it's like bird hunting back home," Ward answered. "You don't aim where they are. You aim where they're gonna be. Lead them a bit and let them fly into the bird shot."

"Here comes one!" Oglethorpe hollered. He swung the machine gun around and fired a long burst at the onrushing fighter. The Zero banked sharply and zoomed away, trailing a thin wisp of smoke.

Ward could barely track the melee as planes flitted across the sky faster than he could imagine possible. He had a quick view of three Zeros attacking the last B-17 in the formation and then another fighter was suddenly turning toward *Little Girl.* He was careful to lead it a bit and let the Zero fly into the stream of his tracers.

The Nipponese warplane suddenly exploded into a huge red-yellow-black ball. Then there was nothing but chunks of junk falling from the sky like smoking hail.

Ward did not take time to celebrate. He grabbed another box of ammo and fed it into his gun. Scanning the sky, he now found nothing to shoot at. Neither could Ollie. As quickly as they appeared, the Japanese fighters had vanished. But he counted only nine B-17s. They had lost three of their planes, crews, and friends in the brief, vicious fight.

Ward took a deep breath as the remaining bombers flew directly into the wall of threatening storm clouds. Nobody complained about the turbulence.

Being bounced around the sky by Mother Nature was a hell of a lot better than taking on more of those quick, maneuverable Japanese fighter planes.

∞

The old *S*-class submarine, *S-55*, cruised quietly with just the periscope protruding into the air above the sea surface. Trip MacLean stared through the lenses at a world mostly painted in blue, deep-blue sea below a cerulean-blue sky. Nothing was moving up there. As far as he could tell, they had this particular sliver of ocean all to themselves.

MacLean sighed, pulled away from the scope for a second to gulp some coffee, and then returned to stare once more at the empty horizon. The patrol had been exactly like this for the past week, ever since the pulse-pounding encounter when the Japanese destroyer inexplicably attacked them. The warship that MacLean first believed to be a cruiser. But after studying the silhouette drawings in the identification manual, he had changed his mind. It was definitely an Imperial Japanese Navy destroyer.

After that incident, the Skipper, Tony DiCarlo, decided that the best place for the *S-55* to patrol was the channel between the Babuyan Islands on the north side of Luzon. The little-used stretch was well off the normal shipping routes. Even in this quiet backwater, DiCarlo chose to patrol submerged during daylight hours, only daring to surface to charge batteries after the sun was well below the horizon and it was completely dark. So far, they had encountered only the occasional Philippine banca boat, fishing the rich waters. That only added to what had now become a very boring patrol.

MacLean was convinced that the Skipper had chosen this out-of-the-way patrol area for no other reason than that it was safe. Their orders said that they were to conduct a scouting mission of the Luzon Strait, the stretch of water between Formosa to the north and Luzon to the south, and their job was to determine the level of Japanese fleet activity in that broad area. While this peaceful, secluded backwater was technically part of the Luzon Strait, to MacLean's mind, only running back and forth through the channel effectively subverted the intentions of the order. And to top off the young officer's concern, Sam Forester, the XO, seemed to agree with DiCarlo.

On the positive side, though, the Skipper had never made good on his threat to call Trip MacLean into his stateroom for a dressing down after the incident with the Japanese warship. Instead, the CO had not even mentioned that eventful evening. It was almost as if he had blanked it from his mind.

That left MacLean with a quandary. Did he talk with someone else back at the base—someone higher up the chain—about how DiCarlo had almost lost the boat and gotten them all killed? There was no doubt in MacLean's mind that had he not taken over and issued the order to stop the mad dive when he did, *S-55* would have ended up on the bottom or on fire or both. But would anybody believe him, a relatively new submarine officer, over a CO and his XO, both of whom had years of experience driving the boats?

DiCarlo walked into the control room and intently studied the navigation chart. "Mr. MacLean, come around to course two-five-five," he ordered. "Make your depth one hundred feet and increase speed to ahead two-thirds. It's time to head home. We've spent enough time out here. When you get clear of Fuga Island, steer down toward Luzon and slow to one-third. Head down the west side of Luzon but stay five miles off the coast. We've got four days to mosey on back home and I intend to take every minute of it."

MacLean was careful not to show his frustration as he issued the orders for the new course, speed, and depth. When he turned around to speak with the Skipper, he only caught a fleeting glance of DiCarlo's back as he disappeared through the hatch, apparently heading toward his stateroom, whistling tunelessly.

∞

Fred Wurster yawned, stretched, and braced himself against the control room chart table to avoid sliding to the deck and napping. He was exhausted. Dead tired. The only thing that kept him awake was draining mug after mug of strong black coffee. And even the potent sludge from the big continually brewing urn in the galley was no longer doing much to help. But when he tried to sleep, no dice. The awful nightmares chased away any chance of getting meaningful rest. Vivid dreams of his CO, Steve Leland, happily settling in on the fairwater, his own cup of coffee in hand, enjoying his new submarine's dash through choppy waters. Then, an image of him suddenly being swept away by the big wave, disappearing over the side, never to be seen again. Except in Wurster's recurring nightmare.

Thankfully, the past week had been an absolute blur, keeping his mind occupied and with little opportunity to reflect on what had happened. Except, that is, until he tried to find dreamless sleep. Someone high up in the chain had decided that the Navy needed *Wolffish* to move up its departure from Mare Island by more than a week and get to Pearl Harbor. For some reason, they needed the submarine there right damn now. There was not even time for a replacement CO to report aboard and assume command. Executive Officer Jim Shelton had been designated the acting Commanding Officer, at least for the transit from Mare Island to Pearl Harbor. Shelton's first act was to appoint Wurster as the Acting XO.

In addition to his duties as the *Wolffish*'s Engineer, Fred now faced all the complications of moving the submarine and crew from San Francisco Bay to Hawaii. Stores loads, weapons load-out, and fueling were all relatively simple, even if all that stuff was time consuming. But the administrative minutiae involved in moving a boat and its crew out of the shipyard and across the Pacific Ocean was more than his sleep-deprived brain could easily handle. It would have been a supreme challenge, even if he had been well-rested. Every waking minute was taken up with some sailor's problems with his landlord, with settling arguments between Cookie and the drivers of the trucks delivering what he saw as inferior produce, or with answering a demand from some pencil-pushing clerk to justify the need to requisition a pallet load of toilet paper.

It just never stopped.

But come high tide this morning, they would slip the lines and be free of the administrative Navy for at least the next two weeks. By Monday morning, 8 December, the *Wolffish* would be tied up at Submarine Base Pearl Harbor. Ready to go to work, yes, but also enjoying tropical breezes and hula girls. The new CO would be on the pier waiting for them. Then

Fred could dump this administrative pile back in Shelton's lap and get busy again learning all he could about how this remarkable new submarine of theirs functioned.

"Eng…er…XO? Jeez, what the hell am I supposed to call you nowadays, sir?" It was Chief Fritz Wankel, and the scowl on his face was even more pronounced than usual.

Wurster looked up from the stacks of files spread across the wardroom table. "Doesn't matter to me. Just say, 'Hey, you,' and I'll answer. What you need, Chief?"

"Fuel load is topped off. Engineering's ready to get underway," Wankel reported. "And the COB asked me to report that the crew is ready to get underway. The new QM1 just reported aboard, too. You remember Clancy Obrien? He's your new Leading Quartermaster. Another former *S-52* sailor following you across the country, looks like. A couple more of the old gang and we'll have enough to keep you straight and out of trouble. Even if we can't tell anybody what we were all doing up there in the North Atlantic."

Wurster laughed. QM1 Obrien had been the Leading Quartermaster on the *S-52* during their recent highly classified adventures while operating out of Argentia Station in Newfoundland. With the *S-52* in the yards for the foreseeable future undergoing repairs after that escapade, there was not much for a Quartermaster to do. And Wurster was certainly glad to hear he would now have Obrien aboard the *Wolffish*.

Grabbing his foul weather jacket, Wurster jumped up and said, "Chief, let's go topside and greet our new QM. We need to make sure the boat's ready anyway, if we're going to convince the CO it is."

Heading forward, he scurried up the torpedo room ladder. Surprised to find the weather cool and crisp, he jammed his hands into the jacket's pockets. He felt something in one of them. A crumpled envelope. He realized at once what it was. An unopened letter from his girlfriend, Ellie Morton. Then he remembered Jim Shelton had handed him the letter—Fred had been in such a hurry and so distracted he had not even noticed who it was from—just before they got underway for sea trials. That was the last time he had worn the jacket in the fickle Bay Area weather. Amid all the hurry, lack of rest, and flustered scurrying about since, it had remained in the jacket pocket, unopened and forgotten.

"What you have there, sir?" Chief Wankel asked, genuinely curious when he saw the look on Fred's face.

"Letter from my girl," Wurster answered. "I guess it got lost and forgotten in all the rush and the whole deal with the Skipper..."

He had already decided he would read the letter later, when he had the opportunity to properly absorb what Ellie might have written. He shoved it back into his pocket and told himself to take an interest in the underway preparations topside.

Chief Wankel grunted. "Excuse me, sir, but for an officer, you sure are dumb."

Wurster pulled up short. "What you talking about, Chief?"

"You just pulled a letter from your girl out of your pocket that has been forgotten for more than a week now. Then you just jam it back in your jacket and say that you'll get to it when you get to it. Sir, case you forgot, we're getting underway in a couple of hours. No mail from nobody for at least two weeks. And no chance for you to reply to that one there unless you bribe some flying fish to deliver it for you. Look, with all due respect, sir, if you expect to still have a girl when we get to Pearl, you need to get your butt down to the wardroom. You need to read and answer that letter before we leave. Don't you worry. We'll take care of topside."

"You sure are romantic for a stinky old Navy Chief." But Wurster did not bother to protest any further. He dropped back down the ladder and grabbed a seat in the wardroom before he ripped the letter open.

"My dearest Freddy," written in the familiar swirling curlicues of Ellie's cursive script, brought a smile to his face. So did the aroma of her perfume from the few drops she usually sprinkled on the envelope before dropping it into the mailbox.

Good start. The next several pages were taken up with descriptions of Ellie's adventures at the Massachusetts General Hospital Training School for Nurses. It seemed that all was going well with her studies. Her grades were good. She even mentioned she had baked an apple pie for the class, like the one she had served Fred that chilly morning when they first met at her father's drugstore in Mystic. That she had gotten a little too much baking powder in the crust and it was crumbly, but she would not make that mistake when she could someday bake another one fresh for him. But

Fred particularly liked her frequent references to how badly she missed him.

Then, on the last page, she dropped a bomb. A wonderful, thrilling bomb.

It seemed that Navy recruiters had visited the school. And she signed up to be a Navy Nurse, even without asking Fred his opinion, for which she apologized. But the best part was that her first assignment would be to the Navy Hospital at Pearl Harbor for her training.

Fred could not suppress a loud, happy whoop! A couple of sailors walking past the wardroom looked at him with puzzled expressions.

"Everything okay, sir?" one of them asked.

"Damn fine! Better than fine! Damn fine!"

The sailors walked on, shaking their heads.

Ellie went on to write that it would take her until spring to finish at Massachusetts General. That meant she should be in Pearl Harbor by the summer. Likely late June.

Wurster was wreathed in smiles as he quickly scrawled out a hasty, happy reply.

Ellie. In the summer. In Hawaii, where he and *Wolffish* would be when not out on patrol.

Damn fine!

∞

Nine B-17Es made a slow, sweeping circle in their box formation around the grass-covered main runway of the US Army's Clark Field on the Philippine island of Luzon. Then they formed a long, straight line as they swung around into the landing pattern above the bright green landscape. An exhausted Greg Tillson eased back on the throttles as *Little Girl* crossed the threshold, gently settling the big B-17 down so that it kissed the sod with barely a bump and rolled down the runway. It took only a few minutes to taxi over to the asphalt tarmac area. A sergeant waving orange paddles directed Tillson and his bird toward a long line of similarly close-parked bombers. Very close-parked. Then he waved what was left of the 30th

Bombardment Squadron into a second tight line, placing them only a scant few feet behind the first row.

Tillson frowned, shaking his head. Why in hell would the bombers be aligned so close together? Then co-pilot Sam Beyers pointed to armed guards who were standing beside each parked plane.

"Looks like somebody must be worried about sabotage," the co-pilot suggested. "Only reason I can think of to park the planes on top of one another like this and station sentries."

"All I know is I don't like it," Tillson said. "Switch the radio over to the control tower for me, Sam."

Beyers reached over and changed the radio to the control tower frequency and gave Tillson a thumbs-up.

Tillson keyed his microphone. "Tower, this is Commander 30th Bombardment Squadron. Request dispersal parking for my aircraft."

The response was immediate. "Commander, this is Tower, negative on your request."

Tillson shook his head. He looked over at his co-pilot and said, "This is nuts. A couple of Jap Zeros on a strafing run could wipe out the entire fleet of Far East Air Force heavy bombers in one pass. It'd take a whole army of saboteurs most of a day to do that much damage." He keyed his mike again and emphatically said, "Tower this is 30th Bombardment Squadron. I want dispersal parking for my birds. If you can't do it, patch me through to Base Ops."

"Happy to patch you through, Captain," the tower operator responded, "but it won't do you any good. The order came down from General Brereton himself. Close-park the aircraft due to increased sabotage threat."

Tillson smacked the control wheel in frustration. They had just flown the squadron halfway around the world, lost three of their aircraft and crews to a squadron of Zeros, only to have everything put at risk by some chair-bound General who happened to command the Far East Air Force. He unbuckled his seat harness and then dropped his parachute before turning to Beyers. "Sam, get the birds all fueled and ready to fly. Get the crews fed and find them a place to grab some sleep. But keep them restricted to Clark. I'm going to go see what enemies I can make with this Far East Air Force bunch."

Stan Ward met Tillson as the pilot started to climb down out of the aircraft, still cursing under his breath. "What's the story, Greg?" the Navy Lieutenant asked. "Looks like you just found a bug in your java."

"I'm heading over to Base Ops," Tillson answered and gave Ward a quick explanation for his vexation. "Look, I'll get you some trucks to transport your boys and their stuff down to Cavite. Given the roads we saw coming in, it's probably a three-hour ride."

Ward found Ollie Oglethorpe sitting in the shade under *Little Girl*'s wing, leaning back against the landing gear, enjoying a fresh pipeful of aromatic tobacco.

"Damn, this tropical paradise is a whole lot hotter and more humid than New London in December," the cryptology group's CO complained from behind a cloud of smoke. "And it looks like it's about to rain, too." Oglethorpe pointed with the stem of his pipe to the dark clouds piling up against the mountains to the north of the air base. Then he abruptly changed topics. "What's got Greg stomping off all red-faced like that, Stan? He's been a pretty cool character in some dicey situations far as I could see."

"He's upset about how his birds are parked here on the tarmac," Ward answered. "He thinks they should be dispersed against a possible air attack. He's heading over to Base Ops to make his point. He says that he'll send some trucks over for us."

The two Navy officers were still chatting under the bomber's wing when a pair of olive-green GMC CCKW deuce-and-a-half trucks lumbered up. A green tarpaulin covered each of the big trucks' beds.

A Sergeant jumped down from the passenger side of the lead truck's cab, considering a piece of paper affixed to a clipboard. "One of you two a Commander Oglethorpe?" he shouted at the two officers to be heard over the truck engines. "I got orders here to take you and your men down to Cavite."

When Ollie responded, the sarge went on. "Y'all gonna wanna get loaded up and outta here then before that storm rolls in." He nodded toward the towering dark clouds still building to the north. "The roads from here out to the Manila North Road are gonna turn into a mud pit as soon as the first drop of rain hits."

A veritable wall of rain had begun to sweep across the north end of Clark Field as the trucks pulled through the south gate. The Sergeant had been accurate in his assessment of the roads and the moisture's effect on them, but the all-wheel-drive Jimmies were more than up to the task. They churned along through a few miles of muddy local village roads until they finally reached the paved Manila North Road. Moving faster now, they were down on the coastal plain just a few miles out of the city of Malolos when the rain stopped as suddenly as it had started. A hot, steamy afternoon sun peeked through the clouds as they skirted off to the east.

Wisps of mist rose up from the blacktop as the trucks began jousting with ever heavier traffic. Stan Ward, sitting in the cab of the second truck, watched with interest the mixed traffic, including everything from new Cadillac touring cars to big, lumbering carabao pulling wooden-wheeled carts piled high with produce, crates of chickens, and some of them even fitted with benches for passengers.

The streetlights were just flickering on in Cavite City as the pair of mud-spattered Jimmies pulled up to the Navy Yard gate. The Marine guard had no idea where some outfit named "Station CAST" might be located. The best he could do was send them to base headquarters. When Stan and Ollie finally found the Base Duty Officer—who had to do some digging to answer their question—they learned that the Station CAST Unit had been transferred to the island of Corregidor, on the other side of Manila Bay from Cavite and Manila. And no, he would not be able to arrange for a boat over there until morning. Maybe by noon.

Ollie turned to Ward. "Toto, I don't think we're in Kansas anymore."

The Duty Officer looked puzzled, but Stan grinned. He, Karen, and Oglethorpe had all gone to see *The Wizard of Oz* together—while one of Karen's nurse friends babysat little Jonathan—the week before they shipped out.

"Yeah, and I suggest we keep an eye on the skies for the Wicked Witch of the West and her monkeys," Ward said with a wink.

"BOQ's two blocks down and to the left," the Duty Officer advised, shaking his head.

Intelligence officers, he was obviously thinking. *Contradiction in terms!*

6

The USS *Tigerfish* pulled away from the short pier jutting out into Sand Island's tiny man-made harbor. In the sky out over the calm, shallow Midway Lagoon, PanAm's brand-new *Pacific Clipper* passenger plane, tropical sunlight glinting off its silver wings, lined up with the long line of buoys marking its landing zone. The big four-engine Boeing 314 flying boat kissed the surface of the lagoon with a rainbow spray of warm seawater.

Brad Johnson stood on the *Tigerfish*'s bridge watching the *Clipper*'s landing while he directed his submarine's maneuvering as it backed away from the pier and then twisted around to line up with the first short leg of dredged channel. The four big Fairbanks-Morse diesels—very similar to the ones the company manufactured for railroad locomotives—burbled reassuringly as they effortlessly pushed the submarine back out to the open Pacific on the next leg of their transit. A thousand yards off to his left, he could see the seaplane as it taxied toward the pier that the *Tigerfish* had just vacated.

Wayne Schacter, the submarine's CO, stood silently behind Johnson, attentively observing how the junior officer handled the boat in these very constricted waters.

"Bridge, XO," the 7MC blasted. "Mark the turn. Recommend come left with a full rudder to course one-eight-five to line up to center channel."

"Left full rudder," Johnson ordered in response. "Steady course one-eight-five. All ahead full."

The *Tigerfish* obediently swung around to the south. The diesels' roar deepened noticeably as the twin screws bit into the water. The bow began pitching mildly as the submarine left the atoll's protective coral reef and headed into the leading edge of the deep, blue ocean.

Schacter glanced around the submarine's topside. Satisfied that everything was in place and secured, he carefully searched the horizon next. Nothing but seawater to the end of the world. Then he turned to Johnson. "Nav, I'm going below. From now on, assume we are on a war patrol and follow all procedures accordingly and to the letter. Dive the boat."

The Skipper disappeared down the hatch as Johnson called out, "Clear the bridge!" then hit the diving alarm. He followed up the "Aoogha! Aoogha!" with, "Dive! Dive!" on the 1MC announcing system. The lookouts had already slid down from the periscope shears and were disappearing through the hatch into the darkness of the conning tower. Johnson followed so closely that he stepped on the last lookout's fingers as he jumped down the ladder and slammed the hatch shut above his head.

"Last man down, hatch secured," Johnson proclaimed as his feet touched the deck of the conning tower. Without a pause, he continued down the ladder to the control room where he would now assume the duties of Diving Officer.

"Depth four-two feet, coming to six-two feet," he called out after checking the depth gauge. And as the submarine sank deeper into the sea. "Four-four feet, coming to six-two feet. Flood negative. Full dive on the bow planes."

The added water in the negative tank and the angle on the planes did what they were designed to, overcome buoyancy and push the boat down. But it still felt much too slow a process to Johnson. Especially if they were ever at war and an enemy destroyer or aircraft was stalking them.

"Five-zero feet, coming to six-two feet."

Finally, *Tigerfish* leveled off at sixty-two feet below the surface of the Pacific. Schacter stepped out from behind the navigation table, studying his stopwatch. "Nav, that dive took one minute and forty-five seconds. Way too long. Let's do it again. I want to dive to sixty-two feet in under a minute. Surface the ship, get the lookouts in the shears, and try again."

The *Tigerfish* bobbed back up onto the surface. Johnson and the lookouts climbed back up to the bridge.

"Sorry about walking all over your fingers," Brad said, apologizing to the young sailor.

"My fault, sir. I should have stomped Smitty when he was so slow goin' down the ladder ahead of me. I done told him I will this time."

They had just gotten comfortably into their positions when Schacter once again ordered Johnson to dive. This time the stopwatch showed a minute and a half. Only fifteen seconds faster.

The Skipper held up the watch, looked at Johnson, and simply said, "Again."

It took four more tries before they finally hit fifty-nine seconds. Johnson and the lookouts were exhausted and beyond frustrated by the time the Skipper was ultimately satisfied that they could dive in under a minute. But that was the time specified by the current standard submarine operating procedures.

"Officer-of-the-Deck, make your depth one hundred feet. Conduct a sonar search. Inform me immediately of any contacts," Schacter ordered. Then, looking at the navigation plot, he went on. "Steer course two-five-zero. Maintain speed ahead two-thirds. We'll surface an hour after sunset. I'll be in my stateroom." He left the conning tower through the control room hatch.

Johnson looked up and saw Isaac Sternman, the XO, who had been standing back in a dark corner. Brad stepped close to him and spoke in a low voice so that they could not be overheard.

"XO, what was that all about? Are we really that close to going to war or something?"

"Brad, our orders are to conduct a simulated war patrol on this transit, all the way to the Philippines," Sternman answered. "Skipper means to do just that. We're going to follow all of the wartime operating procedures. That means that we need to practice them. You can expect a lot more of this kind of stuff as we make the transit. Hell, don't be surprised if he makes us practice torpedoing any freighters we happen to come across."

Johnson rubbed his chin. "Makes sense," he finally said, "but why are we doing a sonar search? Wouldn't we be able to cover a lot more territory looking for contacts while we're on the surface?"

Sternman shook his head and had a "you should know the answer" look on his face. "Procedures say submerged sonar search only if it's daylight. They say we're far too vulnerable to air attack to run on the surface when the sun's up. At least that's what all the war games have shown, so that's what goes in the book."

Johnson thought for a second. He considered letting it ride, but he could not help himself. "Okay, I can understand that, I guess. But we've got an SD radar on this nice new yacht of ours. Isn't that primarily for conducting air search while we're on the surface?"

Sternman nodded. "Yep. But the procedures haven't changed yet. Nothing in there recognizes we have the SD stuff or says anything about using the radar. Skipper's not going to take any chances until the procedures change. He's by the book even if the book is two classes of submarines behind."

"Then I don't suspect he's going to want to hear about some suggestions I have for diving faster," Johnson replied. "All we need to do is run on the surface with safety, negative, and bow buoyance all flooded already. Then we just ride the vents. I guarantee we can dive in under forty-five seconds that way."

When the submarine was operating on the surface and under normal conditions, the safety tanks, negative tanks, and bow buoyancy tanks were kept empty. That provided a safe margin of positive buoyancy. Those tanks were only flooded when the sub dove. The main ballast tanks were kept empty with both the vent valves above and the flood valves below closed tightly to prevent any water from entering. When "riding the vents," the flood valves were left open and only the vent valves prevented the main ballast tanks from filling with water.

Sternman considered Johnson's idea for a long moment but then shook his head. "Lots of risk operating that way. And it sure isn't how the procedures say we do it. My advice? Don't even bother the Skipper with that idea. Or anything else that goes against the way the Navy says we're going to do it. The CO won't be buying what you're selling."

∞

The *S-55* rounded the Bataan Peninsula where it jutted out to form the western side of Manila Bay. Streaks of rust down the gray-painted sides of the ancient submarine looked like long, bleeding gashes in the skin of some huge sea creature, maybe one wounded in an epic undersea struggle with some other prehistoric brute, not just a battered, rusted old ship in bad need of some tender loving care in a shipyard.

Alistair MacLean stood on the bridge, watching as Corregidor Island slowly slid by to port. It would be good to finally get the sub tied up and for Trip to get away from her for a while. Ever since their near-fatal encounter with the Japanese destroyer, the whole atmosphere on the boat had become strange; stilted and uncomfortable, almost as if everyone was walking on eggshells. Meals in the wardroom had become an ordeal. When Tony DiCarlo was present, no one spoke unless they had to answer a direct question. Even then, the answer was usually reduced to monosyllables. And to make it worse, the Skipper seemed to not even notice the testy mood.

MacLean glanced down at his Rolex. 1500. They should be tied up at the pier by 1700. With some smooth maneuvering, he could be off the *S-55* by 1800, giving him plenty of time to shower, change, and catch the launch over to the Manila Fleet Landing. Saturday evening dinner at the Army and Navy Club sure sounded inviting. And Madeleine Forester, the XO's wife, was usually prowling the premises on weekend nights. Even if her husband was just back from maneuvers.

Trip MacLean was dog tired, but not so tired as to miss all the potential opportunities.

"Captain to the bridge!" the 7MC blasted even as DiCarlo's head popped up through the hatch.

"Good afternoon, Captain," MacLean announced carefully, maintaining an even keel despite his now-confirmed impressions of his CO.

"Mr. MacLean," DiCarlo responded with a curt nod. He leaned his elbows on the bridge rail and looked out at the harbor ahead. After a few seconds, he turned to MacLean. "We are tying up alongside the *Canopus*. Have line handlers topside before we reach Sangley Point. And I want them in whites. The Commodore will be watching our berthing. The *S-55* will look sharp."

MacLean had to stifle any comments about the rust streaking down the old boat's flanks or the dents in the superstructure from diving her too deep when they escaped the Japanese destroyer. He had also seen the typed-up notes the yeoman had put together describing the action with the destroyer. Notes that, at DiCarlo's direction, would become an official part of the patrol report. It was fiction. All of it.

But sometimes silence was the best policy.

DiCarlo abruptly turned and headed back down the hatch. Just before he disappeared, he looked back up at Trip.

"Oh, and Mr. MacLean, just in case you thought that I had forgotten your little indiscretion off Caunayan Point, be assured I have not. You are restricted to the ship until further notice."

With that, *S-55*'s Captain disappeared down into the dark hole of the conning tower hatch.

∞

Joto Heiso (Flight Petty Officer) Isokuro Shimizu carefully placed the smoking *ko* stick in the sand-filled bowl in front of the Shinto shrine. The dish was already full of the remains of dozens of smoldering sticks. The scent of incense filled the tiny space.

Shimizu bowed deeply and offered a prayer to his ancestors, asking that they might watch over him and ensure that he acted with honor and bravery during the mission upon which he was about to depart. That he would continue his family's legacy of bravery in battle. Grandfather Isokuro, his namesake, had died honorably when his ship, the armored cruiser *Nisshin*, was hit by a Russian shell during the Battle of Tsushima in May 1905, the last sea battle of the Russo-Japanese War and a glorious victory for the Empire of Japan. Though mortally wounded, Grandfather Isokuro had somehow managed to pull his unconscious and badly hurt gunnery officer from the vessel's mangled gun turret before the elder Shimizu succumbed to his own injuries. That gunnery officer survived and was now Admiral Isoroku Yamamoto, the Commander-in-Chief of the

Combined Fleet of the Imperial Japanese Navy. The grandson's final prayer was that his grandfather would guide him in this day's impending action.

The sacred ritual complete, Shimizu grabbed his soft leather flight helmet and stepped out onto the crowded flight deck of the IJN aircraft carrier *Kaga*. Dodging spinning propellers and ducking around and beneath aircraft, he found his Nakajima B5N2 torpedo bomber waiting for him. Ayumi Inoue, the navigator/bombardier, and Haruki Kato, the radio-operator/gunner, were already in their seats, ready for takeoff, but the pilot had a checklist he was obligated to complete. Shimizu first took a close look at the Type 91 aerial torpedo that hung below his bomber. He carefully inspected the special wooden fins and sheaths, added so that the torpedoes could operate in the shallow waters of a harbor without diving into the mud and serving no purpose. Then he deliberately walked around his aircraft, examining all systems. Satisfied that everything was ready, he climbed up onto the wing and lowered himself into the cockpit. There, settled into his seat and buckled in, he had no choice but to wait until it was his turn to take off.

The sun was about to make its usual daily debut over the horizon when Isokuro finally opened the throttles fully on his torpedo bomber and raced down the *Kaga*'s flight deck. As Shimizu pulled back on the stick, the plane leapt into the air, seemingly as eager to be on its way as her crew was. A raptor freed from its cage. The single-engine bird climbed to its position amid the formation of other Nakajima B5N2s, each loaded with torpedoes. Above them, bomb-laden B5N2s—which would drop heavy, armor-piercing bombs—made a wide, sweeping circle. Off to the left and even higher in the dawn sky, Aichi D3A dive-bombers, easily identifiable with their fixed landing gears, worked around into their own formation. At a still higher altitude, the Mitsubishi A6M fighters swooped about, eager to be off to their mission, primarily protecting the rest of the warplanes before inflicting their own damage on targets below. When all the aircraft had taken off from the carrier, they formed into what most resembled a long arrow, pointing south, toward the Hawaiian Islands, 370 kilometers—about 230 miles—away. Below, the *Kido Butai*—the First Air Fleet Strike Force—with its six aircraft carriers steamed along under high alert, all eyes on the warplanes as they disappeared over the horizon.

A thick, heavy wall of clouds formed ahead of the onrushing attackers. Shimizu was worried. He knew that attacking through the clouds meant that his torpedo assault would become very dangerous and have much less chance to be effective. High-level bombing and dive-bombing would be all but impossible. But he knew they would never consider turning back now. The surprise attack would go forward no matter what the weather offered.

Flight time showed that they were almost to the islands when the cloud bank suddenly broke. Oahu's North Shore formed a long, white line on the horizon with dark-green highlands beyond. Shimizu's squadron swung around to the west and reduced altitude to five hundred meters. They rounded Ka'ena Point and raced down Oahu's leeward shore. The Wai'anea Mountains were a solid wall, towering above them to the east. Then the cleft they were anticipating appeared in the mountains. The squadron banked and flew through the Kolekole Pass. The whole of Pearl Harbor suddenly opened up before them.

Shimizu could see that the harbor was already aflame. Aichi dive-bombers were screaming down into the maelstrom, dropping their 250 kg Type 99 bombs onto the unsuspecting ships anchored below. High above, the Nakajima bombers began unleashing their 800 kg bombs on their designated targets, while the A6M fighters swooped down and strafed airfields, barracks, and any other target that looked inviting. Flames and smoke reached high into the sky.

Shimizu brought his torpedo bomber down until it was just above the palm trees that lined Pearl Harbor's western shore. He steadied the plane up on his assigned target, the first US Navy battleship in the line that now loomed in front of him. The B5N2 lurched upward when Ayumi Inoue toggled the torpedo, dropping it away. Shimizu roared on down the harbor's South Channel, with Ford Island and Battleship Row on his left, but no way to know for sure that his weapon had done its job.

He saw the submarine base and a fuel tank farm flash by as he pulled back on the stick to climb after his attack, to avoid all the anti-aircraft shells directed his way. The submarine base was not on the list of targets. Submarines were of little use in the great sea battle that would lead to the Emperor's inevitable victory. Battleships and aircraft carriers were the weapons that mattered, and they had just struck a mighty blow toward ending that threat. The fuel tank farm was especially tempting, though, but the only ammunition remaining were the few rounds in Kato's 7.7mm machine gun. It would not take much to set off an awful conflagration in the tank farm over which he now passed. But he merely flew on.

That's when he felt something hit his plane. A bump. A nudge. Then loud rattling. For a moment, it sounded like hail striking a metal rooftop. Then there was an anguished scream from behind him. When he quickly scanned the instrument panel, everything appeared normal. The controls felt okay, too. But the elevators did seem squishy. He called back to Ayumi Inoue and Haruki Kato to see if they could see any damage. No one answered him.

Leveling the Nakajima off at one thousand meters, Shimizu swung the plane on around to point north and then looked back over his shoulder. Both of his crew were slumped over in their seats. Blood and flesh were splashed profusely around the cockpit. Then he noticed wisps of smoke trailing behind his bird. Fire was the B5N2's worst enemy, its greatest vulnerability. The plane was built for speed and agility, not to withstand battle damage. It had no armor, but worse, none of those self-sealing fuel tanks that the Americans were using, the technology that helped prevent serious leaking of volatile aviation gasoline.

Shimizu flew on. He did not know what else to do. With his radio operator dead, there was no way to contact his squadron leader or the *Kaga*. With his navigator also dead, he could only guess where he needed to go to locate his ship in a vast sea, unless he could find someone to follow. And with his plane on fire, there was no way to know how far he could even fly, anyway. Muttering a prayer to Grandfather Isokuro for guidance, he aimed north, passing over Oahu's pineapple fields, over the giant, rolling waves breaking on the North Shore.

He was thirty miles out to sea when the fire finally reached the fuel tanks. The B5N2 exploded and instantly became a whirling ball of orange-yellow flame as it fell down, down, toward the emerald surface of the Pacific.

7

Stan Ward found Station CAST located way back in a locked and guarded end of Lateral Number Six on the south side of Malinta Tunnel's main shaft. The tunnels had been constructed deep under Malinta Hill, on tadpole-shaped Corregidor's narrow eastern tail. They had been dug on the cheap during the 1930s, using mostly convict labor, TNT initially bound for disposal as it had been condemned by the Army Bureau of Ordnance, and mostly obsolete equipment rented from the Baguio gold mines. The Army Corps of Engineers even bought the cement from the Japanese on what amounted to the black market.

With the rapidly escalating possibility of war, the tunnels were in the process of being extended and fitted out as a thousand-bed hospital and a modern command center. The place was certainly a hive of activity when Ward and the others arrived. But Station CAST was segregated into its own little world. Major Frank Tanaka, the station's Commander, enthusiastically welcomed Ollie Oglethorpe, Stan Ward, and their team. The facility was undermanned and overworked. The newly arrived members were immediately assigned tasks. Nobody saw much Philippine daylight. They spent their time either inside the station or in their little bunkroom right outside the door. Stan figured that he might as well be on a submarine with one of his Annapolis classmates, as originally planned. But the work they were doing there in the catacombs was so highly classified that he could not share any of it with anyone outside the team. Even Karen, back home, was under the impression that he was mostly just enjoying life in a tropical paradise. That was all he could tell her in his daily letters home.

Ward, being the new guy and junior-most officer, had drawn the dreaded Sunday night midwatch. He sat at his gray steel army desk and pored over a stack of intercepted messages. The CAST team was busy trying to break the Japanese Navy JN-25 code, but they were having little success. On a good day, they might be able to figure out ten percent of the general meaning of the messages and even less of the details. Even those meager results required days or weeks of work, splicing together bits and pieces, often relying more on guessing than actual hard data.

Over the last couple of weeks, there had been a significant increase in the volume of traffic wafting back and forth between Japanese fleet units. Stan had not had time yet to set up his signals analysis system like the one he had developed on the East Coast, but his intuition was yelling at him, telling him that something big was going on. Something truly important. Something that was downright frightening.

"Hey, Lieutenant!" It was Sergeant Gus Arnett. He dropped a thick stack of messages in front of Stan. "Here's the latest we got. Lotsa Jap yakking from what I can see. But I ain't makin' sense outta any of it."

Tanaka had already warned Ward about Sergeant Arnett and his good buddy Stan Lamoille. Both staffers were given to drinking way too much and talking far too loud and copiously. However, for the time being, having the two locked away in the Malinta Tunnel had probably cured that problem. There was no booze, nor could anyone outside the team overhear what they were talking about.

Stan immediately recognized the call signs for some of the messages. They had shown up repeatedly over the last several days. However, that still gave him no idea of where the messages came from or for whom they were intended. All he knew for certain was that there were a lot more of them. And that the direction-finding stations showed that the bulk of them were being transmitted from the island of Formosa, just off the coast of mainland China, six hundred miles to the north of Corregidor and home to the closest Japanese bases.

"Hey, boss, you got to hear this!" Lamoille yelled from across the room. "The Japs are...Jeez! I don't believe it! Sonza bitches are attacking Pearl Harbor! Whoever's keying this is bad shook, too. He ain't even botherin' to code anything. 'Air attack,' he says. And there's hunnerts of Jap bombers. Whole damn place is blowed up!"

Something suddenly clicked in Ward's head. He looked hard at the clock on the far wall. It was 0230 there in Manila. That meant it was 0830 yesterday morning—Sunday morning—in Hawaii. If the Japs were attacking Pearl Harbor early on a Sunday morning, then they should all anticipate the possibility of an attack there in the Philippines in a few hours.

"Arnett, get me Asiatic Fleet Headquarters on the phone!" he shouted. "Then get me General MacArthur's watch officer."

"But, sir," the scruffy Sergeant protested. "It's oh-dark-thirty in the mornin'. They're gonna be sleepin' and mad as a wet hen if I—"

"Sergeant! Get them up! Right damn now!" Ward ordered. "I'm trying to stop the Japs from sticking a bomb up their asses! And Lamoille, run and get Major Tanaka. He needs to see this."

Six minutes later, Frank Tanaka was just walking into the room, yawning and rubbing the sleep from his eyes, when the Asiatic Fleet watch officer finally answered his phone. Without even waiting for what the reason was for the wake-up call, he made known very clearly his displeasure for being disturbed by a bunch of overly excitable spooks. Then he slammed the phone back down.

General MacArthur's watch officer, over at USAFFE headquarters, had a very similar response. But an even more profane one.

Ward gave Tanaka a look of desperation. Here he was trying to warn people that an attack was likely coming, but no one was interested in hearing him. No one was willing to wake up an Admiral or a General to get things moving. Not if there was any possibility that the prediction might be wrong.

Ward was certain he was right, though. Even with limited intel.

Every corpuscle in his body screamed that the Japanese were likely en route to the Philippines—the next largest US Naval facilities in the Pacific after Pearl Harbor—at that very moment. And that they were likely about to do to US military interests in the Philippines exactly what they had just done in Hawaii.

∞

Fred Wurster and Jim Shelton sat back and enjoyed another cup of coffee together. It was an extraordinarily pleasant tropical morning as the *Wolffish* steamed through the Kaiwi Channel, in no particular hurry. The high, green cliffs of Moloka'i reared up out of the sea off to port and the extinct volcano that was Koko Head Crater filled the view off to starboard. They even imagined that they could smell the scent of tropical flowers. The entrance to Pearl Harbor was still thirty miles away, but the submarine nets guarding the channel would not be swung out of the way for them until noon. That meant, after the long ride over from San Francisco Bay, they now had plenty of time to relax, enjoy the sunshine, and be tourists for a few hours.

"Well, we made it," Shelton commented as he lifted his mug. "And even with you navigating, I think we actually found Hawaii." He chuckled and took a sip of joe.

"I won't ever admit that playing XO while also being Engineer was a piece of cake," Wurster retorted, "but I think I successfully fixed all your screw-ups before any damage was done to the taxpayers' new ship. Now, when our new Skipper walks on board, he will find the USS *Wolffish* to be a well-oiled war-fighting machine despite your best efforts."

The two friends shared a laugh and then replenished their cups from the metal carafe. They leaned against the bridge coaming and gazed ahead at the Oahu landscape as the submarine rolled easily in the mild seas.

"Doesn't get any better than this," Wurster said with a sigh. "Sunrise on the bridge. Good cup of coffee, and Oahu off the beam. Wish I could share it with Karen instead of with you, no offense."

"None taken. Only thing better will be the luau tonight," Shelton noted. "Kalua pig, just out of the ground, washed down with plenty of Primo beer, served up for us by dusky maidens in grass skirts."

"Skipper, message from Subbase," the 7MC rudely interrupted. "Pearl Harbor is under attack! It's closed, sir! The harbor's closed. We're to submerge and head back to the east at best speed. And watch for Jap subs!"

Shelton, eyes wide, grabbed a pair of binoculars and looked off toward where the Navy base would be on the horizon. Even though it was still thirty miles away, the rising clouds of smoke were there, easy to see now that he was looking.

Then he spied something else. A bunch of aircraft, Zeros, a formation of angry insects over Honolulu, Waikiki, Diamond Head. And even from this distance, he could tell they were heading in the direction of the *Wolffish* in one hell of a hurry.

"Clear the deck!" Shelton roared. "Fred, dive the sub!" He dropped down the hatch as Wurster hit the diving alarm. He, too, had spied the attacking fighters, even without the aid of binoculars. He dove down the hatch and slammed it closed above himself.

Then he could hear 20mm cannon rounds slamming into his new submarine's fairwaters as it slipped—much too slowly for comfort—beneath the waves toward, hopefully, some semblance of safety.

Unless it was already too late for that.

∞

The crews of the 30th Bomber Squadron were exhausted. Tired from their long trans-Pacific flight, with challenges from weather and the Japanese air attack. Worn out from sleeping beneath their bombers instead of in the barracks at the far end of the base.

They were spending their nights there because Captain Greg Tillson had encountered a brick wall when he requested that his birds be dispersed to make them less vulnerable to an air attack. He had also been unsuccessful when he lobbied for the squadron to be temporarily deployed down to Mindanao, about six hundred miles south, where they would be beyond the range of Jap bombers that would fly in from Formosa should an attack take place.

Greg quickly realized that he was making himself very unpopular with Colonel Arthur Short, CO of V Bomber Command, the Far East Air Force heavy bomber contingent. Arty Short, as he insisted on being called, was adamant that all his birds remain in a guarded little covey on Clark Field to protect against a lone saboteur who might find a way inside the base fence. He was just as convinced that no attack—from Japan or anybody else—was imminent, despite Tillson's most recent deadly experience while passing Truk in the transit over from Pearl Harbor.

"Hell, Tillson, we all know that was just some trigger-happy Nips showin' off for their commanders. The diplomats will rant and shout over it and it'll all get swept under the carpet like the other little dustups we've had with the Japs already. They don't want war with Uncle Sam, you can bet. They just want a treaty of some kind to keep us out of the war while they lay claim to most of Asia."

Tillson frowned, took a deep breath, and was brave enough to say, "That 'little dustup' you mention cost American lives from my squadron, and it's clear that if they intend on going to war, this base will be right behind Pearl at the top of their—"

Short, with a dismissive wave, interrupted the pilot. "Enough, Tillson. Have yourself a nice day. Goodbye."

It was abundantly clear the Colonel was not interested in listening to some Captain who might have a different idea from his own.

The only option that Tillson appeared to have left was to keep his own group of "Flying Fortresses" ready to leap into the air at the first warning of any Japanese attack. That meant the aircrews would have to essentially live in the shadow of their bombers for a few days.

Monday morning, 8 December, found Tillson enjoying a cup of coffee with Sam Beyers and Jim Swits in the shade of *Little Girl*'s wing and fuselage. A warm breeze was blowing gently down from the mountains, promising another hot tropical day and the usual afternoon showers.

A jeep screeched to a halt just short of *Little Girl*. The Sergeant driving the vehicle gave a few quick beeps on its horn and hollered, "Captain! Colonel Short wants all Squadron Commanders in his office right now. The damn Japs have attacked Pearl Harbor!"

Tillson turned to Beyers and ordered, "Sam, get all the crews in the planes. Get them warmed up and ready to go! I expect that we'll be airborne as soon as I get back!" With that, he threw down his coffee and ran to the jeep. It kicked up a spray of mud as the Sergeant skidded it around and raced off to the V Bomber Command headquarters building.

Tillson saw that several P-36 and P-40 pursuit planes were already taking off. A few others were flitting about in the skies, looking for anything that might be up there and coming their way. That was unusual, but not exactly the wall of defensive planes that he would expect to see in the face of a Jap air assault.

Tillson found Bryce Swinson, CO of the 14th Bombardment Squadron, and Leonard Philbert, CO of the 28th, already seated in Col. Short's office. A document marked "SECRET WAR PLAN" lay out on the table between them.

Arty Short was doing his best to wear out the rattan carpet, pacing back and forth from one side of the office to the other. He saw Tillson step in and irritably said, "Now that the 30th Squadron has graced us with its presence, we can get started." He waved toward the document on the table. "The War Plan says that we are supposed to strike the airfields in Formosa immediately upon initiation of any hostilities from the Empire of Japan. I want all the bombers loaded with a full bomb load, fueled, and ready to go. I'm calling General Brereton and General MacArthur to get their go-ahead for this strike."

"Colonel, it'll take hours to load out all the planes for a strike," Tillson protested before even sitting down. "If they've already attacked Pearl, you know they have to be ready to strike our other key facilities in the Pacific. And Clark is key. Half the Far East Air Force and all the heavy bombers are cozied up out there on the tarmac right now. And the Japs are probably already airborne and heading this way. If they took off at dawn, they'll be here in less than an hour. Colonel, I suggest that we get our birds airborne as quick as we can, move them south, and load out for attacking Formosa from there."

"Captain Tillson, I have had about all the fear-mongering from you that I can take!" Short exploded, halting his back-and-forth march across the office, glaring at the Captain. "Nobody's attacking Clark. Intelligence would have told us. And even if the Japs try, our spotters on the north coast will give us plenty of time to prepare to take care of them. Now, if you don't want to be a team player on this, if you're too scared, tell me and I'll get somebody else into the 30th who can handle the load!"

Tillson shook his head and took his seat. He was about to remind the Colonel that an attack on Pearl had come as a surprise already. But he knew he had done all that he could. No one was listening to a "warbird jockey."

Short stared hard at Tillson but spoke to the group. "Now, we'll do what the War Plan tells us to do. Load out your birds and, if we get the nod, and only when and if we do, we'll go drop some holy hell on Formosa."

Tillson glumly rode back to where *Little Girl* was parked. By the time he got to his airplane, bomb trailers were already arriving, parking beneath some of the other squadron birds. Big five-hundred-pounders were being winched up into the cavernous bomb bays. There, the fuses and tail fins would be attached to each weapon. That whole ticklish but necessary process took almost an hour for each airplane, and there were close to forty bombers to load. Tillson's 30th Bombardment Squadron, the new guys in town, were the last ones scheduled to take on bombs. It would be well past noon before the carts even got to his warbirds.

"Sam, our aircraft warmed and ready?" Tillson asked.

"Yeah, boss," Beyers answered. "The Sergeant over at the armory is not going to be singing our praises anytime soon. I had to strong-arm him to get enough .50 cal ammo."

"Good, I think we'll be needing it," Tillson grunted. "Get everyone saddled up. My gut tells me the Japs could show up any minute now and I want to be able to roll, permission or not."

The pursuit planes, already low on fuel from their sorties fruitlessly protecting Clark Field, were now in the landing pattern. Some of them, already short on fuel, were back on the ground, taxiing over to the fuel stands.

That was when a distant, dark swarm appeared as an inky blotch high in an otherwise cloudless morning sky.

By the time the warning sounded all across Clark Air Field, the first wave of high-level Mitsubishi G4M "Betty" bombers was already overhead, releasing their bomb loads. Aichi "Val" dive-bombers were right behind them, screaming down through the thin cloud cover to send their deadly loads plummeting into Clark's hangars and repair shops.

Greg Tillson jumped into the pilot's seat and jammed *Little Girl*'s throttles fully open. Spinning the big bomber around, he aimed it down the sod airstrip. The bird had barely reached eighty knots and he still had plenty of runway ahead of him when he hauled back on the control yoke. Any chance of survival meant being in the air. Staying on the ground was a sure way to die.

Little Girl groaned and grumbled, but somehow, she clawed her way against gravity and was airborne. Tillson heard Anson Hopper, the top-turret gunner, open fire with his twin fifties. They were only a couple of hundred feet off the ground and Tillson was doing all he could to climb out. An A6M "Zero," trailing a thin line of smoke, flashed by the windscreen, almost close enough to touch. The turbulence from the plane pushed the bomber sideways. Then the Nippon fighter suddenly flipped over and crashed in a flaming, smoking ball, spewing fire and bits of what was left of the aircraft across the grassy field below.

Good shootin', Hopper, Tillson thought, then keyed his mike and ordered, "30th Squadron, form combat box on me. Coming to course south." Then he keyed the plane's intercom as he pushed *Little Girl* into a steep, banking turn to a heading that would take them out of the hell being unleashed down there. "Hang on, everyone. Watch for the Zeros. And pray they are more interested in the air base down there than—"

"Here comes another one!" Sam Beyers yelled, pointing straight ahead. Sure enough, a Mitsubishi A6M was swinging around from their right side, standing on its wingtip, then diving at them in a head-on pass.

Jim Swits, in *Little Girl*'s glassed-in nose, opened fire with his .50 caliber M2 Browning at the same time Hopper let loose from the top turret, just above and behind the pilots. Streaks of fire from the Zero's 20mm tracer rounds passed disturbingly close to the bomber. Tillson resisted the natural impulse to duck down behind the instrument panel. The Zero flashed by, missing *Little Girl* by mere yards as the attacker took aim at the next bomber in line.

The sky was full of hundreds of planes, diving or climbing in the noontime sky, mostly concentrating on annihilating Clark Air Base below. All of them sported bright red "meatballs" on their wings and fuselages, proclaiming they flew—and were killing—on behalf of the Emperor and the Empire of Japan. Some planes flew over key targets to disgorge their loads of bombs while others screamed down to make strafing runs on the undefended American bombers, still sitting clustered close together out in the open field. Many already blazed like funeral pyres, black columns of smoke marking each destroyed plane. Smoke and flames also erupted from the hangers and fueling stations.

No one seemed to be shooting back.

Tillson looked around to see where everyone from his squadron—the only ones, apparently, to get off the ground—might be by now, but he could only see six Flying Fortresses in the combat box. And the plane in number four position was streaming a long trail of oily smoke from its number three engine.

"Sam, you see where everyone is?"

"Jones's plane bought it on the takeoff roll," Beyers answered. "Wilson got hit by a Zero and augered in on the climb-out." He searched the skies hopefully. "I'm not seeing Smith's bird. Looks like Jenson's hit in the number three engine, but he's staying with us so far."

Tillson called back to his seventeen-year-old tail gunner, Tim Swigert—"Timmy" to the crew—for a report. "Hey, Timmy, what you seein' back there?"

"Captain, Clark's a burnin'! Most'a the B-17s are burnin' and explodin' where they're settin'. There's Japs ever'where, zooming around like a buncha really mad hornets."

"Anybody chasing us?"

"Not that I can see, sir."

Tillson nodded, then ordered, "Nav, set a course for Mindanao. I think we'll get out of town for a bit."

8

It was late in the afternoon of Tuesday, 9 December, before *Wolffish* was finally ordered to enter port at Pearl Harbor. Because of reports that Jap submarines had been sighted in the area, *Wolffish* was to stay submerged and only surface when they rendezvoused with their escort, a vessel named *Hulbert*, a seaplane tender, and had exchanged recognition signals. That meetup was to take place five miles south of Barbers Point, off the southwest side of Oahu, some distance away from the entrance to Pearl Harbor. The precautions were necessary because most surfaced submarines looked similar. It was hard, even for experienced spotters, to tell an American sub from a Jap one at any distance. Everyone operating around Pearl Harbor was on a hair-trigger, both wary of any more sneak attacks and thirsting to get their licks in if they could. And President Roosevelt had formally declared war against Japan the day before.

Fred Wurster had never heard of a US Navy ship named the *Hulbert*. He had to look it up in their old, tattered copy of the 1935 edition of *Jane's Fighting Ships*. There he found that the ship was originally an old four-stacker destroyer, built in 1919, just missing action in the Great War, and decommissioned in 1934. Somewhere along the line, someone must have decided that the old tin can would make a good seaplane tender, so that was why she had been reactivated, and that was what she was doing now.

Evidently the people in Pearl Harbor were pressing whatever assets still floated into service.

"We have contact on a surface ship, bearing zero-five-six," the JK sonar operator reported. He pressed the earphones to his ears and listened intently. "I'm hearing two screws. Probably a destroyer. Best guess on range is about five thousand yards."

Fred glanced at the navigation chart. That range and bearing worked out to where the *Hulbert* should be. He glanced over to where Jim Shelton stood. It occurred to Wurster that he, acting-Skipper Shelton, QM1 Obrien, and Chief Wankel were likely the only crewmembers aboard *Wolffish* who had ever had to worry about whether or not an unidentified ship might be friend or fire-breathing foe. The look on Shelton's face seemed to confirm he was having the same thoughts. He nodded and said, "Let's go up—up to periscope depth—and take a look."

Wurster shouted down to the Diving Officer in the control room below, "Dive, make your depth five-eight feet. Raising the attack scope."

Wolffish slid smoothly upward until the periscope broke through the surface into the blindingly bright afternoon sunshine. The old gray four-stacker destroyer-turned-seaplane-tender was just off the port beam, steaming a slow circle almost three miles away from the submarine.

Wurster reported, "Have the *Hulbert* visually. One-point-five divisions in high power. Use eighty-foot mast head height."

The QM1 Obrien, already gripping his "Is/Was" circular slide rule, spun the wheel around and adjusted the cursor. "Range four-eight-hundred yards," he called out.

Shelton nodded and ordered, "Fire a white flare from the forward signal ejector." A white flare was the recognition signal that told the *Hulbert* that they were about to see a surfacing submarine and that it was a friendly one.

Wurster called out, "Flashing light from the *Hulbert*." He translated, "'Welcome home. Take station one hundred yards astern.' He sure wants us tucked in close to his skirts."

Shelton ordered, "Surface the boat. Gun crews topside as soon as we're up."

The *Wolffish* lunged to the surface of the Pacific. Water was still pouring down from the free-floods, draining out of the superstructure, when

Wurster led the lookouts topside. They were quickly followed by the gun crew lugging the .50 caliber machine gun up and setting it up on the mount on the cigarette deck. The three-inch deck gun crew trotted out of the watertight door at the aft end of the conning tower. The *Wolffish* looked like she was ready for battle, not for a happy arrival at her new home port.

Then Wurster looked over at the *Hulbert*. Her guns were all trained upward for anti-aircraft use. She bristled with .50 caliber machine guns haphazardly arranged around the deck. Every gun was manned by a crew ready for another unexpected air attack. Fred assumed the vessel had done some shooting of their own on Sunday morning. He hoped that they had, and that they had done some damage to their attackers.

Wurster steered the *Wolffish* around until it was just astern of the seaplane tender. He estimated that they were about a hundred yards astern and about as close as he really wanted to be. However, the conning officer on the *Hulbert* signaled for him to close up the interval. Fred moved the *Wolffish* nearer to the surface ship's churning screws. The conning officer signaled for him to get closer still. Wurster shrugged but brought the submarine up to where the *Hulbert*'s frothy white wake washed up on the submarine's bow.

Wurster shook his head. Whoever was commanding the surface ship certainly did not want any Japanese sub to get in between him and *Wolffish* and sneak past the submarine nets into Pearl Harbor. Not even a porpoise could make such a move the way the two vessels were so closed up.

Fred stole a glance over toward Pearl Harbor. Several columns of thick black smoke rose from fires that still had not been extinguished more than two full days after the deadly attack. He could smell the stench of burning bunker fuel all the way out here.

The ships sailed past the submarine nets, then a small boat swung them closed immediately behind *Wolffish*. Over to starboard, Hickam Airfield was a charred mess of burnt-out hangars and the blackened remains of what once were aircraft. Up ahead, he could see the hulk of the battleship *Nevada*, aground stern first and jutting out into the west side of the channel. Men were working all over the ship, trying to get her afloat and moved to the drydocks for repairs.

Rounding Hospital Point, Fred caught sight of utter devastation. Battleship Row was filled with sunken or badly damaged dreadnoughts. The *California* rested on the bottom with only her superstructure above the murky, oil-covered waters. The *Oklahoma* was capsized at her berth, trapping the lightly damaged *Maryland* inboard. The sunken *West Virgina* had the *Tennessee* blocked from leaving her berth. And at the head of the line, the sunken *Arizona* still burned with heavy black smoke pouring up out of her superstructure into the bright Hawaiian sky.

The airfield and barracks on Ford Island still smoldered. Sweating work crews, blackened with soot and ash, labored to sort through the wreckage, looking for bodies or anything that might still be salvaged and put to use.

Then he noticed the harbor water. Bits and pieces of the battle still floated in oily clots lapping up on the *Wolffish*'s flanks. Bodies were still being pulled from the water by men in small boats. Not at all what Wurster expected to see with his first glimpse of paradise.

He turned and looked at Shelton. Tears streamed down the officer's face. Only then did Fred realize he had tears on his own cheeks.

This was a debt that demanded repayment. Wurster clenched his fists and made a silent vow to himself that he would do all he could to make sure that it was paid in full.

∞

Trip MacLean figured that he was now the *S-55*'s perpetual in-port Duty Officer. Ever since Tony DiCarlo had restricted him to the sub, he had been the Duty Officer while the rest of the officers were over on the beach, sampling the exotic pleasures of Manila. That is, all except Tommy Hilligas, a brand-new Ensign who had just reported aboard fresh from Submarine School. Ensign Hilligas spent his days wandering around the *S-55*, his eyes wide in awe of the complicated machine. MacLean could vaguely remember feeling the same way on his first boat, the old *S-53*.

When the reports rolled in that Pearl Harbor had been attacked and that Japanese aircraft had destroyed Clark Field, DiCarlo ordered that the sub's guns be kept manned and ready during daylight hours. After all, they were now at war with Japan. And that meant MacLean spent most of his time topside. "Working on my tan," he told the crew. "While watching for the Nips to pay us a visit."

DiCarlo and Sam Forester, the XO, spent most of their time over in downtown Manila, at the Marsman Building, in the offices of the US Navy's Commander Asiatic Submarines. There, Captains Red Doyle and John Wilkes were busy planning and briefing the submarine strategy for the boats homeported in the Philippines in anticipation of a possible war. That conflict was now a reality. No one involved had ever taken a submarine to war before, but it was clear, with most of the Navy's battleships out of service at Pearl Harbor and a sizeable chunk of airpower forming mounds of rubble at Clark Field, submarines would have to carry the load of America's counterattack for a while. They just could not agree on how and where to use them.

The absence of the sub's senior officers was fine with MacLean. It left him alone and untroubled by the pair, neither of which had impressed him with their knowledge, aggressiveness, or common sense. They always seemed ready to cover their indecisiveness and lack of leadership with bluster and snap judgments. Like punishing MacLean for doing the right thing.

Trip was sure that the Jap bombers would attack Cavite on Tuesday, the day after they obliterated Clark Field. Especially if it was their aim to cripple the US Navy in the Pacific. He made certain his gun crews were ready, and that they were stocked with plenty of ammunition, just in case they had to take on hordes of manic Japs.

Nothing happened.

All day, the skies were clear, empty of meat-ball-emblazoned warplanes diving out of the sun. Somewhat disappointed, MacLean dismissed the gun crews as the sun dipped below Mount Mariveles over on the Bataan Peninsula. And as he watched, he longed for a cold beer and a warm female human being.

Wednesday, 10 December, brought a flurry of early-morning activity. Admiral Thomas Hart, Commander of the Asiatic Fleet, decided that the sub tenders *Otus* and *Holland* would load up on torpedoes and supplies from the Cavite Navy Yard and then head south, beyond the Malay Barrier. The *Canopus*, the third sub tender, would remain in Manila Bay to support the submarines that would be staying behind. Staying behind but heavily camouflaged over in the shallow waters by the Manila waterfront, far from the Cavite Navy Yard. All the shuffling around became Trip MacLean's headache. As usual, the Skipper and his XO left the boat at sunrise for breakfast ashore and more meetings with the brass. Since the *S-55* was currently tied up outboard to the *Canopus*, all the shuffling meant he would have to get the S-55 underway and then drop anchor out in the bay while the *Canopus* moved to her new anchorage. But between his work and the efforts of the COB leading the crew, Motor Machinist Chief Anthony Watson, the move was accomplished with little hassle.

He had just dropped the anchor when he and the lookouts heard rumbling engines. Then Japanese high-level bombers, swarms of Mitsubishi G4M "Bettys" and G3M "Nells," appeared high overhead. The bombers were far too high for the machine gun to reach, so he ordered the sub's four-inch deck gun to open fire at about the same time other batteries and shipboard weapons—including from Corregidor and other forts around Manila Bay—began shooting. *S-55*'s gun was not specifically designed for anti-aircraft use. It had no gun director for such a fast-moving target. Still, it made a satisfying roar and sent its shells high into the air. Maybe a Jap Betty would accidentally fly into one of them.

At first, the enemy bombers—yes, they would have to get used to Japan now being "the enemy"—ignored the little submarine banging away with no effect on them. Instead, they concentrated on their primary target, the Cavite Navy Yards, with the tightly packed buildings and cramped waterfront, outdated defenses, and almost ten thousand military personnel and Filipino workers. The first wave left the waterfront ablaze. The many wooden buildings burned like kindling. The submarines *Seadragon* and *Sealion*, both in the shipyard for maintenance and unable to get underway, seemed to be special targets for the bombers. The *Seadragon* was set afire while the *Sealion* was hit with a pair of bombs and abandoned.

The second wave of Bettys was working the Navy Yard over when the "Val" dive-bombers discovered the *S-55* and took special interest in her. Two of them rolled over and angrily screamed down toward the diminutive submarine, a sitting duck in the middle of the harbor. MacLean realized they were headed his way and ordered the .50 caliber machine gun to open fire. A stream of bright yellow-white tracer fire arced up toward the onrushing dive-bombers. Some of the crew, desperate to deflect their attackers, grabbed their M1 Garand rifles and started shooting. A couple of sailors even unloaded with Thompson submachine guns. MacLean shrugged, pulled out his M1911 .45 automatic from its holster, and shot at the onrushing dive-bombers. It was all probably futile, but it satisfied the powerful instinct to fight back the only way he could.

He could plainly see one bomber release his bomb and pull up. To MacLean, it seemed that the bomb was following a straight line, aimed right at him. He stood transfixed, watching it growing ever larger. He did not move or dodge as it sailed only a few feet over his head and crashed into the bay a scant twenty feet from the stern of his submarine. The column of water from the explosion drenched everyone topside.

"Sir, you okay?" Chief Watson called up from the cigarette deck where he was supervising the gun crews.

"He missed me, so I reckon so," MacLean responded.

But now the second bomber was diving down at them. For some reason, the pilot was not strafing them yet, nor did he release his bomb or pull up. Instead, he slammed hard into the water at a near-vertical angle, less than a hundred feet from the *S-55* and with a tremendous explosion, sending flames along with bits and pieces of aircraft in every direction before most of what was left of the plane disappeared below the waves.

MacLean could only guess that wildly fired bullets from one of their woefully inadequate weapons had miraculously found its mark. It had hit the pilot before he could release his bomb or pull out of his dive.

And then the attack was over, just as suddenly as it started. The Cavite Navy Yard was ablaze. A couple of ships, in the yards for repairs, were also burning. Secondary explosions and fireballs rocked the Navy Yard. Torpedoes, lined up to load onto the *Otus*, cooked off in the conflagration, sending deadly shrapnel whirling away in every direction.

MacLean realized there was nothing he could do about that. He had a submarine to worry about. A couple of the men topside had been grazed by flying shrapnel either from the nearby bomb or the airplane crash. He called for Doc Jones, the boat's corpsman, to come topside to tend to the injured men.

MacLean was standing off to the side, catching his breath and collecting his wits—reliving watching that bomb coming straight at him—when Seaman Williams looked up and exclaimed, “Mr. MacLean, you’ve been hit! You’re bleeding! Look at your arm!”

MacLean shook his head, about to assure Williams that he was okay, when he looked down. There was a considerable stream of blood dripping from the fingers of his left hand. His left sleeve was soaked with blood. Only then did he feel a sharp, stinging pain in the bicep of that arm. Then, whether it was from the loss of blood or the pain, the dizziness hit him full force. He had to brace himself against the fairwater to keep from collapsing.

Hell, he told himself. *No time to collapse. The Japs might be back in another wave any minute now.*

Then Doc was grabbing hold of him, settling him down to the deck in the shade of the fairwater, leaning him back against the structure. All the while, MacLean protested that he was fine, that Doc needed to work on the guys that were actually hurt. Jones broke protocol and told the Lieutenant to “shut the hell up...sir!” Then he ripped the bloody sleeve off the shirt to expose a deep laceration across MacLean’s bicep.

“Damn, Doc, that was my last clean shirt,” MacLean said, but his words were followed by an involuntary groan as the corpsman dug around in the wound. Then he pulled a big, ugly, jagged piece of aluminum from the deep wound. He wiped it off with some gauze and handed it to MacLean.

“Here, Lieutenant, your first war souvenir. And evidence for your Purple Heart.” He quickly wrapped a bandage around the arm to try to slow the bleeding. “We’ll have to get some stitches in that pretty quick, I reckon. But, sir, if that thing had come at you an inch higher, it would’ve got you in the neck. And that would have resulted in a lot of slow walking and sad singing once they got your carcass back home. Congratulations on cheating death, sir.”

Doc was finishing bandaging MacLean when a small boat pulled alongside. Tony DiCarlo and the XO jumped up onto the submarine’s deck. DiCarlo looked around at the spent shell casings and bloody bandages littering the deck of his submarine. Then he stepped over to where MacLean was struggling to get to his feet.

“Mr. MacLean, what is the status of the boat for underway?” the

Skipper demanded with no hint of concern for the health of his officer or the crew, or for the extent of damage to his *S*-boat.

"Sir, the boat's ready to weigh anchor and get underway," MacLean answered curtly, trying his best to do so in a strong voice. Truth was, he was so dizzy that it was all he could do to stand there without collapsing.

"Very well. Make it so. I want to clear Manila Bay before sundown."

With that, the CO of *S*-55 turned and made a beeline for the hatch.

9

Royal Navy Lieutenant Geoffrey Chandler could not overcome his feeling of uneasiness. Events were moving far too fast, and every one of them seemed to be going in the least desired direction. Mostly, of late, in the favor of the brutally aggressive Japanese. As the Assistant Communicator on the British battleship HMS *Prince of Wales*, he had a front-row seat to everything that was happening in the Far East.

The stew had been bubbling. Chandler feared it was about to boil right out of the pot and become a major mess.

It did just that thing very early on Monday morning, 8 December. Force Z, the group which Chandler and his battleship were a part of, was safely at anchor in Singapore's large and well-defended harbor. He was awakened by Chief Telegraphist Ian Murphy beating on his stateroom door, excitedly shouting, "The Nips, them back-stabbin' samurai! They done hit the Yanks at Pearl Harbor!" Murphy's Irish brogue was normally so thick that it was hard to understand. When he was excited, it was nigh unto impossible. But there was no mistaking the news he was delivering outside the Lieutenant's door in the middle of the night. "Message says they all be sunk! All them Yank battleships done be sunk!"

Chandler forced himself to wake up as he grabbed his robe and opened the door to read the message for himself. He glanced at his alarm clock. It read "0430." He scanned the shocking message quickly and then ordered, "Murphy, get this to the Admiral immediately. Then rouse the whole communications team. I suspect that we'll be at Action Stations in a few minutes."

Then he stepped back into his stateroom and quickly got dressed. There would be no more sleep today. The pot had boiled over. Even though Singapore was more than five thousand nautical miles from Hawaii, the booms of the detonations at Pearl Harbor would reverberate from all sides of the Pacific. The World War had just become worldwide.

Chandler was still tying his shoes when the air raid sirens sounded out in the city. This was quickly followed by the *Prince of Wales* calling away Action Stations for an air attack. He was running to the radio room when he heard the battleship's secondary battery of sixteen Quick Firing 5.25-inch guns begin firing. Then the 40mm pom-pom guns opened up with their characteristic "thump-thump-thump" report.

It did not last long. The "all clear" sounded just before 0500. The report came down from the bridge shortly afterward that no enemy aircraft had been confirmed as hit. Chandler wondered how, with so much ordnance going airborne, none of it had struck any of the Japanese planes. That did not say much for the *Prince of Wales*'s anti-aircraft prowess. But there were no reports of damage or casualties among the British ships, either.

On Monday evening, Force Z got underway. A flotilla of Japanese transports was reported heading to Kota Bharu on the Malay Peninsula. Force Z —made up of the *Prince of Wales*, which served as Admiral Sir Tom Phillips's flagship, the battlecruiser *Repulse*, and a half dozen destroyers—had orders to attack Imperial Japanese Navy vessels to prevent what was expected to be an amphibious landing on the peninsula. There was intelligence that indicated this was likely the first step toward the Japanese attempting to capture Malaysia and Singapore. Force Z had just about reached Kota Bharu at midnight on 9 December when they were abruptly redirected back down the peninsula to Kuantan. To make matters even worse—actually far worse—they were informed that there would be no RAF fighters available for air cover. Force Z was on its own.

Early on the morning of 10 December, they learned that the reported landing on Kuantan—the one that had pulled them away from Kota Bharu—had turned out to be a diversion. A ruse that His Majesty's Royal Navy had swallowed hook, line, and sinker. Force Z did a U-turn and headed back north, retracing their path.

Then, at 1100, the Japanese bombers showed up. The first wave of eight Mitsubishi G3M Nells unloaded on the battle cruiser *Repulse* but initially caused only minor damage. All of the British ships opened fire with their anti-aircraft batteries. Tracers arced across the midday skies. The heavens were littered with black puffs from exploding anti-aircraft shells. The eight bombers, their ordnance delivered, blithely flew on, seemingly unbothered by all the lead and steel being aimed in their direction by the ships.

Then seventeen more Nells appeared and attacked, this time carrying Type 91 aerial torpedoes, the same weapons that had proven so devastating at Pearl Harbor only two days before. Dodging and ducking, the *Repulse* managed to avoid all seven of the deadly fish aimed at her as well as bombs from six more Nells, flying high overhead.

The *Prince of Wales* was not so lucky. One torpedo slammed into the aft port quarter of the battleship. The blast wrecked the outboard propellor shaft. But more importantly, it caused uncontrollable flooding and knocked out the entire electrical system for the after half of the ship.

Geoff Chandler was locked in the radio room where he could not see any of the battle outside. He could certainly hear the gunfire and feel the ship rock as it wildly maneuvered to try to avoid the bombs and torpedoes falling from the sky.

And then the torpedo explosion at the stern shook the whole massive battleship. Chandler was knocked to the floor, hitting his head hard against a bulkhead. The entire episode was unleashing horrible visions in his mind from his time on HMS *Courageous*. Memories had been seared in his consciousness of *Courageous* being sunk beneath him. Of good friend Randall Macallister, the ruddy Scot who died because he could not swim. Recollections of the horribly cold Irish Sea, the screams of the dying men, the great ship disappearing beneath the waves as Chandler treaded water and watched it play out.

Was he doomed to relive that horrible tragedy?

His question was soon answered. As he got back to his feet, rubbing the swelling knot above his eyebrow, he could feel the big battleship begin to list to port. Chairs and desks skidded across the deck to crash into the bulkhead. The lean of the ship was getting progressively worse.

"Mr. Chandler, what we best be doin'?" Murphy asked. His eyes were large and his voice quavered with fear. He had a set of sound-powered phones on, so he was in communication with the rest of the ship. Better than anyone in the radio room, he knew what was going on out there.

"Just stay calm," Chandler said, trying his best to keep his own voice controlled. He had been through this kind of thing before. He knew what raw fear felt like. "The Captain will tell us what he wants us to do."

That was proper procedure. Wait for orders from the Captain. But Chandler would have much preferred getting topside, finding a raft or lifeboat, and getting off what was almost certainly a sinking ship.

Wilkins pushed the headset tight against his ears. As he listened, his face turned white. He started to shake. "She's gone! The *Repulse* is gone! She's sunk!"

With the battle cruiser destroyed, Chandler knew the Japanese would turn their full attention to his already badly damaged battleship and finish her off. It was a foregone conclusion that she would soon join the *Repulse* at the bottom of the Gulf of Siam. The *Prince of Wales* groaned and shuddered—almost as if the vessel knew it was doomed—as more bombs and torpedoes drove home.

"It's time to go," Chandler decided. No reason to wait for word from the Captain. He yelled, "Everyone, grab your life vest. Report to your Abandon Ship stations."

Murphy stood but seemed locked in place. "Mr. Chandler, I'm scared." The usually tough Telegraphist was shuddering. "Sir, I can't swim. What am I going to do?"

Jesus. Not again!

Chandler put his arm around the Irishman. "Murphy, they'll probably pull some destroyers alongside. Or we'll just get on one of the Carley floats. You won't even get your feet wet. But if you do, just cinch up your life vest preserver and float 'til somebody hooks you and pulls you in like an Irish flounder."

"Uh...alright, sir," Murphy reluctantly responded. "If you say so."

Chandler headed out of the radio room and stepped into the middle of bedlam. Panicked sailors ran down the steeply listing deck, vainly looking for somewhere safe, something solid to hold onto. Some simply kept going, jumping overboard. Chandler knew from bitter experience that at this point, the safest place was in the water, not aboard this struggling battleship.

The destroyer *Express* had pulled alongside and was attempting to transfer crew off the *Prince of Wales*, but there were over 1,500 scared sailors on board. Many of them were injured. The cockeyed angle of the ship's deck was a problem, too. It would take too long to transfer the whole crew to the destroyers, especially with the Japanese bombers relentlessly, mercilessly pressing their attack.

In the confusion, someone bumped hard into Ian Murphy, pitching him right over the rail and down into the oil-covered water. Murphy's scream as he fell pierced right to the center of Chandler's soul. In a previous attack in the North Atlantic, he had helplessly witnessed shipmate Randall Macallister, in panic, drowning, simply because he had never learned to swim.

Geoff did not hesitate. He dived over the side.

Chandler's life preserver bobbed him to the surface a couple of yards from where Murphy floated, still screaming in terror, furiously flapping his arms to try to keep his head above water. Chandler swam up behind the panicking sailor, took hold of his collar, and pulled him toward a small Carley float. The little buoyant life raft was unoccupied, probably released and then ignored when the *Express* pulled alongside and offered what someone saw as a better option.

"Don't fight me, Murphy," Chandler ordered. "Keep your face out of the water. Let the preserver do its job."

Only then did the Irishman stop flailing and spinning. The Lieutenant pushed him up onto the little float and then hoisted himself aboard.

"You saved my life!" Murphy sputtered as he retched up the seawater that he had ingested. "Don't tell anybody the Chief was squallin' and snifflin' like a wee chiseller, okay?" He paused to cough some more, then looked wide-eyed at Geoff. The Japs were still strafing the *Prince of Wales* and the ships still attempting rescues. The enemy was clearly trying to kill survivors. "Now, what do we do?"

"We simply sit back and wait to be picked up. There are still three destroyers out here, taking on survivors. They'll get to us soon enough, Chief," Chandler reassured the sailor. "Anyway, looks like the thumpers are going cheerio, thank thee, Lord."

Sure enough, their attackers were departing, maybe out of ammo, maybe low on fuel. But just then, as Chandler looked back at the *Prince of Wales*, the vessel seemed to surrender to its many wounds and rolled over onto its side, spilling men and anything else on its deck that was not tied down into the sea. Then the creaking, moaning vessel slipped beneath the waves in a remarkably short time. There was surprisingly little disturbance on the sea surface—no big wave, no sucking whirlpool—as if the ship was doing its best to not cause any more trouble for what remained of her crew.

Chandler and Murphy looked at each other without speaking. There was nothing to say.

Meanwhile, their raft drifted with the current, either ignored or not spotted by the three British destroyers as they tried to rescue thousands of survivors from the two sunken capitol ships.

Night fell with the two sailors all by themselves on a vast, lonely sea, with no sign of what remained of Force Z. Not even another raft or lifeboat. Chandler had a pretty good idea of where they were, though, so he was not especially worried about their being lost at sea. Finding land or another ship before thirst or starvation became a problem should not be too difficult. He shared his belief with Murphy. It helped keep the Chief calm, even though both men were already thirsty and hungry and knew they would have no protection from a relentless sun when it inevitably made its appearance at dawn.

But Chandler did not share another fact with his raft mate: Finding land or a ship that was not occupied by the Japanese might prove to be considerably more difficult.

∞

The off-watch officers on USS *Tigerfish* had just sat down to their evening meal in the wardroom when RM3 Eric Riegel burst in, excited about something.

"Captain! Captain!" he shouted breathlessly. "The Japs have attacked Pearl Harbor! We're at war!"

Wayne Schacter, the Skipper, held up his hand. "Easy, Riegel. Easy," he told the radioman. "What exactly is it you got there?"

Riegel handed his aluminum clipboard to Schacter, who lifted the overleaf and read the first page. He shook his head and handed the board to Isaac Sternman, sitting next to him. As the XO read the message, Schacter stood and headed out to the control room. The entire on-watch section turned to look at the Skipper as he grabbed the 1MC microphone. Schacter knew that on a submarine, it was next to impossible to keep anything a secret. Especially something as earthshaking as the contents of this dispatch. By the time Riegel's clipboard was carried from the radio room to the wardroom, just about everyone aboard would have heard the gist of the incoming message. Schacter meant to give them an accurate reading before scuttlebutt blurred things and fractured morale.

"Men, it's official," Schacter announced. "We are now at war with the Empire of Japan. Our new general orders are to conduct unrestricted submarine warfare against all assets of that nation. I hereby guarantee you that is exactly what the *Tigerfish* will do. This is no longer a simulated war patrol. We are now embroiled in the real thing."

Loud, enthusiastic cheers rang out all up and down the length of the sub as the Skipper replaced the microphone and stalked off back to the wardroom and his dinner. But Schacter had a deeply worried look on his face. Going to war was not something to be cheered. Certainly not to be celebrated.

By the time he had plopped back down in his seat and loaded a generous helping of meatloaf and mashed potatoes onto his plate, the message board had made its way around the gathering of the seated officers. Then the questions started flying.

Schacter forked a heap of meatloaf into his mouth and chewed for a few seconds as he listened without responding to all the excited babble. Finally, he put the fork down and said, "Guys, what you see there was a general message to all fleet units. The only new information we have is that we are at war. We are authorized to shoot at any Japs we see. But remember, they are also authorized to shoot back at us. By definition, that's what war is."

He forked in a mouthful of mashed potatoes, munching on the meal with no further explanation or answers. That appeared to be all he planned to say about the subject.

"But, Skipper, what exactly are we supposed to be doing out here?" Brad Johnson ultimately asked.

Isaac Sternman, the XO, jumped in as Schacter chewed. "Our previous orders have not been rescinded, Brad. Right now, and until they change, we will follow those orders to the letter, as we are expected to do. Obligated to do. We are to transit to Cavite, conducting a simulated war patrol while on the way."

"But there's nothing simulated now," Brad Johnson said. "We are in a war."

"I expect we can just delete the word *simulated*," Sternman responded with just a bit of irritation. "Understand? And we simply continue on to Cavite, as ordered. That is, unless we see some vessel flying a Japanese flag. A warship, we attack. If it's flying the meatball flag, the new orders say we should attack it, without first having to surface and give them adequate warning to abandon ship, as would have been required by the Geneva Convention if this had not been designated 'unrestricted warfare.' If we see something, and if we have a good shot, and if we have a reasonable avenue of escape, we shoot, duck, and run."

"XO, you are exactly right for the interim until we get specific orders," Schacter added. "I expect the brass in Pearl Harbor are busy with a lot of stuff that's much more important than us and our submarine right now. When they get down to our priority, someone will give us more precise orders. In the meantime, nothing else changes. We stay prepared. We remain submerged doing a sonar search during daylight hours, then we surface after sunset. XO, I want extra lookouts topside any time we're on the surface. Every contact is presumed hostile until proven otherwise and we will respond accordingly. Any questions?"

Even the ice cream sundaes for dessert did little to ease the atmosphere of anxiety that now permeated the wardroom. The meal was followed by a long, uneventful, but sleepless night for the men of the *Tigerfish* as they continued to steam due west.

That changed just after sunrise of the next day, Tuesday, 9 December.

That was when RM3 Riegel began copying a long incoming message. Instead of the general dispatch of the previous day, this one was addressed specifically to *Tigerfish*. It came from Commander Submarine Force Pacific Fleet, COMSUBPAC. In peacetime, orders such as these would come from the submarine's parent squadron, not from the big boss. But this was war and things were obviously being done differently. Riegel had barely finished decoding the first paragraph when he noticed the shadows of someone reading over his shoulder. Both the Skipper and the XO were perched behind him, reading every word as he wrote it down.

With the lengthy message finally aboard, and while the radioman acknowledged receipt, Schacter grabbed the sheet of paper and stepped over to the navigation plot. They were ordered to intercept the Japanese carrier fleet. The same one that had launched the attack on Pearl Harbor. Naval Intelligence calculated that the enemy vessels were heading to either the Wotje Atoll or the Kwajalein Atoll. Both locations were in the Marshall Islands. Their fear was that the Air Fleet Strike Force would use IJN bases on the South Pacific atolls to refuel and rearm, and now that they had a good idea of damage done and what targets remained unscathed, they would hit Pearl Harbor a second time to finish the job. A second hit would almost certainly be fatal for the wounded and fragile US Pacific Fleet.

Tigerfish had been specifically ordered to locate and report on the Japanese fleet, and then to attack it.

The first thing Schacter had to do, however, was to find this Wotje Atoll in the Marshall Islands. He had little idea where to look. After all, the entirety of the CO's previous experience in submarines had been in the Atlantic and on the east side of the Panama Canal. It took a while to locate the tiny little pinprick in the middle of the expansive Pacific Ocean. He measured the distance from his submarine to the atoll as a little over eight hundred nautical miles, almost due south of their present position. But it was over two thousand nautical miles from Hawaii.

"Wow!" Sternman exclaimed as he and the CO worked over the charts. "COMSUBPAC sure threw us into the deep end!"

"Yeah," Schacter agreed with a grunt. "But we'd better figure out how we're going to get the transit down there done." He doodled some quick calculations on the chart. "Way I figure, if those Japs saunter along at a leisurely twenty knots, they'll arrive at the atoll day after tomorrow." He tossed the pencil aside in disgust. "We just can't get there in time to be waiting for them!"

Sternman answered, "Unless we ran at flank on the surface. Then we could be there a day before the Japs."

Schacter idly scratched an itch on his left forearm as he looked hard at his XO. He shot back, "Did you read Admiral Withers's orders? The part where he said to proceed with extreme caution because we don't know enough about the Japanese anti-submarine capabilities. I aim to follow the boss's orders to the tee. Last thing we need right now is some overzealous sub Skippers trying to win the war all by themselves in three days. We are just too vulnerable to air attack on the surface in daylight."

Brad Johnson was standing just behind the two senior officers, watching, listening, seething. He shook his head and stepped backward, farther away, literally and figuratively. Here they had a perfect chance to strike a real blow against the Japs two days into the war. To get some revenge and send the Japs a message that they had messed with the wrong damn navy.

But the Skipper was throwing it away, blowing the opportunity because Schacter insisted on following orders to the letter. Not doing what he needed to do to get the job done.

Brad Johnson's sense of frustration was building. He clenched and unclenched his fists, trying to calm down. Finally, he decided there was probably nothing he could do but smile and follow orders.

Dawn of 10 December was just a glimmer on the far horizon when the *Tigerfish* finally arrived off of Wotje Atoll. The low-lying islands—mostly just rings of coral outcroppings sitting above a long extinct volcano—barely rose above the surf. Schacter carefully eased the submerged submarine in close enough that he could scan the powder-blue lagoon beyond the rim of one of the larger islands. He found it empty. No Japanese carriers lay at anchor in its protected waters. Schacter could see a few seaplanes drawn up on a ramp over on the lagoon side, a few aircraft sitting next to a landing strip, some squatty tin-roofed buildings and big fuel tanks, and the Rising Sun flag flapping proudly at the top of the base flagpole.

For some reason, that flag galled Wayne Schacter. There were no Japanese warships there to sink, or destroyers to shoot back at him, but he could still let the Japs know that Americans were here and willing to fight back. He turned from the periscope and ordered, "Prepare to battle surface, guns!"

The order caught the crew unprepared. They were geared to send their Mark 14 torpedoes into the sides of Japanese carriers, not to attack an island with their little three-inch deck gun. It took a few minutes and some hurried scurrying before the XO could report that the *Tigerfish* was ready to battle surface.

The submarine emerged from the deep three thousand yards from the coral atoll. Johnson and Schacter climbed up to the bridge while the gun crew raced out onto the main deck. It took a few seconds to lower the barrel support, ready the gun, slam a round home, and then train it around and elevate it.

The gun roared.

Schacter saw a splash fifty yards out in the lagoon, beyond the seaplane ramp. He shouted down to the gun captain, "Drop range fifty."

The next round exploded right in the middle of the cluster of seaplanes. A trace of a smile crossed Schacter's lips. He ordered, "Fire ten rounds for effect."

The weapon roared once, then again. The gun crew was getting into a rhythm.

Then Johnson spied troubling movement off to the left. A coastal artillery battery, hidden in a concrete bunker just east of the seaplane docks, was opening fire. The six-inch shell sounded like moving thunder as it roared past, directly overhead. It splashed down a couple of hundred yards beyond the *Tigerfish* just as a second battery west of the other one opened fire. Their first round landed ahead of the boat and short by a hundred yards. A hit from these coastal artillery guns would mean the end for the *Tigerfish*. Even a near miss could inflict fatal damage.

"Brad, I expect we've worn out our welcome," Wayne Schacter said, still grinning. "Secure the gun crew, clear the bridge, and dive."

Johnson just caught a glimpse of one of the submarine's last rounds as it slammed home right at the foot of the flagpole. The Rising Sun banner crashed ingloriously to the ground, lost in smoke and black dust.

As he pulled the hatch cover shut above him, he had a thought. The sight of that flag being obliterated would, he hoped, serve as a powerful symbol—to the Japanese, to the crew of the *Tigerfish* and especially its senior officers—of just what the submarine service would do to fight back against a vicious enemy.

10

The westerly wind blew Geoff Chandler and Ian Murphy and their raft further out into the Gulf of Siam, toward the broad South China Sea. It relentlessly shoved the little Carley float away from the scene of devastation, but that was also away from land, the other surviving vessels, and the possibility of rescue. The first hours after the *Prince of Wales* capsized and sank were the most frightening. Several Japanese planes took an interest in the dark-gray raft floating along on the jade-green water. One of them decided to make a low pass to investigate. The two sailors ducked down in the mesh of the float, trying to make themselves invisible, as the Zero fighter roared overhead and then banked around for a second look. Evidently satisfied that the bit of flotsam down there was unimportant and not worth wasting ammunition, the plane roared off beyond the horizon.

Before it got dark, Chandler carefully inventoried the float's meager supplies. Normally, there would be a wooden box with tins of water and emergency rations, enough for eight men for a week. But that box was missing. There should also have been a canopy of some sort to protect them from the elements but it, too, was not in its zippered pocket. They could only assume it had all been washed away in the rush to launch the raft. He did find the emergency light and a couple of wooden paddles. That was all they had at their disposal.

Then they noticed that the sun, dipping below the horizon to the west, was now obscured by a building wall of dark cumulonimbus clouds. A storm was brewing and obviously heading their way. The gentle, warm breeze that had been relentlessly moving Chandler and Murphy out toward the South China Sea gradually built strength.

At first, the cool wind off the gathering storm provided welcome relief. But soon Chandler watched with worry as the ominous wall of clouds swept across the sky toward them, blotting out the stars and the waning gibbous moon. The strengthening storm began to churn the shallow sea. The float's gentle rocking soon changed to pitching and heaving.

Chandler grabbed one of the painters—a thin manila line tied to the float, primarily intended for men in the water to use to hang on to until they could be pulled aboard—and lashed himself to the float. He tossed another one to Murphy. He now had to yell to be heard over the wind. "Murphy, tie yourself in. If you go over the side in this blow, that'll be the end of it."

The first squall line hit the pair full force just as the Irishman finished tying himself to the raft. The two men clung to the float as the winds sent it skittering across the wave tops, then dropped them into a trough between the waves, only to be heaved up to a crest again. The float repeatedly capsized. However, since it was essentially a floating donut with a rope basket suspended in its middle, the pair only needed to pull themselves back into the basket each time, coughing, sputtering, spitting out seawater.

Because of the storm, the night was pitch black. It was impossible to tell where they were being blown, or even to see the waves before they hit them hard. Between the wind-borne waves, the salt spume, and the sideways deluge of rain, the two felt as if they were engulfed in a world of churning water. All they could do was hang on and pray. Grab a breath of air before once again being submerged by a towering wave. Cramped muscles ached from clutching the rope holds. Eyes stung from the salt spray.

The night had no end. Dawn would never come.

Chandler was exhausted and had just about come to the realization that his strength was spent when he felt—or maybe heard—the wind ease back just a bit. Then a few stars winked at him between the racing clouds overhead. The seas miraculously calmed. By the time the sun appeared, the water was almost flat calm under a cloudless sky. The pair had the entire expanse of the sea all to themselves. Nothing interrupted the blue-green watery wasteland or the brilliant blue canopy above. Had their situation not been so dire, it would have been a beautiful morning to be alive.

Then the rapidly climbing sun replaced the night's maelstrom as their primary enemy. Its unrelenting rays burned down on the unprotected pair. Their throats, already raw from a night of breathing seawater and salt spray, quickly parched to the point where speaking became painful. There was nothing to do but lie in the float and wait. Time seemed to stand still.

The second night adrift at least brought cool relief from the sun, and they were able to sleep a bit. But the following day under the torturous flaming orb was almost unbearable. Any exposed skin was quickly cooked. From their training, both men knew how long a person could survive in a situation like theirs—three minutes without air, three days without water, and three weeks without food—but they also knew that being in such a harsh environment reduced those generalized limits considerably. Besides, they were about to begin their second full day adrift, their third overall on the raft. Without food or water. And there had been no sign of a boat or plane since the Japanese A6M Zeros benevolently decided they were not worth the ammo and to leave them alone on that first afternoon.

Chandler was sure that he was hallucinating when he saw the shimmering image of a sailboat approaching from somewhere beyond the horizon. What in hell was a sailboat doing out in the Gulf of Siam in the middle of a war? Even so, just in case, he feebly raised his hands above his head and waved while hoarsely calling for help from the mirage.

Then his hopeless hallucination improbably turned into reality.

The *banting*, a traditional Indonesian fishing boat, dropped its sails and coasted to a stop alongside the Carley float. Chandler barely felt hands lifting him up and aboard the vessel. The cool water felt wonderful as it trickled down his throat, even if it did cause him to cough and gag. He heard Ian Murphy also hacking and groaning. Chandler was carried down into a small after cabin, one that was wonderfully shaded and protected his badly blistered body from the sun.

"I am Buya," the banting's Captain said, introducing himself to Chandler in fractured, halting English. "This is my fishing boat." The diminutive older man, dressed only in a short sarong, had just stepped into the small cabin. Many years spent fishing in the hot, tropical sun had burnished his skin to the color and consistency of mahogany-colored leather. "I think you must be British Navy sailors. We heard stories about the great battle west near here three days ago."

Chandler struggled to at least sit up. "Where are...?" he asked, but his question ended in a pained groan. He tried again. "The Japanese..." But he had to allow the words to trail off as he fell back onto the little couch, even that small effort exhausting.

Buya ladled up some water for Chandler to sip. "Do not worry. You have drifted far from the Japanese," he assured Chandler. "The storm the other night must have blown you quite a distance. We are almost a hundred miles from where the battle took place. We are sailing back home to Sedanau Island."

"Murphy?" Chandler asked. Geoff had just noticed his raft mate was not in the cabin with him.

"Your friend," Buya answered, "he sleeps. We gave him water and now allow him to rest. There will be a doctor on Sedanau. There you can both rest while the doctor attends to you. Mostly the burns from the sun and the effects of no water or food."

"I need to get back to Singapore as soon as possible," Chandler protested weakly. It was all he could do to keep his eyes open. "I'm an officer in the Royal Navy."

"That may be difficult," Bayu answered. "The Japanese are actively patrolling between here and Singapore. We have been stopped and searched many times. None of us can afford having them find you and your friend on our vessel. Or any evidence you have ever been here." The fisherman paused, a dark look on his face. "Besides, I do not know much about modern battles or warfare, but I fear for the safety of Singapore."

"You mean...?"

"By the time we could get you there, I am certain it will have fallen to the Japanese."

Chandler tried to rise again, to try to make his case. But he knew he should trust the man's judgment. And do whatever he could to assure Bayu and his crew would not suffer for their act of kindness in rescuing him and

Murphy. Chandler agreed the fishermen were taking a huge risk having the Brits aboard.

He started to say more, to agree to go wherever Bayu wanted to take them.

Before he could say anything, though, Chandler was out, lost in deep sleep, dreaming of his home in Plymouth, of a girl he had once considered asking to wait for him, of a calm sea and a favoring wind.

∞

The USS *Wolffish* had barely tied up at berth S-11 on the Submarine Base at Pearl Harbor when a dervish of submarine support personnel descended on her. First across the brow was her new Commanding Officer, LCDR Alphonse Dinnacetti. He was accompanied by COMSUBPAC, RADM Thomas Withers.

Jim Shelton saluted and greeted them as they stepped on board the submarine. "Welcome aboard the *Wolffish*."

"I see the Japs tried to redecorate your superstructure," Withers noted dryly as he pointed to the row of 20mm cannon holes stitched across the relatively new submarine's fairwater. "Hit anything vital?"

"No, sir," Shelton answered. "Just some added ventilation for the bridge. Other than that, we're good to go whenever and wherever you need us, just as soon as we get fuel and groceries."

Withers nodded. "Good. That's why I'm here. Let's go below. I want to discuss our plans for the *Wolffish* with you, your new Skipper here, and your Acting XO."

The three officers dropped through the forward torpedo room hatch and made their way aft to the wardroom. Fred Wurster was sitting there, waiting for them. He immediately stood and snapped to attention when RADM Withers appeared.

"Good afternoon, Admiral," he offered. Then he looked at Dinnacetti, who had followed the Admiral into the tiny space. The guy really seemed familiar to Wurster, but he could not quite place where he had seen him before.

Shelton jumped in. "Admiral, this is Fred Wurster, the Engineer and

Acting XO since we lost Lieutenant Commander Leland." Turning to Wurster, he continued, "Fred, Admiral Withers, COMSUBPAC, and LCDR Dinnacetti, our new CO."

Wurster shook hands with both of the senior officers and offered to pour them cups of freshly brewed coffee from the decanter on the table.

After accepting the offer, Dinnacetti, with a thick Brooklyn accent, said, "Engineer and Acting XO, huh? You must have been one busy guy on the trip over here."

Fred Wurster smiled as he answered and poured. "Not too bad, sir. *Wolffish* is brand-spanking-new and one fine bit of machinery. She runs like a new Cadillac. Not like the old *S*-boat that I came from. The main thing I had to worry about was navigation, but Hawaii wasn't that hard to find. I just followed the sound of ukelele music."

He set the coffee back on the table and then his curiosity got the best of him. He looked at Dinnacetti. "Excuse me, sir, but you look familiar. Have we met somewhere?"

"You mentioned *S*-boats," Dinnacetti responded. "I was XO on the *S-53* in New London. Maybe we were there at the same time."

"That's where it was." Wurster snapped his fingers. "I was on the *S-52*. You were berthed across the pier from us."

Admiral Withers interrupted. "I hate to belay old shipmates before they start sharing sea stories, but time is limited. We need to discuss our plans."

"And something tells me we'll have ample opportunity to catch up, Fred," Dinnacetti said with a nod and a smile.

Finally, all four were seated around the table, each with a steaming cup of brew. Admiral Withers started the discussion. "Gentlemen, as you know, we now only have three aircraft carriers at sea in the Pacific, the *Enterprise*, the *Saratoga*, and the *Lexington*, and not a single operational battleship. That means the submarines will have to carry the load for a while."

Admiral Withers looked at the group and allowed a minute for his words to sink in. "We have been directed to get all of our boats that are seaworthy loaded out for war patrols as quickly as possible. Then we are going to send you out to find and sink as many of those Jap bastards as we can. Any Jap bastard. We don't care if it's a battleship, a carrier, or a load of beef from Borneo. Any damage we can do is a strike against the Empire. A freighter carrying iron ore, bauxite or rubber is about as important to them —and to us—as a warship would be, though God knows, we need to sink as many of those as we can and get this thing over with."

He took a sip of coffee and went on. "We're not sending you out there without firepower. We're going to give you a full load-out of the new Mark 14 torpedoes equipped with the Mark 6 influence exploder. The first truck-load should be arriving here on the pier in a few minutes. My Weapons Officer will be down tomorrow to brief you three on the Mark 6 influence exploder. It's a little bit of a different animal. The Mark 6 is top secret. Only you three will know how it works and what it will do. We think that it is going to be a game-changer against the Japs."

The other three men nodded their understanding. The Admiral took a sip of his coffee, sighed, and sat back in his chair.

"The next thing that I'm going to tell you is even more highly classified, if that's possible. Our codebreakers are making some headway in reading the Jap Navy's mail. We expect to be able to decrypt their messages in time to route you to intercept the bastards. You will know that it's critically important and accurate when you get a message that has 'ULTRA' for a header." Withers spelled the word out for them. "Below that header, the rest of the message will be specially encrypted. You will be the only ones who can break the message. Nobody else—and I mean *nobody* else—can know what is in those ULTRA messages." He looked directly in the eyes of the other three men at the table, one at a time. "Am I clear?"

They all nodded that they understood.

Withers smiled. "Good. Now, I want *Wolffish* fully armed, fueled, and ready to go by Saturday morning. We'll load you up with enough stores for at least a fifty-day patrol, but the selection may be a bit sparse. We're stocking everyone and the larder is getting low. Scraping the bottom of the barrel, literally."

Withers looked around the wardroom and changed subjects. "Workers will be down tomorrow to install a new SJ radar. It's still a prototype for you to try out. I want you to wring it out and report on how to tactically employ it."

He paused to take a sip of coffee. Then he continued, "You will be escorted out by your old friend, the *Hulbert*. You will spend the afternoon making practice sonar and periscope approaches on her and getting familiar with your new ordnance. Then you head to Midway to top off your fuel tanks. After that, you will make your first official war patrol off the Bungo Straits. That's the southern entrance to the Inland Sea. You will be taking the war to the Japanese Home Islands. The more damage you can do, the stronger the message you are sending to Emperor Hirohito and his military, letting them know what a terrible mistake they have made. I don't need to tell you that this is a dangerous mission. You'll be the first boat to patrol this close to the Home Islands. There is a whole lot that we still don't know about the Japs or their capabilities. You need to carefully balance risk against the mission gain. I don't need any of my Skippers trying to win a Medal of Honor on their first run."

He took another sip of coffee as he looked around the table. "Any questions?"

There were none. He slowly rose and turned toward the doorway.

"Good, then I'll expect to see you back in Pearl Harbor in a couple of months with a band playing on the pier and a broom lashed to your periscope."

The "clean sweep" broom, indicating a completely successful mission, "sweeping the seas clean of enemy ships."

From your lips to God's ear, Fred Wurster thought. *But where in hell were the Inland Sea and the Bungo Straits?*

11

Trip MacLean stood in the *S-55*'s cramped control room and watched as "Red" Gray, the submarine's soundman, slowly, deliberately turned the handwheel on his sonar panel, listening for any noises in the depths. The ancient WQB sonar was designed for the deep and relatively quiet North Atlantic. The crowded, warm, shallow South China Sea was full of noises that made it all but impossible for any soundman to detect a ship until it was practically on top of his submarine.

Gray would turn the handwheel a few degrees and stop. Then he would press the headset to his ears and listen carefully. When he was satisfied that he was only hearing fish mating or shrimp snapping, he would frown, turn the handwheel a few more degrees, and listen again. It was excruciatingly slow and boring work. But he had been doing it all day, every day, for the past week. And so far he had not heard one Jap ship. Not any ship at all for that matter. Only fish. And shrimp.

MacLean watched Gray with no real interest. Someone had once told him serving in submarines consisted of hours and hours of boredom followed by a few seconds of sheer panic. That certainly applied to *S-55*'s first war patrol. Though the only panic so far had been caused by a blown fuse in the circuit where the coffee urn was plugged in.

He was not surprised. He had not expected that they would encounter many ships to track. Not where they were operating. The *S-55* had been assigned to a patrol area to the south of Manila Bay. They were to guard against a Jap invasion from that direction, which seemed highly unlikely to MacLean. Then the Skipper, Tony DiCarlo, had decided that the best place to patrol was the Verde Island Passage, a very narrow slice of dingy seawater on the back side of Lubang Island, between it and Luzon. When Trip volunteered his opinion to the CO, pointing out that the passage was only useful for inter-island shipping, that it would be useless as a Japanese invasion route, he was informed by DiCarlo in no uncertain terms that his thoughts on the matter were not welcome.

The *S-55* would patrol where the Skipper directed.

"Mr. MacLean!" Gray called out. "I hear something!"

Trip looked up from the chart he was studying—looking at other bodies of water he would be patrolling, trying to spot potential Japanese invaders, if he were the Commanding Officer of *S-55*—to see the soundman with his headset pressed to an ear. He was moving the handwheel slowly back and forth across one specific bearing. And he had a broad grin on his face.

"Sir, it's a ship. I about forgot what one sounded like. Bearing zero-three-three," Gray called out.

"Let me listen," MacLean responded. He put the headset to his ear. Sure enough, there was a faint *thump, thump, thump*, a rhythmic churning noise that was certainly man-made. "It does sound like engine noise. Or maybe a screw," he guessed.

"Yes, sir," Gray said. "I figure a four-blade screw making about sixty turns."

"It's not a fleet or an invasion convoy, I don't think," MacLean said, smiling as he turned to find the messenger. Gray nodded his agreement with Trip's assessment. "But I'd better inform the Captain anyway."

"Inform the Captain about what?" It was DiCarlo. He had just stepped up behind MacLean as he was listening to the noise from the first ship they had detected in days.

"Captain, we have a surface ship contact on sonar," MacLean reported. "Four-bladed screw, making sixty turns. Probable range one thousand yards. Classified as an inter-island coaster."

DiCarlo gave MacLean a hard look, then grabbed the headset and listened for a moment. Then he dropped the headset, turned nose-to-nose with MacLean, and exploded in anger.

"Bullshit! Any submarine officer worth his dolphins would recognize immediately that that's a Japanese destroyer up there!" he yelled. "Man battle stations! Make all four tubes ready!"

The *gong-gong-gong* of the general alarm presaged the scurry of men rushing to their assigned battle stations. Executive Officer Sam Forester, still donning his sound-powered phone headset, rushed up the ladder to the conning tower. DiCarlo and MacLean followed him up.

"Mr. MacLean, point the target," DiCarlo gruffly ordered. "I mean to shoot with zero gyros. XO, set up to shoot tubes one and two. Set run depth to ten feet."

Wait. The Skipper was serious about launching an attack? He was not just using this convenient but innocent target for a battle station drill for the crew?

Before he thought better of it, MacLean spoke up in protest. "Skipper, shouldn't we at least go up and take a look before we shoot? We could be attacking some innocent freighter hauling coconuts between the islands. Red and I both agree—"

"Mr. MacLean, do as you are told," DiCarlo punched back. "I told you that it was a Jap destroyer. He spots our periscope and he depth-charges us to hell and back and we're no longer here to help fight this war. I don't need some senator's privileged son to tell me how to run a submarine. That's the end of the discussion. Now, do as you are told for once."

MacLean did just that. But he did not feel right about it. He maneuvered the *S-55* around until it was steering zero-three-nine, the current bearing to the ship.

"Steady course zero-three-nine," he reported.

"Shoot!" DiCarlo ordered, without hesitation, but with an oddly exuberant, wide-eyed expression on his face.

"Shoot tube one," Forester ordered via the sound-powered phone to the torpedo room. They all felt and heard the *swoosh...thump* as the Mark 10 torpedo in tube one was flushed out into the sea. Then the XO ordered, "Shoot tube two." Again, there was a *swoosh...thump* as the torpedo in tube two was sent on its way, each weapon giving *S-55* a gentle nudge when it departed.

Now DiCarlo and Forester both concentrated on their wristwatches as they timed the torpedo run. They could expect to hear a pair of explosions in about forty-five seconds if the fish found their target.

"Captain, I lost the target ship," Red Gray called up from the control room. "Don't know if he faded, shut down his engines, or just got lost in all that torpedo noise."

DiCarlo did not even bother to acknowledge the soundman's report. He was too engrossed in staring at his watch, counting off the seconds, anticipating the two imminent explosions.

His watch ticked past forty-five seconds. He frowned.

Then at exactly one minute, everyone aboard the old boat heard a blast. And then, a couple of seconds later, a second one.

DiCarlo shouted and pounded the periscope with a closed fist.

"Whoopee! Hot damn! We did it! We sank an enemy destroyer!"

"Do you want to go up and look for survivors?" Forester asked.

"No, XO. Let's clear the area before his buddies come looking for us. You write the message telling Commander Asiatic Submarines that the *S-55* has drawn first blood. Tell him that we are patrolling back toward Manila to reload torpedoes."

MacLean was about to remind the CO that he still had a dozen more Mark 10 torpedoes available in the torpedo room, but he stopped himself and merely shook his head, stunned at what he had just witnessed.

Tony DiCarlo was claiming to have sunk a ship that he never actually saw. And he was not even willing to go up to periscope depth and take a quick look, to confirm what he was shooting at.

Or even to take a look to see if they might save some survivors from the innocent freighter that he had just sent to the bottom of the Verde Island Passage.

∞

The crescent moon was rising over a quiet, starlit Manila Bay. But to Stan Ward, buried deep back in the Malinta Tunnel and inside the locked and guarded Lateral Number Six, day and night were nothing but abstract terms. To him, there was only work and sleep. Neither of those things had any connection with the journeys of any celestial bodies across the sky. Down there, deep under Corregidor's rocky surface, it was time for Stan to work. Sleep might come later, when the work was done.

Ward glanced over to see Gus Arnett pecking away at a typewriter. The irascible Army Sergeant was wearing a set of earphones, listening to the *dit*s and *dah*s of Morse code. Then he would strike the key for the letter that he heard. But the character that appeared on the paper was not an English letter. It was Japanese. More precisely, a Japanese *katakana* letter. The Japanese used three different but similar writing systems. *Kanji* was the most common one, the one seen in most Japanese books and street signs. Its characters had been "borrowed" from Chinese calligraphy. The other two, *hiragana* and *katakana*, were indigenous Japanese writing systems. Katakana worked particularly well in the transmission of Morse code and so was the writing system that the Imperial Japanese Navy used for telecommunications. Early on, American crypto analysts had taken a common Remington typewriter and modified it so that the operator listening to an IJN message being transmitted would strike the key for the English letter he heard being transmitted. The typewriter would actually print the kana character that the Japanese operator had sent. The RIP-5 typewriter had been a godsend, saving time and reducing errors.

But typing the kana was only the first step in a long and difficult process. A process that Stan Ward and his team at Station CAST had not yet perfected. The JN-25B code, the current Japanese Navy code, was proving to be extremely complex. Even more complex than the BLUE Book that the JN-25 code had replaced. The BLUE Book used almost 100,000 code groups. It had taken years to successfully break that system. Now the Japanese were using an infinitely more complex methodology. And they had already changed it at least twice in the past six months, first from JN-25 to JN-25A in late 1940 and then to the JN-25B system in December of 1941. The changes were likely tied to the secrecy involved with the sneak attacks on US Navy facilities around the Pacific.

The kana code that Arnett was studiously typing was encrypted with the JN-25B code. To anyone attempting to read it and glean some sense from it, the pages were just so much meaningless gibberish. What Stan's team had found was that the JN-25B code was made up of a very large number of code groups. On top of this was something they were calling an "additive book." The book contained random five-digit numbers to super-encipher the code groups. Ollie Oglethorpe, Stan, and the others on their team were trying to figure out a method to strip out the additives so they could work on the code groups themselves. When and if they broke the code groups, the message would go directly over to Frank Tanaka and his Japanese linguists to translate the message into English. Then they would have a useful intercepted message that hopefully contained valuable information.

The primary thing was this all took time. Considering the press of events of late, that was a commodity of which they had very little.

Arnett finished typing and blew on his fingertips as if they were on fire. He wiped a thin layer of sweat from his brow and looked around at Ward.

"Whew! That guy is long winded," Arnett complained. "Long fisted. Whatever."

He looked over at the list on the wall where they were building a reference to the unique characteristics of IJN radio operators: their "fists," or noticeable quirks in the way they sent the Morse code letters. Every radio operator developed his own "fist" when transmitting with a key. To someone experienced at listening, it was every bit as identifiable as someone's voice or fingerprints.

"Good. The more talkative the better," Ward said. "That is, if we knew what he was yakking about."

"That one sounded almost exactly like 'So Solly Sammy,'" Arnett muttered. "Same stutter with his spaces between the dashes."

"We get a DF on him?" Ward asked.

"Yep," Arnett answered. "Picking him up here at Corregidor, from the Guam and Samoan HF stations."

Ward stepped over to the large chart of the Pacific that covered a good bit of one wall in the room. The chart was covered with colored pins, little notes, and runs of string connecting the pins marking the travels of the vessels whose radiomen's unique sending styles had been determined. This was the chart that he was using to develop his ship movement analysis theory. He measured the bearings from each of the DF intercept stations, employed the radioman keying signature to identify each, and marked where they all crossed. It was a spot out in the Philippine Sea three hundred miles south of Okinawa.

Then he grabbed a file of plain-language Japanese ship movement messages. "I saw something in here a few minutes ago that piqued my interest," he mumbled. He riffled through the file until he found the message that he was looking for. "Here we go. *Nissan Maru* outbound from Yokohama, headed for Kaohsuing on Formosa. We figure that 'So Solly Sammy' is the radio operator on the *Nissan Maru*. The interesting question, and the thing that got my curiosity up, is why a merchant ship would be transmitting using the JN-25 code. Makes no sense. That's a Japanese Navy–only code. There is something we don't know about that ship and I'm guessing that it is important."

Ward poured himself another cup of coffee and sat at his desk, staring hard at the chart for several minutes. He noticed several other colored strings connecting from various locations to Kaohsuing. All those strings represented the courses of ships that were sending plain-language movement reports. But a couple of them coincided with JN-25 intercepts. Something was up and there was little chance that it had anything to do with that sleepy port on Formosa.

Then realization washed over him. Kaohsuing was only two hundred miles from Luzon. The Japanese were gathering for the invasion of the Philippines. At least part of the invasion force must be meeting up at Kaohsuing. He sat up straight and grabbed the telephone.

The watch officer at Commander, Asiatic Fleet, was not particularly happy at being awakened in the middle of the night by some staff Lieutenant. At first, Ward was caught off guard by the man's displeasure. Then it hit him. It was three o'clock in the morning. Sure, normal people would be sleeping. The watch officer was even less pleased when Ward refused to tell him why he needed to speak with Admiral Hart or his Chief of Staff. But the guy's instructions were to give priority to anyone from Station CAST—whatever that was—so he scheduled a meeting with Admiral Hart for first thing in the morning but a long four hours into the future. Lieutenant Ward would simply have to be content with that.

Ward was wide awake when, at 0600, he caught the first boat from Corregidor's North Boat Landing going over to the Manila Fleet Landing.

At 0800, he was standing outside Admiral Hart's door on the second deck of the Marsman Building.

By 0820, the Admiral had listened to what the excited Lieutenant had to tell him.

It took Hart only about thirty seconds to decide to send a submarine to investigate this *Nissan Maru*.

And to order the sub's CO to put a torpedo into it if he could get a shot.

12

The weatherbeaten, old banting sailed without celebration into the tiny harbor of Palau Sedanau. The place looked to Geoff Chandler exactly as he had imagined a tropical paradise would be: turquoise-blue waters lapping up on a pure-white sand beach, a lush tropical forest edging the shoreline, then climbing to cover green hills in the background. Dozens of thatched-roof houses built on stilts sprouting from the peaceful, shallow waters of the harbor. Chandler sat in the boat's stern and watched as Bayu, the fisherman and Captain of the little boat, nudged his vessel against one of those thatched-roof houses and quickly tied off.

Bayu and his crew carefully lifted Chandler and Murphy off the banting and into the thatch hut. Cooled by a soft, fragrant sea breeze, Chandler found the hut to be quite comfortable. Banyu cut open a green coconut and offered it to Chandler. The fresh coconut water proved to be remarkably refreshing.

"You can safely rest here for a few days," Bayu assured Chandler. "But then we will need to move you. The Japanese already control French Indochina to our north. Sarawak is under attack now, so it is too dangerous to go that way. The Japanese Malaysian campaign is moving quickly. I fear that Singapore will fall in the next few days, and certainly before the year is out. Then their attention will shift to our little islands, primarily for our fish but also to find those who dare resist their takeover."

"Where will we go?" Chandler asked. The picture that Bayu was drawing looked a lot like a noose that was tightening around them.

"So far the Japanese are not bothering our fishing boats," Bayu answered. "They want us to take as much as we can for when they come to us hungry. That means we can move you around the islands in those boats. South is the safest direction, though no route is truly without hazard. We can hop from island to island until we reach the Dutch East Indies. From there, you should be able to find a ship and move south to Australia."

Chandler was trying to picture in his mind a map of the South China Sea. They would be shooting a very narrow gap between the Japanese forces attacking Borneo to the east and the ones wreaking havoc on Malaysia and Singapore to the west. The sea was bound to be crisscrossed by dozens of Japanese warships moving to support one invasion or the other. But hundreds of tiny islands speckled the sea all the way down to Sumatra. Those islands would be their cover and probably their haven.

Chandler nodded. "The only other option I see is to surrender and spend the war in some Japanese POW camp. That is not something that I would relish."

"No. We have heard of how the Japanese treat prisoners, often with torture or hard labor, or they just shoot them to save food for their Marines," Bayu told him.

Chandler and Murphy stayed with the villagers of Palau Sedanau while Bayu disappeared for a week. When he returned, he was sailing a much larger boat. He explained that the *pencalang*, a traditional fishing and trading ship for his people, was much better suited for the longer trip across the South China Sea. With a covered deck and a deck house, the twin-masted little ship would better conceal its two British passengers and be better protected in the more open waters. Its lug-type sails would move them along smartly, too. The four-hundred-mile trip to Sumatra should take about a week.

The black pencalang hoisted its bright red sails and left Palau Sedanau as the sun was setting back beyond the tree-shrouded mountains. By morning, Mida Island, the first of many rocks that would dot their journey like signposts, passed to starboard.

Noon brought their first encounter with the Japanese. It was a force that Chandler identified as a pair of *Myoko* heavy cruisers with six destroyers. As best he could tell, those were a couple of *Asashio*-class and four *Kagero*-class tin cans, but he could not be sure. The sleek Japanese destroyers were difficult to tell apart, even if he and Murphy had not been keeping their heads down and mostly trying to disappear beneath some smelly fish nets on the deck whenever Japanese vessels were within sight. When he did pop up for a look-see, Chandler could make out a couple of auxiliary ships huddled in the middle of the formation. Oilers, to refuel the ravenous boilers on those warships. Thankfully, the Japanese warships raced on past the pencalang, uninterested, ignoring the little sailing ship.

The fourth day out, just as the first of the large Indonesian Islands, Bangka Island, appeared on the horizon, a big Japanese four-engine flying boat buzzed low over the pencalang. Chandler easily identified the plane as a Kawanishi H6K, a "Mavis." The big bird flew close enough that he could see several machine guns protruding from gunports gouged out of the hull.

As the seaplane made a long sweeping turn for another pass over the sailboat, a pair of Brewster Buffalo fighters screamed down out of the clouds. The orange triangle markings indicated they were Dutch. The fat gray pursuit planes looked like a couple of angry bumblebees harassing a large dragon fly. Chandler watched with interest as the Buffalos dove in, screaming, making firing passes at the lumbering Nippon flying boat. Then, slowly, the two of them would claw for altitude once more, turning for another run. On the second pass by the pair, one of the Mavis's engines burst into flames and the plane's path skewed dramatically.

But the flying boat was not defenseless. And its gunners were deadly accurate. One of the Brewster Buffalos began trailing smoke. It tried in futility to climb away but stalled, and then left a long, greasy trail of smoke and flames as it plummeted into the ocean below. The other Buffalo made a long firing pass at the Mavis. Chandler could easily see the tracers from the Brewster's three .50 caliber machine guns disappear into the interior of the flying boat. The Japanese craft burst into flames and then smashed brutally into the calm, uncaring ocean waters.

The remaining Brewster Buffalo made a victory roll and then disappeared to the west.

Bayu appeared and said, “I think we had better make a landing on Bangka Island today. There are far too many Japanese in the area for comfort. We will put in at Pangkalpinang. It is a major tin port, lots of sea traffic in and out. You should have no problem finding a ship heading to Australia that would be willing to allow you to ride along.”

Early that evening the pencalang eased up to a pier in the bustling seaport. There were no signs at all that a war might be going on. Geoff Chandler bid goodbye to Bayu and his crew. They had saved the lives of the two British seamen but would get no more for their risk and trouble than the most heartfelt thanks from the men they had rescued just in time from that raft. Chandler and Murphy watched the fishing boat with unanticipated emotion as it headed back out to sea.

When the departing vessel was ultimately obscured by the twilight mist, the two men took a stroll into town to take a first stab at finding transportation south. And maybe to locate themselves a couple of cold beers, too.

∞

A thick cloud cover obscured the night sky. Trip MacLean strained to try to see the launch that was guiding them through the protective mine fields stretching across the mouth of Manila Bay. MacLean was well aware that if he did not follow the launch's course exactly, if he did not turn exactly where it did, there was a very real chance that he would drive the *S-55* submarine over a mine. Sweat poured from his brow, and it was not just the result of the warm tropical night.

The launch had met them five miles outside Manila Bay. Its pilot's instructions to the *S*-boat were to stay fifty yards astern and to precisely follow the guide vessel's course everywhere it went regardless how erratic it might appear to be. That was the only way to make it safely through the infestation of lethal mines.

The Skipper, Tony DiCarlo, stood silently and watched as MacLean directed the submarine on the winding route along the channel. DiCarlo, smoking a cigarette, paced back and forth across the narrow bridge. Every half minute, he would lift his binoculars to his eyes and stare out at the motor launch. Then he would mutter something unintelligible under his breath, drop the binoculars, and allow them to hang from his neck.

A flashing light blinked on and off from the launch's stern. MacLean deciphered the message being sent and turned to DiCarlo. "Skipper, they're turning to course north. He says that there is a line of mines fifty yards to port and another one seventy yards to starboard. I'm coming left with a full rudder to follow our guide."

DiCarlo grunted his acknowledgment and then took a long drag on his cigarette. Other than that, he stayed silent as the *S-55* dutifully turned north.

The little two-vessel convoy threaded its way past Corregidor and its dozen protective gun batteries. Those batteries mounted everything from mammoth twelve-inch coastal guns and 305mm mortars down to 75mm artillery. The installations loomed somewhere out there in the inky darkness, protecting the harbor from Japanese warships.

The launch turned northwest and made its way into Mariveles Bay. Soon the signal came that they were safely through the mines and that the little vessel was returning to Corregidor to direct somebody else through the dangling maze of high explosives. MacLean grabbed the small Aldis lamp and flashed out, "Thank you." *And*, he thought, *I truly mean it!*

The frequent Japanese bomber attacks on Manila over the past couple of weeks had effectively driven the *Canopus*, the submarine tender, away from her camouflaged anchorage in Manila out to Mariveles near the high, protective hills of the Bataan Peninsula. That was where *S-55* was headed.

As MacLean carefully maneuvered his submarine alongside the darkened ship, DiCarlo suddenly came alive. But not exactly in a spirited way. He glanced at his watch and announced in a monotone, "Mr. MacLean, it is now midnight. Sunrise is at 0715. I want torpedoes loaded, all stores taken aboard, and the boat fully fueled an hour before sunrise. I want us to be submerged out in the bay before the Japs have a chance to stage an air raid. Understand?"

MacLean snapped to attention and crisply replied, "Yes, sir." He knew DiCarlo still clung to the formal trappings of the surface navy, unlike some of the newer submarine commanders who had happily embraced a more relaxed style on the boats.

"Very well," DiCarlo shot back. "I'll be up on the tender meeting with the Commodore." With that pronouncement, he climbed down from the bridge to the main deck and disappeared up the brow to the *Canopus*.

It was 0615 when DiCarlo, freshly showered and wearing a clean uniform, stepped across the brow, back aboard his submarine. "*S-55* arriving," the 1MC announce system blared as MacLean trotted over to the brow to greet his Skipper.

Saluting, he said, "Morning, sir. Ship is ready to get underway. Request permission to cast off lines."

DiCarlo grumbled, "Have coffee sent to the bridge for me. Get the ship underway, Mr. MacLean." The CO stopped and looked out into the harbor. "Where is that damn motor launch? They expect us to navigate that mine field on our own going out?"

"He's on the other side of the tender," MacLean responded, trying to remain upbeat and pleasant despite DiCarlo's surly demeanor. "He'll come around as soon as we're clear of the *Canopus*. Coffee's on the way to the bridge." Turning to Motor Machinist Chief Watson, the Chief of the Boat, he ordered, "COB, single up all lines." Then he turned to trail DiCarlo up to the bridge.

They were halfway between Corregidor and Fort Drum, obediently trailing the guide launch, when they heard the air raid sirens begin to wail from various places along the shoreline. Almost immediately, large anti-aircraft guns on both places began to bang away. Guns over on Bataan and around Cavite soon joined in. Through the clouds, MacLean caught just a fleeting glimpse of bombers flying in formation high overhead.

DiCarlo decided that the only safe place for the *S-55* was to dive in the shallow water and rest on the bottom. He ordered MacLean to dive the boat and then scurried down the hatch into the conning tower.

MacLean turned and yelled, "Clear the bridge!" He announced, "Dive! Dive!" over the 1MC and hit the diving alarm twice.

MacLean suddenly spotted a Zero screaming down out of the clouds, heading right for the *S-55*, its 20mm cannons winking bursts of gunfire as it dove. The Japanese fighter blasted by, missing the periscopes by scant feet.

MacLean was sure that he could see the pilot grinning just before he dove through the hatch and slammed it shut above him. Apparently unhit, the *S-55* sank below the murky water and settled down to rest on Manila Bay's muddy bottom.

With nothing to do but wait out the air raid, DiCarlo decided that it would be a good time for the wardroom to gather and discuss their next mission, just delivered during his meeting with the Commodore. Sam Forester gathered all the officers in the cramped space. Everyone had to grab up their coffee cups and hold on to them as the CO unfolded a chart of the South China Sea and spread it out, covering the table.

"Gentlemen, we are going south on this patrol," he began. He used his finger to trace a track out of Manila Bay, down past Mindoro, and then west of Palawan. He went on, "COMSUBS Asiatic Fleet wants us to see what the Japs are doing down there. There are reports that they have already landed in Sarawak, likely intending to start grabbing their oil and antimony."

Ensign Tommy Hilligas, the youngest officer on board the *S-55*, asked, "Where's Sarawak? And what's antimony?"

Forester looked at the young officer with undisguised scorn and shook his head. "I don't know what they teach in school these days but it's not geography or chemistry. Sarawak's on the west side of Borneo," he explained, pointing to the chart. "Belongs to the Brits but word is they've bugged out. Or at least their military has, off to help defend Singapore. The Nips probably want it for all the oil wells down around Kuching. Rumor has it that the oil is pure enough coming out of the ground that they can pump it straight into their ships' bunkers for fuel. And antimony. They use it in batteries and as a fire retardant."

"We going all the way down there?" the young Ensign asked. Valid question. Kuching was over a thousand miles from where they now lay in the silt at the bottom of Manila Bay.

"We're going a whole lot farther than that," DiCarlo answered. "Once we do some reconnoitering, we'll go on through the Karimata Strait between Borneo and Sumatra, and then down through the Java Sea to Surabaya, on Java." Using his finger, he traced out their intended route and then tapped a point on the chart. "That, gentlemen, will be the new homeport for *S-55*."

"What about Manila?" MacLean asked. "We bugging out?"

"Admiral says it's not safe to operate out of Manila anymore," DiCarlo said, shaking his head, his neck and face flushing red. "Daily air raids and no good way to get parts or supplies in. And some say the Jap sons of bitches will invade pretty soon. We're moving everything south to where it's safer to refuel and rearm. Then we'll come back north as needed for patrols. And that's about all I can tell you right now."

Since it was clear the Skipper was becoming irritated with the questions, no one dared ask any more. The meeting broke up as each officer found something to keep him busy for the rest of the day. The *S-55* emerged from the bottom of the bay shortly after sundown. By midnight, with the help of the motor launch, they had once again successfully negotiated the mine barriers and were on the surface, headed south. Way south.

At sunrise, and with a full battery charge, the submarine dived fifty miles west of Mindoro and headed toward the long, skinny island of Palawan on a course of south-southwest at five knots.

∞

Del Monte Airfield, on the north shore of the Philippine Island of Mindanao, was little more than a grass pasture with a few shacks hastily thrown up to house a meager store of tools and spare parts, mechanics, and support personnel. The parts were mostly salvaged from B-17s that had limped back from missions to this airstrip but were too damaged to try to put back in the air. About the only things Del Monte had a good supply of were bombs and machine gun ammunition for the B-17s, all cached in an old pineapple storage building. The closest thing anyone had to creature comforts were the crude wooden floors that had been hastily thrown down in the sleeping tents. That, at least, kept the legs of their cots from sinking into the omnipresent quicksand-like mud.

But at least the squadron could now get caught up on their sleep. That is, until Captain Greg Tillson charged into his crew's tent and shook Sam Beyers awake. "Come on, Sammy. Time to rise and shine."

Beyers, Tillison's co-pilot on *Little Girl*, sat straight up, wiping sleep from his eyes with both fists. “Dammit, boss! Why’d you go and wake me up? Me and Betty Grable, we was just about to get very personally acquainted.”

Tillison laughed and shook his head. “See, I’m always looking out for you, Sammy. Protecting your virtue for that sweet thing you left behind back in Lubbock. Now, get everybody up. We’ve got a mission that does not involve Miss Grable.”

“Whole squadron?” Beyers asked. The 30th Bombardment Squadron had left the States with twelve planes and full crews. They were now down to six B-17s, thanks to the Japanese deciding to give themselves a head start on the war.

“Yep, everybody. We’re heading up to the Philippine Sea. Seems Navy Intelligence believes there are some Nip ships heading toward the Luzon Straits and they’ve ramped up some interest with the brass in Manila. Could be the first wave of an assault force. They were going to send a submarine up to sniff out what was going on, but they couldn’t get one there in time to do any good. Damn ball fell into our court.”

“Philippine Sea would be just about the ragged edge of our combat radius from here,” Beyers said as he pulled on his trousers. “Please don’t tell me they want us to carry a full bomb load.”

“Whoever said you weren’t very sharp?” Tillson quipped. “Yep, full load. We’ll just have to do a quick pit stop at Clark Field or Nichols on the way back to grab some gas. Now, let’s make sure everyone has a full load of coffee and has been briefed up. I want all the birds airborne and heading north by 0300. Sunrise is 0715 and we really need to be in the search area by daylight.”

A row of jeeps used their headlights to mark the runway for the pilots as they charged down the grass runway and then over vast pineapple fields before climbing up into thick rain clouds. As they climbed out, they finally broke through the overcast and into a beautiful starlit night at about ten thousand feet. The six bombers formed up into a combat box and pointed due north. The cloud cover dissipated from beneath them shortly after they crossed over Luzon’s east coast, offering a good view of the dark land giving way to the even darker waters of the Philippine Sea far below.

The sun was just showing itself on the eastern horizon when Jim Swits, *Little Girl*’s navigator, called out, “Hey, boss, X marks the spot.”

Tillson radioed to the squadron, "Spread out and look for ships. And keep a sharp eye out for any Zeros that might be aiming to get lucky."

Five minutes later, Sam Beyers spotted the first ship. They were soon looking at dozens of vessels, their wakes forming long white lines into the distance. They were all steaming together in a loose formation.

"Looks like we found ourselves a Jap invasion fleet," Tillson proclaimed. "Form up on me. Let's see how many sons of Nippon we can send to the bottom of the sea."

The six bombers tightened their formation and pointed their noses directly toward the Japanese convoy. They were still a couple of miles out when Anson Hopper, the top turret gunner, called out, "Here they come! Pair of Zeros, twelve o'clock high!"

Almost immediately, his twin .50 caliber machine guns chattered for a couple of seconds as a pair of green-painted Japanese warbirds flashed past, the meatballs on their fuselages and wings mocking the Americans. Then Tim Swigert, the tail gunner, opened up as the fighters flew away. But now more Zeros attacked the bombers from all directions. The fast, flitting planes were trying to destroy the B-17s—or chase them away—before they could unload their cargo of death on the ships below. Black puffs of smoke, flak from the anti-aircraft guns on the vessels, began leaving small but deadly dark clouds in the sky around them.

"Steady, guys, just like we practiced," Tillson reminded as he did his best to keep *Little Girl* straight and level on the bomb run despite the turbulence from the ack-ack.

He felt the plane lurch upward just as the bombardier hollered, "Bombs away!" Tillson immediately threw the B-17 into a steep banking turn to try to avoid another Zero. He glanced out of the cockpit long enough to see his stick of a dozen five-hundred-pound bombs walk across the water directly toward what appeared to be a freighter. But the ship steamed on, completely unscathed as the last one fell well short of the intended target. He looked to the right to see a Zero trailing smoke and flames arcing down toward the sea. At least they had done some small degree of damage!

But then he saw the number six plane in his squadron, *Lizzy the Legend*, explode in midair.

"Guys, let's get the hell out of here!" he ordered, voice husky, pulse pounding. "Tight combat box. Let's protect each other."

The bombers made a sharp turn to the south and suddenly, surprisingly, they had the sky all to themselves. Tillson looked back over what remained of his squadron. One plane no longer existed. *Pouting Paula*, flying in the number five position, had its left outboard engine feathered. *Sammy's Sister* flying just to *Little Girl*'s left, was reporting two wounded and a dead radio operator. Nobody had any hits on the Japanese ships to claim.

Tillison smashed his fist into the control yoke in frustration. Then he ordered, "Sparks, contact V Bomber Command. Report the convoy location, course, and speed. Report our bomb attack with no hits. Repeat, no hits. Returning to base with five birds, two crewmen injured, one KIA."

After a quick stop for fuel at Clark Air Base—where they were more worried about excitable anti-aircraft gunners than they were about another Jap air raid—a very subdued 30th Bombardment Squadron touched down on Del Monte Field that afternoon.

Tillson was surprised to find the rest of the B-17s based there were in the process of being fueled and armed. Some were already airborne. Where were these birds headed? It was too late in the day for a re-attack on the convoy. He had heard no squawking on the radio about other possible missions launching this close to nighttime. Tillson was mystified, but he figured that he would find out soon enough.

Then, once they were back on the ground and Tillson was climbing from his airplane, Arty Short, CO of V Bomber Command, came rolling up in his jeep.

"Captain, sorry about your losses," he told Tillson. "Get your guys some chow right quick and we'll get your tanks topped off." The CO ignored the puzzled look on Tillson's face. "Orders just came down a couple of hours ago. General Brereton has ordered all the B-17s to evacuate the Philippines. You're to take your squadron and fly down to Darwin, Australia. Del Monte Field, they've decided, is just too damned vulnerable."

Tillson stretched mightily, trying to get the blood moving again in his legs and arms after sitting in his B-17's cockpit for more than twelve hours.

"Okay, then I guess I got some navigatin' to do," the pilot responded with a sideways grin. "First to the head to drain the lizard, then to the chow line, and finally to figure out the most direct route to Darwin, Australia."

13

Brad Johnson lay back in his bunk on USS *Tigerfish* and read the tattered letter from Debbie Schultz for what felt like the ten-thousandth time. He had long since memorized all the words. The faint lavender aroma of her perfume had been overwhelmed by the smell of the diesel boat. But out here in the middle of the war-torn Pacific Ocean, this piece of well-consumed correspondence was his only connection to her and to home. There was no way to know when he would receive another one, but it certainly would not be until they pulled into Cavite.

There was a faint knock at the door. Seaman Wasterman, the messenger, stuck his head in.

"Mr. Johnson." His timid voice was little more than a squeak, barely heard above the throb of the engines. "You have the midwatch on the bridge."

Johnson grunted, "Thanks, Wasterman. On my way."

He swung his legs out of the bunk, slipped on his shoes, hit the head, and then made his way to the wardroom for a cup of coffee before he climbed up to the bridge. Isaac Sternman, the XO, was sitting at the table, munching on a bologna sandwich as he read the latest message traffic. He nodded to Johnson.

"Anything interesting in the morning mail?" Johnson asked as he topped off his cup.

"Nah, just admin crap," Sternman retorted. "And a bit of college football news. They're moving the Rose Bowl to North Carolina, thanks to the Japs. No big gatherings on the West Coast, they decided. I did get some intel earlier. Manila and Cavite have been bombed pretty hard. We'll probably have a warm welcome when we come sneaking in. I bet guys there are shooting at everything that moves and checking their flag later." He pulled the intel message board from the bottom of his stack and scooted it across the table to Johnson. "Biggest news is it looks like the Jap invasion fleet's been spotted, headed for Lingayen Gulf."

"Don't we steam right by there?" Johnson asked.

"Yep," Sternman confirmed. "Need to keep our eyes open and be ready to attack those heartless bastards. Every damn one of 'em we dump in the ocean is one less samurai on the beach plugging our Marines. And besides, they made 'em move the Rose Bowl out of Pasadena. Bastards!" He chewed his sandwich for a bit, then asked, "You look at the charts yet?"

"Not since last watch," Johnson said, enjoying a chocolate chip cookie off a platter on the table with his coffee. "But in twelve hours, we ain't gone very far. Should be just short of the Luzon Straits unless Miller and Lawson got lost and spent their watches steaming in circles."

Sternman chuckled. "Those guys would resent your aspersions against their navigational capabilities. We're about a hundred miles short of the Straits. You know there's gotta be Jap patrols all around. I want you to station extra lookouts topside. Skipper wants to dive at first light. He said if you can see your hand on the railing, it's past time to pull the plug. Call me an hour before sunrise so I can get a fix before we go under. Now, you'd better get to the bridge before George gets all upset."

Johnson headed out of the wardroom, aft to the control room. After checking that everything was as he expected, he climbed up into the conning tower and then on up to the bridge, carefully avoiding spilling any precious coffee from his topped-off mug. The nearly full moon illuminated a cloudless night. That allowed a full array of bright stars to provide a Christmas-tree-light canopy over a calm sea.

LTjg George Lawson was yawning when Johnson appeared. "I see that you finally deigned to bless us with your presence, Brad." He waved his arm around and reported, "No contacts, steaming on four diesels, ahead full. Course two-nine-zero. Just completed a normal battery charge. About as boring a watch as I've ever stood, but I ain't complainin'. I stand relieved. What's for mid-rats?"

Johnson looked around. He noted that there were a pair of lookouts up in the shears and two more on the cigarette deck scanning the horizon. "I relieve you," he said to Lawson and then, over the 7MC, he said, "This is LT Johnson. I have the deck and the conn." George Lawson was already halfway down the tower to the conn when Johnson answered his last question. "For mid-rats, sliced horse-cock sandwiches again, if the XO hasn't eaten it all yet."

Johnson sipped his coffee and settled in for what remained of a long night. For the next six hours, he had the stars, occasional phosphorescence in the water, the four lookouts, and an ocean empty of vessels to keep him company. He wondered how he might describe the beauty of steaming on the surface of a placid sea at night to Debbie. He was working on composing the letter in his mind when the mood was interrupted by one of the lookouts.

"Mr. Johnson, I have a contact!" the young sailor standing high in the starboard sheers called out. "One point off the starboard bow. Low down on the horizon."

Brad grabbed his binoculars and stared out in that direction. He could not see anything. Not surprising since the lookout, up in the shears, stood a good ten feet higher. He grabbed the 7MC and said, "Conn, possible contact bearing about three-zero-zero true. What do you see?"

The 7MC blasted back, "Aye, wait." Then, after the watch below looked through the raised scope, which added even more height to the observation, came, "Bridge, warship bearing three-zero-five. Best range six-five-hundred yards. Port thirty angle-on-the-bow."

Johnson formed a quick mental picture. The contact was a warship, and out here, almost assuredly a Japanese one. It was coming at them and, if the port thirty angle-on-the-bow was anywhere near accurate, it would pass within a thousand yards ahead of the *Tigerfish*.

"Conn, Bridge, aye," he acknowledged. "Ahead one-third." It was time to slow down and see how the problem developed. "Conn, wake the Captain, and call away Battle Stations!"

The *bong-bong-bong* of the General Alarm had barely died away when Wayne Schacter, the Skipper, climbed to the bridge. His puffy eyes confirmed he had been awakened from a hard sleep.

"What you got, Brad?" he asked groggily as he scanned the horizon.

Johnson pointed to the contact, now barely visible through his binoculars. "Possible warship, bearing three-zero-zero, range six thousand, port thirty angle-on-the-bow, drawing left."

Schacter spent a few seconds looking at the contact, then he said, "Yep, Jap tin can. Let's see what we can do to help him realize his dreams of dying for the Emperor and going to meet his ancestors. Come left to two-seven-zero and dive the ship." With that the CO disappeared down into the conning tower.

"Clear the bridge!" Johnson hollered. He counted the lookouts as they went through the hatch. Then he ordered, "Dive! Dive!" and hit the diving alarm.

Johnson dropped down into a flurry of activity in the cramped space below. Schacter was already at the attack periscope, watching the unsuspecting Japanese destroyer as it steamed toward them. Sternman was organizing the approach party and setting up the torpedo data computer, the stack of whirring gears and spinning dials that took the crew's best guess of the target's course, speed, and range, along with the *Tigerfish*'s speed and course, and delivered a solution to the torpedoes. Brad was sure that there was some magic involved in all that whirring and spinning, but after some time, the TDC would spit out to the torpedoes the precise course they would follow when launched. The course that would most likely result in a kill.

George Lawson had grabbed the "Is/Was," the circular slide rule that the TDC largely replaced, then scrunched back in a corner. His job was to back up the XO and the TDC. If the computer went down or its solution was way out in left field, Lawson was supposed to be ready to instantly step in and provide the real solution, using outmoded technology.

Stan Miller was busy plotting out the situation on the geographic plot.

He was trying to solve the attack problem by plotting each range and bearing and then fitting the best course and speed between them.

The COB, TMC Alonzo Heinrich, called up from the control room, "Ship is manned for battle stations."

Schacter barely grunted as he locked in on the target. "Observation on the target," he called out. "Bearing, mark!"

Eric Riegel, the Periscope Assistant, read the dial and announced, "Bearing two-nine-seven."

"Range, mark."

Riegel read the stadiameter dial, "Range five-five hundred."

"Down scope." The attack periscope slid down into the scope well. "He's not varying or zigging at all. He has no idea we're watching him steam right into our sights."

Sternman looked at the TDC readings and confirmed, "Checks with solution." The TDC was sending courses down to the torpedoes that agreed with what the Skipper was seeing through the periscope.

Schacter leaned back from the periscope and said, "Okay. This is definitely a Japanese destroyer. Probably *Fubuki*-class. That's a mean son of a bitch but there's no sign that he's alerted. I want to shoot when he is broad. Make tubes one and two ready. Set run depth twenty feet, speed to HIGH. We'd have to screw up bad to mess this up." He paused for a moment and looked around the conning tower to make sure everyone understood the plan. No one had a question. "Mr. Johnson, get me on a normal approach course. I want to shoot this bastard at two thousand yards."

Johnson did some quick mental calculations and ordered, "Come left, steer course two-six-five."

Sternman looked at the TDC and the stopwatch hanging there. "Skipper, recommend an observation."

Schacter nodded, then squatted in front of the periscope and said, "Observation on the destroyer, up scope." He flipped the training handles down as they cleared the well, put his eye to the eyepiece and rode the scope up, aiming his view at where he expected the enemy destroyer to be.

"Bearing, mark."

"Two-nine-two."

"Range, mark."

"Range three-zero-hundred."

"Down scope. Angle-of-the-bow port four-five."

Two more observations were made as the Japanese destroyer boldly steamed across the sea directly in front of them, enjoying the same nice night as Brad and the lookouts had been doing. Then the CO, satisfied that they were in the best possible position, said, "This will be a shooting observation."

Finally, it was time to quit looking and start shooting. The raw tension in the conning tower had reached a peak. Johnson could feel a trickle of sweat running down his back.

"Up scope." The periscope slid up. Schacter spun it around so that he had the crosshairs right on the destroyer's bridge and called, "Bearing, mark."

"Bearing two-eight-seven."

"Set," Isaac Sternman called. The bearing was input to the TDC.

"Down scope."

Sternman turned to the firing panel and flipped up the switch for tube one. Then he pressed the firing key and ordered, "Shoot tube one."

Down in the forward torpedo room, the Mark 14 torpedo in tube one was flushed out into the warm ocean waters. The alcohol-fueled steam turbine quickly pushed it up to a speed of forty-five knots as the gyro steered it directly toward the intercept point with the target. The depth sensor pushed the torpedo down to twenty feet where it would just run under the Japanese destroyer at just the right depth for the Mark 6 influence detonator.

Sternman waited five seconds and then ordered, "Shoot tube two." He flipped up the switch to select tube two and pressed the firing key. The second Mark 14 torpedo followed the first one but with a course offset of half a degree.

Sternman and Schacter both watched the stopwatch next to the TDC. If their solution was good, they should hear a satisfying explosion in twenty seconds. The clock ticked higher. Twenty seconds. Twenty-three seconds. Twenty-six seconds.

Thirty seconds and still no explosion. Perfectly quiet.

"Up scope," Schacter ordered. He looked out into the night. The

Japanese destroyer was still there, not ablaze, just steaming along, fat dumb and happy. He had not changed course or done anything to indicate he was aware of just how close to catastrophe he had just been.

"Observation on the destroyer. Bearing, mark."

"Bearing two-eight-one."

"Range, mark."

"Range one-two-hundred yards."

"Checks with solution," Sternman called out. "No way we could've missed him."

"Okay," Schacter said with a long sigh. "It's still a good shot. Make tubes three and four ready. Run depth twenty feet, speed HIGH."

Again, the Captain raised the periscope and sighted on the destroyer. Again, two torpedoes raced out at the target as the crew of the *Tigerfish* endured the agonizing wait for them to explode this time.

Again, nothing.

Schacter ordered, "Up scope." He angrily slapped the training handles down and stuck his eye to the eyepiece as it rose higher. The top of the scope had just broken the surface when he shouted, "Oh, shit!" Then he hollered, "Down scope! Make your depth two hundred feet. Left full rudder, steer course south. Ahead flank!" Turning to Sternman he said, "He's turning toward! The bastard must have seen those last two torpedoes. Let's skedaddle!"

Then, "*WHOOMP*!"

The first depth charge explosion caught the *Tigerfish* by surprise. The horrendous slam knocked the boat over, breaking light bulbs and brutally hurling crew members into the bulkheads. That was quickly followed by two more detonations that threatened to tear the submarine apart.

Then, silence.

"Skipper, maybe we should go deeper and sneak out of here," Johnson muttered as he stood beside Schacter.

The CO was shaking—whether from fear or frustration—and sweat poured off of him. "Make your depth three hundred feet, ahead one-third. Rig for quiet. Turn off everything we don't need. Don't even fart."

The *Tigerfish* slowed until it was barely crawling and slipped even deeper into the sea.

"Destroyer screws," the soundman said, headset clenched to his ears, barely whispering, as if he feared his counterpart on the Japanese warship above might hear him. "Here he comes again."

Four more horrendous explosions in rapid succession, and then, again, eerie quiet.

The *Tigerfish* did all she could do, slinking away toward the south, trying to evade the enemy's powerful charges. Again, the destroyer dropped four more depth charges. Thankfully, these were a little further away, noticeably less jarring. Were the Japs guessing now? And guessing wrong?

Gradually, the submarine eased away as the destroyer's attacks were further and further astern, bothering nobody but a few unfortunate fish. But they were slow to give up. It was afternoon when the last depth charge, well astern of the submarine, detonated. Schacter chose to continue quietly leaving the area to the south, not returning to the surface until a dark, blanketing night had once again descended.

When they were satisfied they had successfully eluded their stalker, Schacter called the XO, Johnson, and the COB into the wardroom to discuss their frustrating attempt at sinking the Japanese destroyer. He was vigorously scratching a red, scaly spot on his forearm. His hands were shaking, and his face was flushed a brilliant red.

"I don't understand what went wrong," the Skipper opened the discussion, shaking his head. "But I aim to find out. We shot four damn torpedoes on what should have been a dead-nuts solution. The bastard should be on the bottom four times over. Instead, we've wasted four torpedoes and damn near got ourselves sunk. COB, get the torpedomen together and go over those fish with a fine-toothed comb. Brad, same thing with the TDC and the periscope. Something made us miss and I want to know what it was. Even if it was me, somehow. Now, get busy and get me some answers."

"Will do, Captain," the XO said.

"Meantime, I'll be in my stateroom punching the hell out of my poor innocent pillow with both fists. Else I'm gonna explode like them damn Mark 14s did not!"

As the others filed out, Issac Sternman held back. "Skipper, want me to get Doc to look at that arm? It's starting to look nasty."

"Naw, just some rash I've picked up. It's nothing."

14

Debbie Schultz truly enjoyed her regular Saturday morning meetup with her little group of friends at Morton's Pharmacy in Mystic. The lunch counter was a perfect place to get away from all the worries of daily life, the biggest being that the attendees' men were off in some distant part of the world. Sailors' wives down through history had learned to cling to each other for mutual support when their boyfriends and husbands were gone and they had no idea where they were gone to or for how long. All they knew for sure was that whatever the guys were doing, it was dangerous work. Especially now that America was officially a part of what had already been dubbed the Second World War by President Roosevelt himself. Whether they admitted it to themselves or not, the women left behind knew there was a possibility they might never see their loved ones again. All they could do was keep the faith and the home fires burning. Even when others they knew—thankfully so far, none of the members of their group—had already gotten that ominous knock on the door and the bad news it foretold.

Debbie was usually the first to arrive. Other than Ellie Morton, of course, who came down on the bus each week from her nursing school in Boston specifically for the gathering at her dad's drugstore. She—as well as the others—felt they were closer to their distant men when they were all together. Indeed, Ellie was behind the counter when Debbie rushed in, seeking not only comradeship but shelter from the morning's nasty weather.

"All this war work going on everywhere you look," Debbie exclaimed. "Makes it impossible to find a place to park, even in Mystic, Connecticut, on a miserable Saturday morning!"

Ellie slid a cup of hot coffee and a Danish over to Debbie.

The two of them were already sipping their coffee and nibbling on a pastry when several of the other women came in, red-nosed, brushing sleet off their coats. Debbie and Ellie were the only non-wife regulars in the group, though both women had plans to change that when Brad Johnson and Fred Wurster came home from the war.

"Here you go," Ellie said as she passed out coffee and Danishes down the counter. "Hey, I got a letter yesterday from Karen. She and baby Jonathan are doing great, even if they did get a foot of snow out there in Kansas this week. She told me to say hello to everybody."

"I got one, too," Debbie said. The other girls offered that they had as well. "But sorry to say I just have not had time to open it yet. I don't see how she has time to write us all, what with the hospital job and the baby. And she says she writes Stan twice a day, sometimes three times."

"A letter every time that precious baby burps or poops?" one of the others asked. They all had a good laugh. "Heck, I would, too, if I had one of those cute little tykes. Chuck and I tried, which was fun as hell, but no luck. When that man gets back, though...well...he better be eatin' his Wheaties!"

Another laugh around the table. Debbie Schultz leaned back, closed her eyes, and massaged her temples.

"You look bushed, Deb," Ellie said. "Late night at the bar last night?"

"Yeah, those sub sailors don't want to go home, afraid, I guess, that it could be their last night at Solomon's for a while." She took a sip of coffee. "Ummm. That's good. And you know, for some of them, it's the truth. They show up. They go to school. They come get drunk at Solomon's and flirt with me. They go to war. We had three 'last calls' tonight. Oh. Last night. We got out of there at four and I haven't been to bed yet."

She did not mention she had spent some of that post-work time conspiring with the Naval Intelligence officer she was helping to try to frustrate and eventually prosecute a German spy ring operating around New London and Groton. No one knew how much stress that was putting on her, too.

"Honey, sit back and relax," Ellie told her. "Margaret wants to tell us all about her big, mysterious idea."

Debbie took a bite of the Danish, looked up, and asked, "What? I hope it's fun."

Margaret, easily the oldest of the group, was the wife of a longtime submarine Skipper on patrol in the Atlantic but based in New London. That meant he was home often. She picked up a well-thumbed copy of *Vogue* magazine and flipped to an article near the back.

"This is the latest thing," she said with a sly grin. "Socks! Personalized socks. See, Myrna Loy and Agnes Moorehead, they're knitting socks and sweaters for our boys in the war and urging everybody else to do it. I say we all get together for popcorn a couple of nights a week and knit our guys some warm socks for the cold decks of those nasty old submarines."

Ellie, Debbie, and the other women scanned the article and photos, then looked up at each other. All had odd expressions on their faces. Once again Margaret had shown how little she had in common with this particular group of Navy wives and girlfriends.

"Great idea, Margaret," Ellie Morton said half-heartedly. She did not want to offend Margaret. The older woman's intentions were good. And word was her husband was angling for Captain and probably a Squadron Commodore job pretty soon. "But between nursing school and working at the hospital and making the bus trip down here every week..."

Debbie Schultz offered, "I'd love to do the popcorn and knit Brad some socks, but I work nights. Long nights. And cook and clean for my dad, who's on double shifts over at EB." She did not mention the time spent meeting with LCDR Klemp a couple of days a week and with the German spies at least once each week.

Margaret looked hurt.

"Okay, then. I'll just make sure my Herbie doesn't get cold feet," she told them.

"And let's just hope Brad Johnson and Fred Wurster don't get cold feet either," Ellie offered, setting off another round of welcome laughter.

Then they changed the subject.

∞

Naval Intelligence agent LCDR George Klemp had long since found a spot where he could comfortably observe Miss Schultz during her regular Saturday morning get-togethers with the other Navy wives. He was seated inside a cramped but warm and dry newsstand/bookstore with a couple of small tables and a decent cup of coffee, and it offered a good view of Morton's Pharmacy across the street. The coffee was especially welcome on winter days like this one.

Klemp also took great pleasure in seeing that the other character who took special interest in Miss Schultz—a sinister individual known to be affiliated with several East Coast Nazi Party groups—had not yet found such a hospitable observation point. This morning, he stood beneath an awning near the street corner, as if waiting for a bus. Maybe it was the guy's way of showing his willingness to suffer for der Führer. Of course, the Nazi agent did not constantly follow Miss Schultz as Klemp or an associate always did. But the spy regularly made it a point to reach out to her on Saturdays after the coffee klatch at the pharmacy, just in case one of the talkative wives may have heard something of importance from their husbands and felt the need to share it with her friends. The agent seemed to have a special interest in the Ward woman, who was known to be a member of this group. Her husband was rumored to be in a high position in a key Naval Intelligence station somewhere. Klemp had suggested that Debbie not mention to her German "friend" that Karen Ward was and had been back in Kansas for a while now, staying with her folks, and not at the gathering each week. Unless the creep asked, of course.

Still, a single bit of information could have great value to the Reich. And to the Japanese. Or at least enough to make their operative stand out in the cold wind and sleet early on a Saturday to be sure he spoke with Debbie Schultz immediately after the get-together.

Klemp smiled. He had already given Debbie a couple of false bits of useless information to share with the bastard this time, primarily to convince the spies that she was still willingly working for them and that she continued to be able to contribute important information to them, even if Debbie's father—because of his job building submarines at Electric Boat—had far more usefulness.

Klemp rubbed the fog off the window where he sat so he could see the women in the drugstore. They seemed to be having a good time, laughing, swapping around a magazine.

He could not imagine what might be so amusing, but it was good they could forget and have a good time, if only for a few minutes, without worrying about the men they loved and what they might be going through.

That devotion to the man she loved gave Klemp even more resolve to protect Miss Schultz as best he could.

∞

It took a couple of days, but Geoff Chandler managed to convince someone to give him and Ian Murphy passage to Australia. He worked to convince *Commanduer* Daan de Bakker, and it was the communications skills of the two Brits that sealed the deal.

De Bakker was the Captain of the destroyer HNLMS *Van der Groot*, an *Admiralen*-class destroyer, a 1920s era vessel built for the Royal Dutch Navy. It had been assigned to patrol the Karimata Straits, the stretch of water that separated Sumatra from Borneo. Until very recently, the aging destroyer's job was policing shipping through the straits for pirates operating out of the hundreds of small islands that dotted the area. Piracy had historically been a major source of livelihood for the natives and a plague on commerce. But in the last week, the *Van der Groot*'s mission had been changed. With the unstoppable Japanese horde charging south, down the Malaysian Peninsula and having already landed on the British portion of Borneo, it was only a matter of time before they swarmed into the Dutch East Indies in their relentless search for natural resources to fuel the Empire's aggression. The *Van der Groot* was now assigned to patrol the vital straits against the Japanese fleet. They were to sound the warning when the Japanese attacked. That meant they would necessarily drop down to Surabaya on the south side of Java, for refueling and reprovisioning. They could drop off their two hitchhikers there if they did not encounter a British ship in the meantime.

With almost sixty thousand square miles of ocean to patrol, De Bakker knew that he was in over his head. However, in keeping with Dutch Navy tradition, he vowed that he and the *Van der Groot* would do their very best or die in the trying.

Chandler reasoned that De Bakker and the *Van der Groot* would be very likely to cross paths with the Royal Navy somewhere out there. Then he and Ian Murphy would be back on one of His Majesty's warships. And, since the *Van der Groot* would eventually be heading down to the shipyard at Surabaya, Java, for some much-needed maintenance, that would only raise the possibility of it happening.

Happening soon, Chandler hoped. He had family back home who by now knew he was missing in action. As the days passed without word, they would assume he was dead.

Daan de Bakker welcomed the pair on board primarily because they were both experienced communicators, conversant with the latest Royal Navy equipment and procedures. He promptly assigned them to help out in the ship's antiquated radio shack. They had no more than gotten settled in on board—borrowing uniforms and kit since everything they owned that they were not wearing now rested on the bottom of the Gulf of Siam in the wreckage of the *Prince of Wales*—when the *Van der Groot* headed out to sea, leaving the crowded port of Pangkalpinang astern.

The *Van der Groot* was steaming through the Gaspar Strait, the stretch of water that separated Bakgka Island from its neighbor, Belitung Island, when they received yet another change in their orders. Chandler was the one who received the message. He knew it meant their "rescue" was likely going to be once again postponed for a bit. A Japanese convoy had been sighted steaming through the narrow stretch of water separating Serason Island from Sarawak. The old Dutch destroyer was to scout out this reported convoy and report back. If it really was an invasion fleet, the heavy ships of the Dutch Navy, and hopefully the American cruisers *Houston*, *Boise*, and *Marblehead*, would steam out to attempt to repel it.

De Bakker pointed the *Van der Groot* north-northeast. He calculated that at thirty knots, it would take about nine hours to intercept the Japanese force. If it even existed, of course. More than one fishing fleet had already been reported as a likely Japanese flotilla. That meant any intercept would happen in the middle of a moonless night. Since neither he nor the IJN were blessed with that newfangled radar invention, the technology that the Americans were so proud of, he could steam right past a Japanese ship in the dark without either side seeing the other. But if the Japanese really had an invasion fleet, there would be dozens of ships clogging the narrow seaway. That heightened the chance that though they might not see him, one lonely little destroyer, he would have a good chance of seeing them. Besides, there was no option. Nor time to waste waiting for daylight. He had his orders.

The *Van der Groot* charged north through the Karimata Straits looking for Japanese while the two Brit survivors spent most of their time in the radio shack, hoping to detect a signal from a Royal Navy ship.

∞

Kaigun Chusa Akito Saito stood proudly on the bridge of the *Asashio*-class destroyer *Kasumi* surveying the convoy of troopships that were his responsibility to protect. With his heavy Nippon Kogaku 10X80 night vision binoculars, it was easy to make out the ten *marus* stretched out in two lines astern, even on such a dark, moonless night. The marus, heavily laden with troops, supplies, weapons, and ammunition, rode low in the water as they slogged slowly south-southwest toward Sumatra. Two other escorts, the torpedo boat *Chidori* and the destroyer escort *Kunashiri*, steamed in circles out on the flanks. They most resembled two sheepdogs guarding the flock, an image from Saito's childhood on the family sheep farm near Shibestu, up on the north island of Hokkaido.

Saito lowered his binoculars and took a sip of strong green tea. The beverage's tart bitterness was invigorating on such a languid tropical evening. He took a second sip and then resumed scanning the dark horizon. Even with reports that the Karimata Straits were clear of any enemy warships—updates from both the scout planes flying out ahead and from the I-boat submarines cruising the sea—Saito knew that he must keep his little escort force alert, ready for any surprise attack. He also knew the only way to make sure his men stayed alert was to always be alert himself.

"Captain!" Kaigun Chui Kato, the Officer-of-the-Deck, called out. The OOD stood on *Kasumi*'s port bridge wing while Saito, as was tradition, was stationed on the starboard wing. "A ship on the horizon, two points off the starboard bow."

"Hai!" Saito grunted an acknowledgment. He scanned over and, thanks to the night vision binoculars, immediately saw the shadowy image of the ship that Kato had spied. It certainly appeared to be a warship, probably a destroyer, and it was coming fast toward them. Saito's orders had said nothing about any Imperial Japanese warships being anywhere nearby. And it did not look like any IJN destroyer with which he was familiar.

His decision was an easy one.

"Kato-san, come right to point the contact. Report optical rangefinder range," Saito ordered.

The Captain estimated the range to this mystery warship at seven thousand meters, but the Type 94 director's optical rangefinder, located on the deck above them, would measure the range to the warship based on two telescopes mounted exactly three meters apart. The difference in bearing between the two telescopes was measured and the range computed geometrically. It was much more accurate than even a trained eye, and that data was fed right down to the men manning the forward gun mount.

Kato reported, "Rangefinder range six-seven-hundred meters."

Saito, never taking his eyes off the approaching warship, ordered, "Take the warship under fire with the forward mount."

Seconds later, the two 12.7cm 50 caliber guns in the forward turret barked loudly, shattering the quiet, calm night at sea. Saito watched for the splashes of misses, but they were impossible to see on this moonless night. On the other hand, there were no fiery explosions either, so no hits so far.

The guns belched again. Still no splashes. No hits sighted. But no return fire either.

"Kato-san, prepare for a torpedo attack with the number one launcher," Saito ordered. Could it possibly not be a warship? Were they raining hell on some freighter? He could not afford to take the chance. His task was to defend his convoy, not worry if some ship in the night was innocent or not. "We will use four torpedoes. Launch when range is four thousand meters."

The *Kasumi* charged on through the night, drawing closer to the target. The forward twin guns blasted away about every fifteen seconds. Then Saito saw a flash of light from the oncoming warship. It was finally answering fire. The battle was on.

"Captain, range four thousand meters, coming left to unmask number one launcher," Kato yelled above the noise from the guns.

Almost immediately the *Kasumi* heeled over as her rudder bit in. The IJN destroyer had just steadied up on the new course when the launch charges in the forward Type 94 Quadruple torpedo tubes shoved four Type 93 Sanso gyorai torpedoes over the side and into the water. The massive twenty-four-inch-diameter, thirty-foot-long torpedoes hit the water with their motors already running. Their kerosene and oxygen motors quickly shoved the three-ton monsters up to fifty knots as they turned toward the targeted oncoming warship.

Another quick flash then distant boom erupted from the approaching vessel's forward gun. Saito heard the shot whistle overhead and splash fifty meters to port. He fought the instinct to flinch. None of his crew should see their Captain show any fear, though.

Then Saito saw an explosion and fire on the target ship. At least one of his guns had found its mark. With the *Kasumi* now racing at right angles to the target ship instead of head-on, Saito decided to give the number two and number three gun mounts some target practice, too. With all six main guns blasting away and the range down to four thousand meters, he could now easily see where the shots were falling around or into the enemy vessel. And also confirm they were indeed shooting at a warship, a destroyer.

Which navy it belonged to did not matter. It was not IJN. Therefore, it was "enemy."

He could also see the target ship start to turn away, maybe to dodge, maybe to race for safety, but it was already too late. More shots found their target as fires broke out all along the length of the destroyer. And the target was now perfectly visible, afire, a beacon in the night.

Then the *Kasumi* suddenly shuddered. One of the incoming rounds had struck them. Saito was thrown to the deck by the force of the explosion. He looked up to see the forward gun director torn away. The deck above his head was a shambles of twisted metal and flaming bits of debris. Both the helmsman and the lee helmsman were down, lying on the deck, motionless. The ship's wheel was spinning on its own with nobody at the helm. The *Kasumi* lurched drunkenly, out of control. Saito stood, stepped over the body of the helmsman, grabbed the spinning wheel and held it steady, once again the Captain of his ship.

Just then, a tremendous explosion tore the night over where the target ship was. At least one of the Type 93 torpedoes had found its mark.

The enemy destroyer was no match for the IJN torpedoes' thousand-pound warhead.

∞

Chandler heard the roar of the first two shells as they passed overhead. Close! Damn close! He rushed out of the radio room and onto the *Van der Groot*'s bridge.

Commanduer Daan de Bakker was rushing his men to their action stations. He yelled to Chandler in frustration, "We can't see them! How do we shoot back at an invisible attacker?"

Just then a pair of bright flashes off to the northeast illuminated the night sky. The guns on the enemy warship. De Bakker used the compass ring to get a quick bearing to the flashes but he had to guess at the range. Then he ordered, in Dutch, "To the gun director, take hostile under fire. Bearing zero-three-five, range three-five-hundred meters."

However, it took almost a full minute before the forward guns reported that they were loaded and ready. On the *Van der Groot*, the 120mm guns were in individual superfiring mounts, the "B" behind and above the "A" mount. The mounts themselves were completely open, exposing the gun crews to the elements as well as enemy fire. The "A" gun fired first, quickly followed by the "B" gun.

De Bakker stared into the dense, dark night. There was no way to see if his shots were landing anywhere near the enemy unless they hit the ship and set it afire, but it was important to keep shooting. For moral support, if nothing else. And in hopes of getting lucky. The two forward guns reloaded and fired again.

Chandler grabbed a pair of binoculars and strained his eyes to see the enemy in the darkness. Nothing there but the flashes of gunfire. And he knew the attacking vessel could easily home in on the Dutch ship.

Then the Brit saw a glimmer, the ghost of a ship coming broad. That gave the warship a much larger profile and removed all doubt of who their attacker was. It was a Japanese destroyer, low and sleek and deadly dangerous.

Chandler yelled and pointed, "There he is! One point off the starboard bow, best range four thousand meters! He's turning to unmask his after batteries! He will shoot at us with all he has!"

De Bakker immediately saw the problem, too. The Jap destroyer was "crossing the tee," turning to a course that would take him in front of the Dutch warship so that he could rake it with all his guns. Meanwhile, the *Van der Groot* could only use its forward two guns to answer. A classic naval maneuver that dated all the way back to the age of sail.

"Left full rudder!" De Bakker ordered. Two could play this game. They would come broadside to broadside and slug it out, again like a couple of sail-driven warships in the nineteenth century but firing shells instead of cannonballs.

Then one of the Japanese rounds found its mark.

A brilliant flash and massive explosion rocked the *Van der Groot* mightily. Chandler half dived and half tumbled behind the bridge coaming as shrapnel, broken glass, and jagged debris zinged through the air. When he raised his head, he could see through the smoke that the "A" gun mount had ceased to exist. In its place was a pile of twisted and blackened metal and the ripped-apart bodies of the crewmen who had been manning the weapon. Despite that direct hit, the after "X" and "Y" mounts now joined the "B" mount in the fight. It was their only hope: outgun their attacker. But with more opportunity to determine range and bearing, more shots from the Nippon ship were now landing closer to the Dutch destroyer. Spray from the near misses drenched Chandler on the bridge.

Then the Japs scored a hit all the way aft, on the fantail. It penetrated the deck and detonated in the after-steering room, destroying the *Van der Groot*'s steering gear. That meant she had lost all control of the rudder.

Fifteen seconds later, a pair of rounds crashed one after the other through the forward funnel and exploded in the forward fire room. The lucky members of the "black gang" manning the fire room were killed instantly by the explosion. The less fortunate died a bit more slowly, horribly, from being scalded by high-pressure steam from the vessel's ruptured Yarrow boilers.

The *Van der Groot*, with no rudder control and only one screw, began to make a slow, aimless circle in the calm waters off Borneo.

"Captain, the fire forward is threatening the forward magazine!" the Officer-of-the-Deck yelled above the cacophony of noise and shouting. "The fire main is broken. We have no way to fight the fire."

Commanduer Daan de Bakker shook his head in disbelief. If the fire reached the forward magazine, the explosion would sink whatever would be left of his ship. Less than an hour ago, they had been peacefully steaming through a quiet tropical night. Now he was about to order that his ship must be abandoned. There was no way to save it.

The Captain was just opening his mouth to utter the dreaded words when the *Van der Groot* was rocked by an impossibly violent explosion.

Chandler felt himself flying through the air, propelled by the concussion of the blast. He had a quick, fleeting vision of the Dutch destroyer breaking in half below him. Then he crashed hard into the water, shoved deep by the force of his landing. He grabbed handfuls of water, clawing his way toward where he thought the surface might be. His head popped up just in time to see the ship, now split in half, sink beneath the waves.

Then all around him there was nothing but darkness. And a few human voices, plaintive calls in the darkness, shipmates calling out for help.

My Lord, he thought. *It all seems so familiar*. He had been through this too many times before. Was he cursed to be dunked into the sea from any ship on which he rode?

At least he had once again survived having a ship sunk from beneath him. He swam over to a sizeable piece of floating planking and grabbed on. A pair of searchlights flashed on a few hundred meters away. A ship was slowly approaching, its lights darting through the wreckage.

Chandler instinctively knew that vessel was not looking to rescue men in the water. Then, as if to confirm his suspicions, he heard the chatter of a machine gun. Then others. Rifle fire, too. Bullets tore apart the body of a dead sailor floating faceup nearby.

Chandler ducked beneath his planking as one of the searchlights danced around the water very close to him. There was no doubt about what was happening. The Jap destroyer was steaming through the mess they had caused and were deliberately shooting survivors.

It seemed like forever to Chandler, but after about ten minutes of such blatant brutality, the Japanese destroyer seemed to lose interest in the sunken Dutch destroyer and its surviving crew. It steamed away over the southern horizon, its convoy safely in tow.

Chandler, finally able to stop ducking the searchlights and bullets, began a slow, plodding swim to a place he had noticed a bit earlier, a little island a couple of miles to the east. Every few minutes, he stopped to tread water, to rest, and to call out for Ian Murphy.

There was no response. Not from his radioman friend. Not from anybody.

15

The mountains of Sarawak on the western coast of the island of Borneo were just visible on the horizon. From the bridge of S-55, Trip MacLean could see a loom of light that indicated a bit of civilization on the otherwise dark coastline. Checking the charts, he determined that it had to be Kuching, the capital of the nation of Sarawak. Obviously, Kuching was not darkened for war. Of course, with the city in Japanese hands, and since the only bombers anywhere within range belonged to Hirohito and his far-flung Empire, there would be no reason for a blackout. Even the Tanjung Po Lighthouse, out on the northern tip of Bako Point, was lighted to warn mariners approaching Kuching Harbor of the jut of land in their way.

"Left full rudder," MacLean ordered over the 7MC. "Steady course one-nine-zero."

MacLean's instructions were to approach the harbor at Kuching so they could conduct a reconnaissance mission. He was to close to within three miles of the coast and then dive the submarine. Captain DiCarlo had been very explicit. He expected the *S-55* to be in position at first light to get a good look at what might be happening in the harbor, most of which was on the mouth of the Sarawak River.

MacLean had no idea what to expect. How many patrol craft or shore guns might be there, guarding against any attack or incursion? How dense was the ship traffic that they would have to avoid? But he did suspect that the bottom of the harbor, constantly being fed by silt from the river, would not necessarily match the old charts that the S-55 carried.

MacLean checked his watch. Sunrise would be in ninety minutes. He still had ten miles to go before he would get to the ordered dive point. And he still needed to thread his way on the surface through a host of small fishing boats, as well as several cargo ships waiting for morning light so they could enter the harbor. All without being seen or reported. Any one of those ragged fishing boats could be a picket boat just waiting to report that an American submarine was steaming toward Kuching.

MacLean shook his head. The cargo ships were sitting ducks, just begging to be shot. Especially the bigger freighters, likely loaded with supplies and ammo for Japanese troops. But DiCarlo had been insistent. They would recon the harbor first, as ordered. Only then, after they had safely left shallow water and had room to go deep after firing torpedoes, would they even consider attacking any shipping.

Ensign Tommy Hilligas was next to MacLean on the bridge, standing watch as the Junior Officer-of-the-Deck. He pointed out four large freighters, all huddled in a tight cluster, two miles off the port bow, effectively blocking their way. MacLean immediately thought, *A spread of torpedoes and we could get all four of those bastards.* But he had his orders. They would have to find a way to maneuver the submarine carefully around those juicy targets if they were to get into position by sunrise.

MacLean slowed the boat and swung wide around the freighters. He was depending on the low, dark silhouette of the submarine being invisible in what remained of the dark night. Then he caught sight of a patrol boat slowly weaving its way between the freighters, likely more concerned about pirates or pilferage than mounting any kind of anti-submarine defense. It still took the better part of an hour to skirt around the resting ships and then get back on track to the entrance to the harbor.

Those freighters gave MacLean another reason for worry. He did not like the idea of putting the *S-55* in line between those big vessels and the harbor mouth. Most likely, at first light, the ships would all weigh anchor and traipse on into Kuching, right over top of where the submarine would be reconning. Heavily loaded as they were, they would run deep while *S-55* was sitting shallow, with no deep water beneath the sub's keel. It was not a good position to be in.

MacLean checked his watch. "Mr. Hilligas, drop below and inform the Captain that we are ten minutes from the dive point. Recommend that he come to the bridge to view the situation."

DiCarlo huffed and puffed his way up the ladder and onto the bridge. He pulled out a cigarette and flicked his lighter. The flash of bright light all but blinded MacLean, whose eyes were night-adapted from his long watch on the bridge. DiCarlo did not seem to notice MacLean's grunt of pain or the OOD vigorously rubbing his eyes. Nor did he seemed to be concerned that even that quick bit of light might alert the Japanese that a submarine was steaming into their harbor.

"What's the problem, Mr. MacLean, that you are so anxious to show me?" DiCarlo sarcastically asked.

MacLean quickly explained his concern with the freighters, with the chance of being run over while they were trying to reconnoiter. And of the risk of their charts not being accurate enough to allow them to safely exit the harbor under duress.

"Our orders were to see what was happening in Kuching," DiCarlo growled. "And that, Mr. MacLean, is damn well what we will do. Now, get this boat dived so we can do what we are supposed to do." With that, the Skipper took a last deep drag of his cigarette and flipped the glowing butt over the rail into the dirty brown water, just before he went down the ladder into the conning tower.

MacLean closed his eyes, bit his tongue, then ordered the *S-55* submerged. When he came down the ladder into the conning tower, he saw DiCarlo at the attack scope, swinging it around as the boat leveled off at periscope depth.

"Okay, I have Kuching Harbor entrance on this bearing," DiCarlo called out.

Seaman First Class Thurgood Williams, the Periscope Assistant, called out, "Bearing two-five-one."

Sam Forrester, the XO, was bent over the navigation chart. He slapped down the parallel motion protractor and called out, "Bearing checks with middle of Sarawak River mouth."

"Steer course two-five-one," the Skipper ordered without taking his eye from the scope.

DiCarlo was locked in, watching as they slowly steamed toward the river mouth. He kept up a running commentary of everything he was seeing. The muddy water, the docks with ships tied up, the lighthouse high on the promontory. All of it.

But, MacLean noticed, he never looked behind them. Not once had he made a "safety sweep" to see if anyone was coming up on their stern. But how could he say something to someone as pig-headed as Tony DiCarlo?

MacLean had learned from bitter experience not to make any suggestions to the Skipper. Instead, he slipped over to where he could whisper to Forrester while the Captain was on the scope, giving a running guided tour of Kuching Harbor.

"XO, recommend the Captain make a safety sweep," Trip told the XO. "We know we have ships behind us, and they're probably on the move by now."

Forrester nodded but made no motion to tell DiCarlo anything. MacLean waited a few seconds to be sure Forrester had heard him. Nothing happened.

He whispered louder, "XO, we need a safety sweep."

"Damn it! Silence on the conn!" DiCarlo angrily shouted. "Mr. MacLean, if you can't keep your suggestions—"

The soundman interrupted DiCarlo, his voice urgent. "We have a contact! Close aboard! Astern! Astern!"

DiCarlo quickly swung the scope around, then stepped back. His eyes wide, his face showed near panic. He yelled, "Down scope! Make your depth one hundred feet! Left full rudder!"

"My rudder is left full," the helmsman called out.

"Depth sixty feet coming to one hundred!" the Diving Officer yelled. "Sixty-five feet, coming to one hundred! Seventy feet—"

The boat heeled over sharply to starboard. There was a horrible grinding and crashing sound of agonized metal somewhere above their heads. Men fell hard against bulkheads or to the deck.

Then, just as abruptly, the boat popped upright. MacLean looked around, fully expecting to see massive flooding, dingey water rushing in to fill the conning tower. But amazingly, everything seemed normal.

"Depth eighty feet coming to one hundred," the Diving Officer called, his normally calm voice now shaky.

"Skipper!" Forrester yelled. So, now he was going to speak up. "Chart only shows eighty feet of water here."

"We just need to get to—"

The submarine ground to a sudden, complete halt. Men who had just gotten back to their feet—some bleeding or bruised—once again tumbled.

No doubt what had happened. They had run aground in the mud at the mouth of the Sarawak River.

DiCarlo stood, looking at the periscope as if it had offended him. Forrester stared down at the chart, quickly found the spot where they had found bottom, then drew a neat ring around it.

The COB, Anthony Watson, called up from the control room below. "Captain, all stations report systems normal. But the soundman reports that he lost the lower sound head."

Tony DiCarlo finally spoke. "I thought I ordered 'down scope.' Scope's still partially up. Why's the scope still up?"

Thurgood Williams was doing his best to finish lowering the attack scope, but nothing was happening. Something was wrong with it topside.

DiCarlo leaned against the chart table and took a deep breath. Then he said, "I think that we've completed our recon. Let's carefully get ourselves out of the mud and slip out of here before anyone up there is any the wiser."

It took almost two hours of carefully pumping tanks to lighten the sub without suddenly, uncontrollably popping to the surface, backing down, then easing forward to wiggle loose, before they finally broke free of the sucking muck at the bottom of the harbor.

"Steer course north," DiCarlo ordered, as if nothing had happened.

Forrester immediately called out, "Captain, recommend course zero-five-zero. North will run us into Bako Point."

DiCarlo threw his hat on the deck in frustration. Then he growled, "Hell, steam course zero-five-zero if that is what you want!" He stomped over to the control room ladder. As he started down, he said, "Mr. MacLean, you have the deck. I'll be in my stateroom."

It was time to get out of town, but they soon found that any speed above three knots resulted in a very loud banging from someplace topside. MacLean ordered a speed of two knots and carefully watched the charts as they crept to the northeast.

It was well past noon when they were clear of Bako Point and could come around to course north. By sundown, they were still only fifteen miles off the Sarawak coast, but MacLean surfaced the *S-55* and climbed up to the bridge to check the damage. The attack periscope was bent over a couple of feet above the top of the shears at a nearly ninety-degree angle.

The bad news? They had seriously damaged their old submarine in an incident that should never have happened. And, at least for right now, they would need to remain on the surface to make any speed at all.

The good news? They might be able to work on the scope, rigging some temporary repairs so they could make better time while submerged. And they could still dive the boat if necessary. Best of all, they were now making their way for the shipyard in Surabaya to get the old girl repaired.

∞

Kaigu Shosa Riku Ito, Commander of the Imperial Japanese Navy submarine *I-53*, was sitting in his tiny stateroom, enjoying a cup of tea as he composed a letter home to his wife, Akemi. Ito was tired. It had been a long, slow, boring day spent patrolling an empty stretch of water off Borneo. But composing a letter to his wife, and writing it using traditional Japanese *shodo* methods, always served to refresh and revive him.

He carefully arranged his *fude* (brushes) and his *suzuri* (inkpot) on the tiny desk. Then he pulled a sheet of *washi sumi* paper from the box that Akemi had given him as a departure gift and carefully smoothed it out on his desk. He sat back and relaxed, seeking calm as he pictured the shodo, the way of writing Japanese calligraphy, in his mind. As he did, Ito carefully put a dab of water in the suzuri and began grinding the *sumi* (ink stick) into a thin paste.

He had just chosen his first fude when the speaker above his desk rudely buzzed. "Captain, please come to the bridge."

Riku Ito closed his eyes and sighed. Something about the submarine required his attention. Composing the letter to Akemi and its usual therapeutic effect would have to wait. He stowed the writing implements and walked out to the *I-53*'s control room. There he grabbed his pair of binoculars and continued on up the ladder to the bridge. Moving from his fully lit stateroom to the midnight black of a moonless night left Ito blinded for a few minutes.

The watch officer, Ensign Sato, pointed to the east-southeast and said, "Captain, there is a submarine on the surface at bearing one-two-one, range three-five-hundred meters. He is coming almost directly toward us."

Ito could see nothing, but he smiled. Suddenly, a long boring day was not at all boring anymore. To find an enemy submarine—and it had to be an enemy submarine since there were no other Japanese subs operating anywhere within a thousand miles—gave him a very tempting quarry. But it was also a very challenging and dangerous one. It could bite back. And it had ways to avoid detection and destruction that a surface warship did not. It was all a matter of who could get in position and shoot first without the other being any wiser. And it was still a deadly game of cat-and-mouse.

"Sato-san, dive the submarine and come to normal approach course," Ito ordered. He went back down through the hatch into the darkened control room. Enough time had passed that his night vision had cleared. Through the attack periscope, he could now clearly see the submarine. It appeared to be an American *S*-class, although it could just as easily be a Dutch *O*-class. It really did not matter. He would attack it, no matter whose navy owned it. It was a threat to the Empire and must be destroyed.

By the time the *I-53* was settled out at periscope depth, the target submarine—now confidently identified as an American *S*-class boat—was still apparently unaware of any impending danger. The vessel had steamed toward them so that the range was down to two thousand meters. It was time to start the attack routine.

Ito called out, "Observation on the submarine." He centered the crosshairs on the target and said, "Bearing, mark."

Sato read the bearing off the repeater. "Bearing zero-three-six."

Ito said, "Range one-eight hundred meters. Angle-on-the-bow port thirty."

Ito stepped back from the periscope and considered the process for a moment, much as he had pondered the initial shodo in the letter to his wife. Then he confidently announced, "We will let the American submarine get to eight hundred meters before we shoot. He is on a course of two-zero-five. Sato-san, steer to be broad on his beam at eight hundred yards."

"Hai!" Sato responded. There was not much for the young Ensign to do. The *I-53* was already heading at ninety degrees to the target *S*-boat's track. His job was easy, unless the American abruptly maneuvered.

"Make the torpedoes in tubes one and two ready," Ito ordered. "We will shoot them as a spread, five seconds apart."

Ito looked through the periscope. The American was still there, still nonchalantly steaming along on a straight course. Still obligingly on the surface. He would pass a few hundred meters ahead of where the *I-53* hid, waiting and ready.

Ito stepped back from the periscope and wiped the sweat from his forehead. He willed his heart to stop pounding, his voice to remain strong and even. He needed to stay calm. But most importantly for his voice and demeanor to stay controlled so that his crew sensed that all was normal and their Commanding Officer was firmly in control.

Ito glanced at the clock. It should be about time to shoot. He stepped up to the periscope and looked out.

The American had changed nothing.

Ito put the crosshairs on the firing bearing, zero-two-two. When the American submarine was centered on that bearing, he would shoot.

The unsuspecting American *S*-boat plodded across the width of the periscope view until the crosshairs finally centered on its sail.

"Shoot tube one," Ito calmly ordered. He could just as well have been telling his wife, "Good morning."

There was a *whoosh* and a *clunk* as the Type 95 torpedo was flushed out of tube one and sent on its deadly journey.

Ito counted off five seconds and then said, again with quiet assurance, "Shoot tube two."

The torpedo in tube two raced out to chase the first shot toward the doomed target.

Ito allowed himself the slightest of smiles as he calculated that it would take each weapon thirty seconds to reach their target. His gaze once again fell on the vessel's clock. He was not aware that he was holding his breath, but when an explosion suddenly rocked the submarine, he involuntarily exhaled strongly. He looked through the periscope just in time to see the second torpedo hit and explode spectacularly.

The enemy vessel, the American submarine, her stern blown off, quickly sank beneath the waves.

"Sato-san, surface the boat," Ito ordered. "We must report our success to Submarine Command. And recharge our batteries to prepare for our next victory."

∞

Trip MacLean stood on the *S-55*'s bridge and scanned the dark sea around them. Ever since they passed a couple of native fishing boats an hour or so before, they had the South China Sea all to themselves.

The COB, Anthony Watson, and a couple of his machinists were up in the shears doing their best to lash what was left of the attack scope down so that it would not bang around when they were running at more than two knots while submerged. If they were limited to such a crawl, it was going to be a very long trip to Surabaya. Or a very risky one if they tried to run too much on the surface. The Motor Machinist Chief's colorful language filled the night air as they struggled to make the emergency repairs. Everyone agreed the damaged scope would never be operational again. It was far too badly bent. That meant they were concentrating on lashing it down to keep it quiet so every Japanese destroyer in the region would not hear them banging along.

Seaman Thurgood Williams climbed up the ladder from the conning tower, carrying a fresh pot of coffee. MacLean grabbed his coffee cup, threw the dregs over the side, refilled it, and thanked the sailor. Even a hundred miles north of the equator, a steaming mug of coffee was just what the midwatch called for.

Williams looked around, breathing deeply of the fresh night air. Red Gray and Doc Jones followed him up the ladder. After the collision and spending all day slinking out of Kuching, it was good to get topside and see the horizon, to verify that there was still a world beyond the submarine's confining hull, and to breathe the cool, refreshing night air. These old boats, built without air conditioning, certainly had not been designed for crew comfort in tropical climes.

Suddenly, Tommy Hilligas yelled in a panic, "Torpedo! Torpedo track broad on the port side!" He pointed excitedly toward the arrow-straight trail of bubbles. Arrow straight and headed right at them.

MacLean grabbed the 1MC microphone and yelled, "All ahead emergency, right full rudder! Torpedo in the water, port side!"

The twin MAN diesels roared in response. Thick black smoke poured out of the exhaust as the *S-55* jumped ahead, her bow swinging to starboard.

But she could not respond quickly enough. It was already too late, even before Hilligas saw the incoming weapon.

The first Japanese torpedo slammed into the *S-55*'s rudder. The explosion blew away both rudders and screws. It punched a mammoth hole through the after trim tank and into the motor room.

The second torpedo exploded five seconds later in the wreckage caused by the first. But the *S-55* was already doomed even before that blow.

MacLean, seeing the boat quickly settling by the stern, and seeing the stern mostly blown away, grabbed the 1MC and yelled, "Abandon ship! Abandon ship!"

As fast as the boat was going down, he knew instinctively that there was very little chance for anyone belowdecks to get out alive. He looked at the dozen men who happened to be topside at the time. He ordered, "Everybody in the water! Stay together. Closest land is due east about twenty miles."

Anthony Watson stood beside MacLean as the rest of the men dropped down to the main deck and then into the water. "Well, sir, you're in command now. What in hell do we do?"

"Chief, I'm going to tread water. Suggest you do likewise."

Then both men stepped off the bridge of their stricken submarine and into the South China Sea.

∞

Fred Wurster sat hunched over the ECM Mark II encryption machine as he worked to decipher the incoming message. This was the first ULTRA message that the submarine had received, and its contents had spiked everybody's curiosity. Jim Shelton and Alphonse Dinnacetti were crowded into the tiny radio shack, watching over Wurster's shoulders.

No pressure, Wurster thought. However, rivulets of sweat dribbled down the back of his neck, further soaking the already sodden khaki shirt as he carefully read each of the letters from the message that the *Wolffish* had just received into the machine, then typed it onto a piece of paper. Slowly, the meaningless gibberish of letters was transformed into useful information.

ULTRA – CO EYES ONLY

Expect battleship NAGATO in vicinity of 27-10 N X 143 E. 25 Dec. WOLFFISH tasked to search area for 48 hours to arrive on or before 0200Z 25 Dec. Mission is to sink NAGATO. At FINEX resume transit.

Wurster tore the sheet out of the typewriter and handed it to Dinnacetti. The Skipper had already read it. He rushed out of the radio shack and over to the chart table. It took him only a couple of seconds to find 27 degrees 10 minutes north latitude by 143 degrees east longitude.

"That's over five hundred miles off our track," he growled. "Fine Christmas present SUBPAC sends us. 'Haul ass and happy holidays!' It's going to take all day at flank just to get there. I sure as hell ain't running at flank on the surface when we're only six hundred miles from Japan. Somebody explain how we're supposed to do this?"

All of Alphonse Dinnacetti's years of submarine training screamed against this operation. He had it beaten into his head over and over again. "A submarine does not run on the surface in the daylight! That is suicide! A submarine is just too vulnerable to an air attack!" It was universally accepted submarine tactical dogma. There was no way that he would dare challenge that dogma.

They had a little over twenty-four hours to get in position to shoot the Japanese battleship. There was just no way to do the mission without running as fast as they could go from now until dawn tomorrow. That meant charging ahead all day today on the surface at twenty knots. A submarine running on the surface during the daytime was just wrong. That would leave them far too vulnerable to an attack from the air. An image of a Japanese dive-bomber suddenly plunging down at them from out of the sun, gun blazing as it rammed a death-dealing bomb right into the deck of his submarine, flashed across his mind. The shiver was totally involuntary. So were the trembling hands.

Shelton took a pair of dividers and walked off the distance on the chart from their current location to where they were ordered to go locate and sink the *Nagato*. Then he grabbed a pencil and a scrap of paper to scratch out some figures.

As he worked, he mumbled, half to himself, "0200 Zulu. That's 1100 local time." He grabbed the nautical almanac and did a couple of quick calculations. "Sunset tonight is at 1650 and sunrise tomorrow is at 0620. That gives us thirteen and a half hours of darkness. That's 270 of those 500 miles. But we still got to find the time for the last 230, which would be accomplished in daylight. Where we going to find those, Skipper?"

Dinnacetti looked over Shelton's shoulder, doing more calculating in his head. He said, "We have about five hours of daylight tomorrow morning, but we sure don't want to get there with our batteries drained. Let's say we do six knots submerged. That's thirty of your miles." He shook his head. "Unless we can make ourselves invisible, there is just no way to get the last two hundred."

Shelton shook his head as he stared at the chart. "Skipper, we got another problem." He pointed to a tiny speck on the chart. "That's Ogasawara Island. You can bet it has an airfield and patrol planes out guarding the Emperor's deep blue seas from rascals like us." He used his dividers to measure the distance from the tiny island to their potential rendezvous spot with the *Nagato*. "It's only fifty miles to the west of where we're supposed to be raising all this ruckus."

Dinnacetti slammed his hands down onto the chart table. The control room fell silent. All eyes turned to the Skipper. No one, except for the XO and Wurster, had any idea what was being discussed, but they knew it was important and that the Skipper did not like the way the conversation was going.

"Well, here's what we'll do. We'll do the best that we can," the exasperated CO finally said forcefully. "Sunrise is in an hour. We'll run at flank until then. Make sure the batteries are topped off before we dive. If we run at six knots submerged all day, we can make up eighty miles of those two hundred, but the batteries will be totally drained."

"That all adds up to us being 120 miles short of that oversized tugboat at 0200Z tomorrow," Shelton answered. "What do we do about that, Skipper?"

"Nothing we can do," Dinnacetti answered. "But I plan to use that new SJ radar that they strapped on us before we left Pearl. That should extend our eyes out another thirty miles or so. Maybe our friends will be cooperative and steam somewhere closer."

The *Wolffish* charged ahead, spending the day submerged and running on the surface all night. 0200Z on 25 December found the submarine still one hundred miles short of the rendezvous spot, still a long way from where they had been ordered to be. When the *Wolffish* was back at periscope depth and took a long look around, they found that they were all alone in this bit of ocean. The fancy new SJ radar did not have any contacts either.

The *Wolffish* spent a frustrating Christmas Day at periscope depth, fruitlessly searching the ether for a radar return on a Jap battleship.

As the sun dropped below the horizon, the *Wolffish* emerged from the depths. It was a little after midnight when they finally arrived at 27-10 N x 143 E and commenced their slow search for the Japanese battleship. The only contact they had all night was from the SJ radar painting the high mountains of Ogasawara Island.

Dawn of 26 December found the *Wolffish* submerged, but still searching for the *Nagato*. Fred Wurster stood in the conning tower, his eye to the periscope as he slowly swept the horizon, wishing he might catch a glimpse of the distinctive pagoda mast structure of the battleship appearing. Then he saw a dark speck just above the horizon. Something coming toward them very fast. He had just an instant to recognize a four-engine flying boat before he quickly lowered the periscope and ordered, "Make your depth one hundred feet! Jap flying boat coming this way!"

Wurster turned to find Dinnacetti standing beside him. "Jap flying boat coming right at us," Wurster reported again, breathlessly. "A Mavis, I think. But I don't think he saw us."

The Skipper nodded. "Just to be safe, let's stay down for half an hour. Then we can get back to searching."

Thirty minutes later, *Wolffish* was back at periscope depth. Wurster was once again staring out at a vast, lonely ocean. By sundown, Dinnacetti and Shelton were becoming restless. All the tension and excitement of the first ULTRA message and the possibility of sinking a truly major target had dissipated. Now they were just tired and frustrated. Either the Japanese battleship had steamed through the area before they could get there, or the intelligence was bad from the get-go and the *Nagato* was nowhere near. Still, they spent the night slowly zigzagging across the area in the vain hope that the errant battleship would suddenly show up, steam broadside to them, inviting a spread of torpedoes for a wake-up call.

When dawn found them still sailing in an empty sea, Dinnacetti chose to slowly depart the area to the north and resume course to the Bungo Straits.

"XO, make sure that the patrol report logs this wild goose chase," the Skipper grumbled. "And use those precise words. 'Wild goose chase.' No telling how many marus escaped while we were farting around down here wasting time, patience, and diesel fuel looking for a damn phantom."

16

It was a pitch-black night. A thick layer of clouds, pushed by a westerly wind until they were jammed up against the highlands of Borneo, hid the moon, but delivered the promise of a morning shower. Only the deep rumble of an explosion and flashes of light, off to the north, disturbed the tropical night's silence.

Hadi bin Sinaga—literally "the good and handsome son of the dragon" —steered his *sandeq potangnga* around to try to see what was making all the noise and flashes of light. The explosions and flickers on the horizon grabbed his interest far more than just idle curiosity. Hadi and his crew alternated between being fishermen and acting as pirates, depending on which opportunity presented itself and promised to be most lucrative. Lately, with the Japanese invading his home waters and punishing both fishermen and pirates with equal cruelty but also presenting plenty of opportunities for profit, he had added "freedom fighter" to his job description.

The traditional sandeq potangnga was a large outrigger capable of carrying a dozen or more men out into the open ocean to fish or to transport purloined cargo. Its sleek lines and large triangular sails made it an exceedingly fast vessel. Over the years, Hadi had modified this one with a powerful diesel engine so that he could outrun any pursuer, no matter how softly or strongly the wind blew, or even if it was not cooperating at all.

Regardless of what may have happened on the horizon, Hadi bin Sinaga smelled opportunity. There might be a wounded ship to easily take. Or wreckage to salvage. Whatever, it demanded investigation. But with caution. The Japanese, easily provoked, were not to be taken lightly. A few quick words to his crew had them all armed and hunkered down, hiding below the ship's gunwale. He secured the diesel so that the sandeq was almost silent as it sliced through the water using the westerly wind, its black hull and dark red sails all but invisible in the cloud-darkened night.

It took Hadi almost an hour to get to the wreck site. The only way that he could discern that anything had occurred at this particular location was the overpowering reek of diesel fuel that offended his nose and the oil slick that lapped up to sully the hull of his vessel. He saw nothing floating in the water that was worth salvaging. Just a few bits of wood decking and some rags of clothing. Not even any bodies floating in the oil amid the wreckage.

Then Hadi heard voices out there in the darkness. Plaintive cries, coming from somewhere off to port. He steered toward the sound. It took a few minutes to find the survivors, huddled together in the water, clinging to whatever they could to stay afloat.

Hadi had a quick decision to make about what he should do with this bunch before he hauled them aboard his ship. If they were English or Dutch, then he could pull them from the water, hide them from the Japanese patrols, and then take them to Sumatra, hoping for a generous reward. The Dutch colonial government was paying a handsome bounty for rescued mariners.

But if they were Japanese, he would simply shoot them in the water and sail away. That is, if they did not shoot first.

Then Hadi recognized that they appeared to be speaking English, but with a much different accent from his missionary schoolteacher. That was where he had learned English. From the missionaries who believed one could best worship God in English.

"What ship?" he called into the darkness.

The answer came back, "American submarine, *S-55*. We were sunk by a Jap sub, we think."

That added another level of complexity to Hadi's problem. A Japanese submarine hiding in the area could easily pop up at any second and take issue with him rescuing enemy survivors. His sandeq would be no match for the Japanese boat.

Still, there might be money here. And he had no qualms about helping any enemy of the Japanese. Hadi ordered his men to quickly get the Americans aboard and hidden belowdecks. It took almost half an hour to pull all of the sodden men, a couple of them injured, out of the water. Then the American in charge of the group insisted that they take time to search for any other survivors. Hadi reluctantly agreed, but it proved to be a fruitless and disappointing outcome. The sun had just emerged over the eastern horizon when Hadi finally sailed away from the area.

When he felt strong enough to stand and move about, Trip MacLean found Hadi bin Sinaga sitting by the rudder. He was steering with his toes as he enjoyed his morning meal, using his fingers to pull chunks of steamed rice and fish from his bowl. He waved MacLean to sit and offered him the opportunity to dig into the bowl.

"It's steamed rice and *ikan asin*, salt fish," he said. "Perfect food for a fine morning on the water."

MacLean was certainly hungry. He had not eaten since going on watch the previous day at 1800 hours. He pulled up a small handful and took a tentative bite. The fish was indeed very salty. He fought hard not to choke.

Hadi laughed and handed the American a cup of a thick, greenish liquid. "Drink this," he said. "It will cut the salt."

MacLean took the cup and eyed it suspiciously.

"It's called *jamu*," Hadi answered the unasked question. "Turmeric, ginger, tamarind, and some secret spices." He motioned for MacLean to drink. "Go ahead. It tastes good and it will make you feel better."

MacLean sipped the spicy concoction. "Not bad," he offered. Then, realizing how ravenously hungry he was, he grabbed another portion of rice and salt fish. "Where are we headed?" he asked as he munched.

Hadi was quiet as he thought. Then he answered, "With all the weapons my crew is carrying, you have probably guessed that we are not exactly fishermen. Some people might say that we are pirates, but in these times I prefer 'freedom fighters.' We fight the Japanese when it is safe for us and, hopefully, where we can also make a generous profit. Right now, we are heading to our home. It is a little island that does not appear on many of the charts. It is called Pengiki Besar Island, down in an area called the Karimata Straits. We will rest there and decide how to get you back to your navy so you can fight the Empire of Japan."

"How soon?" MacLean asked. He took another sip of the jamu. He found that he liked the taste, and it was surprisingly refreshing. He could already feel a boost in both stamina and spirit.

"Tomorrow," Habi answered, leaning back in impressive contentment, stretching. "Maybe the next day. It all depends on the whim of the winds and the Japanese."

This guy really enjoys life, such as it is, Trip MacLean thought as he, too, settled back against the deck rail. *And here I am, on the deck of a pirate ship in the middle of nowhere bound for some place that doesn't even show up on the damn map.*

It certainly was not the pavilion of the Manila Army and Navy Club. Only a few hours before he had been washed off the bridge of a doomed, sinking submarine, faced with the prospect of being cut to pieces in the water by enemy guns, a twenty-mile swim in shark-infested waters, and the likelihood of either being eaten or drowning.

But he had survived. There was that.

Sometimes life throws you a Bob Feller fastball, he thought. *Sometimes it gives you steamed rice, salt fish, and jamu.*

∞

Geoff Chandler had to force himself to wake up. Then he was not at all sure why he had wasted the effort. Truth was, it had been the blazing morning sun that demanded that he open his eyes. After two days adrift, clinging to a bit of unidentifiable floating wreckage, with no food or water, the Royal Navy officer knew that he was now very near the end. There was no way that he would survive to see another dawn. It would be so very easy just to lose his grip on this bit of flotsam and sink into the deep, surrendering to the sea.

Then Chandler shook his head and freed one hand from the floating junk long enough to slap himself in the face. There was no way he was going to take the easy way out. He was too much the stubborn Yorkshireman to take that path. He would float along out here in the South China Sea until the bitter end came, the victim of sun, sea, hunger, and thirst, not of the loss of the will to live.

The startlingly loud screech of seagulls shook Chandler from his revery. He lifted his head to try to find the offending birds so he could give them what-for. That's when he spotted something far more interesting. It was a thin green line on the horizon. For a few seconds, he thought that he might be imagining it. Or maybe it was some fluke prism effect from the new morning sun. There was the appearance of the gulls, though. They would not be far from land.

He blinked, shook his head, then looked off to the east again. He could still see the green line. Could it possibly be an island? He realized he might soon find out. The constant wind was pushing him in that general direction.

With the little strength that he had left, Chandler started to paddle. At first, it did not seem that the green sliver on the horizon was getting any closer. Gradually, though, he was able to discern individual trees. Tall palms. Then he could see that they were swaying in the breeze. But his progress, even with the attempt at paddling, was maddeningly slow. The sun was well over his shoulder to the west when the water started to change color from deep blue to a lighter turquoise hue. Then, when he looked down, he could see coral and a sandy bottom through the crystal-clear water. The sun was just dipping toward the horizon when he felt sand beneath his feet. When he could, he began slowly crawling up onto the beach.

Finally, totally spent, beyond exhaustion, he collapsed on his belly in the warm sand and promptly passed out.

It was the sound of voices—sweet, lyrical female voices—that brought Geoff Chandler abruptly awake. He moaned softly, opened his eyes, and tried to roll over. He did not have the ability to do so. He summoned all the strength he could just to be able to raise his head to look around.

Three women stood there, silhouetted against a brilliantly colored sunset. Only a few feet away, they were chattering at each other, pointing toward him, as if he were some kind of odd sea creature that had washed up onto their beach. Maybe they were considering shoving him back into the sea or putting him out of his misery.

"Where am I?" Chandler groaned. He was sure that he was dreaming. That in his sad shape, his brain had made him the centerpiece in a bawdy fable. Washed ashore on some tropical isle. Greeted by a bevy of dusky-skinned young maidens who attempt to nurse him back to health in their own unique way.

"You have drifted ashore on Pengiki Besar Island," one of the women said. She spoke surprisingly good English and appeared to be the leader of the trio. She stepped a little closer to where Chandler lay. "Our village is across the island. Are you able to walk?"

Chandler tried to rise but immediately collapsed back onto the sand with a groan. In his present state, he would not be walking anywhere anytime soon.

"Wait. Rest a moment. We need to carry you to our village." She turned to one of the other women and engaged in a lightning-fast conversation in a language that Chandler did not recognize, one that involved plenty of hand motions to match whatever was being said. The woman who the leader had been speaking with nodded and scurried off through the trees, into the gathering darkness.

"I have sent Ayu to get the men," the woman explained. "They will carry you back. Here, drink this." She knelt down, helped him to roll over onto his back, and put a small cup of water to Chandler's lips. "Drink slowly so you do not get sick."

Despite the warning, Chandler gulped the refreshing liquid and almost choked. Then he drank more slowly.

With the cup emptied, he lay back with a sigh. "Who are you?" he asked hoarsely.

"My name is Sri Wahyuni," she answered. "My father, Hadi bin Sinaga, is the chieftain of Pengiki Besar. It is fortunate that my sisters and I were over on this side of the island checking our turtle nets. And that we cache water in a jug over here. You might well have died. So, who are you and why are you drifting across the sea only to become snagged by Pengiki Besar?"

Chandler started to tell her his story but quickly gave out. He listened as Sri Wahyuni explained where they were in the wide sea. Then a brightly painted outrigger pulled up on the beach. Four men hopped out and ran over to them.

"Our *jukung* has arrived," she explained. "Much easier to paddle to the village than to walk over to the other side of the island."

The men easily lifted Chandler into the boat. Wahyuni jumped in as they pushed off from the beach and raised the vessel's crab-claw sail. They employed the wind to quickly sail around the southern point of the island, along a foliage-lined shoreline, and then turned into a narrow entrance into a deep cove encircled by thick flowered bushes and palm trees. Beyond the vegetation, Chandler could just make out thatch huts of some kind. And maybe a herd of children watching them from behind the bushes.

As they came to a sliding stop on the beach, a much larger, ocean-going outrigger sailed into the tiny harbor and promptly dropped anchor.

"Father has returned early," Sri Wahyuni exclaimed. "Either the trip was a good one or we have a problem. One thing is for certain. We shall know which shortly."

17

A smoky pall hung in the air, shrouding Manila Bay like some evil man-made fog, effectively hiding the waning moon and any lingering stars. The stench of the stuff caused Brad Johnson to cough and sneeze as he climbed up to the *Tigerfish*'s bridge, even though they were still more than ten miles from the mouth of the bay and some forty miles from Manila or Cavite. Despite Manila having been declared an open city two weeks before, the Japanese continued their unrelenting daily air attacks. They had already left both the city and the naval yard little more than burning ruins. Though Manila was still too far away for the *Tigerfish* crew to see the damage from where they were, the fires illuminated the eastern horizon.

"Mr. Johnson," the port lookout, Seaman Ronnie Wasterman, called out, "I see the recognition signal out on the port beam."

Johnson turned his gaze to port. There it was: four quick flashes, pause, and then two quick flashes. He grabbed the Alidade light and flashed the answering challenge for this day. However, his reply message was a bit more complicated: short-long-long, pause, short-long, pause, long-long-long. Johnson was deliberate, making sure he got it correct the first time. Those guys were likely shell-shocked by now and not in the mood to tolerate too many mistaken attempts at responding to their challenge.

The answering message directed *Tigerfish* to heave to. The escort would be coming alongside shortly.

Indeed, the motor launch appeared out of the dark and smoke only a minute later. It pulled alongside the submarine as the Skipper climbed through the hatch. Schacter nodded to Johnson and frowned as he glanced down at the dirty gray boat coming out to meet them. The vessel looked like it seriously needed some maintenance. Or at least a good scrub down.

"God only knows what these guys have been going through lately," Schacter conceded. "I'll be happy to get in, make my case to the Commodore, and haul ass back to sea, to be honest with you." He rubbed the bandage on his left arm against the bridge coaming in an effort to relieve the itching.

"Where did the bandage come from, Skipper?" Johnson asked.

Schacter laughed self-consciously. "Doc says I have eczema. He's overreacting as usual. He insists that I keep it covered and treat it with some concoction called Zemo Ointment. And boy does it stink!"

The coxswain in the launch, wearing a khaki kapok and a dishpan tin helmet, yelled up to Johnson. "Sir, follow me exactly. Stay fifty yards astern of me the whole way. The channel is only fifty yards wide and mined to the gills on both sides."

"We'll probably follow your suggestion then," Johnson assured.

Schacter nodded and said, "Okay, Mr. Johnson, let's get a move on. I hear a cold beer calling my name."

Johnson blinked hard. Following that little motor launch from fifty yards astern through a narrow, twisting channel, in darkness and swirling smoke, was going to be a challenge in ship handling. A challenge where even a minor mistake could result in striking a maritime mine and losing the submarine in what were supposed to be friendly waters.

His mouth was dry when he answered, "Yes, sir." Then he ordered, "Ahead one-third, steer course zero-sixty-two."

The little two-vessel convoy slowly corkscrewed its way toward the island of Corregidor at the mouth of Manila Bay, and then on up into Mariveles Harbor. Since it was almost dawn by the time they were finally in the harbor, and since Japanese air raids lately had been punctually executed each day with the rising sun, the *Tigerfish* would submerge and nestle down onto the muddy bottom for the day. But before they hid beneath the waters of the bay, Wayne Schacter and XO Issac Sternman hopped off onto the motor launch. Brad Johnson was left to handle the submarine while the CO and XO motored over to the submarine tender *Canopus* to meet with the newly designated Commodore Submarines, Manila, Captain Roger Mount. Sternman clutched his small leather satchel that contained the carefully typed patrol report from the just completed run.

Capt. Mount, tall, balding, and tending to a bit overweight, had a well-earned reputation as a gruff, direct straightshooter, an officer with no sympathy for excuses or obfuscation. He was standing at the head of *Canopus*'s Jacob's ladder, ready to greet these members of his newly assumed submarine empire. After a quick, perfunctory introduction, he turned on his heels and led the pair up to his cabin on the tender's O-1 level.

Stepping into the spacious compartment, he waved toward the coffee urn and the small conference table as he said, "Grab a cup and a seat. Let's get started. We've got about an hour before our Nipponese friends come back around to wish us a fine morning. You may have noticed that the crew is putting the finishing touches on today's camouflage. Busy shifting from using foliage to now looking like a derelict, abandoned hulk, not worthy of their precious ordnance. That means nobody can be out on deck until the sun goes down."

Schacter nodded as he poured himself a cup of coffee. "Yes, sir. Not like we have anywhere to go. At least, until *Tigerfish* is back on the surface, and that'll be after sunset." He took the satchel from Isaac Sternman and removed the sheaf of papers that formed the patrol report. He handed them to Mount and then took a seat at the conference table to the Commodore's right. Sternman took the chair on the left.

The CO and XO stared across the table at each other as the Commodore silently scanned the report, occasionally nodding. Why did it feel like Mount was a particularly stern professor back at Annapolis, reviewing the test papers of a couple of struggling plebes? Schacter felt the itch of his eczema kick into high gear. It seemed to be spreading, creeping up his arm, even as they sat there.

When Mount got to the section about the unsuccessful torpedo attack, he slowly read it in detail, turned back and reread it, using a forefinger to follow each sentence. As he read, he started to slowly drum his class ring on the mahogany tabletop. Then Schacter noticed that Mount's neck was turning crimson from his collar up. The blush moved up the Commodore's face to his hairline. He most resembled a thermometer dropped into boiling water.

Both submarine officers swallowed hard.

"Bullshit!" Mount finally roared as he slapped the offending document down on the table. Pages scattered. "This is all crap! Schacter, you're trying to defend your bad shooting by blaming your failure on the torpedoes. That Mark 14 is a fine weapon. Ask me how I know that to be a fact." He did not wait for the question. "I spent five years in Newport working to develop and test the Mark 14. I should know!"

"Sir, we—" Schacter started, but Mount pounded his fist on the table, squelching any comment.

"I will not endorse this! You will go back and rewrite it. Either you can't shoot straight or the *Tigerfish* has some other problem. Either way, it must be fixed."

Wayne Schacter sat up ramrod stiff. He boldly returned Mount's livid stare and firmly stated, "Commodore, the shots were at a ninety-degree angle-on-the-bow at a thousand yards to the target. It would be near impossible to miss, even if we were incompetent. Which we are not. We went over the boat's systems and the remaining torpedoes thoroughly and found no issues. Everything checked out. With all due respect, I'm telling you that there is something seriously wrong with the Mark 14s."

"No there's not," Mount countered, simmering. "Now, get out of here. I want *Tigerfish* back at sea tomorrow morning. Pick up your orders on the way out. Find a place to hang out until dark and work on making that an accurate patrol report. We got guys who can type it up for you when you're satisfied you got it right. And if either of you try to blame a failed patrol on your torpedoes again, I'll have you both in the surface navy in a red-hot minute. Meanwhile, you'd better work on your aim or I'll find somebody who can shoot straight."

With that he stood and waved the pair toward the door. The meeting was over. The coffee in their cups had not even gotten cold yet but it had certainly become very bitter.

As they walked out, Schacter turned to Sternman and said, "I'm going to go find sick bay on this tub. Get a real doctor to look at this eczema rash stuff so I can think straight." He disappeared down the passageway.

∞

Stan Ward sat back, put his hands behind his head, and stared up at the rock "ceiling." This far back in Malinta Tunnel's Lateral Six, the walls, floor, and low ceiling were all solid rock, which, along with plenty more rock and dirt of Corregidor Island, almost completely isolated Ward from the outside world. He had no idea if it was night or day, sunny or raining. He was in his own little world. A world of intercepted Japanese messages, a large map on the stone wall covered with colored pins and string, and an endless flow of strong black coffee. The work that occupied most of his time and attention, trying to break the JN-25B code, was going slowly. Frustratingly slowly. It still typically took him several weeks just to break the headers on intercepted Imperial Japanese Navy traffic. Ward calculated that they were gleaning useful intelligence from maybe ten percent of each message.

On the other hand, his signal traffic analysis was progressing. Using his pushpins and knitting yarn to track and predict enemy warship movement, he had been able to warn of the Japanese invasion at Lingayen Gulf at the end of December. Unfortunately, General MacArthur disregarded the warning and thus was unable to mount a defense. The Filipino troops were undertrained and ill-equipped. Then they were outmaneuvered, outnumbered, and outfought. Those that survived the battle either fled south or simply disappeared into the jungle. By the end of December, a full-scale retreat to the Bataan Peninsula was well underway. That meant the battle for the Philippines was effectively lost. From his vantage point in Lateral Six, Stan Ward could see the inevitable defeat coming, but no one was listening to that prognostication either.

Then he watched with interest as more and more of his colored pins undeniably moved farther south, down toward the Dutch East Indies. The

Imperial Japanese Navy was on the move again. Ward studied his maps, pins, and strings, until the story he pieced together was a virtual certainty, not just an educated guess. He could see that they formed a rough arrow that pointed down past the South China Sea, on toward Sumatra, Borneo, and Java. Maybe even Australia, beyond those islands.

Using the little bits of intelligence that he could scrape from the ULTRA decrypts and adding that to his signal traffic analysis process, Ward put together a rough order-of-battle of the ships that he could reasonably identify. The list was long and alarming. Half a dozen heavy cruisers, at least ten light cruisers, thirty destroyers, at least one carrier, and a seaplane tender.

He had to get a warning out to someone in the Asiatic Fleet who might put some stock in his analysis. Ward sat down at his typewriter and began to peck away. It took most of the day—or was it the night?—and a wastepaper basket full of mistakes before he ripped the last page out of the machine and hurried off in search of Ollie Oglethorpe.

The Navy Commander was sitting in the walled-off area with his team of cryptologists and all their secret gear. As usual, Oglethorpe was wearing a tattered old cardigan and slippers, and he was wreathed in a cloud of sweet-scented pipe smoke. He quickly leafed through Ward's document, went back and read some parts again, then studied the conclusion on the last page. Finally, he looked up at Ward and asked, "Are you sure, Stan?"

Ward nodded and said, "Yes. Damn sure."

"Good enough for me," Oglethorpe said as he pulled out his old Parker fountain pen and scratched his endorsement on the cover page.

To: Admiral Thomas C. Hart

From:CDR Ollie Oglethorpe

Enclosed is classified ULTRA. This analysis is most important. I judge it highly reliable. Urge you to act on it soonest.

— Ollie

"Wow, Ollie!" Ward exclaimed. "I didn't know that you were on a first name basis with Commander, Asiatic Fleet."

"Yep." Oglethorpe smiled slyly. "He calls me Ollie and I call him sir. We were shipmates on the old *Mississippi*. Now, we need to get this down to his headquarters at Surabaya." He looked at his watch and nodded. "Just enough time. We're expecting a B-17 flying in supplies and picking up some wounded tonight. Get your butt over to Mariveles Airfield. Looks like our old Flying Fortress chauffeur friend Greg Tillson is leading the mission."

The boat ride over to Mariveles was crowded. Half a dozen young Army officers clutching the latest instructions to their battalions from MacArthur's headquarters crowded the little launch. A Navy nurse escorting a badly wounded sailor on a stretcher took up most of the rest of the space. The only way Ward got on board was to crowd in next to the coxswain and substitute for his line-handler.

Thankfully, Ollie had arranged for a jeep to meet him at the pier. He shared the ride with the nurse and wounded sailor. He glanced at his watch as they bounced down the rutted dirt road. It was going to be close. Very close.

Sure enough, he could just see the bomber making its final approach. The jeep's driver had the old shot-up jeep on two wheels as he skidded through the gate and out onto the airfield.

"Gotta hurry, Lieutenant," the driver grunted as he shifted gears. "These birds are on the ground just long enough to toss off their load of bullets and bandages and grab up all the wounded and VIPs they can stuff on board. Then they are out of here. That minimizes the chance for the Japs to hit one of them."

Ward recognized *Little Girl*, patched up and much the worse for the wear, but still looking the part of a proud warbird. The plane braked to a halt fifty yards away from where the jeep was approaching. Greg Tillson left the props turning as supplies were dumped out through the hatches and the side gun ports. A dozen people waited off to one side, including three on stretchers, ready to get on board their flight out to safety.

Ward apologized for not offering to help as he hopped out of the jeep and ran as quickly as he could manage over to *Little Girl*, leaving the nurse and driver to carry the stretcher over to join the other three wounded men.

Ward pulled himself up through the forward boarding hatch and stuck his head into the cockpit.

"Hey, Greg, what time's dinner on this flight?" He had to yell to be heard above the rumble of the four Wright Cyclone engines. Tillson grinned and gave him a quick wave.

"Check with the flight attendant, my friend," Tillson shot back. "I'm just in charge of aiming this old bird to where she needs to go. You riding with us today?"

"No, no. I just need you to hand deliver this envelope to Admiral Hart. Personally. Not an aide or messenger. Personally. It's very highly classified and really, really important."

He handed the envelope containing his analysis to Tillson. The young pilot took it, folded it in half, and stuffed it inside his flight jacket.

"Since you put it that way. Good to see you, too, Stan," he said with a grin. "Now, unless you want a free flight down to Surabaya, you'd best get your ass off my airplane."

Ward had just enough time to climb down from the plane and limped—the injuries that kept him out of submarines prevented him from doing much more than a quick limp—back to the jeep when he heard the roar of Greg Tillson shoving the throttles of his B-17 all the way forward. He watched as *Little Girl* shot down the gravel runway and lifted smoothly away. Ward could still hear those Wright Cyclones well after the plane had disappeared into the ebony night sky.

∞

Trip MacLean was fascinated by the tiny village hidden on the tiny tropical island, just one of the thousands of rocks and coral atolls that dotted the Karimata Straits, the broad, shallow stretch of water connecting the South China Sea on the north with the Java Sea to the south. Standing on the village's tiny dock, he stared out at placid turquoise-blue water that stretched out to the horizon. In his mind, though, he could picture the peaceful sea beyond that horizon cluttered with Japanese warships. It did not take a strategic naval genius to figure out that the Empire's latest efforts, bearing the innocent sounding title of the Great East-Asian Co-Prosperity Sphere, would come pouring through the Karimata Straits in an effort to grab the Dutch East Indies' vast troves of oil, rubber, and other raw materials, all to feed its ravenous war machine. He knew he was standing looking out at a critical choke point for this war.

A soft female voice broke into MacLean's thoughts. "Father asked that you come join him at our *bolae*...that is, our house."

Trip smiled at the pretty young woman. Sri's bright orange sarong perfectly offset her raven-black hair in a very pleasing way. *In another place, at another time*...He shook off his typical thoughts when in the presence of such a beauty.

Sri Wahyuni smiled shyly and waved him toward a wood and thatch structure built on stilts at the water's edge. He followed her into the cool shade provided by the bolae's broad, overhanging porch.

Hadi bin Sinaga sat in front of a compact shortwave receiver. He had a pair of headphones pressed to his ears. Hadi looked up and smiled as the pair walked into view. Removing the headset, he waved MacLean to a cushion lying on the woven bamboo floor covering. As the marooned submariner plopped down and attempted to bend his legs into a comfortable position, Sri Wahyuni disappeared somewhere into the bolae's dark interior.

"Welcome to my home," the islander said.

"Hadi bin Sinaga, I want to again thank you for rescuing me and my crew," MacLean said as he shifted his weight again in an effort to get comfortable on the cushion.

The pirate/fisherman/freedom fighter waved his hand in dismissal. Then he laughed and said, "*Tau laingnge* MacLean, would you be more comfortable in a chair?" He clapped his hands. From out of nowhere, one of his crew produced a chair and placed it for MacLean to sit on.

"It seems that we have suddenly become a haven for shipwrecked sailors," Hadi told him with a chuckle. "My daughter found an Englishman washed up on the beach on the other side of the island just last night. The man says that he is a Royal Navy Lieutenant and that his name is Geoff Chandler, off of the *Prince of Wales*. He has had a rough time of it. It will be a few days before he is up and around. Thankfully, other than a really bad sunburn and some dehydration, he will survive. Our medical capabilities for anything more severe are quite limited."

"Interesting. We'll have to compare notes with Mr. Chandler and make reports to our navies about our survival. Loved ones will soon hear we are lost in action and probably fear the worst." MacLean pointed toward the shortwave receiver. "The radio way out here is a bit unexpected. Business or pleasure?"

"From the Dutch," Hadi answered with a smile. "We do get news and music, at night mostly. But they also send us intelligence on Japanese shipping. I have another set, both a receiver and a transmitter, on the sandeq potangnga, when we want to talk, to report our own observations. We take the boat out to a different spot each time we transmit. That way, the Japanese cannot use their direction finders to locate our island or associate the signals with our homes here."

Through a window, MacLean could see a large room. Surprisingly, one whole wall consisted of bookshelves. And they were full of books.

Hadi noticed the look on the American submariner's face. "Yes, my personal collection. But it serves as the library for the others on our island. When I visit ports, I try to find bookstores. Or libraries. Sometimes I steal them. Most times I pay for them. Sri has read all of them. I've read maybe half. My anti-Nippon efforts have greatly restricted my reading, I'm afraid."

"Very impressive."

Hadi offered MacLean a cup of jamu. The American gratefully accepted it, took a healthy swallow, and sighed. "Almost as good as a gin and tonic."

Hadi laughed. "I'm afraid that your taste for alcohol will not be requited for some time. As long as you remain a guest on our island. We are good Muslims here on Pengiki Besar. You will not find any gin. And what you call 'tonic water' we only use to avoid the malaria."

Hadi bin Sinaga settled back on his cushion, clearly changing the subject. "I have a little proposition for you. With all the Japanese in the area, it is going to be a while before we can safely move you and your men down to Surabaya. The newly arrived Englishman, either. Meanwhile, the Dutch are asking us to double our efforts as 'freedom fighters.' I can acquire the use of another sandeq potangnga, but I do not have the crew required to man it. If we add in your dozen men and perhaps ask the British naval officer who washed upon our beach to join us, we would then be able to crew the two boats."

It was MacLean's turn to laugh. "The Pengiki Besar Pirates. The scourge of the Karimata Straits, ready to strike fear into the hearts of every sailor in the IJN war fleet." Then Trip got serious. "Hadi, my men don't have any idea how to sail a sandeq potangnga. Give them a submarine and watch them go. I've sailed racing yachts all my life thanks to the good fortune of my dad, but even I would be hard pressed to sail one of your vessels."

Hadi bin Sinaga nodded, a slight smile playing at his lips. "The Pengiki Besar Pirates? I like it. Perhaps we should acquire one of those skull-and-crossbones flags the English pirates flew on their vessels back in the days of the Spanish Main. At any rate, I have a suggestion that I believe would work well. We mix your crew in with mine. Your men learn to sail from my men. My men can learn from your men how to use the American weapons that the Dutch gave us."

Maclean finished his jamu, smacked his lips, smiled, and said, "When do we sail?"

"As soon as the sun drops below the horizon and night makes us as nearly invisible as it can."

18

The *Wolffish*, its periscope barely exposed above the wavetops, cautiously approached the coast of the Japanese Home Islands. The headlands of Shikoku were just visible to the northwest. The Bungo-suido—Bungo Straits in English—opened out to the west. They formed a very busy shipping artery that led directly to the Inland Sea and the manufacturing heart of Japan. Whether it was ships built in Kure, manufactured goods from Kobe, or tanks and heavy equipment from Fukuyama, it all necessarily flowed out through the Bungo Straits to create havoc wherever Japan sought to extend its growing empire.

Wolffish was there to disrupt that vital flow.

"Mark this bearing," Alphonse Dinnacetti called out. His eye was on the eyepiece for the submarine's attack periscope.

QM1 Clancy Obrien, the periscope assistant, read the dial at the bottom of the periscope eye-box and called out, "Bearing three-zero-one."

"Ship, hull down, on that bearing," Dinnacetti announced. "Looks like a maru, but he's too far out and it's too damn foggy to say for sure."

The submarine CO slowly swung the periscope through a full 360-degree circle. He stepped back and ordered, "Down scope." As the shiny silver tube lowered into the periscope well, he said, "That maru is the only ship I can see. But we got a dense fog bank across the entrance to the straits. I can't see more than a couple of miles in that direction. They may have a couple of dozen destroyers waiting up in there in all that pea soup for all I know."

"What's your plan, Skipper?" Jim Shelton prodded his CO, but he already had a pretty good idea of the answer.

Dinnacetti looked at the navigation chart, grinned, and ordered, "Officer-of-the-Deck, come left to course two-five-zero, make your depth two hundred feet, speed ahead full. I think we'll just sink the SOB. But first, we need to get out in front of him."

The OOD was Fred Wurster. He jumped to give the orders that caused the submarine to dive deeper into the sea and sprint ahead to the southwest. Meanwhile, Dinnacetti took his dividers and walked off the distance on the chart to where he wanted his boat to go.

"Freddy, run at full for forty minutes, then we'll slow and go up to see where the maru is by then," the Skipper explained. Turning to Shelton, he continued, "XO, here's the plan. We'll get out in front of the maru and then close him while we're at periscope depth. I plan to shoot when I have him broad at a range under a thousand yards. Make tubes one and two ready in all respects. Set twenty-foot run depth and speed to HIGH. We will shoot tube one with tube two as the backup. That close, this should be about as close to a sure shot as we'll ever get."

After precisely forty minutes, Wurster slowed the submarine and coasted up to sixty feet. They had just slowed to four knots when the sound man called out, "I have contact on bearing two-nine-six." He held his headset tightly to his ears for a few seconds and then confirmed, "Heavy screw beat, single screw. Sounds like our maru."

Dinnacetti stepped back up to the attack periscope. "Up scope." He slapped down the training handles as it emerged from the scope well and rode the thing up. Then he swung around to the reported bearing to see the maru exactly where he expected the vessel to be. No zigzagging. Apparently, the Japanese were not yet convinced US Navy submarines could or would be operating this close to the Home Islands. The Skipper immediately called out, "Bearing, mark," then, not waiting for Obrien to announce the bearing, he said, "Range, mark," and then, "Down scope."

As the periscope disappeared, Obrien announced, "Bearing two-nine-three, range nine hundred."

Dinnacetti then calmly said, "Angle-on-the-bow port seventy." He grinned again and said, "He's right where we want him. This will be a shooting observation."

Shelton carefully looked over the torpedo data computer to make sure everything was set before he confidently said, "Ready!"

Dinnacetti ordered the periscope raised again. He swung around to the bearing for the maru and carefully lined the crosshairs up with the bridge on the unsuspecting target vessel. "Bearing, mark."

Obrien called out, "Bearing two-nine-zero."

Shelton checked the bearing input to the TDC and called, "Set." He then turned to the firing panel and flipped up the switch to select tube one. Shelton pushed the firing key, a plunger topped with a round brass plate curved to fit the hand. He then ordered, "Shoot tube one!"

The *whoomp-whoosh* of the torpedo in tube one being flushed out into the sea announced that the attack was underway. A shot had been fired.

Shelton hit the button on the stopwatch and said, "Forty seconds, torpedo run."

Dinnacetti looked down the trail of bubbles from his launched torpedo and saw that it was traveling perfectly to intersect the still-unaware ship. But even if someone on the target saw the approaching torpedo now, there was nothing they could do about it.

The CO was counting off the seconds when the sound man yelled, "New contact, bearing three-five-four. Heavy screw beat, multiple screws. Sounds like a warship!"

The CO spun the scope around in the direction of the new contact. He saw at once a large gray ship emerging from the fog.

"Looks like a cruiser, maybe a battleship," he announced. Neither was a good thing.

Then they heard an explosion on the bearing of the maru. Dinnacetti spun the periscope around in time to see a cloud of fire and smoke erupting from the stern of the targeted merchant ship. One fish, one hit.

However, there was no time to watch it sink. Not even time to assess if it might need another shot to finish it off, to send it and its likely load of war materiel to the bottom. The cruiser or battleship or whatever it was had now become the primary target and there was not much time for a shot on the new arrival.

"Observation on the battleship," Dinnacetti announced. He swung the periscope back around to the north. When he saw the huge grayish wall of steel steaming directly toward them, he called out, "Bearing mark, range mark, down scope."

Obrien announced, "Bearing three-four-seven, range three thousand."

Dinnacetti said, "Angle-on-the bow port twenty. He's closing fast. Looks like he's headed for the *maru*. I aim to stick two fish in him when he's broad at a range of fifteen hundred yards. Make tubes three and four ready. Set run depth twenty feet, high speed."

"Observation on the battleship," Dinnacetti said. The conning tower fell silent. "Up scope." He rode the periscope up and swung it to center on the target. "Bearing, mark." A slight pause. "Range, mark." Then, "Down scope."

"Bearing three-four-zero, range two-five-hundred," Obrien called out.

"Angle-on-the-bow port twenty-seven. He's picked up speed and still heading for the maru. Probably going to pick up survivors since he has no idea where we are, assuming we've left the scene by now. Damn good thing, too. He's a *Myoko*-class heavy cruiser. It's gonna irritate the Emperor if we sink one of his—"

A sudden yelp from the sonar operator interrupted the Skipper's pronouncement.

"Skipper, I'm hearing several more screws to the north!" the sound man hollered. "They sound light and fast. Best bet, destroyers!"

"Getting crowded up there. Up scope for a look around," Dinnacetti ordered. As the scope once again rose out of the well, he grabbed the training handles and began to swing it around in a circle. He stopped at a point and said, "Bearing, mark!"

Clancy Obrien immediately announced, "Three-five-three."

Dinnacetti swung the scope just a bit to the right and said, "Bearing, mark."

Again, Obrien announced, "Three-five-seven."

Then, for a third time, "Bearing, mark!"

"Zero-zero-three."

"Down scope." Dinnacetti stood, stretched his back, and said, "Destroyers on those three bearings heading this way. Bet they're pissed. But we got just enough time to shoot the cruiser, then we skedaddle."

Turning to Shelton, he asked, "XO, we have a shooting solution?"

Shelton's eyes were wide. Then he looked at what was tracking on the torpedo data computer before he answered, "I think so, Skipper. Recommend a spread of four."

"Alright. Up scope for a shooting observation," the CO directed.

The periscope rose smoothly upward until the top was out of the water. Dinnacetti put the crosshairs directly on the cruiser's bridge and said, "Bearing, mark!"

Shelton selected tube three on the firing panel, pressed the firing key, and ordered, "Shoot tube three!"

Whoomp-whoosh!

The torpedo in tube three was on its way. Shelton timed out five seconds, then shot tube four. "Shoot tube four!"

Whoomp-whoosh!

The Mark 14 torpedo in tube four had been launched. Only a few seconds later, just as the command to fire the third weapon was about to be given, there was a tremendous deafening explosion, near enough to the *Wolffish* that it rocked the submarine mightily. Several men were knocked to the deck. Dinnacetti, still looking out the periscope, saw a tall plume of water only a couple of hundred feet from the bow of the *Wolffish*. He yelled, "Premature! Damn first weapon prematured! Check fire, XO. Report any damage or casualties. It's time for us to vacate the premises! Down scope!" Turning to Fred Wurster, he ordered, "Make your depth three hundred feet. Come around and steer course zero-seven-zero, ahead flank. Rig ship for depth charge!"

The *Wolffish* dove into the deep and turned to the east as the crew strapped down everything that they could. Everything that might become a flying missile if a depth charge exploded too close.

The sound man yelled, "Destroyers picking up speed! Zero bearing rate! They're headed this way!"

Dinnacetti, sweat pouring off his forehead, turned to Shelton and said,

"XO, let's run for ten minutes, then slow to two knots and slink on out of here. We know when we're not welcome."

Shelton noticed that even though the Skipper's words were calm, even almost jovial, his hands were shaking. The XO chose not to say anything. He just nodded and confirmed with, "Sounds like a plan, Skipper."

The first string of depth charges—four detonations in total—rattled the submarine brutally, slamming into its hull like someone hitting a metal barrel with a sledgehammer. With people inside the barrel. Several light bulbs shattered. Electrical breakers popped open. Cork dust hung heavy in the air, almost as thick as the fog bank across the strait entrance above.

Then all was silent.

But not for long. Another string of four depth charges hammered the submarine. Just as the reverbs from that string died down, another string of four more detonated. Maybe even closer than the previous ones. Every man aboard knew the next round could be right on top of them. Or, even worse, just beneath them, their most vulnerable point to such a pounding.

"They're taking turns working us over," Shelton mumbled to Dinnacetti. Everyone spoke in the lightest of whispers, as if they were afraid that the Japanese were listening and their conversation might give away the boat's position.

Dinnacetti nodded, and then he asked, "Water depth?"

"Chart says one hundred fathoms," Shelton answered.

Another string of four depth charges lambasted the submarine. Men grabbed whatever they could to remain upright. Paint chips fell like hail, and cork dust hung even heavier in the air, making it hard to breathe. At least when they were not holding their breath in anticipation of the next blasts. The air in the sub had quickly become strength-sapping hot and humid. All the fans had long since been secured.

"Fred, make your depth four hundred feet," Dinnacetti whispered.

Wurster turned and looked questioningly at him. "Captain, you know test depth is three hundred feet."

"Yes, I know," the CO replied. "It's time we tested just how good Mare Island was at welding the hull of this boat together. Make your depth four hundred feet and see if she springs any leaks."

The next string of four explosions was a little farther away, and, thankfully, not quite so jarring. The enemy destroyers likely had their depth charges set to explode at no more than three hundred feet, never expecting a US Navy submarine to go any deeper.

It took four hours for *Wolffish* to get far enough away so that the explosions were only distant rumbling noises in the water. They had moved back above test depth after an hour, apparently with no damage from the intense pressure of sea water at that depth. After six hours and plenty of wasted ordnance, the Jap destroyers finally gave up. The ocean was once again quiet.

The night was pitch black and Japan lay a mere thirty miles to the north of them when the *Wolffish* finally surfaced to recharge the depleted batteries and to flush out the fetid air, replacing it with cold, fresh sea air. Jim Shelton and Alphonse Dinnacetti sat at the wardroom table behind mugs of coffee, rehashing the day's adventure.

The XO said, "Partial success, Skipper. At least we got the maru."

"Didn't see him go down," Dinnacetti answered glumly, shaking his head. "We can only claim him as damaged. That I saw for damn sure. I wish we'd had time to get a photo through the scope, but we didn't. Or maybe we'll claim a probable sunk, but that might be stretching it. Depends on what kind of mood the Squadron Commodore is in, what he'll be willing to endorse. But we know we got the target with one fish. Damn good shootin', I say." He took a sip of coffee, a deep frown taking over his face. "Truth is, Jim, I'm more interested in what happened when we shot at the cruiser. What could have made that damn weapon premature. Not only did it mean a miss, but it also pointed those damn destroyers right at us. We're damn lucky that didn't turn out real sorrowful for us, you know."

Shelton shook his head. "No idea, Skipper. Solution was good. That torpedo checked out fine before we shot it, just like all the others did. We just ought to thank our lucky stars that the thing ran a couple of hundred yards before it went boom. Think what would have happened if it had gone up while it was still in the tube."

"I know. That would've been sorrowful, too. 'Eternal Patrol' for *Wolffish* and her fine crew. Praise the Lord for small miracles," Dinnacetti said, making the sign of the cross. "We just got to make sure the patrol report talks enough about the premature. That can't get lost in the paperwork. Somebody needs to know."

Shelton nodded, then grinned. "These fish keep malfunctioning, they'll have us launching attacks on the surface with deck guns and tossing hand grenades."

The Skipper rubbed his unshaven chin. "Deck guns? Not a bad idea in the right situation. Sure a better chance to do damage to the enemy than some of the torpedoes we're carrying these days." He took another big swallow of coffee and smiled. "But be quiet about the grenades, okay, XO? Somebody back at HQ might hear you."

∞

Trip MacLean was enjoying a deep dreamless slumber, the first really restful night that he had experienced in a very long time.

Then Hadi bin Sinaga rudely shook him awake. "It's time, *tau laingnge* MacLean."

MacLean groggily came awake, muttering, "Whaat?... Where am I? Time for what?" He slowly rose, yawning, and swung his legs out to sit on the makeshift cot. Sleep-drugged and bleary-eyed, he cocked his head and looked up at the Indonesian freedom fighter.

"Hurry, *tau laingnge* MacLean," Hadi coaxed. "Our second sandeq potangnga has arrived and the Dutch coast watchers just reported several Japanese freighters heading into the Karimata Straits. If we sail immediately, we can catch them tonight before moonrise."

"What is this *tau laingnge* that you keep calling me?" MacLean asked as he grabbed his clothes and began to get dressed.

"It's an honorific in Buginese, our language," Hadi answered. "It translates as 'foreign visitor.'"

MacLean laughed. "Well, if I'm about to go out raiding with you, I hardly classify as a *tau laingnge*."

Hadi nodded and thoughtfully rubbed his stubbly chin. "True, true. We need a better title for you then." He thought for a few moments while

MacLean tied his shoes. Then he said, "How about *pappirate mappoji*? It translates as 'honorable pirate.'"

Trip MacLean laughed and slapped Hadi on the back. "*Pappirate mappoji*. 'Honorable pirate.' Back in high school, we would have called that an oxymoron. But I like it! *Pappirate mappoji* MacLean it is."

The two paddled the little jukung out to where the two larger vessels floated easily at anchor. MacLean noticed at once that the Americans had already divided themselves up between the two trimarans. Chief Anthony Watson, Doc Jones, Red Gray, and Thurgood Williams stood looking over the gunwale of the first boat while Tommy Hilligas along with Billy Mutter and Igor Tomlivich, the two machinists who had survived the sinking of their submarine, were on the other one. Hadi explained that the Brit naval officer was eager to join the bunch but would require a few more days of recovery time after his ordeal.

Then MacLean spotted a couple of sign boards that had been added to the two sailing ships. One said *PB Seddi* and the other said *PB Duwa* in big gold letters, painted with a flourish onto the black sign boards.

Hadi bin Sinaga saw what had grabbed the American's interest and laughed. "Since we now have two ships in the Pengiki Besar Pirate Navy, we need to name them. I wish I could tell you that we have been creative in that process, but their names are *PB One* and *PB Two*. You and I and Chief Watson will sail on the *Seddi* while Bintang will sail on the *Duwa* with your Ensign Hilligas."

Bintang, MacLean had learned, was the equivalent to Sinaga's Executive Officer in their little dozen-man navy.

Hadi jumped out of the small jukung, up onto the *Seddi*. The two black-hulled sailing ships set their large red sails and quickly left the island of Pengiki Besar behind. It was picturesque, like an image off a travel magazine cover, MacLean observed. They headed briskly out to the northeast, toward what they knew to be the main Japanese shipping lanes around the western side of Borneo. It was a beautiful tropical day with a light wind blowing from the southwest, only a few clouds in the sky, and not another ship in sight.

"It is time to test our weapons," Hadi declared when they were all well out of range of the island.

Sailing the *Seddi* to within shouting distance of the *Duwa*, he yelled orders to Bintang. Soon, the men were scurrying to break out an impressive hodge-podge of weapons from their hiding places on the two sandeq potangngas. MacLean recognized the Thompson submachine guns and several ancient Mannlicher rifles. A pair of Browning M2 .50 caliber heavy machine guns, one on each boat, came as a welcome surprise, as did a brace of Lewis guns. Those were Great War vintage but very effective light machine guns. The submariners were familiar with all of these weapons. But then MacLean spied a contraption that he had never seen before.

"What's that thing?" he asked as he looked it over. As near as he could tell, it was a short pipe mounted on a heavy steel rod and then a small baseplate. A lever halfway up the rod appeared to be some sort of trigger.

"I see that our knee mortar has caught your interest," Hadi said. "Japanese. It will shoot a hand grenade over five hundred meters. Not really very accurate, but it makes an impressive boom. And if we somehow land a few of the grenades on the decks of our targets, they can do some damage as well."

The men spent a couple of hours firing the weapons, checking their accuracy, and cleaning them, before carefully re-stowing them and their associated ammunition where they could be reached quickly.

The sun dropped below the horizon a little before 1900 local time. That allowed them to enjoy a typical brief but impressive tropical sunset, a quick display of yellows, oranges, and brilliant reds on the horizon for a few seconds, and then complete darkness, as if someone had slammed the drapes shut.

The sun had only been down for an hour when a lookout on *Duwa* yelled, pointing toward the north. A small freighter with no lights showing was steaming toward them, just like the coast watchers had told them to expect. The ship was making no more than five knots but belched out a tremendous cloud of smoke from its stack. It could only be an ancient coal-burning freighter, a vessel too slow to keep up with any convoy and not valuable enough to rate an escort of its own.

Hadi sent the *Seddi* on a wide sweeping course to pass ahead of the Japanese freighter, then approach it from the freighter's starboard side while Bintang pointed the *Duwa*'s sharp bow directly at the oncoming freighter. The two attackers used their significant speed advantage and surprise to suddenly pull up alongside the freighter. Hadi lobbed a grenade from the knee mortar up onto the freighter's deck while both boats sprayed its bridge with machine gun fire. There was only one brief burst of return fire that did not hit anything, then no more.

Hadi eased the *Seddi* alongside the hapless ship and signaled for MacLean and his team of shipwrecked submariners/Pengiki Besar Pirates to climb up onto the freighter. MacLean, clutching his Thompson and ready to plug anyone who moved, trotted across the freighter's main deck and climbed up to the tiny wheelhouse. It was a shambles. The .50 caliber rounds had torn through the thin steel bulkheads as well as through the men who had been on watch there. The master and the helmsman were both sprawled on the deck, lying in pools of their own blood, clearly dead. One deck hand, apparently slightly wounded, cowered in an after corner, shaking violently but unable or unwilling to move.

The ship was theirs. The Pengiki Besar Pirates had their first victory on the high seas.

It took a couple of hours to herd the rest of the surviving crewmen into a lifeboat and shove them off, search the cargo for anything of value, and then set the scuttle charges to sink the vessel. MacLean expressed his appreciation to Hadi for not just executing the freighter's crew.

"We are not savages. Unlike the Japanese. These men are not warriors. They will survive with the supplies we gave them and being adrift in an area of high traffic," the islander said. "We do not know who their rescuer will be, friend or foe. Nor do we care."

The freighter's cargo seemed to mostly be bags of rice and many boxes of dried, salted fish. Supplies for Japanese troops, no doubt. But they did find several crates of small arms and ammunition. However, Tommy Hilligas made the most important find. The ancient freighter had a modern radio room with an almost new HF receiver and transmitter. And there, on the desk by the radio equipment, were the latest Japanese merchant codes. All they needed now was someone who could read and speak Japanese and they could easily track ships that were in these waters to support the Japanese bases that were springing up all around the region. And being sent back to the Home Islands loaded with agricultural cargo and raw materials.

The two sandeq potangngas were a mile away from the freighter when the scuttling charges detonated. There was a cloud of grayish-brown smoke that poured out of the stack to punctuate the blast. It took twenty minutes for the freighter to finally slip beneath the waves and plunge toward the sea floor.

Then the Pengiki Besar Pirates turned and headed toward home.

19

The USS *Tigerfish* slowly cruised along twenty miles west of Palawan, the westernmost island of the Philippine Archipelago. It had been very quiet since they slipped out of Manila Bay almost a week before. Quiet both because the South China Sea around them was practically empty of enemy shipping and because neither the CO nor the XO was in any mood for joviality. Even the meals were solemn affairs, eaten mostly in silence. Gloom generally permeated the atmosphere up and down the length of the submarine.

Then *Tigerfish* received the ULTRA message a little after midnight as they were running on the surface, recharging the batteries. RM3 Eric Riegel copied the encrypted message and promptly handed it over to the CO. It took Wayne Schacter more than an hour, and several aborted tries, before he finally had a decrypted message that made some kind of sense. Serious sense.

Clutching the sheet of paper, Schacter hunched over the navigation chart in control, glancing from one to the other, making sure of the numbers. The dim red light, the only illumination in the darkened compartment, made seeing the chart difficult, but it preserved everyone's night vision.

Schacter took his dividers and walked off the distance down to the

Balabac Strait and then on into a point in the Sulu Sea a couple of miles west of Cagayan de Sulu. Then he grabbed the nautical slide rule and spun the dial.

Looking up at Sternman, he said, "Two hundred forty miles total. We run at flank until sunup, dive, and run at six knots all day. Surface and run flank again at sunset. My calculations, we arrive at about 2330 tonight."

The XO nodded, "I agree. That gets us in the area an hour early. Time to look around before we get down to business."

Schacter reached up for the 7MC microphone and said, "Officer-of-the-Deck, Captain. Come to ahead flank. Steer course two-one-zero." Turning to Sternman, he continued, "We should be just short of the Balabac Straits when we dive at first light. Slink through the Straits submerged at six knots. Then we make the final dash when the sun goes down. I want the fish all backhauled and checked over by the end of the day. And the TDC checked out. No glitches tonight. Get the COB busy with the rest of the torpedomen to get that done."

Sternman nodded and answered, "Yes, sir. Right on it." But he was already talking to the Skipper's back. Schacter had marched out of the control room by then. A bit of a smile flashed across the XO's face. The Skipper was starting to sound more like the confident warrior that had left Pearl Harbor three months before. But the Skipper's first stop was to see the corpsman, Doc Mahon. He sighed with relief as Doc slathered on a fresh coat of Zemo's Ointment and zinc oxide.

Then the *Tigerfish* charged ahead through the night.

∞

Kaigun Chusa Akito Saito watched the sun rise in the east. For a moment, the red orb on the horizon looked almost exactly like the rising sun on the empire's distinctive battle flag. The *Kasumi* had joined up with Rear Admiral Shoji Nishimura's 4th Destroyer Flotilla. The sea, all the way out to the horizon, was dotted with ships. There were a dozen destroyers, including the *Kasumi*, herding twenty marus, all laden with troops, weapons, and supplies for the upcoming invasion of Dutch Borneo, another bold thrust south. And there, in the center of the formation, the cruiser *Naka* sailed serenely.

Saito's heart swelled with pride. He was commanding a warship entrusted with a task that was vital to his nation's entire war effort. Some were saying that this invasion was the real reason that the *Daihon'ei*, the Imperial General Headquarters, had initiated this war. The oil wells at Tarakan, and then those at Balikpapan, were critical to Japan, and especially to the Imperial Navy. Petroleum was the lifeblood of the IJN. The *Kasumi* was guarding the troops that would soon seize the precious oil that colonialists, European corporations, and rich capitalists had been stealing from Pacific Rim nations for centuries. All the 4th Destroyer Flotilla needed to do was to evade the few American submarines that were known to still be in the area. But those submarines had proven to be mostly ineffective so far.

Saito allowed himself a quick smile as he sipped his tea and watched his men operate his ship. All was well.

Kaigun Chui Kato, standing watch as the Officer-of-the-Deck, walked over to where Saito stood on the starboard bridge wing and snapped to attention. "Captain, the flagship has signaled to change course to zero-eight-zero and to slow to three knots while the seaplane tenders conduct flight operations."

Saito nodded and told him, "Make it so."

It was good to have the two seaplane tenders along as part of the invasion force. Their Aichi E13A seaplanes effectively extended the Admiral's eyes—and his reach—out to several hundred miles in all directions. Of course, that came at the expense of slowing the invasion force while the seaplanes were launched, and then, later, retrieved.

In the grand scheme, the *Sanuki Maru* and the *Sagara Maru* having to slow down really did not matter when all the marus they were shepherding had slowed the entire flotilla down to about six knots anyway. He looked at the clock on the after bulkhead and then glanced at the navigation charts. They were due to rendezvous with an oiler in the lee of Cagayan de Sulu at first light tomorrow to take on fuel. At this pace, they should just make it on time.

His teacup was empty. First thought was to go below and refill it, maybe get some *dango* dumplings. But no. He was the Captain of the ship. He would dispatch a sailor to fetch tea and sweets.

Meanwhile, he would remain there on the bridge wing of his warship, enjoying the clean air and the promise offered by the first early hours of another successful day in service to his Emperor.

∞

After sailing through the Balabac Strait without any excitement, the *Tigerfish* turned southeast. When asked, the sound man reported that all he had heard was shrimp snapping. Then, when Ensign Miller asked the question for the sixth time, he reported he could hear mermaids, playing their harps, plaintively singing his name.

Just as the sun dropped below the western horizon, out toward Banggi Island, the *Tigerfish* emerged from the deep to quickly surface so they could make a surface run of the final forty nautical miles to a spot in the Sulu Sea, their new patrol area. They were to be just to the west of a remote rock named Cagayan de Sulu.

Wayne Schacter chose to cautiously reconnoiter the area, at least until he had a better idea of what he might be facing. The ULTRA message that had sent them to this location had only said to expect Japanese warships, and that among them there would be at least one "high value" unit. That could mean anything from a lone cruiser to a task force made up of battleships and aircraft carriers. He knew he would simply have to wait and see.

The waning crescent moon glimmered weakly on the horizon as the *Tigerfish* slowly explored the waters to the west of Cagayan de Sulu. Schacter stood on the bridge with Brad Johnson as they scanned the night. So did the four young, sharp-eyed lookouts above them in the shears, each scanning his quarter of the horizon. But none of them saw what the sonar operator was about to report.

"Bridge, Sonar," the 7MC blasted. "I'm hearing multiple screws to the north. Too many to classify."

"Here we go!" Schacter yelled, pounding the bridge enclosure with the heel of his hand. "Brad, dive the ship." The Skipper dropped through the hatch just a step ahead of the lookouts and seconds before the urgent twin warnings of the dive klaxon.

By the time the submarine was beneath the surface, steadied out at periscope depth, and with all hands at battle stations, the first masts of the approaching enemy vessels were just visible on the northern horizon. Schacter, watching through the attack periscope, waited as the Japanese ships slowly steamed almost directly toward the *Tigerfish*. Gradually he could discern several destroyers and a host of merchant ships, all taking advantage of the calm weather to run along clustered tightly together. Then he spied the two seaplane carriers steaming very near to what appeared to be a cruiser. Those, he deduced, had to be the promised "high value" targets. The cruiser was lagging along behind one of the seaplane tenders, so Schacter decided to make the tender the first target. Then he would shift to the cruiser in the confusion he hoped to generate from his first attack.

"Observation on the left-hand tender," Schacter ordered. He swung the periscope around until the cross hairs bisected the target ship. "Bearing, mark."

Eric Riegel, the periscope assistant, read off, "Three-five-six."

"Range, mark."

"Range, three-two-hundred."

"Down scope. Angle-on-the-bow port ten."

As the scope slid into the well, Schacter looked around the conning tower and advised, "We've got three really juicy targets steaming straight at us. Two look to be seaplane tenders, the other a cruiser. I'm going to put four fish into the right-hand tender, then two into the cruiser. If he's still afloat when we swing around, I'll put two more into him. Any torpedoes left will go into the left-hand tender. Let's put some Japs on the bottom!" Then he said the words that let everyone aboard the submarine know the attack was on. "Make all tubes ready. Set run depth at thirty feet. Speed to HIGH."

All tubes. Six at the bow. Four at the stern. Loaded, flooded down with the outer doors open, and ready to fire.

The submarine slowly headed in the direction of the oncoming Japanese. The conning tower was silent, except for the ticking of the clock. There were only whispers from the control room directly below. Everyone was intent on making this a successful attack. Sternman watched the clock and then said, "Time for an observation, Skipper."

"Observation on the right-hand tender," Schacter said. "Up scope."

He swung the scope only a few degrees to the right and said, "Bearing, mark." A pause. "Range, mark, down scope."

As the scope slid down, Riegel announced, "Bearing, three-five-two. Range, two-six-hundred."

"Angle-on-the-bow port forty," Schacter said. "Target has zigged. But I think they've come to all stop. They must be recovering aircraft or something. Regardless, the bastards are giving us a perfect shooting setup. This will be a shooting observation. Up scope."

Schacter carefully centered the crosshairs on the seaplane tender's bridge. Then he said, "Bearing, mark."

Riegel called out, "Three-five-one."

"Set." Sternman confirmed that the TDC had generated the right bearing. He selected tube one and then pressed the firing key as he ordered, "Shoot tube one."

The torpedo in that tube was immediately flushed out and sent on its way. Then its own internal steam turbine took over. The next three followed the first one with five seconds between each.

Sternman grabbed the stopwatch and said, "Time to first impact, one minute, twenty seconds."

"Observation on the cruiser," Schacter said, already turning attention to the second target. "Up scope."

"Bearing, mark." A short pause. "Range, mark. Down scope."

"Zero-zero-seven, range three-two-hundred."

"Angle-on-the-bow port eighty. He's at all stop. Like he wants to get shot."

Schacter grabbed a rag and wiped the sweat from his forehead as he looked over at Sternman. "How much time on the first fish, XO?"

"Still have...forty seconds, Skipper."

"You ready to shoot the cruiser?

"Yes, sir! Let's get the SOB!"

The periscope went up once again. "Shooting observation on the cruiser. Bearing, mark. Down scope."

"Bearing zero-zero-seven," Riegel called out.

Brad Johnson stood back in the shadows of the cramped conning tower, listening while he kept the solution updated on the "Is/Was." It all sounded like a well-rehearsed choir performing a beautifully complicated hymn.

Sternman selected tube five, pressed the firing key, and ordered, "Shoot tube five." Five seconds later, he did the same for tube six. Then he checked his stopwatch once more. But as he looked at the timepiece, there was the thunderclap of a terrific explosion. The *Tigerfish* was rocked hard a second or two after. Then, while everyone was still holding on to something solid, that one was followed by a second blast.

Sternman smiled. "I think we got one of 'em," he said.

"Let's take a look," Schacter said. "Up scope for a look around."

When the periscope broke through the surface, he saw the seaplane tender ablaze and sinking quickly from the bow. He spun around to look at the cruiser but something else filled his view.

"Damn! Destroyer heading our way! Down scope!"

∞

The long day and night of steaming through the Balabac Strait and then down to Cagayan de Sulu was finally over. All that was left was to wait for the oilers to arrive in the morning to refuel all the warships. Akito Saito was tired, but the *Kasumi* and the other destroyers had been assigned to guard the anchorage while the remainder of the ships rested. Saito would make sure that his crew were properly doing their job protecting the flock before he turned in for a few hours' sleep.

The *Kasumi* was steaming past the *Naka* when *Sanuki Maru*, the seaplane tender, suddenly erupted in a tremendous explosion of smoke and flames and ear-numbing detonation.

Torpedoes! There had to be a submarine close!

Saito looked out to sea. Nothing.

Then he spotted the twin streaks of white in the water, and they were heading directly for the *Kasumi*. More torpedoes! And their obvious target was really the *Naka*, the cruiser behind him, since Saito's ship had only just now wandered into the course of the oncoming weapons, likely after they had already been launched.

Saito closed his eyes, not to deny what he was seeing but to make certain in his own mind of the decision he had already made. He had no choice. He was charged by IJN command, by the Emperor, by his ancestors to do whatever it took to protect the cruiser and the life of Admiral Nishimura. There was only one way to do that. And it was not to scurry out of the way of the torpedoes to save his own warship.

No, he would use *Kasumi* to block the deadly fish. This action would surely destroy his ship and kill many of his sailors, but the *Naka* and Admiral Nishimura would be spared. Saito smiled as he gave the order that made certain his destroyer was in position to be hit by the torpedoes.

It was, after all, the samurai way.

The first torpedo exploded directly beneath the *Kasumi*'s engine room. The second one was detonated by the blast of the first, short of the vessel, but it did not matter. The destroyer was already doomed.

Akito Saito felt himself being tossed high into the air, tumbling, then falling. He landed in the water a few feet from where his stricken ship was already in its death throes. When he bobbed back to the surface, he watched and could feel the heat as the flames lit up the night and the *Kasumi*, groaning, belching, hissing, slipped inevitably beneath the waves. As her crew—his crew—trapped in the wreckage, screamed, cried. As they were all dragged down along with their doomed ship.

20

The Pengiki Besar Pirates were barely halfway back home from the night's successful activities when they heard a low-pitched buzzing sound off to the northeast. The buzz soon mutated into a roar as a dark-green twin-engine plane zoomed very low overhead. The aircraft bore the bright red Rising Sun of the Japanese Army on each wing.

Hadi bin Sinaga stood and waved a friendly greeting as the plane roared by. He instructed the rest of the "fishermen" on deck to do the same.

"Mitsubishi Ki-46," Hadi said. "Americans call them Dinahs."

"I'm impressed," MacLean told him.

"I've observed and reported most of the ships and aircraft the Empire has," Hadi responded. "I'll show you my collection of identification charts someday. Right now, I just hope he believes we are innocent fishermen. And he's coming back for another look at us just to be certain before he flies on to somewhere else."

Sure enough, the plane had flown out to the horizon, banked high, and was now circling back, this run even closer to the wavetops and mast-tops of the two vessels. However, the pilot merely waggled his wings as he flew overhead, a friendly response to the smiling and waving fishermen in the two outriggers. Then, thankfully, he disappeared back to the east.

As the Japanese reconnaissance plane disappeared, Trip MacLean doffed his *topi caping*, the conical, woven bamboo hat he was wearing to disguise his decidedly Anglo features and blond hair. He looked over at Hadi and asked, "What is a Japanese Army recon plane doing way out here fifty-some-odd miles from land? You think he's searching for some sign of the lost freighter?"

Hadi bin Sinaga sat on a fish basket and took a long swig of water from a flask before he answered. "I can tell you all you need to know about the Dinah and its capabilities, but I can only guess an answer for your question about why he is out here. The Japanese High Command must have forgotten to include me on the distribution of the pilot's mission orders. I doubt, though, that he is looking for a lost freighter. I would also doubt that they have even figured out yet that this particular ship is lost. My guess is that he is—what is the term you would use?—reconnoitering the area. The missionaries did not include that word in our vocabulary when they taught us English. Anyway, he is likely here to make certain there are no Dutch or American warships anywhere nearby."

"And just why would he be doing that?" MacLean inquired, but he thought he could see where the Indonesian freedom fighter was going. And he liked it.

"Only reason would be if the Japs had something in the works," Hadi answered. "Something of interest to the Allies heading this way. And..."

"And we're going to find out what it is," MacLean finished Hadi's thought. "Why don't we come around to the north and see if we can find out what's new in the neighborhood?"

Hadi took another swig of water, grinned, and ordered his crew to do just that.

The *Seddi* and the *Duwa* tacked around and beat into the north wind. This was where the two sandeq potangngas really excelled. Sailing close-hauled, they could still make good headway pointed almost directly into the wind. No need to employ their smoky, noisy diesel engines.

Sailing in a line abreast, with lookouts up on the mainmast, the two vessels could search out a line almost twenty miles long. It was near sunset when Bintang, over on the *Duwa*, signaled that they had spotted ships out on the horizon. The lookout was reporting two ships visible and the smoke from several more.

Hadi immediately ordered the two boats around so that they carefully approached the oncoming ships obliquely. The sandeq potangngas were small enough that they could remain unseen. Even if they were spied, a couple of fishing boats would not be of any concern.

Anthony Watson, *S-55*'s burly, gruff COB, stood beside MacLean as they sailed toward the Japanese ships, but spoke quietly enough that Hadi could not overhear. "Boss," he said, "Hadi does know that we're not some kind of native-islander battleship, armed to the teeth, right?"

MacLean laughed. "Somehow, I don't think he does."

Watson pointed MacLean toward one of the crates of weapons they had captured on the previous night's adventure with the coal-burning merchant ship. "Well, just in case, we got a couple of things in these crates that may be useful." Grabbing another of the rescued submariners, Doc Jones, the COB said, "Hey, Doc, give me a hand with this."

They proceeded to pull the largest rifle that MacLean had ever seen from the crate. "What the hell is that, a cannon?" Trip asked with a gasp.

"Near as I can tell," Watson answered, "it's some kind of anti-tank rifle. Must be at least a 20mm. Damn thing's bore is almost the size of my thumb. A shot or two from this thing will get somebody's attention real quick."

The COB slapped a round into the chamber, extended the bipod and butt supports, and then lay down behind the impressive weapon. Sighting down the barrel, the COB gently squeezed the trigger. The cannon thundered as it recoiled sharply against Watson's shoulder.

He slowly stood, rubbing his shoulder. "That's gonna leave a bruise, but you see what I mean about it being a real attention grabber." He winked at MacLean. "And the other thing we got is even better."

Then Watson and Jones grunted and groaned as they struggled to lift a heavy tube and base plate out of another crate.

"Near as I can figure, this is an 81mm mortar. If I can figure out how to put this thing together and fire it, the *Seddi* will be one bad-ass pirate ship. Or battleship. Take your pick."

MacLean laughed and shook his head. He left the COB with his crew to figure out the weapons. But he felt a bit better knowing they had at least something more than rifles and pistols to use if they needed to defend themselves.

Sundown found the Pengiki Besar Pirates a couple of miles west of what they had now determined was a relatively small Japanese convoy. The pirate ships were far enough away, it was doubtful anyone on the Japanese merchant ships could even see them yet. MacLean shinnied up the *Seddi*'s skinny mainmast for a better look before it got dark. From that perch, he could make out six ships steaming together. There did not seem to be any type of escort, just the six marus in a cluster. They almost certainly carried self-protection weapons, though, to fend off an attack by enemy patrol boats. Or, more likely in these waters, from pirates.

When the sun slipped below the horizon, Hadi deftly steered the *Seddi* into a spot less than five hundred yards from the closest Japanese ship while Bintang took the *Duwa* around to a station just off the convoy's port flank.

Watson opened the assault with a mortar round that fell harmlessly a hundred yards beyond the targeted vessel. The second round exploded somewhere near the ship's forward kingpost. The seven-pound high explosive round was enough to topple the kingpost and start a fire on deck. They could see men moving around, trying to control the blaze.

While the COB was busy with the mortar, Trip MacLean sat behind the M2 .50 caliber machine gun and peppered the ship's bridge. The COB's third round struck home, hitting the merchant vessel midships. There was a quick flash of fire, and then a tremendous, roiling, smoky inferno engulfed most of the target. There was no fighting that blaze. The ship disappeared below the surface with stunning quickness. Even from five hundred yards away, the crew on the *Seddi* recoiled and shielded themselves below the gunwales against the heat.

Hadi quickly brought the *Seddi* around and headed for the next nearest ship. "He must have been hauling gasoline. Probably avgas," he shouted to MacLean. "Let's see about eliminating the next ship."

The burning remnants of the maru and the pool of burning gas served to light up the night with eerie flickering light. The remaining five ships were easily visible, but now so were the Pengiki Besar Pirates. Two of the ships began to lob shells in all directions from their deck guns. At the same time, all five of them disgorged heavy black smoke from their stacks as they tried to run away from their attackers.

Hadi pulled away, beyond the light from the fires, and raced out ahead for another run at the fleeing convoy. As they did, they saw the darkness off to the east suddenly erupt in flame.

"Looks like Bintang scored, too," Hadi said with a following falsetto. "Whoop! Whoop!"

It took almost an hour for Hadi to get into an attack position again. He steered to the best place to launch another slashing assault, coming at the convoy from out of the darkness. Watson, now that he had figured out the mortar, found the range to the next ship with the second round. This time, it took three direct hits—and the last of Watson's supply of purloined mortar shells—to set this maru afire.

Hadi called out that it was time to end the battle. All the fire might attract a quick visit from their airborne friend or one of his buddies. The two sandeq potangngas were sailing over the horizon when the last ship exploded spectacularly, illuminating a bank of thunderclouds like sheet lightning.

Trip MacLean sat with Hadi as they both enjoyed the breeze and a refreshing jamu.

"I expect we made sure tonight that some Jap fighter planes are going to be short on avgas," MacLean said with a laugh.

Hadi held his cup out for a happy toast. "Yes, they will." Then his face, lit only by starlight and phosphorescence in the water, grew serious. "And who knows how many Japanese sailors on those ships will never return to their families?"

"You're not getting soft on me, are you, Captain Kidd?" MacLean asked. "Neither you nor I started this war, and the sooner we can end it, the fewer the people who will die."

"Not hardly," Hadi replied. "But we have always been a peaceful people. Even when we liberate cargo from colonialists invading our seas and islands. We've mostly spared their lives and set them adrift in the hopes they would one day give up on finding lands to plunder and peaceful people to dominate." He offered another toast and a modicum of a smile. "So, Mr. MacLean, here's to killing to stop the killing. What say you?"

"Aye, aye, Captain Kidd. Aye, aye."

"And, since we have a long voyage home, tell me. Who is this Captain Kidd of whom you speak?"

∞

Cookie Ramirez was frantic. He searched through the *Wolffish*'s dry storeroom under the galley, emptying it of every can, crate, and bag of food stores. Then he searched the lockers stashed outboard in the forward torpedo room. In a last, desperate effort, he emptied all the lockers in the wardroom pantry. That's where Jim Shelton found him.

"Cookie, what you doing?" the XO asked the head cook, who was rummaging through the last locker.

Ramirez, flushed and sweating heavily, turned to Shelton. "XO, we got a real problem. It's bad enough that we ran out of Spam, but this is a disaster." He wiped the sweat from his forehead with a greasy dish towel. "We're down to the last bag of flour. There should still be half a dozen bags. I just opened that last bag of flour and it's got weevils!"

Shelton was shaking his head. Weevils in the flour sounded like something from a Herman Melville story about early sailing ships. Salt beef and hardtack. Everyone knew that flour came in sealed five-gallon cans precisely so it would not end up contaminated. "But how in hell could...?"

Ramirez interrupted the Exec. "Remember when we loaded stores in Pearl? They weren't kidding when they said they were scraping the bottom of the barrel. All they had left was bagged flour, and don't even ask me what date was stamped on those bags. I think you might not have been born by then."

Shelton sat down and thought for a second. "Can't you just sift out the bugs?" he asked.

"Probably most of them. And the oven should kill any of the ones that make it through. Still, if the guys find out them's bugs in their bread and not sesame seeds..."

Truth was, they did not have any option. Midway Island, the closest place to restock supplies, was three thousand miles away. That was well over a week's worth of steaming if they turned and headed that way right this minute.

"How long will that last bag of flour last?"

"The way this crew goes through bread and sticky buns, a couple of days, maybe three at best. If we carefully ration it."

"Well, do all you can with what you got, Cookie. Look on the bright side. The bread will have a little added protein and a bit of a crunch to it now."

Ramirez could only scowl and look disgustedly at first the XO and then the bug-infested flour.

Shelton knew he had no other option. He found the Skipper, Alphonse Dinnacetti, sitting at the tiny desk in his stateroom, writing. He looked up as Shelton knocked.

"Just writing a letter to my wife. Telling her what a fun time we're having out here," Dinnacetti told him as he stowed the letter and fountain pen in a drawer. "So, what you got, XO?"

"Skipper, we're going to have to come off patrol," Shelton said flatly, directly.

"And why would that be?" the CO responded. "If something's broke, it better be something that prevents us from scootin' or shootin'. We still have a couple of weeks scheduled before we turn east."

"Food," Shelton said flatly. "We're out of canned meat and powdered eggs."

"Neither one of those is a really big loss, much less something to stop the war over," the Skipper said with a chuckle. "Ramirez has doctored up and served canned mystery meat about every way it can be fixed, I reckon. He can try something else."

"Worse than that," the XO went on. "Cookie says we only have enough flour for three days and that what little we got left is full of weevils. The only thing we have enough of is ice cream mix. By Wednesday, we could be eating ice cream for breakfast, lunch, and dinner."

"Okay," the CO relented after a long moment's consideration. "I guess Napoleon was right. An Army does move on its stomach. A Navy, too. Draft up a message to SUBPAC. Tell them the situation and make sure they have a stores load ready for us at Midway. Tighten your belt. We're going on a diet. Looks like we're heading to port." He reached up to punch the 7MC button. “Bridge, Captain, come around to course one-zero-zero, all ahead full.”

∞

Trip MacLean awoke with a start. After the long, tiring night spent attacking the Japanese convoy and then sailing away before any other Japanese showed up, he had finally fallen asleep, shortly after sunrise. He checked his Rolex and then looked at the sun. The bright orb was not where it should be. The wristwatch said it was midafternoon. That should have put the sun on the starboard beam. Instead, it was almost dead ahead. That told him that they were not on a course for Pengiki Besar, for home, at all.

“Hadi,” he called to Hadi bin Sinaga, who was sitting quietly by the *Seddi*’s tiller. “Where we headed?”

“Good afternoon, *Pappirate mappoji*,” the Indonesian pirate replied with a smile. “Did you have a nice sleep?”

“That I did. That I did.”

Hadi slipped a rope to the tiller to hold it steady and in position, then stepped over and sat down next to MacLean before he explained. “I fear that too many Japanese saw us last night and lived to tell the tale. It would not be safe for two vessels fitting our description to arrive at Pengiki Besar. The Japanese have a nasty habit of arriving unexpectedly and with a lot of firepower should they find those who have done them harm. They would certainly destroy not only our boats but everything else on the island. We are heading west, out to the Tambelan Archipelago. There are many small islands with little bays and coves where we can hide for a few days. And many of the islands are uninhabited.”

MacLean felt a quick pang of disappointment. He had been looking forward to spending some time with Sri Wahyuni, getting to better know Hadi’s delightful young daughter. But bin Sinaga’s words made sense. If the Japanese found two sandeq potangngas resembling the ones that attacked the convoy suddenly showing up at the tiny island, they would simply level the place with an immediate and very deadly air attack. No questions or inquiry. Hiding the boats in some out-of-the-way cove far from Pengiki Besar was the only sure way to prevent that.

MacLean nodded that he understood, then he remembered that he had not eaten since before daybreak. His rumbling stomach was reminding him that he needed food. Hadi laughed and waved at a basket of fruit in the forward hold.

MacLean sat back and cut open what he had been told was a cempedak. The thin, leathery, greenish-brown skin gave way easily, revealing the sweet edible orange-yellow fruit inside. Yellow juice was soon trickling down his forearms onto the deck as he enjoyed the fruit's honey-lemon sweetness.

He had almost finished it when an ominous buzzing noise caught his attention. It quickly grew to an even more frightening roar of something rapidly coming their way from the northern horizon. MacLean did not need Hadi's guidebook or charts to recognize the pair of Japanese Zeros that flashed by, close enough that he could see the faces of the fighter planes' pilots looking down at them from not quite directly overhead. They flew on, though, out to the south a mile or so.

"Not good," Hadi said. "If they are looking for us, they have found us."

Sure enough, the fighters were already doing a steep banking turn.

"They're going to come back shooting!" MacLean yelled.

Hadi swung the tiller over hard in a vain attempt to avoid the attacking fighter planes. Anthony Watson yanked off the spare sail that hid the .50 caliber heavy machine gun and swung it around toward the onrushing Zeros. The right-hand fighter seemed intent on shooting up the *Seddi* while the left-hand one, trailing the other Zero by several hundred yards, concentrated his interest on the *Duwa*.

Watson pulled back on the charging handle, flipped off the safety, and jammed down on the thumb triggers. Their only hope was to shoot their attackers out of the sky.

The heavy machine gun bucked and roared as a stream of .50 caliber rounds flew out to meet the onrushing Japanese fighter plane. It would be a tough target to hit.

The Zero was now clearly shooting back. Twin lines of splashes from its 20mm cannons walked across the water and then crashed into *Seddi*'s thin wooden sides. In seconds, the Zero flew overhead, barely avoiding the vessel's mainmast.

MacLean could see a faint trail of blueish-black smog trailing from the aircraft. Apparently, some of the COB's rounds had struck something. Trip prayed it was something vital or flammable.

Then MacLean stole a quick glance at the other Zero. It trailed behind the first and was only beginning its run at Bintang's *Duwa*. Somebody on the *Duwa*—most likely Tommy Hilligas—was hammering away with their machine gun. And doing a damn fine job of it. The line of tracers from that weapon was intersecting with the speeding Zero. The plane was a couple of hundred yards from the *Duwa* when it suddenly burst into flames. They got him!

But MacLean stifled a cheer when he realized the doomed plane was somehow managing to maintain its dive, still charging directly at the outrigger, despite the flames pouring from the engine and trailing far behind the plane.

MacLean gasped and, instead of a rousing cheer, shouted a useless warning as the flaming wreckage of the fighter plane smashed ferociously into the wooden boat. A couple of hundred gallons of high-octane avgas exploded, instantly incinerating everything and everybody on the *Duwa*. Nothing was left but some bits of burning debris, both on the surface of the sea and raining down from a bright sky.

Anthony Watson, tears streaming down his face, jumped up and begged the fleeing Zero, now leaving a distinctive trail of smoke, to "come back and fight like a man."

Hadi swung the *Seddi* around to sail through the debris in a vain effort to search for any survivors. After a few minutes, he shook his head. There was nothing. Not even any bodies to bury.

Trip MacLean felt an almost overpowering wave of sadness. Tommy Hilligas, Billy Mutter, and Igor Tomlivich—three men with whom he had shared so much in the past months—were gone, never to have a grave or marker to commemorate their cut-short lives, their ultimate sacrifice to their country. And Hadi's men, with wives and children back at the island, waiting for those who would never return.

The remaining vessel's journey on over to Uwi Island, on the outer reaches of the Tambelan Archipelago, was conducted in somber silence, but with eyes always on the sky and with the .50 caliber constantly manned.

21

A huge, frigid polar air mass poured down out of arctic Canada and spread over the western Atlantic. When it did, it slammed into the warm ocean currents of the Gulf Stream, the river of Caribbean water that rushed north and then eastward, toward Britain. The collision of different temperature water and air resulted in a massive nor'easter, or *naw-eastuh* if spoken by pretentious Bostonians. Freezing cold, hurricane-force winds drove a massive snowstorm deep into New England. Roads were too treacherous to drive, schools closed, and the Thames River railroad drawbridge froze in the up position, effectively snarling rail transportation in the region. New Englanders, imbued with a sense of long suffering, hunkered down in front of warm stoves and fireplaces to ride out the storm.

Debbie Schultz shivered as the howling wind rattled the house, which stood up on an unprotected hilltop on Groton, Connecticut's Cottage Street. It seemed at times that the blizzard might blow the house right off its foundation. She pulled her sweater around her as she puttered about in the kitchen, brewing herself a cup of tea. The weather was far too treacherous for her to venture out to her job as barkeep at Solomon's Tavern, even if it was only a couple of miles up Military Highway, just outside the Submarine Base. She had been housebound for almost a week, waiting for the storm to finally blow itself out. But Heinrich Schultz, her father, only had to walk a few blocks down to the Electric Boat Shipyard where he worked. The wartime submarine production could not slack in the slightest, no matter the weather.

That left Debbie in the unusual position of playing homemaker during the day. However, puttering around the house, doing dishes and laundry, or cleaning out long forgotten closets had lost their appeal. She tried to speak with her girlfriends, and especially those who had husbands or boyfriends away fighting the war. But in her neighborhood, she had to share a multi-family telephone party line, and Mrs. Crutchfield down the street became quite surly if Debbie interrupted her chats with her sister over in Waterford.

About the only thing that kept her going were letters from Brad Johnson, but even those were few and far between lately. He could not tell her much, but she knew he was at sea most of the time, out on war patrols on his submarine. Without his letters to look forward to, she was now just plain bored.

She grabbed a Groton Public Library copy of Edna Ferber's *Saratoga Trunk*—it was already a week past due for return because of the blizzard, so she wanted to get her seven cents' worth from it—dropped two lumps of sugar in her tea and sat back to read the antebellum adventures of the scheming Clio Dulaine.

The Creole heroine had just arrived in sun-dappled New Orleans when the jangling telephone interrupted. Two long rings and a short one. And then it repeated as Debbie walked over to the phone stand. Two longs and a short was the ring for the Schultz house on their ten-way party line, but who would be calling her this afternoon? Had Dad been hurt? Was there bad news about Brad? She answered before it could ring a third time.

"*Guten tag*, Fraulien Schultz." The guttural voice was not the usual shadowy German spy who had tasked her and her father to work for the Nazis. The one who urged her and Dad to learn details of secret technologies put into the American submarines being built down the street. Or to pass along any overheard conversation from sub sailors at Solomon's. No, this voice seemed younger, the accent a bit thicker. Always in the back of her mind was the fear that the Germans would learn they had been dealing with US Naval Intelligence, and that all information they fed back to the spies was bogus.

"Yes?"

"This horrid weather prevents us meeting," the voice said, giving the reason for an unusual telephone call. "But it also keeps the FBI warm and snug in their offices and away from our efforts on behalf of our common Fatherland, fraulein. We have a very simple assignment for you and Herr Schultz. Ask *dein vater* to listen for any rumors he may hear about problems with the *Amerikanish* Mark 14 torpedo. Understand, Mark 14 torpedo. And we will ask you to listen to what the sailors might be saying about the weapon at your Solomon's Tavern. You will be contacted in the usual manner in two weeks, and we anticipate valuable results."

Then Schultz was listening to the hum of a dead phone line. The German had hung up. She placed the receiver back in the phone's cradle while she thought for a bit.

But while she was putting her thoughts in order, the phone rang again. Fully expecting to hear the German voice once more, she was momentarily disconcerted to hear George Klemp's clipped Yankee accent.

"Are you all right, Miss Schultz?" the Naval Intelligence agent, whose job it was to assure nothing happened to the young woman or her father, inquired. "We recorded the entire call. Our spies are becoming very bold, using a regular phone on a party line. Or maybe they just don't like leaving correspondence under your doormat when there's more than a foot of snow. But this tells us that the information they're asking for must be very important to them."

"Did you figure out where the call came from?" Debbie asked. She would feel much safer if the call had emanated from someplace far away. Or someplace the Navy men already had under surveillance. They had already hinted that finding the spies' "nest" would be key to making arrests and shutting the ring down.

"Yes, he called from a payphone over in the New London train station. They like that spot. By the time we got someone over there, he was long gone," Klemp told her. "Don't worry, though. We have you under constant surveillance. You're safe."

"Even in this nor'easter?" Schultz shot back. "You tell me all is well just after sharing that your men have already let the Nazi get away."

Klemp laughed. "Yes, even in this nor'easter. The couple that moved into the rental house at the end of your block a few weeks ago? They're our agents. You want your walkway shoveled, just give them a call, New London 5-1234. Ask for Harold."

∞

A thick pall of smoke hung low over the port city of Surabaya. The air was heavy with the pungent smell of burning sugar from the still-smoldering sugar mills that lined the harbor. The drizzling rain did little to wash it away. The fires that still burned out of control amid the wreckage of the extensive Royal Netherlands Navy dockyard illuminated the night, eerily reflecting off the dense clouds overhead. A pair of Dutch destroyers, fires aboard them still raging after the afternoon's Japanese attack, had settled low in the water alongside the dock. The black harbor waters reeked of bunker oil and diesel fuel.

Brad Johnson stood on *Tigerfish*'s bridge and carefully threaded the submarine around the wreckage that littered the devastated harbor. The young Lieutenant shook his head in disbelief. "This is where we're supposed to refit and repair so we can go fight the Japs?" he asked, despair and disgust both heavy in his voice.

Skipper Wayne Schacter replied, "Damn Jap bomber raid sure didn't add to our merry welcome now did it? But these poor guys here had to live through the real thing, not just the aftermath. I think we'd best get refueled, loaded with groceries, and be out of here by daylight." He glanced aft at his gun crew manning the lone .50 caliber machine gun on the sub's cigarette deck. It would provide meager protection if the Jap bombers returned.

"Looks like we do have a little welcoming committee." Johnson waved toward the pier. A couple of dozen sailors in dungarees, but wearing tin pot helmets, stood at the pier ready to tie the submarine up. Three officers in khakis, but also wearing steel helmets, stood apart from the line handlers.

Johnson eased the *Tigerfish* alongside and brought her to a stop. Tying the submarine up consisted merely of dropping the lines over the associated bollards.

The senior of the three officers stepped over to the head of the brow and shouted to Schacter on the bridge, "Welcome to Surabaya, Captain. Hope you're not planning a liberty port. We want to get you fueled, fresh stores loaded, and back underway tonight. Captain Wilkes sends his regrets at not meeting you himself. He got caught up in a staff planning session with Admiral Hart up at Lembang."

Schacter shouted back, "Sounds about right. Come aboard. I think we can rustle up some coffee in the wardroom." He turned to Johnson and said, "Brad, get the fueling and stores load going. I want to keep the guns manned, though, just in case the Japs come back. I'll be down in the wardroom."

Johnson was already talking with the COB, Alonzo Heinrich, about how to go about getting the fueling and stores load underway as the Skipper climbed down from the bridge. Schacter met his guest as the officer stepped on board the *Tigerfish*.

"Good evening," the tired-looking Commander said and offered his hand. He was dressed in dirty khakis that were heavily sweat-stained and had a couple of bloodstains on the torn left sleeve. "I'm Jerry Thickstun, Captain Wilkes's Ops Officer when I'm not busy trying to fight off Japanese bomber raids. You'll have to forgive the uniform. Those murderous bastards didn't allow me enough time to change after they left. I'm leaving my two junior officers up here to help with the load-out. They both speak a little Dutch, especially cuss words, just enough to keep the stevedores motivated."

Schacter took the Ops Officer's hand and answered, "Quite all right. I understand that there's a war on. Come on down to the wardroom and let's get you a cup of coffee. You look like you need it."

When the two were seated at the wardroom table with steaming mugs of black coffee and Issac Sternman had joined them, Thickstun finally got around to asking, "How was the trip down from Corregidor?"

"Well, we had a little run-in with a Jap invasion force a couple of weeks ago, up in the Sulu Sea, around the Balabac Strait," Schacter shared. "I'm pretty sure we got a seaplane tender and got hits on a cruiser, too, but we couldn't stick around to verify anything. Damn Jap destroyer got in the way." Turning to Sternman, he asked, "XO, you have the patrol report ready for Commander Thickstun?"

"Yes, sir," the XO replied and scooted a heavy manila envelope across the table. "It's right here."

Thickstun took the envelope. "Thank you. Anything in particular in here that I should know about?"

Schacter and Sternman shared a quick glance. Neither of them knew if Thickstun was cleared for ULTRA traffic or not, so they made no mention of the message or what set off the mad dash through the Balabac Strait to rendezvous with the Japanese invasion force. That information would not be shared.

Schacter shook his head. "Nope, other than it was a pretty boring trip with two cases of diarrhea and two more of skin irritation treated by Doc and a coffeepot that kept blowing fuses until we found the short in the carafe warmer." He didn't mention that he was one of those cases of "skin irritation."

Thickstun smiled, sat back, and replied, "Well, Skipper, I don't believe you'll consider your next trip to be boring." He reached into a pocket and pulled out a sheaf of papers. In actuality, more a wad of papers. "You're going back up to Corregidor. We're loading you up with all the ammunition that we can spare and several crates of medical supplies for the troops that are still stuck there."

"Got it. Guess we're mostly a three-hundred-foot-long delivery lorry these days, but whatever it takes."

The Commander smiled and took another sip of coffee. "That's the easy part. We need for you to be a taxi, too. Pull out the Station CAST people. It's vital we get those Intelligence guys out of there before Corregidor falls. And believe me, Corregidor will fall, and soon."

Thickstun stopped and looked around, obviously making sure no one could overhear what he was saying. In a voice so low it was almost a whisper, he added, "Skipper, it's critical that the Japanese do not get their hands on those people you're hauling out of there. If you get into a situation in which there is any chance whatsoever that they might be captured alive, your orders are to make absolutely certain that does not happen."

It took Schacter a moment to digest just what CDR Thickstun was telling him. "Do you mean that I...we...should...?" He left the rest of the question unasked. He felt the uncomfortable itching on his arm and back rising to a crescendo.

"Yes, sir. That is exactly what I am saying," he answered emphatically. "We cannot allow the Japanese to capture them. They have intelligence vital to the war effort. And the Japanese have creative and effective ways to get it out of them."

∞

Geoff Chandler set a stiff pace with his exercise walk. Pengiki Besar was only two miles in circumference, but the soft sand beaches made the fast walking he was doing very difficult. That was on purpose. A week of bedrest, under Sri Wahyuni's care, had been just what the castaway Royal Navy Lieutenant needed to recuperate after his latest shipwreck experience. But now that he felt he had recuperated as much as needed, a restlessness was setting in. He wanted to restore his body to fighting fitness and to get his mind back into the war. This tropical island interlude had been nice, but for as long as the Japanese threatened British interests in the South Pacific, downtime could only be temporary. Duty called, beckoning in a way that could be quite persuasive for a man dedicated to fighting for his country.

"Geoff," Sri Wahyuni yelled from some distance behind him. "Wait for me!" The young self-appointed nurse was struggling to keep up with his pace. She had plopped down on a fallen coconut log to catch her breath. She had tried to convince their convalescing guest that long-distance walking was not something that Pengiki Besar islanders did. And Chandler already was on his third lap this morning. She was simply no longer able to keep up.

Chandler doubled back and sat down beside her, a grin on his face. The truth was, he was dragging as well. And the view there where she rested, at the edge of a palm-tree-fringed beach, was about as lovely as from any spot along his walking route. Especially for him since that view included Sri. They had spent much time here the last few days, talking, learning of the vast differences in their lives to this point, satisfying her curiosity about the vast world outside the bay and beyond the coral atoll.

As they caught their breath, they could enjoy the gentle breeze off the ocean. They gazed out over the turquoise-blue waters. A pair of black-headed gulls wheeled gracefully on the wind as they searched the clear, shallow waters for their lunch. And a patchy rain squall, way out in the sea, meandered across the distant horizon.

Then Sri pointed. A red sail out on that same horizon. The black hull had just become visible when Sri stood and waved excitedly. She called out, "I thought so! That's Father's boat. They are back." She paused for a second, then added, "But I see only one boat."

She immediately turned and, apparently revived now from trying to maintain Chandler's walking pace, ran down the beach toward the island's sheltered harbor. "Hurry, Geoff," she called over her shoulder. She had begun calling him "Geoff," not "Lieutenant" or "Mr. Chandler." "Father is home. He may bring us news. Hurry!"

Chandler did his best to keep up, but he caught only quick flashes of her orange sarong as she darted through the trees, quickly leaving him behind. It occurred to him then that she might not have been so winded after all, that she merely wanted to sit on the log and talk with him.

When he finally caught up with her at Hadi bin Sinaga's thatched-roof bungalow, Chandler had to bend over, gasping for gulps of air. When he looked up, he could see the Indonesian pirate bring his sandeq potangnga around the point, dropping the red mainsail as he turned. The *Seddi* silently glided across the little lagoon. Hadi dropped the anchor at precisely the right moment, which brought the boat to a smooth halt only a few feet from the beach. Close enough they could wade to the dry sand without getting wet above the knees.

As the villagers raced out to greet the arriving outrigger, Chandler saw that there were white men aboard. Sri had mentioned there were other castaways on the island now, and that they were assisting her father in some special activities. For his part, Hadi was obviously pleased to find Chandler recuperated and rearing to go. He pulled the Royal Navy officer aside and made quick introductions, then went to meet the islanders and share the sad news with them.

Within minutes, Chandler and Trip MacLean determined that they had acquaintances in common, that both knew the American submariners Brad Johnson and Freddy Wurster. That indeed, those two were some of Trip's best friends since their days together at Annapolis. And that Chandler had gone to war in the North Atlantic with the two men, even before the US had entered the war. All agreed it was a small world. Chandler and MacLean were soon sharing sea stories about the two other submariners, wondering where they were currently sailing, what they might be doing to try to defeat the Empire of Japan.

The joy of the reunion was tempered with sorrow with the news of the loss of Bintang and the crew of the *Duwa*, including several men from the island and three of the American submariners. Within the tiny village on Pengiki Besar, everyone was related to everyone else. The sorrow was shared by everyone. Hadi, as the village elder, called for an *appanreng tedong*, a communal feast, to respect and remember the departed. With no water buffalo on Pengiki Besar, however, the bounty of the sea would replace the traditional sacrificial water buffalo.

That night, as the last embers of the bonfire died out and a thin red line on the eastern horizon promised the dawn of a new day, Hadi bin Sinaga gathered his crew, including Chandler, MacLean, and other surviving US Navy submariners. He explained that they needed to replenish the food and water on *Seddi* and make their goodbyes. That is, if they all wanted to continue with him and his pirates, observing the enemy, reporting what they saw, and doing damage where they could. Regardless of their choice, the vessel, now familiar to the Japanese in the area, needed to be very far from Pengiki Besar before the enemy patrols found it again. Found it and made sure everyone in the area paid the price for harboring the vessel that had caused them so much pain of late.

Geoff Chandler glanced at Sri. Was that a frown of worry on her face? For him? For her father? For both of them? Or for one of the Americans, who had been shipwrecked here longer than he had. Whatever, he had already made up his mind. Until he could be back with the Royal Navy, he would do everything he could to strike a blow. He would help Hadi and his pirates, just as his American Navy counterparts, Alistair MacLean and his rescued crewmembers, had decided to do.

∞

Stan Ward pulled back the green Army blanket that served both as a wall and a door for Ollie Oglethorpe's office at the far end of Malinta Tunnel, Lateral Six, deep in the rock that formed the island of Corregidor.

"You wanted to see me, boss?" Ward asked as he slumped down into an old metal chair.

Oglethorpe fiddled with his pipe for a moment. It was never clear to Stan if the man was performing a ritual or just postponing whatever conversation was about to take place. He applied a match to the pungent tobacco mix in the bowl of his pipe, then puffed mightily until his head was shrouded in a cloud of aromatic smoke. Only then did he speak. "Stan, we got orders out of here. A submarine will take us off this island. We got a couple of weeks to wrap things up here."

"Submarine, huh? Looks like I'll finally get my wish," Stan said, almost wistfully.

"How's that?"

"Remember, out of the Academy I was approved for submarine officers' school at Groton. Then I got hurt on the way..." Ward had become an instant hero, saving lives when the bus on which he was riding across Kansas crashed and caught fire and, despite his own serious injuries, he helped fellow passengers get out and to safety. But those injuries had kept him from submarine duty. Now he—and even more so his boss, Ollie Oglethorpe—felt his shift to Naval Intelligence had been best for all involved. Except for the Germans and the Japanese.

The conversation paused as blasts from Japanese bombs overhead shook the tunnel. A thin rivulet of dust drifted down from the rock ceiling. Oglethorpe's big coffee cup was jarred a full inch sideways and framed maps attached to the rock wall behind him gently swayed.

He murmured, "Damn Japs! Won't even let us carry on a civilized conversation." He turned back to Ward. "As I was saying, we have a couple of weeks but it's not nearly long enough. We won't be able to take any of our equipment with us and damn few of our records. I need for you to figure out how to destroy the gear so that there is absolutely nothing that the Japs can use. Anything we don't want them to know we have. Then we'll dump that junk in deep water, just to be sure. I've already started sorting through the paperwork." He glanced around at the mounds of paper littering the cave. "Gonna be one massive bonfire."

"I'm with you. I don't think we can do it all in two weeks either."

"Oh, and one other directive from the good folks up the chain of command," Ollie went on. "We are to maintain our efforts with decoding ULTRAs and predicting ship and troop movements and...well...business as usual even as we burn the place down and take a sledgehammer to all our gear."

"Where we headin' from here, boss?" Ward asked.

"Message says we're going to Australia. We are to form up something called Fleet Radio Unit, Melbourne. FRUMEL, for short."

Ward chuckled. "Australia. From what I've heard, we're going to need to learn an entirely new language. They say they speak 'Aussie' down there. Any similarity to English is entirely accidental."

Oglethorpe laughed. "I guess we'll see soon enough."

Another string of Japanese bombs shook the tunnel.

"Not soon enough for me!" Ward replied with a sideways grin.

22

The moonless night was almost totally black. Thick clouds and lingering smoke absorbed what little ambient light there was. The *Tigerfish* appeared out of the darkness, nudging up against Corregidor's South Pier. The lines had barely been slipped over the bollards when the crew started passing crates of ammunition, medical supplies, and food topside from their stowage locations on the submarine. Even as the submarine's diesel engine exhaust continued to burble away in the night, Alonzo Heinrich, the COB, had a couple of lines of sailors efficiently manhandling everything off the submarine and over to the small pier. There the soldiers and sailors stranded on the island loaded the supplies onto carts and moved them off to storage tunnels bored out of solid rock.

Wayne Schacter nervously paced around the submarine's tiny bridge and back to the cigarette deck where he could observe the activity. With the guns manned and loaded topside and the diesels idling belowdecks, the *Tigerfish* was ready to fight or to run at an instant's notice. There was not much more the Skipper could accomplish, but the combination of nervous tension and the annoying itching of the rash from his persistent eczema would not allow him to simply sit back and rest.

As the last of the ammo was carried over to the pier, a group of twenty sailors, each toting a half-empty seabag, appeared from a nearby tunnel and crossed the brow to the *Tigerfish*. Their passengers were now on board.

Brad Johnson, standing up on the bridge, immediately recognized one officer's ungainly limp. He hopped down to the main deck and jumped out to grab Stan Ward in a tremendous bear hug as he passed by.

"What the hell are you doing here, Stan?" he asked. "You're supposed to be back Stateside enjoying your wife and that new baby boy of yours. Not out here on this rock, bumming rides on subs."

Once freed from Johnson's embrace, Ward pumped his Naval Academy roommate's hand and said, "Great to see you, Bradley. I've been looking forward to our little sea cruise. If you could just have the steward take my bags, I understand there are cocktails and light snacks on the Ledo deck."

Johnson cuffed his friend on the shoulder. "Oh, you're about to cruise in style, buddy. You always wanted to ride one of these things. Now you get your chance. But you best get belowdecks. We should be casting off as soon as we get you all loaded."

Even as Brad was speaking, a pair of four-by-four trucks led by a battered jeep pulled to a halt at the head of the pier. A harried-looking Army Major climbed out of the jeep and trotted down the pier to the *Tigerfish*. A dozen soldiers piled out of the trucks and began unloading what appeared to be small but very heavy cloth sacks.

"On the sub," the Major yelled. "Need a working party to load this stuff aboard your vessel."

The COB looked across the brow at the Major, effectively staring him down. He shook his head and informed him, "We weren't told about any cargo and we ain't got time enough to load it now." He turned to find Schacter standing on the cigarette deck just above him. "Skipper?" he asked.

"What you got, Major?" Schacter asked.

"Philippine thousand-peso silver coins," the Major replied, "about fifty tons of silver worth well over a million dollars US. Orders are to ship as much out of Hell as we can before the Japs can just come in and take it."

Schacter nodded. With ten torpedoes gone from the forward torpedo room, there was plenty of room and reserve buoyancy to handle the load of silver. He yelled at Heinrich, "COB, get it aboard as quick as you can. Stow as much of it as you can down in the bilges, as low as you can get it for stability."

The sailors and soldiers passed the bags of coins from the trucks, across the brow, and down the hatches into the *Tigerfish*. The fastener from one bag broke open as it was being passed across the brow from shore to sub. Bright new silver coins flashed in the meager light as they fell into black, oily bay water. The line did not even hesitate. There were simply too many bags to get loaded before the sun came up to worry about one being lost.

Wayne Schacter checked his watch as the last bag dropped down the after engine room access hatch. They had one hour until the first sunlight appeared. It would take that long to get out to water that would be deep enough for *Tigerfish* to dive and hide. The eczema was starting to drive him mad as he climbed back up to the bridge. His back was one ugly mass of itching and burning skin. He thought he would very much prefer a Japanese air attack to another night of this kind of suffering.

But of course, the Skipper had no choice in the matter.

∞

Fred Wurster was excited. This was supposed to be their last night at sea for a while, running on the surface, hurrying to home port while getting a battery charge accomplished. It was a moonless night, so he had a dazzling canopy of stars overhead to enjoy. He could easily pick out Pollux and Castor, the bright stars in Gemini. Pearl Harbor was only two hundred miles to their southwest. He thought at times that he could already smell the scent of plumerias drifting along on the warm evening breeze. But that could also be from Kauai, the "Garden Isle," which was only forty miles to their south at the moment.

Being ashore for a while was not the only reason he was so excited. When they arrived at Pearl Harbor, Ellie Morton, his fiancée, was supposed to be waiting for him on the pier. Fred had a very difficult time hiding his smile.

"Mr. Wurster, I been seein' somethin' low on the horizon out yonder," Billy Bob York yelled down from his lookout post up in the periscope shears. His position had him covering the *Wolffish*'s after port quarter, so he was looking to the north-northwest. Out to sea and away from Hawaii.

Wurster grabbed his binoculars and looked in the direction that York pointed. "I don't see anything, Billy Bob."

"Mr. Wurster, it's gonna be reeeaaal smaaall." York's East Tennessee drawl got even more pronounced when he was excited. "No lights nor nothin'. I figger maybe five thousand yards."

Wurster still could not see this contact, but, according to the patrol order, there should not be any friendly ships in the area. They were supposed to have this bit of sea entirely to themselves. He grabbed the 7MC and said, "Conn, Bridge. Take a look out around three-four-zero. Billy Bob says he sees something out about five thousand yards. And have the sound man listen out that way, too."

QM1 Obrien's reply was quick. "Bridge, I see a submarine on that bearing. Best I can tell, it's a big one. Bigger than any of ours. Maybe one of those Jap seaplane-carrying ones."

Without hesitation Wurster grabbed the 1MC and yelled, "Man battle stations! Captain to the bridge!" Then he grabbed the 7MC and ordered, "Left full rudder, steady course three-four-zero." He swung the *Wolffish* around to point the Jap sub to both minimize their own profile and thus the chance of being seen, and to start the attack that was surely coming.

The *bong-bong-bong* of the general alarm had barely stopped echoing throughout the boat when Alphonse Dinnacetti climbed up to the bridge. He had obviously been asleep when the call came. "What's all the excitement, Fred?" he asked, rubbing his eyes. "Some sort of Pearl Harbor welcoming committee convened just for us?"

"Not unless the Japs are heading it up," Wurster told him as he pointed dead ahead. "Low down at a range of four thousand or so."

At the same time, the bridge speaker rattled, "Bridge, Conn. Sound reports a contact, bearing three-four-five. Screw noises and a very loud diesel."

Dinnacetti turned to Wurster and said, "Fred, my eyes aren't night-adapted. I'm not seeing anything. Dive the ship. We'll shoot this bastard from periscope depth when we can see him. That'll limit his chances to shoot back."

The *Wolffish* slid smoothly beneath the waves. The Japanese submarine still seemed to be unaware that an American sub was stalking it. But attacking another sub was a problematic business. Not only were there the usual two-dimensional parameters, but there was the vertical dimension. A submarine could always pull the plug and disappear. Then the hunter could never be sure whether or not he had, at that point, become the hunted.

Even as the *Wolffish* slipped below the waves, Alphonse Dinnacetti was already on the attack. "Observation on the Jap," he called out as he squatted before the attack scope. "Up scope."

The attack periscope slid up. The Skipper centered the cross hairs on the enemy submarine and called out, "Bearing, mark."

"Three-four-six," QM1 Clancy Obrien reported.

"Range, mark."

"Three-six-hundred."

"Angle-on-the-bow starboard six-zero. Down scope."

Jim Shelton dialed in the observation into the torpedo data computer. Watching the projected solution generate, he said, "Skipper, recommend coming to course zero-two-three for best approach course."

Dinnacetti glanced at the TDC before he ordered the new approach course and then ordered, "Make tubes forward ready in all respects. Set run speed to HIGH, run depth to twenty feet."

As the *Wolffish* maneuvered to intercept the Jap sub, the target obligingly steamed nonchalantly onward, seemingly oblivious to the predator only a few thousand yards away. Tension in the *Wolffish* conning tower was palpable, though. Dinnacetti wiped the sweat from his forehead with an already sodden towel. Wurster fiddled nervously with the "Is/Was." Meanwhile, Shelton concentrated on the whirring dials and flashing lights of the electro-mechanical TDC.

"Observation on the Jap sub!" The Skipper's announcement only heightened the tension. "Up scope!"

The periscope had barely broken the surface when Dinnacetti called out, "Contact is zigging toward! Bearing, mark. Range, mark. Down scope."

"Bearing three-five-two," Clancy Obrien announced. "Range two-three hundred."

Dinnacetti stepped back and rubbed his chin in thought as Obrien called out the range and bearing. Finally, after Shelton looked at him expectantly, he said, "Angle-on-the-bow starboard forty. He was still swinging."

With the target making a course change, it was fruitless to do anything until the guy steadied up on a new, stable course. That could take a couple of minutes. Minutes when the tension within *Wolffish* would only escalate.

Finally, Shelton checked his stopwatch. "Skipper, it's been two minutes. He should be steady by now."

Dinnacetti nodded and said, "Observation on the Jap sub, up scope."

In quick succession, he called out, "Bearing, mark. Range, mark. Down scope."

"Bearing three-four-six, range one-five-hundred," Obrien responded.

"Angle-on-the-bow port six-zero," Dinnacetti said, then added, "People were clearing the bridge. Looks like he's getting ready to dive. This will be a shooting observation, spread of four."

Dinnacetti used the towel to again wipe his face as the scope emerged. Obrien had jockeyed the scope so that it came up on the expected bearing. Dinnacetti stared hard through the eyepiece.

Nothing! Not a damn thing but a dark, tropical night with a sky bedecked by brightly winking stars. The Skipper swung the scope to the left and then to the right. Still nothing!

He stepped back and growled, "The bastard's gone! He's disappeared! We got nothing out there!"

Now, there was a very real possibility that the Jap sub could be lining up at that very moment to shoot the *Wolffish*, turning the tables in a deadly direction. It was time to break off the attack and get out of town. Or at least head on down to Pearl.

"Dive, make your depth two hundred feet. Right full rudder, steady course one-two-zero. All ahead flank!"

As *Wolffish* sought the safety of the deep, Dinnacetti turned to Shelton. "Jim, we came so damn close to bagging ourselves an I-boat," he complained, throwing the towel the length of the conning tower in frustration. "Now, the son of a bitch is still out here. No telling who he might stumble on and shoot. Get an Ops Urgent message drafted up to SUBPAC telling them about our friend out here. Maybe they can send some tin cans to make his life miserable."

Shelton nodded and said, "Yes, sir. I'll get right on it. We'll send it as soon as we surface."

Dinnacetti slumped down on a stool and rested his head in his hands. "God, I will be so very glad to get a full night's sleep in a real bed tonight."

∞

With twenty extra passengers milling about the strange, compact undersea world of the *Tigerfish*, and with fifty tons of Philippine silver coins crammed into her bilges, the submarine had become an even more crowded and claustrophobic place. The COB, Alonzo Heinrich, did everything he could think of to make their guests comfortable, but twenty extra men shoe-horned into a space that was barely adequate for the existing crew taxed even his considerable logistical skills and personal diplomacy. Even moving about the boat was a chore, dodging around or stepping over bodies sprawled everywhere. Thankfully, the forward torpedo room was empty of its usual load of reload fish.

The day spent sitting on the bottom, hiding just outside Manila Bay, offered the opportunity to explain to the passengers what they could touch. And, more importantly, what they should not touch. Especially important was demonstrating the complexity of flushing a submarine head the proper way. That chore required explanation and demonstration. A mistake could be very ugly, and smelly. And, of course, Doc Mahon had to check everyone and make sure they were healthy. Any kind of communicable disease they might have brought aboard with them could wreak havoc in the close confines of a submarine.

As the sun finally dropped below the western horizon, the *Tigerfish* was able to emerge from the deep and meet up with the motor launch that would guide them safely through the maze of the outer minefields. It was well past midnight when the motor launch signaled that they were clear of all that potential mayhem and then turned back toward Corregidor.

Wayne Schacter watched them go, wondering what the immediate future held for the guys aboard the little guide vessel. For all the others still manning US Navy facilities around Manila. It was a foregone conclusion that the Japanese were coming, and they were coming hard and mean. The thought of spending the rest of the war in a Jap POW camp must weigh heavily on their minds.

But the Skipper could not wait around to ponder the inevitable. He had passengers and silver to deliver to Darwin on the northwest coast of Australia. He ordered up "Ahead flank." It was important to be well away from Manila and Corregidor and as far down the Philippine coastline as he could get before he dove with the first hint of morning sun.

The days soon took on some regularity as the boat raced south on the surface all night and then slowed to a crawl for submerged travel during the day. They transited down through the Mindoro Strait and out into the island-laced Sulu Sea. Isaac Sternman, the XO, calculated that they were averaging two hundred fifty miles a day. At that rate, Darwin was two weeks away.

The third night out found the *Tigerfish* slipping through the Simisa Strait, a narrow passage between the Simisa and Balanguingui Islands, two links in the chain of a thousand small bits of dry land that separated the Sulu Sea from the Celebes Sea to the south. It was a calm, peaceful tropical evening. There had been no sign whatsoever of the Japanese since leaving Manila Bay behind. And very little other shipping traffic or aircraft.

LTjg George Lawson was enjoying the peaceful night air, happy to be away from the crowded submarine's interior. Up here on the bridge, he could turn around without bumping into half a dozen people, most of whom were strangers on his boat.

The 7MC disturbed his pleasant, quiet night. "Permission for Seaman Wasterman and Cookie to open the engine room access hatch and dump trash."

Necessary stuff. Seemed increasing the number of men on the boat by a third had led to the generation of five times the garbage. Lawson answered, "Open the engine room access hatch and dump trash."

He looked aft just in time to see the hatch pop open and two men emerge. They dragged several big bags behind them and were soon tossing the weighted garbage over the side.

Lawson was enjoying watching the guys do their dirty work when suddenly, out of nowhere, the throbbing roar of a runaway freight train passed directly over the boat, not fifty feet above his head. A phosphorescent column of water erupted a hundred yards ahead of their bow.

Damn! Somebody was shooting at them!

Then, before Lawson could order a dive, two more whistling roars went by overhead. And led to two more massive pillars of water, even closer to *Tigerfish*.

Lawson yelled, "Clear the bridge!" He hit the diving alarm and ordered, "Dive! Dive!"

Looking back toward the main deck, he saw the two crewmen stand transfixed for a moment and then scramble for the access hatch.

The next round hit home. It smashed into the periscope shears, tearing away both scopes and all the other masts. The four lookouts, in the process of hurrying down from the shears, had no chance. The explosion threw bits and pieces of shears, masts, and sailors out into the black water.

Lawson, suddenly realizing that he had been shredded by whirling shrapnel, lost all strength in his legs and fell hard to the deck. But he could still crawl, using his elbows. He left a trail of blood as he pulled himself to the hatch and did the only thing he was still able to do.

With his last ounce of strength, with his last breath, Lawson slammed the hatch shut.

The *Tigerfish* was already descending beneath the waves as Wayne Schacter rushed into the control room and started up the ladder to the conning tower. Water was cascading down from above and it was difficult climbing. At first, the CO thought the hatch to the bridge was still open, but no. Somehow, it had gotten closed though nobody on the bridge or in the shears had come down.

The CO realized that all the flooding came from both periscope packing glands. It threatened to inundate the vital electrical equipment in the conning tower and in the control room below. Schacter slammed the hatch to the control room shut from above. That would at least isolate the flooding to the conning tower but essentially trap him and the others who were still in the conning tower. Then he went to work, trying to help COB Heinrich, who was already doing his best to stem the deluge. They would worry about emptying the water that had already flooded into the conning tower once they had stopped the in-rush of seawater.

"Flooding! Flooding in the pump room! Flooding from the periscope wells!" was the frightening report ringing up and down the submarine. The passengers understood at once they were in deadly peril. Stan Ward closed his eyes and did the only thing that he knew to do. He prayed.

The first report was followed almost immediately by, "Flooding! Flooding in the after engine room from the access hatch!"

By then, the COB had climbed up into the overhead area of the conning tower, lugging a large spanner wrench. Fighting his way through the salt-water torrent, he found the nuts for the periscope packing glands and twisted them as tight as he could. It took a powerful turn on the wrench before the waterfall subsided. Finally, it was reduced to a manageable stream. Still, Heinrich and Schacter had to wade in more than two feet of water that remained trapped in the conning tower. That was more than enough to do damage to the sub's systems in the control room below even if they could open the hatch to the control room. There was no way to do so because of the weight of the water.

With the conning tower isolated and the Skipper obviously stuck up there—and with no idea if he and the COB were okay—Isaac Sternman, the XO, was left to fight the rest of the ship. He ordered, "Line up the drain pump to empty the after engine room bilge and commence pumping." Next, he directed, "Line up the trim pump to the pump room bilge. Commence pumping."

Looking around the control room, he spotted Brad Johnson. "Brad, get down to the pump room and take charge. Find out where the flooding's coming from and get it stopped."

The speaker near his ear interrupted the XO, the voice near frantic. "Control, Maneuvering, zero grounds on all main motors. Zero grounds on the battery bus. Answering all stop. Opening the battery breakers."

Sternman recognized with that report that they were now in a major fix. There was still flooding that they had not isolated. Water was still pouring into several compartments. The bilges, packed with silver coins, took up much of the room that could have taken on some of the flood waters. And now they had lost propulsion and the ability to pump water overboard. At least until they could shut the battery breakers again.

As the XO considered the situation, emergency battle lanterns clicked on, providing just enough light to see by.

Stan Miller was standing by the depth gauge. He called out, "Depth two hundred feet." Then, "Two hundred ten feet."

They were sinking. With no propulsion, there was nothing Sternman could do except blow the ballast tanks.

Not a viable option. Blowing the water from the ballast tanks would pop them to the surface in a hurry. The surface, where someone up there was gunning for them. Sternman immediately ruled out that potential course of action.

Then the XO had an idea. Maybe settling on the bottom for a while was an alternative. If the bottom was not so deep here that the pressure of seawater would crush their already vulnerable vessel like squeezing the shell of a raw egg.

"Report water depth," he requested.

The Quartermaster called out, "Chart depth three hundred feet."

God, let the chart be accurate!

"Prepare to bottom," the XO ordered.

In the condition that *Tigerfish* was now in, with no propulsion and no way to pump water, there was not anything else to do except allow the boat to sink and brace for the lurch when they bottomed. Hopefully, on a smooth, soft, muddy but level plain. Not a hard, steep slope cluttered with jagged volcanic rocks.

Johnson climbed back up out of the pump room. His uniform was soaked, grease-stained and badly torn. Blood dripped from his left hand as he tried to tie a temporary bandage around an ugly cut.

"XO, flooding in the pump room is stopped. We jammed DC plugs into both scopes. It sure ain't pretty, but it's keeping the water out for now. Can't make any promises if we go much deeper..."

"Thanks, Brad," the XO said. "Now I need you to go back and see what you can do about the after engine room. We need to get power back soon as we can."

The *Tigerfish* abruptly settled onto the bottom with a powerful jolt and a couple of ominous groans from the boat's superstructure. She started to roll to port. Every man held his breath. But then she settled at about a ten-degree list. Just enough to be annoying. Now, if she could just stay there and not drop off a cliff into some unmarked underwater ravine.

Sternman ordered the drains to the conning tower opened, and then when that space was drained, he ordered the hatch to be opened.

As a soaked and ragged Schacter slowly climbed down the ladder, Sternman looked up and asked, "You okay, Skipper?"

Schacter nodded. "Doc said I should try saltwater baths for my rash." He gave a wry laugh. "I don't recommend this method, though." He glanced around the darkened control room, illuminated only by a few battle lanterns. "What's the status of the ship?"

As if someone elsewhere in the submarine had heard him, the 7MC answered the CO's question. "Control, Maneuvering. Flooding in the after engine room is under control. After trunk is flooded. Four feet of water in the bilge."

"As you just heard, flooding is under control. No propulsion and no power until we can dry some circuits out and clear the electrical grounds. Until then, we are stuck here in the mud," Sternman reported.

"Muster the officers and the COB in the wardroom in five minutes," Schacter said. "And make sure the officer riders, uh...Oglethorpe, Ward, and Tanaka? Make sure they're there too. This could affect them as well. I'm going to go see if I have a dry uniform. That sea salt is really, really starting to sting."

The officers crowded into the tiny wardroom, but George Lawson's seat was sadly left empty.

Schacter started the meeting.

"The way I see it, we have some work to do to get the *Tigerfish* up and moving again. Brad, I want you to take charge in the engine room. Get the generators dried out and get the grounds cleared as quick as you can. That's the only way we can bring the batteries back online."

"Skipper," Johnson interrupted, "there's five feet of water in the engine room bilge and it's still leaking in slowly. I can't do anything until the water's out of there."

Schacter glanced over at Heinrich. "COB, get a bucket brigade to bail the engine room bilge. Put as much in the other bilges as we can. Then we'll have to get creative."

Stan Ward had been sitting there quietly. Now he looked around the room and asked, "Skipper, what happens if we can't get the batteries back online? Can we do one of those free ascent things like they teach at sub school?"

Schacter's face became even more serious. "Mr. Ward, my orders are to deliver you and your guys to Darwin, Australia. I fully intend to do that. But there is one very serious proviso in those orders. I have been told that under no circumstances am I to allow you or any member of your team to be captured by the Japanese. If it gets to the point where the only way out is a free ascent, and if there is any chance the Japanese are waiting topside for us to come up, I cannot authorize that. Bottom line, we either get the *Tigerfish* moving south while submerged, or we all sit here and die. Any other questions?"

There were none.

23

The sea buoy marking the entrance to the Pearl Harbor ship channel was only a mile ahead. Their old friend, the *Hulbert*, was guiding the *Wolffish* back home. Fred Wurster, dressed in his best set of khakis—even if they were a little grease-stained and wrinkled—stood proudly on the bridge, carefully driving the submarine into port. As they steamed past Hickam Field and the little Hickam Harbor where the Army Air Corps kept their crash boats, Wurster saw that the beach was lined with people out to greet them on their return from war. If submarine movements were supposed to be super-secret, someone had certainly let the cat out of the bag to all the families and friends of USS *Wolffish*.

Wurster steered around Hospital Point, revealing the vista of Pearl Harbor. Much had changed since they had left here in December, but much was still the same. The battleship *Nevada* had been refloated and was now riding at anchor, awaiting her turn in the number four drydock. Two more battleships, *Maryland* and *Tennessee*, looked like they were ready to head out to sea, to go to war. Work was clearly underway on the *California* and the *West Virginia*. It appeared salvage work was still underway on the *Oklahoma* and the completely submerged *Arizona*, but surely they would never float again. The harbor remained littered with debris and wreckage.

The water still had a black sheen from all the oil that had been spilled there on 7 December.

Wurster realized that he needed to wipe tears from his eyes. *Must be the lingering smoke*, he thought. Then he noticed that Dinnacetti was having problems with eye irritation, too.

Then they made the turn into Southeast Loch. The band was playing on the pier at berth Sierra One in Quarry Loch. Flashbulbs were popping as Wurster twisted the *Wolffish* around smartly and coasted over alongside the berth. Lots of eyes watching, some with an abundance of ribbons and medals on their uniforms, but he had nailed the landing. It took a couple of minutes to secure the diesels and to get the brow across while Wurster made his way down from the bridge. Then he had to wait while Admiral Thomas Withers, COMSUBPAC, walked on board to greet them. Wurster realized that the Captain who was walking a step behind the Admiral looked very familiar.

"Commander Flynn?" he said questioningly as he saluted the pair.

Roderick Flynn, the former Commanding Officer of the Sub School, looked over and smiled as he returned the salute. "Well, if it isn't Freddy Wurster. Still up to your old goldbricking tricks? You know, to be honest, I always figured you'd make as good a submarine officer as you did a football player at the Academy." Then he touched his shoulder boards with four gold stripes. "It's Captain, now, by the way. And pleased to inform, I'm your new Squadron Commodore." His smile warmed and he winked. "And, Freddy, I ran into somebody down there on the pier just now who seems really anxious to see you. Some Navy nurse."

Wurster ran over the brow and onto the pier. As usual, it took him just a moment to get accustomed to a solid foundation under his feet after weeks at sea. Then suddenly, as if in a dream, with the band still playing and flashbulbs popping, Ellie Morton was in his arms, smothering him with kisses. He had so many questions for her but he had now forgotten every one of them.

At least for right now and right here, the world was perfect again, and he did not want to do or say anything that might change that.

∞

The atmosphere was thick and heavy. Brad Johnson had to exert all the strength he had left just to pull in enough air to remain conscious. After forty-eight hours of sitting on the bottom of the Simisa Strait, surviving on the fetid air, his head was pounding. They had long since used all of the lithium hydroxide powder, spread about the deck to absorb the carbon dioxide. If he did not get the main motors dried out and the battery back in service, this area of sea floor would end up being their grave. And the truth was, that could be the case before the day was done.

The COB's bucket brigade was continuously emptying the after engine room bilge, first by filling the torpedo room bilges up to the lip for the hatches. Then they had removed the manhole from the negative tank and dumped the water there. They were running out of places, as well as men with strength enough to do the backbreaking work without clean, breathable air.

"Mr. Johnson, we're ready to megger the port bus," Harold Wurtz, the leading electrician, wheezed. He cranked the handle on the side of the megger, a portable instrument used to measure the electrical resistance of insulation. "Let's cross our fingers."

Johnson replied, "I'm not sure I got the energy left." He looked down at the dial on the megger. A thousand ohms. Normally not nearly enough, but today it would have to do.

"Shut the battery breakers," Johnson ordered, mostly as a gasp. There was a quick flashing, sputtering arc across the breakers as they slapped shut. The lights flickered and then came on. He grabbed the 7MC and said, "Control, Maneuvering, battery breakers are shut. Ground's one thousand ohms. You should be able to use the trim and drain pumps."

Gradually, the *Tigerfish* came back to life. The extra water was pumped overboard. To break free from the bottom, they had to pump all of the trim tanks dry and then they still had to blow some water out of the main ballast tanks. Gradually the submarine righted herself and slowly lifted out of the mud.

And so far, there was no sign of the sub's batteries shorting out, exploding. No fires.

"Shift propulsion to the main motors," Schacter ordered. "Ahead one-third."

The shafts had only just started turning when there was a loud banging outside the hull, aft.

"Control, Maneuvering, loud noise, port shaft," the 7MC blasted, not sharing any news they could not hear quite well for themselves. "Port shaft vibrating excessively. Answering bells on the starboard shaft."

"Probably bent something when we hit bottom," the CO guessed.

The damaged submarine inched forward, though. They had no choice but to get to the surface and replenish the air if they were going to survive. And there was no way to know what was waiting for them up there when the *Tigerfish* suddenly reappeared from the deep. And with both periscopes gone, there was no way to peek before they popped up and revealed themselves.

Schacter leveled the sub off at sixty feet. He turned to Sternman and said, "Well, XO, this is it. We could pop up in the middle of a mad Japanese battle fleet, tired of waiting for our asses to come back for more. Or it could be empty seas. Stand by to battle surface and let's see what kind of luck we got today."

The gun crew mustered in the crew's mess, ready to charge up through the access hatch to man the sub's three-inch gun and the .50 caliber machine gun on the cigarette deck. Those weapons would be a meager answer to any Japanese warship, but the *Tigerfish* would at least go down fighting, not squatting on the bottom while its crew and passengers suffocated.

The *Tigerfish* popped to the surface. The bridge hatch and the after battery hatch slammed open almost simultaneously. The gun crew raced up on deck, sliding a three-inch shell into the breech and banging the breechblock shut even as the trainer and pointer jumped into their seats that still dripped seawater. In less than a minute, the gun was ready, its crew peering into the murky darkness for any sign of the enemy. The .50 caliber team was almost as fast. They dropped the gun down on its pintle mount, fed the ammo belt into the breech, and pulled the charging lever, ready to unleash all they had on an attacker.

Schacter followed Johnson up to the bridge. They both breathed in deep gulps of clean, sweet, cool sea air as they scanned an empty horizon for any threat. Except for a couple of small islands, dark on the horizon astern, they appeared to have the sea all to themselves.

Now, they could turn their attention to the damage. The bridge and fairwater were in shambles. The periscope shears and everything above that were gone. The bridge compass repeater, the target-bearing transmitter, and even the announcing system box, were all shot away. The fairwater was littered with holes punched through the mild steel by shrapnel.

And there were no signs of George Lawson or the four sailor lookouts.

They could feel the vibration in their feet when the diesels rumbled to life. Exhaust smoke poured from beneath the main deck, burbling as the sub moved forward through the slight swell. Air whistled down through the hatch, a relief for all the men below who so desperately needed to take in gulps of the precious stuff.

"Bridge, Control, answering bells on the starboard shaft with four main engines. Commencing a battery charge."

"Helm, steer course one-three-zero, ahead standard on the starboard main engine," Johnson ordered. And with that, they were once again on their way to a distant Darwin.

Even up on the bridge, Schacter and Johnson could feel the heavy, drumming vibration as the sub came up to speed. Then the clanking eased, but the sub also slowed markedly.

"Bridge, Maneuvering, excessive vibration starboard shaft, answering ahead one-third. Recommend limiting to ahead one-third."

Schacter looked over at Johnson and said, "Well, that confirms one thing, Brad."

"What's that, Skipper?"

"At ahead one-third, if you got any knitting to do or a novel you been meaning to read, here's your chance. It's going to be a long, slow ride to Darwin."

∞

Debbie Schultz sat in her beat-up old Ford and watched the workers from the day shift traipse out of the shipyard gate like a herd of cattle. It was startling for her to see how many of the people who were building submarines at Electric Boat were now women. She had no idea of the exact numbers, but by watching them emerge through the gate, it had to be about half of them. Prior to the war, there were practically no women doing the job. But they all, men and women alike, clutched their coats tightly around themselves for warmth from the cold winter wind blowing in off Long Island Sound. And many of them—again both male and female—quickly ducked into one of the many bars that lined Thames Street, seeking an after-work beer or two and an hour or two of relaxation after a rough day bending steel and welding joints. Each opened door emitted happy noise and smoke before being slammed shut to keep out the elements.

Then Heinrich Schultz walked out through the gate, carrying his lunch bucket. His distinctive red-and-black mackinaw was easy to spot. So was his green Bavarian alpine hat, pulled low over his face against the biting wind. He immediately spotted Debbie's car and walked more quickly as he made his way down the street to where she had parked.

He slid into the passenger's seat and promptly shut the door to avoid letting in the cold and the bits of blowing snow. He smiled at his daughter and shook his head.

"There was no need for you to come pick me up, *tochter*," he told her. "I could easily walk home. And it's about time for you to get to work yourself. Especially since you carry more of the phony paperwork to those *böse männers*. They may get suspicious if you are late to get there. Or your usual parking spot may be taken."

"I know, *vater*," she answered. "About coming to pick you up. But it's cold out. It's nothing for me to come by the shipyard and give you a ride home. Then I'll drive up to Solomon's. We won't be busy for a couple of hours yet. And those Nazi bastards...evil men...they can wait in the cold for a bit. They have no cause to distrust us, Dad."

She slowly pulled into traffic and aimed the car toward home. She could tell he had something else he wanted to say.

"Your father can read you like a book, Deb. I see the worry in your eyes. You are concerned about tonight's message drop, aren't you?" He spoke in a low whisper, as if those trudging along the street from Electric Boat might be able to hear what he was saying if he did not. She had to struggle to hear him over the rumble of the car's busted muffler. "This...this work for the Naval Intelligence...it is dangerous for you. I am your father. I know you worry about it. About them realizing we have been messing with them. We must stop it now. We have done all they have asked. The Nazi spies and Admiral Johnson's men alike. It is only a matter of time before the Germans discover we have been feeding them useless information all along."

Debbie shook her head. "No, vater! What we are doing is important! Brad and all the other young men are out doing the really dangerous work. We have to keep doing everything we can to help win this war and bring them all home safely. If that means that I take a risk or two throwing a spy ring off track, then I will happily continue to do it."

He shook his head again. "Darling, I will gladly do what I can as well. But I'm afraid the Nazis will soon grow desperate, even if most all our submarines are in the Pacific, aimed at Japanese targets. Hitler's men know our new submarines have systems they could employ on their U-boats. And share with the other Axis powers. No, I can continue to pass the fake documents, but you must stop dealing with them. Tell them they must deal directly with me from now on." She slowed the car in front of their little house on Cottage Street, then, with a quick goodbye, she dropped her worrying father off.

Before he slammed the car door shut, he bent over and said, "And one more thing, my baby girl. With the money they have given you, please have this muffler replaced. I love you."

"Yes, Dad. I will. Love you."

She watched as he shuffled up the icy walkway and front steps, checked the mailbox next to the door, and finally went inside. Only then did she hurry on toward Solomon's Tavern.

She noticed a dark car pull out from the driveway of the house down the street as she drove by and then fall in thirty or forty feet behind her. That would be Lieutenant Commander George Klemp or one of his men, out to protect her. It was a precaution that Debbie thought was totally unnecessary by now, but Klemp disagreed.

The sun had been down for almost two hours when she parked at the far end of the bar's parking lot off Crystal Lake Road, back where there was no overhead light and precious little illumination spilling over from other parts of the lot, from distant streetlights or a waning moon. She deliberately left the car unlocked. The documents—official and accurate-looking but completely and expertly contrived—were in an envelope lying on the floorboard behind the passenger side seat. This was all according to the standing precise instructions that her German spymaster had given her months before, when all this double-agent activity started.

What was not according to the German's instructions was the Navy Intel agent who was carefully hiding in the bushes several dozen feet away, huddled in the cold, but watching the loud, newly arrived car and the pretty young woman as she parked it in the dark. Watched as she killed the headlights, hopped out, leaned into the biting wind, and trotted toward the front door of the bar.

An hour after Debbie tied on her apron and started her shift as barkeep, back in the parking lot, a shadowy figure dressed all in black approached her car in the thick darkness. It took only seconds for him to open the unlocked back right-side door, grab the envelope from the floorboard, and to leave an identical one stuffed with cash and future instructions. Then he disappeared back into the woods.

The hidden agent watched the German the entire way, until the spy disappeared. He waited five more minutes to make sure that the man did not circle back to check if he might be followed or under surveillance. Then the agent stood and walked down to Debbie's car. He carefully removed the package the spy had left and briefly inspected it with his penlight before tucking it into his jacket pocket and walking on to his own vehicle.

Meanwhile, the German spy emerged from the woods a quarter mile away, alongside Route 12, where he had parked his car. Then, when he cranked it up and headed north toward Norwich in the early evening traffic, he did not notice a car emerge from a driveway a couple of hundred yards farther south. The second Naval Intelligence agent managed to follow the German all the way to a run-down house on the outskirts of Norwich. When the German pulled into the driveway—joining several other cars there—the intel agent slowed, smiled, then drove on past.

He noted the address as he did. They finally had the primary location for the spy nest to go with the complete list of all of its participants. All the receipts from the bank where they withdrew cash to leave for Debbie Schultz and her submarine-building father. Marked bills from the bank, left in Debbie's car, while agents watched. Recordings and transcripts of numerous phone calls between the Nazi spy ring members and the Schultzes.

There would be no need for testimony from the hardworking German immigrant or his daughter, who just happened to be the girlfriend of Admiral Devin Johnson's son. Admiral Johnson, close advisor to President Roosevelt.

Now all the intel agent had to do was report the address of the spy nest. Indictments could be drawn up as early as the next day. Newspaper reporters and newsreel photographers would be notified so they could be present when the spies were brought in wearing manacles and handcuffs. A dastardly group of spies operating right here on American soil, broken by the FBI, so far as the public would ever know.

All good for morale. Good for the country. Bad for Hitler and Hirohito.

But it was especially good for Heinrich and Debbie Schultz. Unbeknownst to them, an intercepted message that very day indicated the Nazis had begun to question the detailed information the two had been providing. People in high places back in Germany now believed much of it was bogus, manufactured. It was only a matter of time before the spies would have paid them back for the time- and money-wasting subterfuge and do so in a very bloody and final way.

Now, with the arrest of the cell members, the danger was greatly reduced for them. Admiral Johnson could personally deliver the good news and explain why their services were no longer required. And that they would still be under the watchful eye of his men for a while, just in case. But he would also remind them that no one could know what had been going on or just how crucial their help had been in catching this huge spy ring. That there was no way to calculate how damaging those many documents, blueprints, and plans had been to the Axis powers. Their contributions would necessarily remain secret.

Then he would remind them that not even Brad Johnson, the Admiral's submariner son, wherever he might be, could be told what Debbie and her father had been doing. Maybe someday, when the war was over.

But not now.

∞

The *Tigerfish* plodded across the Celebes Sea at a maddeningly languid pace. The nights were dedicated to trying to repair the damage and to restoring vital systems while dawdling along on the surface. The days were spent running submerged, even slower, as they rested and planned. And speculated about who or what had shot them, not only damaging their boat but claiming lives of their shipmates. Most were certain it had been a Japanese destroyer or cruiser that caught them on the surface. Some guessed a dive-bomber, but unlikely at night. As the Skipper pointed out, it did not matter if it was Thor, the god of thunder, who had pounded them with his mighty hammer, they were in ragged—and perilous—condition.

The first order of business—after a brief remembrance of the lost men —was to do whatever they could to keep the water out of the "people tank," the compartments inside the submarine's hull where the crew lived and worked. The problem with the after engine room hatch was reasonably simple to resolve. In the cooks' panicked rush to get back belowdecks when the shooting started, they had managed to foul the upper hatch with a bag of garbage. Then they had somehow found a way to slash the rubber gaskets on the lower hatch. With the upper hatch cleared, that problem was solved. However, they would have to wait until they got to Darwin to replace the gaskets. It was not a big problem.

The periscopes, or at least what remained of them, were an entirely different matter. The COB tightened the packing glands down as best he could. That slowed the water flowing into the conning tower to a bare trickle. But the periscope tubes themselves had been blasted wide open. The scope internals, never designed to be subjected to full sea pressure at depth, were essentially open to the ocean. The entire eye-box of both scopes leaked like sieves and threatened to give way completely. If that happened, the periscope would become an open-ended pipe all the way from what remained of the bridge to the pump room. They could not submerge if that happened. Brad Johnson and the COB spent hours in the pump room trying to improve on their hastily installed damage control plugs. They were finally forced to recommend that *Tigerfish* be limited in depth to no more than one hundred feet. Any deeper and the plugs might not hold. And if they failed, it could be catastrophic.

At the same time, Harold Wurtz and his band of electricians struggled to dry out the sub's electrical circuits. Gradually, wire by wire, system by system, *Tigerfish* came back to life. Even the coffee machine was working again. That set off much celebration in the Chiefs' quarters.

On the third night after the attack, CO Wayne Schacter decided to heave to and send a diver down to inspect both of their shafts and screws. He knew there was likely nothing they could do to fix anything they might find, but at least they would have an idea of what was going on with them. Johnson, by dint of his having swum the four hundred freestyle on the Academy swim team—and his lack of judgment in bragging about it one night at dinner—was chosen to do the inspection. Even with Johnson's swimming experience, Isaac Sternman insisted that he have a line tied around his waist and held topside by a tender.

"Sorta like we're baiting a hook for some big old shark or tuna," the XO noted with a straight face.

Lying just a couple of degrees north of the Equator, the Celebes Sea was thankfully bathwater-warm and crystal clear. Johnson, with the thought of that big old shark constantly on his mind, spent over an hour free diving. Going under, coming back up for air, going back down. Taking his time, he performed a careful hand-over-hand inspection of both shafts and both screws. Finally, he surfaced alongside the boat and signaled for the crew to haul him back aboard before he became shark supper.

Drying off, he reported, "Skipper, the port shaft is bent badly. No way we're going to be able to do anything with it out here."

Schacter nodded glumly. "I expected as much. Must have hit something when we bottomed. What about starboard?"

Johnson rubbed his hair dry and tossed the towel down the hatch. "Starboard shaft is fine, as near as I can tell. One of the blades on the screw has a pretty good-sized ding in it. That's most likely the vibration we're getting when we go faster than ahead one-third."

Schacter nodded. "I suppose we could eke out a couple of more knots if we pushed our luck. Probably not real smart or worth the risk, though." Turning around, he yelled up to Stan Miller on the bridge. "Mr. Miller, come to ahead one-third and steer course one-one-zero. We still have a long way to go and sitting here ain't getting us any closer."

The water aft of the submarine churned white as the *Tigerfish* slowly accelerated. A long line of bioluminescence glowed brightly far behind the boat. Schacter climbed up to the bridge where Miller stood amongst the shattered wreckage. The young Ensign had only his lookouts and a phone-talker to rely on. His sole means of communication was a sound-powered phone cord hanging down through the hatch. Steering orders would have to be done the old-fashioned way, by seaman's eye.

The phone-talker, Seaman Wasterman, said, "Excuse me, Captain. COB's requesting you to meet him in the goat locker." The Chiefs' quarters.

Schacter hurried down from the bridge to find out what the COB might want to discuss. He found Alonzo Heinrich and RM3 Eric Riegel waiting for him.

"Skipper," the COB started the discussion, "Riegel here has an idea. One of the things we don't have working yet is a radio since we lost our antennas."

"I was thinkin', Skipper," Riegel said, picking up the conversation, "the radio room gear is all dried out and seems to work fine. But it does us no good without any antennas. I figure if we could rig up a wire from the bridge to the jackstaff, we could have us an antenna. Only wire that I can think of is maybe some sound-powered phone line. I think I could tune it to receive VLF."

"Any way we can transmit HF on that little stuff?" Schacter queried.

Riegel shook his head. "I don't think the line will handle the power to transmit a signal to do us any good at HF way out here. I need some heavy copper for that, at least twelve-gauge. And maybe twenty feet of piping to get it up away from the hull."

Heinrich looked thoughtful for a minute and then said, "The periscope hoist motors use twelve-gauge wiring. I don't think we'll be needing those for a bit. And we can probably find twenty feet of auxiliary bilge piping."

Schacter smiled for the first time in a couple of days. If Riegel could get the VLF antenna working, then at least they could copy incoming messages on the *Fox* schedule. And if a jury-rigged HF antenna functioned, they could even contact Darwin and see about getting some help to come meet them.

"Start riggin', Sparky!" the CO told the radioman. "I'm ready to hear some Morse with an Aussie accent."

24

Kaigu Shosa Riku Ito was mystified. He could not quite fathom why the Imperial Japanese Navy would order his submarine, the *I-53*, away from their patrol area, guarding the northern entrance to the Makassar Strait, to a new area somewhere north of Papua New Guinea. It did not make sense to the submarine Commander. This move would leave the back door open to the Imperial Navy's most important fleet movement of the war so far, only to run two thousand kilometers east and set up patrol off some forgotten, prehistoric jungle island.

But, as he well knew, his concerns did not matter. The Admirals had spoken. The *I-53* had obeyed their orders.

"Pardon me, Captain." Ito's frustrated revery was interrupted by Ensign Sato. "It is near daylight. Should we dive and run submerged?"

Ito laughed. "Sato-san, the nearest American ship is over a thousand kilometers away and the nearest American aircraft is even more distant. We will cross the Celebes Sea on the surface and enjoy the sunlight for a change."

Sato made a quick bow and sharply answered, "Hai!"

The *I-53* charged across the deep blue sea, the tropical sun reflecting off the frothy, pure-white bow wave. Riku Ito stood on the bridge, face to the sky, enjoying the warm sunshine. He reached into his shirt pocket and pulled out a pack of Kinshi cigarettes. Shaking one of the slender cylinders from the moss-green pack embossed with the image of a golden bat, he applied a match and deeply breathed in the acrid smoke. Almost immediately he felt the boost from its nicotine. He slowly exhaled as he stared at the empty horizon. Nothing but blue sea below, blue sky above. Too peaceful to believe the world was at war. A Zen moment, but one marred by the submarine Commander's conviction that he, his crew, and his boat were being wasted, not serving the cause at all. Sometimes, he thought, he could better serve the Emperor and the Ancestors by doing as his brother did. He harvested seals off Hokkaido, their skins to be used to make flight jackets for Nippon aviators.

"Captain, the sonar watch is reporting a contact," Sato said, yet again interrupting the Commanding Officer's musings. "Bearing zero-eight-six. He says that it sounds like screw noise and that it is quite loud."

Ito looked out on the bearing. Nothing but empty sea. He grabbed his binoculars and searched that quadrant more thoroughly. Still nothing.

"The sonar watch is certain?" Ito inquired.

"Yes Ito-san," Sato quickly replied. "I asked him the same question myself. It is definitely a ship's screw and it is within a few thousand meters."

Ito knew that could only mean one thing. They were being stalked by a submarine. There was only one place to hide, one place to mount a counterattack. One place where he would be on equal footing with another submarine. That was in the deep.

"Sato-san, dive the ship immediately!" he exclaimed as he headed down the hatch. "Order battle stations."

Even as the *I-53* was submerging, Ito ordered, "Make all forward torpedoes ready! Set run depth ten meters. Set a spread of two degrees. Open the outer doors." The submarine was quickly ready to shoot at the invisible foe. Ten meters run depth should be just right against a submarine at periscope depth. The six-torpedo spread would cover enough ocean to make it very likely that at least one weapon would strike home. And that would be all it should take to violently end this particular threat.

Turning to the sonar watch, Ito ordered, "Go active. Give me a range to the enemy submarine!"

"Captain-san, active return," the sonar operator yelled. "Range two thousand meters, bearing zero-eight-six."

Within fifteen seconds, six Type 95 torpedoes were racing out of their tubes, off to destroy the target.

This new threat was moments away from being forever eliminated.

∞

"Active sonar, bearing two-six-four!" the sound man yelled. "Sounds like a Jap submarine sonar!"

The *Tigerfish* was cruising one hundred feet below the surface, heading southeast at three knots, toward the Molucca Sea. Most of the crew were resting after a hard night spent repairing as much of the damaged submarine as they could. Wayne Schacter was sitting in the control room discussing those repairs with Isaac Sternman and the COB.

At the sound man's alert, Schacter jumped up and ordered, "Man battle stations! Make forward tubes ready, set speed to HIGH, run depth to sixty feet. Open outer doors forward. Steer course two-six-four."

The badly battered submarine could not go any faster or dive any deeper. He could come around to point the Jap sub. That would at least minimize the size of the sonar return and make *Tigerfish* a much narrower target should the other sub decide to shoot.

Whatever else they did, it would have to be done blindly. All they could manage was to try to dodge and duck, and shoot back, and pray. There was not much else remaining in his bag of tricks. His usual maneuvers in such a dire situation as this were just not available.

He scampered up the ladder into the conning tower, followed closely by Sternman. The XO had just slipped on the sound-powered phone headset when the report came up from the forward torpedo room. "Tubes forward ready, outer doors open!"

A quick glance at the TDC and the torpedo firing panel confirmed that all was set.

"Incoming torpedoes!" the sound man suddenly yelled. "I can hear at least four! Bearing two-seven-zero!"

"Shoot tubes forward, five-second time delay!" Schacter ordered. The enemy sub already had weapons in the water. With that half-minute head start, Schacter and his crew might never know if any of *Tigerfish*'s torpedoes fired now struck home or not, but he was damned determined to fire a volley.

One after another, in rapid succession, the forward six torpedo tubes were emptied of their deadly load. Then, it was time to pray.

"Incoming torpedoes bearing two-six three!" the sound man cried out. "At least four!" A few seconds' pause. "Hearing at least six now!"

Then they could all hear the incoming torpedoes, roaring menacingly at them. Schacter gripped the chart table with both hands, as if that bit of support might save him from a direct hit. Sternman stared fixedly at the TDC, concentrating on their own fish, not the half dozen hurtling toward him. As they grew ever closer, the clamor of those onrushing torpedoes built to a crescendo. One passed almost immediately overtop of the *Tigerfish*. The others seemed to zoom past really close.

To a man, they held their breath, even after it was obvious the attacking torpedoes had all missed. The torpedo sound was miraculously fading into the distance.

Isaac Sternman was wide-eyed and breathless. "Jesus! They must have figured we were at periscope—"

BOOM!

Tigerfish was brutally rocked by a tremendous explosion, quickly followed by a second one, even more horrendous.

No one moved. Few breathed.

The CO waited for damage reports. There were none. He grabbed the microphone and quickly requested them. A few minor issues from the concussion and shaking from the nearby blasts, but nothing serious.

It would be more than a full minute after the pair of explosions before the reverberations died down enough for the sound man to hear anything. But there was nothing out there to hear. Even the usually ever-present biologic sounds of the ocean remained deathly quiet.

"I don't hear the Jap sub anymore," the sound man reported.

"Should we surface and take a look?" Sternman asked.

Schacter rubbed his back against the bulkhead to relieve the fierce itching from his eczema. Somehow, he had forgotten it altogether for the last five minutes or so. "What for, XO? All we would see would be an oil slick, maybe."

"At least we could claim one Jap I-boat if we got some pictures."

"Right now, I don't really give a damn about claiming anything, XO. Let's just slink out of town while the slinkin' is good."

∞

The *Tigerfish* was on the surface. The shootout with the Jap sub was now a week and five hundred miles behind them. The crew was still slowly bringing the beaten and battered submarine back together. Admittedly not exactly back to fighting trim but at least she would be better able for her crew to defend themselves should the need arise.

A couple of new cables fouled the bridge hatch. One thin line stretched back to the cigarette deck and then all the way aft to the jack staff. It took Eric Riegel several days to tune the jury-rigged antenna so that they could receive the *Fox* VLF broadcast. The news was pouring in, most of it bad. Along with several other US Navy submarines, the *Tigerfish* was reported as late to check in and presumed lost with all hands.

The main job the last two nights had been rigging an HF antenna so that they could transmit. Then they could tell Darwin that *Tigerfish* still floated and that they were all still alive, even if they might be late for dinner. Both torpedo rooms were now missing their auxiliary bilge drain piping. Those were lashed together and then bound to the wreckage of the periscope shears. The pipes reached up some twenty feet into the air. The periscope hoist motor cabling had been stripped from the periscopes and strung from the antenna connector on the HF radio, up through the hatch, and then up the pipes to form what would have to serve as an HF antenna.

Eric Riegel and Harold Wurtz spent several miserable hours during a tropical rainstorm splicing and taping the stiff twelve-gauge copper lines to make sure they could carry the wattage needed for broadcasting HF. Even with their best efforts, the first time Schultz tested the circuit, one splice, right at the bridge hatch, arced and sparked for a second before it quickly burned through. Repairing and replacing that section of cabling took several more hours.

After lots of spits and sparks from the transmitter itself, Riegel finally got it working and raised Darwin almost immediately. Hopefully before the word of their assumed demise had been delivered to kinfolks and other loved ones. Schacter speculated that had likely not happened yet, but it was not to prematurely spare the feelings of those waiting back home. The Navy simply did not want the enemy to know of any ship losses at this point in the war.

At first COMSUBSOUWESPAC would not believe that *Tigerfish* was up on the circuit. They were certain that it was some Japanese trick since the submarine had officially been reported as sunk. It took a lot of back and forth, including some silly questions about Major League Baseball team nicknames and college football bowl games before COMSUBSOUWESPAC would believe they were who they said they were. And then they were incredulous about *Tigerfish*'s reported condition, including just how these radio transmissions were being conducted if the antennas had been blown away by some mysterious attacker.

The Captain then rather pointedly suggested they limit transmissions. No need to strain Riegel's makeshift antenna system. Or to risk some stray Japanese warship hearing them and homing in for another abrupt attack, like the last two, each unexpected and coming from nowhere, and that had come frighteningly close to violently concluding what Schacter had already labeled a "snake-bit cruise."

He also told the crew to try not to eat so much since they had twenty extra mouths to feed on this run. They likely would not care to chomp down on any of that silver in the bilges. And he okayed allowing the passengers to go up on the deck at night to stretch and catch some fresh air. Maybe even stop for swim call at dusk or dawn, but to be sure to put guys with rifles up and down the length of the boat to watch for hungry sharks. Submariners and their riders were rumored to be a special delicacy highly sought after by those critters.

"Just keep us chugging along toward Australia, boys," Schacter told them. "Be alert, but we can almost pretend there is not a war going on way out here. If you need me, I'll be in my stateroom for the next couple of weeks, catching up on my sleep."

EPILOGUE

The moonless night shone with a billion stars as the sub cruised across an empty Banda Sea. Brad Johnson stood on the bridge of *Tigerfish*, resting his elbows on the fairing, staring up at the spectacular sky. Stan Ward was there next to him, taking in the peaceful beauty of the warm night.

"Only a thousand more miles to go before we get to Darwin," Brad noted. "At least according to the Skipper. That means two more weeks of days and nights just like this one, I'm afraid."

"No complaints from me," Ward responded. "Lot better scenery than what I've had in the last few places Naval Intelligence told me to spend the bulk of my time."

"Now that we've done about all we can to fix the damage, I've at least gotten caught up on my letter writing," Johnson said. "I've got about a dozen ready to mail to Debbie. Let me know if you see a mailbox somewhere along the way."

Ward laughed. "Same with me. God knows I miss Karen and baby Jon so bad it hurts. He'll be driving tractors and spooning girls by the time this damn war is over. But at least they're safe and got family around them."

"Yeah, Debbie's doing okay, I guess. Her dad's still working at Electric Boat, and she takes care of him, too."

"You are going to make an honest woman out of her, right?"

"Better believe it. If I can find a preacher right there on the pier, we'll get it done at the first port where I can meet up with her." Johnson used his sleeve to wipe something from his eye. "Whether this damn war is over or not. I should have taken care of that before we left Groton, dammit. I'll not sail off again without a ring on my finger and another one on hers."

"You and Freddy had talked about a double ceremony once upon a time. Fred and Ellie. You and Debbie."

Johnson shook his head. "Can't let logistics get in the way. I'm marrying Debbie at the first opportunity. You can bet on that."

Ward laughed again. "So you saying you're no Trip MacLean then? I think his plan is to nail every female of the species before he even thinks about settling down with just one of them."

Both men were quiet for a moment. Both knew their friend and his boat, the *S-55*, had been reported missing.

"But you know, if Trip were to wash up on a desert island somewhere..." Brad said.

"And if there was just one girl there on the whole island..." Stan added.

Again, they were quiet, lost in their thoughts, the rumble of the diesel engines and the hissing wash of the sea against the submarine's flanks providing the only soundtrack for this calming scene they were enjoying.

"They're sending the *Sargo* out to escort us home," Johnson finally said. He stopped and stared at the dark sea for a while. Then he added, "A thousand miles to go and mostly through Jap-held waters the whole way."

"Yeah, but you know, on nights like this, it's really hard to believe there's even a world war going on out there," Ward offered, waving his arm to take in the seascape stretching out in all directions from the *Tigerfish*.

"You see the message boards?" Johnson asked. "They certainly confirm there's a war on. Bataan and Corregidor are still holding, but barely. MacArthur's still there, though. Couple of major battles down in the Java Sea and the Sunda Straits. Looks like we lost a bunch of ships. The *Houston*, the *Perth*, couple of Dutch cruisers, all gone. And the Japs are landing on Java. Not any better news out of Europe, either. The Krauts are holding onto France and bombing the hell out of England. Is anybody going to stop this madness? Every way we turn, evil seems to be winning, big-time. It's almost like a pitch-black night fell over the whole world and there's no daylight in sight."

Ward stared at the dark horizon for a long moment. Then he said, "Yeah, Brad, you're right. It does look pretty dismal. But remember what they say."

"What's that, shipmate?"

"The night is always darkest just before the dawn."

A Code for Victory
The Tides of War Book 3

Reeling from the Java Sea catastrophe, four friends in the Silent Service wage a desperate campaign against a surging Japanese Empire.

Spring 1942. Japan's conquest of the Southwest Pacific is nearly complete. Allied fleets lie shattered on the ocean floor, and America's submarines—armed with faulty torpedoes and led by overcautious commanders—are all that stand between victory and total defeat.

Four young officers, bound by friendship and forged in the fires of war, fight on separate fronts.

Trip MacLean, survivor of a sunken warship, leads a guerrilla band from a remote tropical atoll, striking at Japanese supply lines. When his fighters recover the Imperial Navy's most closely guarded codebooks, the fragile balance of power begins to shift.

Stan Ward, deep in the shadows of naval intelligence, races to crack the JN-25 code before the Japanese realize it has been compromised—and before time runs out.

Beneath the waves, Brad Johnson aboard the battered *Tigerfish* and Fred Wurster in the *Wolffish* press the attack against overwhelming odds, carrying the weight of a failing campaign on their shoulders.

And as Japan prepares its next move, a massive invasion of Australia, these four officers—scattered across islands, intelligence offices, and hostile seas—are drawn together by a mission that could decide the Pacific War's first year.

ABOUT GEORGE WALLACE

Commander George Wallace retired to the civilian business world in 1995, after twenty-two years of service on nuclear submarines. He served on two of Admiral Rickover's famous "Forty One for Freedom", the USS John Adams SSBN 620 and the USS Woodrow Wilson SSBN 624, during which time he made nine one-hundred-day deterrent patrols through the height of the Cold War.

Commander Wallace served as Executive Officer on the Sturgeon class nuclear attack submarine USS Spadefish, SSN 668. Spadefish and all her sisters were decommissioned during the downsizings that occurred in the 1990's. The passing of that great ship served as the inspiration for "Final Bearing."

Commander Wallace commanded the Los Angeles class nuclear attack submarine USS Houston, SSN 713 from February 1990 to August 1992. During this tour of duty that he worked extensively with the SEAL community developing SEAL/submarine tactics. Under Commander Wallace, the Houston was awarded the CIA Meritorious Unit Citation.

Commander Wallace lives with his wife, Penny, in Alexandria, Virginia.

Sign up for Wallace and Keith's newsletter at
severnriverbooks.com

ABOUT DON KEITH

Don Keith is a native Alabamian and attended the University of Alabama where he received his degree in broadcast and film. He has received awards from the Associated Press and United Press International for newswriting and reporting. He is also the only person to be named Billboard Magazine "Radio Personality of the Year" in two formats, country and contemporary. Keith was a broadcast personality for over twenty years, owned his own consultancy, co-owned a Mobile, Alabama, radio station, and hosted and produced several nationally syndicated radio shows.

His first novel, "The Forever Season." received the Alabama Library Association's "Fiction of the Year" award. Keith has written extensively on historical subjects including World War II, submarine warfare, and fiction, biographies, and non-fiction works on a variety of subjects. He has published more than forty books, two of which—HUNTER KILLER and COLORS OF CHARACTER—have been adapted for the screen.

Mr. Keith lives with his wife, Charlene, in Indian Springs Village, Alabama.

Sign up for Wallace and Keith's newsletter at
severnriverbooks.com